A
GREAT
BEAUTY

Also by A. O'Connor

This Model Life

Exclusive

Property

Ambition

Full Circle

Talk Show

The House

The Secrets of Armstrong House

The Left-Handed Marriage

The Footman

On Sackville Street

The Legacy of Armstrong House

By Royal Appointment

A
GREAT
BEAUTY

A. O'CONNOR

POOLBEG

Published 2019
by Poolbeg Press Ltd
123 Grange Hill, Baldoyle
Dublin 13, Ireland
E-mail: poolbeg@poolbeg.com
www.poolbeg.com

A catalogue record for this book is available from the British Library.

ISBN 978-1-78199-797-0

Typeset in Sabon 11pt on 15pt by Poolbeg Press Ltd
Printed by SCANDBOOKS, Sweden

www.poolbeg.com

About the author

A graduate of the National University Maynooth and Trinity College Dublin, A. O'Connor is the bestselling author of thirteen previous novels including *The House, The Secrets of Armstrong House, The Legacy of Armstrong House, The Footman, The Left-Handed Marriage* and *By Royal Appointment.*

He had also written children's books on Kilmainham Gaol, Martin Luther King, James Joyce and the Irish patriot Michael Davitt. (Also published by Poolbeg)

Acknowledgements

A big thank-you to the team at Poolbeg – Paula, Kieran, David, Lee and Caroline. Also, my gratitude to my editor Gaye Shortland. As always, a big thank-you to the book buyers and the readers.

For Laura Byrne

In 1921, Michael Collins travelled to London as part of the Irish peace delegation, where he met the famous society hostess Lady Hazel Lavery.

This novel is the author's interpretation of actual events.

PROLOGUE

1909

New York came into plain view as the ocean liner continued to reduce speed.

"We're nearly there – home," said Hazel Lavery as she and her five-year-old daughter Alice looked out the porthole of their stateroom.

"It's so big!" cried Alice, her eyes wide in amazement at the view of the city.

"Indeed it is," said Hazel, smiling. "Now, we want you to look as pretty as possible for our arrival, so go with Nanny and change into your nicest dress. Nanny, can you take Alice to her room and dress her for her arrival, please?"

"Yes, Mrs Lavery," said the nanny as she took Alice by the hand.

Hazel's husband John Lavery was seated in an armchair smoking a cigar and he smiled indulgently at Alice as she walked past. Alice ran to her stepfather and hugged him.

Hazel looked at the two and her heart filled with joy. It was not just a relief, but an absolute pleasure to her that her daughter adored John and he returned that love in equal measure.

As romances go, hers and John's had the most tumultuous journey possible before they had finally married two years previously. *'The course of true love never did run smooth,'* Shakespeare said, but Hazel thought that the Bard of Avon could not have imagined the twists and turns she and John had to endure before finally being allowed to marry.

She sat down on the couch opposite him once Alice and her nanny had left the room. "You spoil her, John," she chastised him.

1

"I delight in spoiling her," he said, smiling, then his smile drooped slightly as he thought of his own daughter, Eileen, from his first marriage, and how he had neglected her during her childhood by putting his career before everything.

"I know you do." Hazel's smile suddenly turned to a frown. "I do hope the press haven't discovered we are returning to the States. I have sworn everyone I know to secrecy. I couldn't bear it if a gaggle of reporters were waiting for us at the port."

She remembered the last time she had travelled to the States, a week after her marriage to John. She had come back to settle the estate of her mother who had recently died. The press had been waiting in full force to report the arrival of one of Chicago's most famous society debutantes and her new husband, the world-renowned Irish artist John Lavery. Due to the gravity of their reason for travelling to America this time, Hazel wanted to avoid such a circus at all costs. Any such publicity would only add to her sister Dorothy's fragile state.

As if reading her thoughts, John rose from his chair and came to sit beside her, putting an arm around her.

"Stop worrying about Dorothy, Hazel – she'll be fine," he reassured her.

Hazel took his hand. "I hope so." The doctor had said she was very bad this time.

"It is just more amateur dramatics on her part. She'll do anything to get your attention. She, and your mother beforehand, have done everything possible to prevent your happiness. And now Dorothy just can't bear to see us together, happy at last."

"Well, I'm all she has in the whole world, John, since Mama died."

"That does not mean that you have to sacrifice your life to take care of her. Dorothy needs to start acting like an adult and learn to take care of herself. She could start by stopping this ridiculous continual starvation of herself and eating a proper dinner occasionally!"

"The doctors insist the fasting is somehow tied up with her insecurities," said Hazel.

John sighed and raised an eyebrow. "Everything is down to her insecurities!"

"It hasn't been easy for her, John, especially after Mama died and we discovered she had squandered all of Papa's fortune."

"That is no reason to take it out on the rest of us. We invited her to come and live with us in London – she lasted but a couple of weeks and returned to Chicago. And here we are again, putting our lives on hold for your sister."

Hazel kissed him. "You've had to contend with a lot for me, John Lavery."

"You have no idea how much more I would contend with for you, Hazel."

His words filled her with joy. She looked into his kind face which always seemed to have an underlying seriousness. Although he was over two decades older than her, he was still handsome, with neat brown hair, a distinguished air and immaculate tailoring. He always made her feel so protected, so safe. When she thought of the turmoil of her life in the past few years, she felt she had found the safest of harbours with John Lavery. She squeezed his hand before standing up.

"I had better go and change. I want to look my best when we arrive."

"My dear Hazel, you will always be the most beautiful woman wherever you go, whatever you wear."

She smiled and bent down to kiss him before walking to their bedroom.

As he watched her go, the smile left John's face, to be replaced with concern. He sighed and walked to the porthole where he stood, watching New York looming up ahead as the liner approached it.

Dressed in furs, Hazel led the way through the crowd at the pier on the Hudson River, followed by John, Alice and her nanny. Porters followed them with their luggage.

"Where *is* she?" cried Hazel in frustration, unable to spot her close friend Grace who was due to meet them. They had arranged to spend a couple of nights at Grace's home in Manhattan before travelling on to Chicago and Dorothy.

"*Hazel!*"

Hazel swung around and saw Grace waving frantically as she pushed through the crowd to her.

"Grace!" Hazel embraced her friend warmly. "Oh, it is so good to see you! And so good to be back on solid ground after that voyage! We seemed to be at sea for ever!"

"It's good to see you too, Hazel," said Grace as she pulled back from her.

"I cannot wait to get away from these dreadful crowds, get to your house and have a nice cup of tea!" said Hazel. "How's Dorothy? What's the latest news from the doctors?"

Grace stared at Hazel and bit her lower lip as tears came to her eyes.

"Grace?" said Hazel, squinting in concern.

"I'm sorry, Hazel," said Grace, shaking her head slowly. "It happened while you were still at sea. Just a couple of days ago … there was no way of contacting you … she slipped away. They said it was peaceful … at the end."

Hazel stared at Grace in disbelief, trying to comprehend what she was saying.

"What do you mean … slipped away?"

"She's dead, Hazel – Dorothy is dead."

Hazel's eyes widened as she felt her legs buckle under her. A loud cry was coming from somewhere but she wasn't sure from where. And then she realised it was coming from her.

"*John!*" she cried as he bent to raise her from the ground.

"She's in shock," said Grace. "My chauffeur has the automobile over there – let's get her out of these crowds."

"*John! John!*" Hazel cried over and over again as he and Grace supported her and pushed through the crowds, trying to get her to the waiting automobile.

The Laverys spent the night in New York before travelling by train to Chicago the next day with Grace. Time passed Hazel by in a haze.

She was indeed in a state of shock, unable to accept that Dorothy had died. But when she finally saw her sister's lifeless body, emaciated from years of fasting, there was no denying she was gone.

John took care of the funeral arrangements as Hazel was lost in a grief she hoped never to experience again. It was grief accentuated by awareness of a wasted life, of the knowledge that something had happened that might have been avoided.

The funeral was a small affair. Dorothy had lost contact with all their old friends after their mother died and Hazel hadn't lived in the city for a number of years. As Hazel pulled her fur coat closer to ward off the October Chicago chills and looked at the small crowd assembled around the grave, she felt depressed at how times had changed so much for them. There was a time when her family had been one of the most prominent in Chicago. They had lived in a fabulous mansion on Astor Street, her father had been a very wealthy and respected businessman and her mother a famous socialite. Both Hazel and Dorothy had been celebrated debutantes, famed for their beauty. Hazel herself had been nicknamed 'The most beautiful girl in the Midwest'.

As Dorothy's coffin was lowered into the grave to join their parents, Hazel felt very alone. There had been only two children in the family. But what depressed her even more was the family's fall from grace – where had the wealth gone, the prestige, the friends?

After the service, Hazel accepted the condolences of the few who had gathered and then she, John, Alice and Grace made their way to the automobile that was waiting for them outside the graveyard, John's arm around her at all times.

She was getting into the automobile when she heard a man call her name.

"*Hazel!*"

She turned and saw a man standing there with notebook and pen.

"Hazel, I am reporter from the *Chicago Sun Times* – could I have an interview with you about your sister's death?"

"What – what is this?" asked Hazel, confused.

"No comment!" snapped John as he ushered Hazel into the automobile.

"What does he want an interview for?" asked Hazel.

"Drive on!" John ordered the chauffeur and the automobile quickly drove away.

"Well, sadly, nobody could do anything for her in the end," said Grace.

She and the Laverys were sitting in their hotel suite.

"I shouldn't have let her come back to Chicago," said Hazel. "I should have forced her to stay in London."

"She was a grown woman, Hazel," said John. "She had a right to choose how to lead her life as she wanted to."

"And choose her own death?" Hazel asked. "She wasn't able to look after herself. I let her down."

"Dorothy was a very strong-willed girl, Hazel," said Grace. "There was nothing you could do to stop her from returning to Chicago if that's what she wanted to do."

There was a knock on the door and John went to answer it.

A waiter wheeled in a trolley with tea, sandwiches and cakes.

"Thank you, you can leave it just here," John directed as he reached into his pocket and tipped the waiter handsomely.

"Shall I be Mother?" said Grace, standing and lifting the teapot.

As she poured the tea she spotted a photograph of Hazel on the front page of the evening *Chicago Sun Times* which was placed on the trolley. She quickly put down the teapot and reached out to remove the newspaper, but she was too late. Hazel had grabbed it, having spotted the headline.

DOROTHY MARTYN DIES ABANDONED BY SOCIETY SISTER

"*What is this?*" cried Hazel.

"Don't read that trash, Hazel," begged Grace as she tried to snatch the newspaper away, but Hazel held on to it firmly.

Hazel read the article aloud.

"*'The Chicago Sun Times has learned of the tragic and untimely death of Miss Dorothy Martyn, daughter of one of the city's once most influential families. Aged just twenty-three, it is understood Miss Martyn died as a result of years of physical neglect. Chicago society was shocked to learn Miss Martyn died alone in a public hospital with neither relative nor friend present. Miss Martyn's one surviving sister, Hazel, lives in London in considerable style and comfort. Previously the widow of top New York surgeon Ned Trudeau, Hazel is now married to world-famous artist John Lavery. It is thought the relationship between the two sisters had been fraught with difficulty for years. A family friend says the sisters were not close and while Hazel continued to live the high life in London, her sister sank further into a life of misery, poverty and depression ...'"*

"That's enough!" said Grace and she snatched the newspaper out of Hazel's hands. "How dare they write trash like that! I'm going to ring the editor first thing in the morning and give him hell! And then I'm going to get on to our lawyers and get a retraction. They can't write things like this!"

Hazel stared into the distance. "They can ... because it's true."

That night Hazel stood at the window of their suite, looking out at the city of her birth and upbringing. Grace had gone to her room and Alice and her nanny were in bed.

John came into the room and, finding it was in darkness, went to turn on the light.

"No, John, don't – don't turn on the light."

He walked over to her and, standing behind her, placed his hands on her shoulders.

"I'm never coming back here, John. I've no reason ever to come back, now Dorothy is gone. I'm closing the door on Chicago and the States. My home is Europe now – London and Ireland. I don't want anything to do with America again."

BOOK 1

1920

CHAPTER 1

Winston Churchill, Secretary of State for War and Secretary of State for Air, was as ever, enraptured by his hostess as he sat across the table from her. Hazel Lavery, or Lady Lavery as she was now styled since her husband had been knighted the previous year, held everyone's attention at her dinner party at 5 Cromwell Place, Kensington. Her delicate hands moved gracefully as she spoke, deftly emphasising the points she was making. Her hazel eyes, more green than brown, moved from guest to guest as her soft American accent hypnotised everyone present. They said an invitation to Hazel Lavery's dinner table was the most sought-after in London. As Winston finished his delicious pudding, he fully agreed.

Hazel ended her tale and all present burst into laughter.

"Did that *really* happen with that young gentleman, Hazel?" asked Winston's wife Clementine.

"As true as I am sitting here! My father forbade me ever to go to a dance in Chicago again after the incident!"

"But that didn't stop you, Hazel?" asked Winston.

"Of course not! Whenever my father forbade me from doing anything, it only made me do it twice as much!"

"It's the poor chap who asked you to dance that I feel sorry for!" said Winston. "I'd say he never recovered from the experience."

"Oh, he recovered fully I can assure you and went on to have two wives, though not at the same time I am glad to say – and several mistresses, occasionally at the same time I am not glad to say – after that unfortunate encounter with me!" said Hazel, causing all at the table to erupt into laughter again. "Though I hasten to add, I take no responsibility for his unfortunate love life from that point on!"

"Where was the gentlemen from?" enquired Clementine.

"He was raised in Chicago, but I believe his family had emigrated from Ireland," said Hazel.

"*Huh!*" grunted Winston with disdain. "Well, that explains it all!"

"And what is that supposed to mean?" snapped Hazel, her jovial nature suddenly suspended.

Winston looked across the table at Hazel's husband Sir John and realised he had been indelicate. Not only did John hail from Ireland, hut it was a well-known fact that the Laverys, particularly Hazel, had espoused Irish Independence, a *cause célébrè* they had identified with. Everyone knew that Hazel, an Irish American, had almost completely rejected her American nationality in favour of her Irish heritage. In her pursuit and love of all things Irish, she had almost reinvented herself as a 'simple Irish girl', as she called herself, as opposed to what everyone knew her to be – the daughter of a well-known Chicago society family. The whole thing left Winston bemused, as he knew that the Martyns had emigrated from Galway to Chicago more than two centuries before. Still, he saw no harm in this idealised love affair Hazel had decided to have with Ireland. She was a romantic, he knew, and this love of Ireland was just a whimsical phase she was going through.

"I apologise, John, I did not mean to offend," he said.

"Oh, none taken, Winston," said the ever-congenial John, more concerned that his guest would be concerned than anything else.

"But what *did* you mean, Winston?" pressed Hazel.

"Nothing personal against anybody Irish, I assure you," said Winston, his temper rising. "But this unfortunate young man you are discussing at that dance in Chicago demonstrates all the arrogance and pig-headedness the Irish continually show ... which is why we are still bogged down in that bloody war in Ireland!"

"Well, the solution is simple, my dear Winston," said Hazel. "Just give us Irish our independence and the Anglo-Irish war will be over, simple as that."

Thelma Grey, a society wife who was a neighbour of the Laverys, was seated at the end of the table beside Clementine Churchill. She raised her eyes to heaven, leaned towards Clementine and whispered, "Oh dear, and here she goes! She won't shut up about Irish politics for the rest of the night!"

Clementine giggled and sat back to watch her husband do battle with Hazel.

"You *know* it's not as simple as that, Hazel!" snapped Winston.

"What I *know* is that two sides in a war will never find peace if they continue to refuse to *talk* to one another!" said Hazel. "I am certain that if the Irish and British could just sit around the same table then a compromise could be reached. If people just *talked* to each other!"

Winston became animated. "How can we talk to shadows? Men who hide in the shadows or behind women and children and then come out and ambush our troops and commit murder before disappearing back into the shadows just as fast? At least the Germans in the Great War came and fought us head on!"

"Well, I am sure the Irish Republicans would come out of the shadows if they were confident your men wouldn't shoot them or arrest them and fling them into gaol – without trial!" said Hazel.

"It is they who are shooting us without trial, Hazel, without warning, without shame," said Winston. "And all this is being organised with military precision by this monster Collins."

"Michael Collins is not a monster," declared Hazel. "The press and the government have portrayed him as something he simply is not."

"And how would you know?" demanded Winston.

"Because I have met him," declared Hazel.

There was silence around the table as everyone stared at Hazel in disbelief.

"*You* ... met Collins?" said Winston incredulously.

"Indeed, I did. Quite a number of years ago, but I remember him well. I have a very good memory for interesting faces – it is the artist within me – and he had the *most* interesting of faces."

"But how could you possibly have met him?" pressed Winston.

"It was before the Great War, when he lived in London. I can't quite remember all the details – it was so long ago and so much has happened since. But I remember him well. He worked for the General Post office and he had been invited to the theatre by the Solicitor for the Post Office, Crompton Llewelyn Davies, and his wife Moya who is Irish – you know, her father was on the Supreme Council of the Irish Republican Brotherhood so, politically, she and Michael had much in common. He loved the theatre as we did and we were sometimes in his company. If my memory serves me right – and it usually does – he lived with his sister Hannie who worked in the Post Office as well."

"That is correct, Hazel, bless your memory," confirmed Winston. "Indeed, Hannie Collins is still living here in London."

"And no doubt being watched carefully by British intelligence," said Hazel knowingly.

"What's he *like,* Hazel?" demanded an excited female guest at the end of the table, anxious to bring the conversation back to Michael Collins and away from his sister.

"Yes, do tell – is he as handsome as they say?" asked Thelma, who had been jolted out of her apathy on hearing Hazel had met the elusive revolutionary.

"Michael was gentle –"

"*Gentle!*" roared Winston. "How can you describe a cold-hearted assassin as gentle?"

"But that's how he came across to me, during the time I met him. Gentle and kind and quite charming." She smiled at the memory.

"You said he liked the theatre – then obviously he was also a very good actor!" said Clementine.

"Perhaps." Hazel shrugged her shoulders.

"So, you would recognise him if you saw him again?" asked Winston.

"I would," said Hazel.

"I ask because no one knows what he looks like. We don't have one good photograph of him – that's how he continually escapes our troops and walks around the streets of Dublin undetected while he plans the war against us."

14

"Perhaps Hazel could go to Dublin and help track him down," suggested Thelma acidly.

"Oh, no, I couldn't possibly do that," Hazel said.

"Why ever not? You would be helping to put the most wanted man in Britain behind bars," said Winston.

"Oh, no, it just wouldn't be the right – etiquette, you know!"

"What?" Winston looked at her.

"Well, he was an acquaintance – hardly a friend, but he *was* an acquaintance – and I couldn't just shop him to the authorities any more than I could have pointed you out to the Germans, Winston, if we had lost the war!"

There was a sharp intake of breath around the table.

"Hazel!" admonished Clementine.

Hazel looked around the table and shrugged. "Well, it's true! What ails you all?"

"Hazel!" snapped Thelma. "You simply cannot draw comparison between Winston and that – that – murderous thug!"

"The one you were dying to know whether he was handsome or not?"

She turned to Winston and saw his face was red with rage.

"Madam!" growled Winston.

"Yes, Winston?" she asked sweetly, her eyes wide with innocence.

"I–I–" he stuttered.

"Yes?" She smiled at him, making a small guilty pout.

He drew a deep breath before saying, "I am glad that I can always rely on your loyalty – even if there had been the unlikely event of a German victory!"

His cracked a wide smile and Hazel blew him a kiss as the rest of the table heaved a sigh of relief and began to laugh.

They had left the dining room and were now having drinks in the sumptuous upstairs drawing room which was located at the front of the house.

All the men at the party now had gravitated towards Hazel and literally surrounded her as she held court. Thelma studied Hazel and felt the familiar pang of jealousy she always inspired in her. She wasn't sure if it was Hazel's auburn hair, her delicately refined features or her porcelain skin that unnerved her more. Or it could be the fact that all this was polished by Hazel's glamour and style, and accompanied by a witty and sparkling personality. The fact was that Thelma was always left feeling inadequate after an evening in Hazel Lavery's company.

"I must say you are very brave or very patient – I'm not sure which is the right word to use," said Thelma to Clementine Churchill as she watched Hazel and Winston laugh over some private joke across the parlour.

"In what way?" asked Clementine.

"Allowing the friendship between Hazel and Winston."

"But why ever should I mind?"

"Well, you know what they say about her? That no man is safe from her?"

"I should think Winston is quite safe – from any woman!" chuckled Clementine.

"Well, if it were my husband I would most certainly be concerned!" said Thelma.

"Well, if it were your husband you probably would have every right to be concerned!" said Clementine with a smirk.

Clementine viewed Thelma's pretty features, her wavy black hair and chic clothes and wondered how a woman as fetching as her could allow herself to be jealous of another. But she realised what an untamed monster envy could be once it got a person in its clutches. And it had certainly got Thelma in its clutches.

Thelma became annoyed at Clementine's nonchalance. "I'll have you know some of the wives in Kensington are so concerned about the matter that they have formed a husband protection society!"

"And I believe you are a founding member of that society, Thelma!"

"I would not trust Hazel as far as I could throw her with any man, and I don't mind who knows that!" said Thelma.

"Hazel isn't a threat to me or to any other woman … and those who feel threatened by her are just jealous of her in my opinion."

Thelma scoffed. "What is there to be jealous of? She parades around pretending to be from some noble Irish family, when we all know she's just another American nouveau-riche social climber!"

Clementine frowned. "You mustn't speak so unkindly of Lady Lavery, Thelma."

"Well, it's true. She has very cleverly used her husband's talent as an artist to infiltrate the very top level of society. She even managed to wrangle him a knighthood and herself a title along with it through this infiltration … he paints the great and the good, and *she* sneaks in behind his easel and makes them her friends. She gives new meaning to the words *social climbing*!"

"If she manages to become friends with the 'great and the good', as you put it, that is because they want to be her friends. And they want to be her friends because of her many wonderful qualities. I'll never forget the great kindness Hazel showed Winston in the past."

"What kindness?" asked Thelma dismissively.

Clementine's large eyes became misty as she recalled that awful time in their lives.

"It was during the war, after Winston's disastrous military campaign at Gallipoli. When he had to resign from the Admiralty and we had to leave Admiralty House, we came to live here on Cromwell Place with Winston's brother. We were political and social pariahs at the time. Winston was in such a dark depression. We rented a small country house, Hoe Farm, to spend time there at the weekends. To try and distract him from his troubles, Winston began painting. One day he ran out of some oils and was wondering what he could use as a substitute. Then I remembered that John Lavery lived on the same road as us here in Kensington. So, I telephoned looking for advice but the Laverys were out. Two hours later Hazel Lavery arrived at our front door at Hoe Farm." Clementine smiled at the memory. "On hearing about our query from her butler, she had got into her automobile and driven herself down to Hoe Farm with the missing oils that Winston needed."

"How energetic of her." Even Thelma was impressed.

"Not only that, but she then proceeded to spend the rest of the day tutoring Winston on his painting. I can see her still out in the garden at Hoe Farm ordering him not to be afraid of the canvas and to be dynamic and dramatic with his colours. I think painting saved Winston's life at the time, and the Laverys were a big part of that. Why, Winston practically lived in John's studio here, being encouraged with his art."

As Thelma watched Hazel float and flit around the room, she wondered what benefit it would have been to a social climber like Hazel to befriend the socially expelled Churchills at the time. She decided that Hazel was such a shrewd operator she probably knew the Churchills would come back into fashion one day and wanted to be their best friend when they did.

CHAPTER 2

Hazel was at her writing desk in her sitting room as she finished penning a letter. The comfortable room was on the first floor, at the front of the house, overlooking Cromwell Place. When at home she preferred to spend her days there as opposed to the main drawing room downstairs. For a start, the window overlooked the busy street so she could keep an eye on the comings and goings of her illustrious neighbours. Secondly, as this was her own private room, she could be sure of every item always being where she had left it and not being misplaced.

She reread aloud the last paragraph of the letter she had just written to a Member of Parliament.

"*'And that is why I beg you as matter of urgency to change your opinion and to stop supporting this vicious and fruitless war the British are conducting in Ireland. The Irish have already established a parliament (the Dáil), government departments and a court system and the British presence in Ireland, and the terrible acts of violence being committed by the new constabulary forces there, are looking more like an illegal occupation as each day goes by. I would be more than happy to meet you in person to discuss this matter further and I offer you an open invitation to high tea at my home in Kensington at a time and date suitable to you. I look forward to meeting with you.'*"

Hazel nodded in approval and finished it off by signing *Lady Lavery* with a flourish at the bottom of the page.

There was a knock on the door and Gordon the butler entered.

"Sir Shane Leslie is here to see you, Your Ladyship," said Gordon.

"Ah excellent! Show him in," said Hazel, rising from her desk.

A dapper man in his mid-thirties, with a large frame and slicked-back hair atop a long oval face, came bounding into the room past the butler with his arms outstretched. Shane was Winston Churchill's cousin and, unusually for an Anglo-Irish aristocrat, a believer in Irish independence. He was a firm friend of Hazel's and made no secret of the fact he was besotted with her.

"Hazel!" he declared, coming around to her behind the desk and embracing her tightly.

"Shane, I wasn't expecting you today."

"Well, I was in the neighbourhood and thought I'd drop by."

"Tea, my lady?" asked Gordon, disapproval evident in his voice.

"Yes, please, Gordon," said Hazel and the butler retreated as Shane continued to hold her.

Hazel tried to wriggle away from Shane's ever-tightening embrace. "Shane! Your cologne is quite overpowering me!"

"But I put it on especially for you!"

"Perhaps use a little less next time then, my dear?" she said, pushing him away, forcing him to release her.

He glanced down at the letter on the desk and picked it up, his eyes scanning it.

"What are you writing to *him* for? He's a lost cause – you'll never convert that fellow to the notion of Irish independence." He then burst out laughing as he read the ending of the letter. "And you've invited him to high tea! What are you expecting to do – convert him by crumpet with cream and strawberry jam?"

"I've often found a little tenderness and hospitality can change the way a man views the world. And I'd try anything, Shane, to try and stop this dreadful war in Ireland. If I could meet this MP in an informal setting and express to him what the situation on the ground in Ireland is, then perhaps he could be converted."

"*Hmmm* – you mean flutter your eyelids and widen your big hazel eyes and he will do your bidding as the rest of us do?" Shane smirked at her. "Well, I think even your charms will fail with this fellow – the man is an imperialistic warmonger who will never believe in Irish Independence ... *Empire before all else!*"

"Well, we can but try ... And did your mother never tell you it was rude to read other people's letters?" She took the letter from Shane and, folding it over, placed it in a drawer of her chesterfield desk.

She then drew him away from the desk to the centre of the room.

"Where's John?" asked Shane.

"He's out on a commission – he's painting an exiled Russian count." She clasped her hands in glee. "I can't wait to hear later how the man escaped the Bolsheviks!"

"Well, as long as the chap escaped the Bolsheviks with enough money to pay John his commission!"

"My heart goes out to the Russian nobility – they have been treated in such a beastly fashion by everyone," said Hazel.

Shane's voice was full of mockery. "Do not tell me that your next cause is going to be the Russian nobility and their plight in exile! Are you about to abandon the Irish peasants and start campaigning for Russian aristocrats ousted by their own peasants?"

"No – I am not!" She feigned anger at his mockery. "I am just curious to hear what the Russian has to say about his escape, that is all! Do not mock my involvement in Irish affairs, Shane. It is the issue most dear to my heart and I am determined to do my best to resolve the situation."

"Oh, I know, Hazel dear! We all know how you cut short your stay at your villa in Tangier to come back and try to use your influence to end the Irish war. Not that it was any great sacrifice on your part – the fact that you never particularly liked Tangier whenever John forced you to stay there is entirely beside the point, is it not?"

"If you are going to continually mock me then I suggest you just leave!" she said, now genuinely annoyed.

"I'm sorry – I apologise!" He held his hands in the air. "I am only teasing. Nobody appreciates your interest in Irish affairs as much as I do. Why, Winston was only telling me yesterday that he was at a dinner party here a couple of weeks ago and all you did was try to twist his arm to start negotiations with the Irish."

"Did Winston really say that?"

"He most certainly did – he said he went home with a headache after listening to you wittering on for the whole night about it."

"Good! He deserves a headache for presiding over this disastrous campaign in Ireland."

"Well, I've haven't made any headway with him – so if you can, then good luck!" said Shane.

Shane was a constant source of fascination for Hazel. By background, family and education, he should automatically be on the side of the British in their continued control of Ireland. But along the way Shane had had a conversion and now fully supported Irish independence, had converted to Catholicism and even befriended some of the fugitive republican leaders. All this made Shane one of Hazel's heroes, despite his faults, and she relied on him for information and instruction on Irish affairs.

He stood admiring her, seeing all anger now removed from her beautiful features.

"I've written you a new poem," he said.

"Another one?"

"Yes." He reached into his pocket and took out a page of paper, unfolding it he walked across and handed it to her.

She smiled broadly as she took it and read it. The poem was a whimsical ode to love. The wording was bordering on immature, describing all of Hazel's features in an adoring fashion.

"Well?" asked Shane as he saw her finish reading the cringeworthy verse.

Hazel sighed. "It's beautiful."

"Really?" Shane was delighted.

"The words, the sentiment, the emotion – it's all magical!" she whispered in a breathy voice.

Suddenly Shane reached out and, grabbing her shoulders and pulling her close to him, kissed her on the lips.

Momentarily stunned, she pushed him off and backed away from him.

"Shane! Have you forgotten yourself!"

"Yes, I have forgotten myself! I freely admit I forget myself whenever in your company!"

She fixed her hair and said, "Shane, I've told you before – you must get over this infatuation."

"It is *not* an infatuation. I am in love with you, Hazel. I always have been!"

"Nonsense, Shane. Besides, being in love with me is a waste of your emotion – as we can never be together. I never could and never would leave John. I adore him."

"But he's thirty years older than you, Hazel. What kind of marriage can you have with a man like that? He never laughs, he never jokes – how can somebody as vivacious as you be happy with somebody like John?"

"He is not thirty years older than me – he's only twenty-four years older. And you are being quite cruel about him. I won't have you say a bad word about him!" However, she was not looking too upset by Shane's words. "Are you seriously suggesting that I leave him, and you would leave Marjorie on the basis of this infatuation?"

"Yes!"

"You are deluded. Besides, you can put any such notion out of your head as I am about to follow your example and convert to Catholicism – and we Catholics, may I remind you, do not believe in divorce!"

"Convert to Catholicism! But why are you doing that? You aren't even religious!"

"It's just something I feel I need to do," she said. "For my identity – to make me more Irish and connect me with my Irish roots."

"I see!" said Shane, rolling his eyes.

"Heavens above, Shane! *You* converted! Why shouldn't I?"

He began to pace up and down in frustration, ignoring her question.

"Hazel, I'd do anything you asked me to do. Anything! Why are you so loyal to him? Why won't you have an affair with me at least? I mean, it wouldn't be the first affair you've had, surely? I shall accept whatever terms you dictate to be with you."

Hazel showed mock horror. "I have never been unfaithful to my husband! Ever!"

"But all the men you know –"

"Are just friends. No more – and no less. If their feelings are more than that or they wish to spread lies – or their *wives* wish to spread lies – then there is nothing I can do."

"But everyone takes lovers, Hazel. You must be the only wife in our circle who's never had a lover!"

"Perhaps I am, I can only speak for myself. Now you must put all this nonsense behind you, Shane. Your poor wife Marjorie is fully aware of this infatuation and continues to look daggers at me whenever I am in her company, as if I am responsible for provoking you!"

"Marjorie, like all other wives in London of our class, fully accepts and expects her husband to have a mistress," Shane said dismissively.

Hazel looked cynical. "Marjorie, unlike the other wives in our circle, is an American, may I remind you, and I can assure you that as an American she certainly does not condone the louche behaviour of the British upper class."

Shane's expression became very serious and he embraced her again. "Hazel, I can't live without you!"

The door suddenly opened. "That Russian count is the most peculiar man –"

John Lavery stopped speaking abruptly as he saw Shane Leslie jump away from his wife.

"Oh, good afternoon, John."

"Good afternoon, Shane – and how are you?" asked John, noticing Shane's face had become beetroot-red.

"Very good," said Shane.

John looked at Hazel who was smoothing down her hair.

"So tell us about the Russian count?" she said.

"Yes, Hazel was just telling me all about your latest commission," said Shane. "I hope you got paid upfront, John – I don't think many of these Russian nobles managed to flee with much money out of their country!"

"Oh, I think my commission is quite safe with this fellow," said John.

"I was just telling Shane that we're travelling to Ireland next month," said Hazel, "for you to paint religious and political leaders for an Irish Collection – to be displayed in a new national art gallery when the country gets independence." She turned to Shane. "I was hoping, Shane, that you could use some of your subversive contacts to arrange for us to meet some of the rebel leaders, to do their portraits?"

"Oh, I don't know about that, Hazel," he said, taken aback. "I can't imagine any of the rebel leaders agreeing to a sitting for an oil canvas when they're doing everything to hide what they look like from the authorities!"

"Well, the paintings wouldn't be for public viewing – certainly not until the war in Ireland is over. We wouldn't show them to anyone, we would guarantee that."

"I really can't see any of the rebels agreeing to that. If the paintings fell into British hands, they would have an up-to-date image of what they look like!"

Gordon walked in through the open door with a tray.

"Tea, my lady," he announced.

"Actually, we'll have tea in the main drawing room, Gordon. Come along, Shane – we can discuss this further downstairs."

Hazel led Shane out of the room, Gordon following.

John spotted a paper on the floor. Walking over to it, he picked it up. It was a love poem to Hazel, written by Shane. He read it before folding it over and putting it in his pocket.

He looked at the door through which their laughter was drifting back, and he began to frown.

CHAPTER 3

Michael Collins was seated at a kitchen table in a house in Harold's Cross on the southside of Dublin. Sally Owens, who owned the house, thought he was like a king holding court – as she had countless times when she'd watched him with the other men sitting around her kitchen table. She smiled to herself at the thought of her ordinary kitchen being likened to a royal court, but that's how Michael's presence there made it feel.

Sally's house was one of the safe houses that Michael frequently stayed in. She was a young woman of thirty whose husband had died the previous year of the Spanish flu that had taken so many lives. She now lived alone in the house as they didn't have any children. Her husband had been a close friend of Michael's and she was delighted to be able to assist in the struggle for independence and offer her home as a safe house to him. Michael could never stay long in the one house in case the British got wind of the fact he was there, so he was always on the move, never staying in one house for longer than a few nights.

Sally wondered at his energy – that he could lead such a life continually on the run – but he seemed to thrive on it. She watched him talk to the other men around the kitchen table and was amazed, listening to him issue instructions, at how he could organise a whole war hiding in a kitchen. Not only could he organise a war, but by the looks of it be on the winning side.

"When're those arms arriving in Wexford, Jack?" asked Michael.

"Tomorrow night."

"Make sure you get them to Dublin as fast as you can," said Michael. "Did you organise the milk lorry to transport them?"

"Yes, Mick – the local creamery has already lent us a lorry and it's on standby."

Mick reached into a big bag beside him and took out a wad of cash. He wrote out a receipt and put it into his pocket before handing the cash to Jack. "Give that to creamery owner and tell him he'll have his lorry back the next day."

"Yes, Mick," said Jack, taking the wad of money and putting it into his pocket.

"Anything to report on that new chief of police staying at the Gresham Hotel, Francie?" asked Michael, directing the question at the blond man across the table.

"Yes, the telephone operator at the hotel said he made three calls to London today. He demanded reinforcements to deal with the – quote – 'ever worsening situation'."

Michael laughed. "He'll find his own situation worse in the morning when he wakes to find his automobile burned outside the hotel!"

"It's an ill wind that blows nobody any good! His driver will have the day off!" said Sally as she went around the table with the teapot, filling everyone's cup.

"Never a truer word said, Sally!" laughed Mick as she cut a big slice of fruit cake and put it in front of him.

Michael reached into the bag and took out a five-pound note. Again, he wrote a receipt and placed it in his pocket before handing the money to Francie.

"Make sure the hotel receptionist gets that."

"I will surely."

Sally had seen the same thing happen time and time again. Michael would arrive with a bag of money and distribute it during the course of the evening to the men, to be paid to those helping and advancing the war effort.

"Everyone needs to be extra-vigilant over the next few days," said Michael. "They will want revenge for that ambush we carried out on the Tans today in retaliation for what those Black and Tan bastards did last week."

The 'Black and Tans' were a force of temporary constables recruited in a hurry to help the Royal Irish Constabulary – an idea of Winston Churchill's. Many of them unemployed veterans of the Great War, they were given a rushed three months' training. Then, because of a shortage of RIC uniforms, they were issued with 'uniforms' made up of a mixture of army khaki and black or dark-green RIC jackets, caps and belts. A journalist wrote that they reminded them of a certain pack of beagles nicknamed the 'Black and Tans' from their colouration. The nickname stuck.

"Tell everyone to be on their guard. The British have stopped any time off for their Tans, so the city will be teeming with them."

"Right, Mick," they all responded.

"Right, off home with all of ye and I'll see ye tomorrow," said Michael.

They all stood up and waited at the back door for Sally to open it. She went into the back yard and walked to the gate that led onto the lane at the bottom. Unbolting it, she glanced up and down outside before waving to the men. They silently slipped out of the house and filed past her into the laneway. She watched them disappear into the night like shadows.

Back inside, she poured herself a mug of tea and refilled Michael's mug.

"Will you have another bit of cake, Mick?" she asked as she went to cut another slice.

"I will not, Sally. I'll explode if I have another bite to eat. Sure, I'm full after the stew you made earlier. I always say, out of all the cooks in all the houses I stay in, Sally Owens is the best!"

She laughed and came and sat beside him.

"Do you want something stronger in that tea?" she asked, moving her small round figure closer to him and speaking in a conspiratorial whisper.

"I do not! Are you trying to get me drunk?" he said with a scowl.

"I most certainly am not!" she said, affronted.

28

His scowl faded into a large grin and she realised he was joking.

"Oh you!" she said, slapping him on the arm.

"I'd better get to bed. I've an early start – the Squad will be arriving for me at daybreak," said Mick.

'The Squad' were a handpicked team of twelve republicans who went with Michael everywhere and whose loyalty was so unwavering they would lay down their lives for him. The British press called them ruthless assassins, cold-blooded murderers who enforced Collins' death warrants. The British press said many things about Michael Collins.

"Do you never get tired of it, Mick? All this running around – you can't ever even get a decent night's sleep!"

He shrugged. "Somebody's got to do it, Sally." He stood up, bent down and kissed her forehead. "Thanks for everything, Sally. You're a great girl."

He stopped as he reached the doorway and, turning, smiled at her while he studied her. She gazed at his large frame in the doorway, his handsome face, brilliant eyes and brown hair.

"What is it, Mick?" she asked.

"Tell me, Sally, how did a nice girl like you get mixed up in all this?"

She smiled back at him. "Probably the same way you did, Mick – it was my fate!"

He nodded and laughed, running a hand through his thick hair, before leaving. She could hear him walk heavily up the stairs to his bedroom and close the door. She sat sipping her tea for a while before going to bed herself.

Sally's eyes sprang open as she heard a loud bang. When she heard another, she jumped out of bed and rushed to the window.

Black and Tans were smashing into the house next door. Throwing a shawl around her shoulders, she ran out onto the landing.

Michael was already there.

"It's the Tans – they've smashed in next door!" she hissed.

They could now hear shouting and screaming outside.

"They'll be here next," said Michael. "They'll search every house in the street."

"You hide," she said, pushing him back into his bedroom. "If they come here, I'll try and distract them."

Michael rushed into the room and to the window which looked out on the yard at the back of the house. He knew nothing Sally could do would distract them. And they would be there any minute. They had obviously got a tip-off that he was staying locally, and they wouldn't stop till they found him. He opened the window. He could make out Tans coming down the back laneway and breaking into houses from the back as well.

Michael climbed onto the window ledge, jumped down onto the roof of a shed that ran from the house to the back laneway and lay there motionless, waiting for a hail of bullets. But none came.

There was a loud knock on the front door and Sally steadied herself. She pulled her shawl tightly around her and went down to open the door. As she unbolted the door, it suddenly swung forcibly open as a group of Black and Tans stormed into the house.

"What is the meaning of this?" she demanded.

"*Where is he, you Fenian bitch?*" demanded one of the Tans.

"Who are you –?" but before she had time to finish her sentence the Tan had struck her across the face, sending her flying to the floor.

Stunned, she lay on the floor, the blood flowing down her face.

Michael could hear the commotion going on inside the house as the troops stormed through it. He could hear Sally's screams. He knew he had to move whatever the risk. At any moment a Tan would look out the open window. More Tans ran through the yard below and in through the back door. He raised his head cautiously and glanced up and down the laneway. Seeing no one there, he slid from the roof of the shed into the laneway and sprinted away. He could hear Sally's screams behind him.

He stopped running. His heart beating quickly, he reached inside his coat for his gun. He could hear Sally begging them to stop whatever they were doing.

Shaking and trembling, he fought the overwhelming urge to return to the house. Wiping away tears, he forced himself to continue into the night.

Michael spent the next three hours stealthily stalking through the back alleys and laneways of Dublin. Everywhere he turned there seemed to be a military presence. Finally, he arrived at the back of a house in Phibsboro. The house was in darkness and he began to throw small stones up at a window. At last he saw some movement inside. The window opened and the head of his cousin Gearóid emerged.

"*Gearóid – it's me!*" he hissed.

Gearóid quickly closed over the window and seconds later the back door of the house opened.

Michael rushed in and stood panting against the wall.

"Mick – what's going on?"

Michael stumbled to the table and sat down. "There was a raid on Sally Owens' house where I was staying. I barely got out." He sank his face into his hands as he remembered Sally's screams as he escaped into the night.

"Fuck's sake!" said Gearóid, going to the cabinet and pouring a large glass of whiskey. He placed it in front of Michael who grabbed it and drank the whiskey back.

"Either they didn't know exactly where I was or they got the address wrong – they barged in next door first, waking us up – otherwise they would have caught me for sure."

"How did they know? Sally's was the safest of safe houses."

"It's obvious, isn't it? An informer – somebody is giving us away. I want that person found, Gearóid, and I want him taken out."

Gearóid nodded. "And what about Sally?"

Michael's eyes filled with tears. "I don't know ... I heard her screams ..."

Gearóid grabbed his arm. "There was nothing you could do, Mick. You had to escape – the country has to come first."

"I know. I want a report first thing tomorrow on what has happened to Sally. If she's in prison, I want her sprung – if we can spring De Valera from an English gaol then we can spring an Irishwoman from a Dublin one."

"I'll find out first thing," said Gearóid.

"And – she has a mother – a widow who has no other children. I want her looked after. She lives down the country in Tipperary. Make sure she has enough money to get by if Sally has been taken away."

"Right. Mick, you need to get out of the city for a while. With three of their men killed, they're hunting everywhere for you."

"Will you be quiet, man! I'm not leaving Dublin!"

"What good will you be to anyone if they capture you or shoot you? Will you see sense and lie low for a few days? Just until we find out if there is a spy in our camp and get on top of the situation? If there's an informer, as you say, then nowhere you go in the city will be safe for you until we find out who it is and take him out."

Michael looked at Gearóid who was his second cousin but often felt more like a brother, they were so close. Gearóid was very youthful-looking and his eyes had an innocence about them which belied the role he had played in the 1916 rising. Michael knew he could trust Gearóid with his life and he often did.

Michael nodded, accepting the sense of what was being said. "Where can I go?" he asked.

"I'm going down to Longford to visit Maud – come down with me. Nobody in the organisation needs to know where you have gone."

Michael digested the suggestion. Maud Kiernan was Gearóid's girlfriend, one of the daughters of a wealthy merchant family in the town of Granard in Longford. She was also the sister of the woman Michael was in love with.

"Granard?"

"Yes – come on down with me to Longford. It will be like the old days. We can relax and enjoy ourselves with the girls."

The girls ... even after a night like the one he had just had, Michael could smile at the reference. That was how they always referred the Kiernan sisters – as *the girls*.

An oasis of glamour, fun, charm and beauty in the midst of these dreadful times. Michael closed his eyes for a few seconds and allowed himself the luxury of floating back to all the happy times he'd had with the girls, and one girl in particular.

"Well?" said Gearóid.

Michael nodded. "Fine, we'll leave tomorrow."

CHAPTER 4

Inside the Laverys' beautiful home, down the long wide hallway, up the magnificent staircase to the landing above and to the left were the double doors that led into John's art studio. This gigantic room, with three windows at the front overlooking Cromwell Place and a glass dome above which allowed in the most wonderful light, was the jewel in the crown of the house. A spectacular studio, it was considered the best in London. Stunning artwork decorated the walls while unfinished paintings rested against walls, surrounded by ornate furniture.

As she had done on so many occasions, too many to remember, Hazel was posing – for this painting she was stretched out on a chaise longue. It was a happy co-operation. Hazel enjoyed modelling for John every bit as much as he enjoyed painting her. He had used her as a model so many times that she had become known as the most-painted woman in London. As John brought her face to life on canvas, he was as fascinated by her as he was on the first day he had met her, many years ago in France. He had been there painting – she had been on vacation with her recently widowed mother and her sister Dorothy. It had been love at first sight for both of them, to the horror of everyone. Hazel, from one of the most respected families in Chicago, a stunning debutante with intelligence to match, was expected to marry a dashing young East Coast, Yale-educated WASP, not an Irish widower twenty-four years her senior. He frowned as he thought of the obstacles that were put in their way, the battles they had to fight. At the time, he would never have thought it possible that she would ever be here living with him as his wife.

"I wish Shane would let us know when he plans to visit, instead of constantly dropping in unannounced – and uninvited," said John as he worked away on the canvas.

"Oh, Shane would not be Shane if he stuck to protocol, John – he is a spontaneous creature. Besides, we are so near Harrods and he just drops in when he is out shopping."

"Well, I can't imagine many women who would tolerate his constant intrusions as you do – he can make quite a nuisance of himself."

"I wouldn't describe Shane as a nuisance, John. He's a dear friend and he is on our side when it comes to Ireland – in fact, I wouldn't know what to do without him. As you know, he is my chief informant on what is happening over there – my eyes and ears."

"*Hmmm*," said John, his face stiffening with irritation.

Seeing his expression, she stifled a giggle. "And he can be quite charming and amusing ... I imagine many a woman would find him very attractive company and enjoy his dropping by when he felt like it."

John tightened his hold on his paintbrush as he tried not to let his emotions show.

"I don't know what his poor wife must think – writing another woman love poems all the time," he said.

"Oh, I'm sure Marjorie Leslie knew what she was getting when she married Shane and, if she didn't, then she was a fool who must live with the consequences."

"He can't even write good poetry," muttered John under his breath.

"I do believe you are jealous, John Lavery!"

"I am not! Although if I didn't keep finding love notes from him to you around the house it might make his visits less ... uncomfortable."

"*I* couldn't agree more!" said a young female voice.

John turned around to see his fifteen-year-old stepdaughter Alice enter the room. She was pretty girl with brown ringlets and intelligent eyes. John often thought they were eyes that belonged to an older woman they seemed so knowing and wise.

"It's far more than just *uncomfortable* watching Shane Leslie's antics around Mama – it's downright *embarrassing*!" said Alice as she leaned forward and kissed John on the cheek, then inspected the painting he was working on.

"You are far too young to understand these things, Alice, and nobody has asked for your opinion in any case," said Hazel, her face turning sour.

"I think John is far too tolerant! Shane Leslie should be banned from the house and his ridiculous love poetry along with him!" said Alice.

"I don't know how everyone has suddenly become a reader, nay an expert, on Shane's *personal* poetry to me," said Hazel. "Has it been published in *The Times* without my knowledge, perchance?"

"It is left all over the house, Mama," stated Alice. "One can't go into a room without finding one of his outpourings of love to you on a shelf or mantelpiece ... goodness knows what the servants think!"

"Don't you have French lessons to attend to, Alice dear?" asked Hazel, irritated by her daughter's company.

"No, that was this morning."

Gordon entered the studio carrying a letter on a silver tray.

"This has arrived for you, my lady."

"Thank you, Gordon," said Hazel, sitting up from her reclining position and opening the envelope. "It's from Sir Philip Sassoon."

Sir Philip was a well-respected art collector who was also an MP. Hazel had become friends with him through the art world and he had recently been appointed Prime Minister Lloyd George's private secretary.

"Wonderful news!" said Hazel, jumping to her feet. "Philip has arranged for me to meet the Prime Minister at his home on Thursday! I have been trying to meet Lloyd George since we got back from Tangier, to no avail ... I knew Philip would not let me down!"

"Bravo!" said John.

"What shall I wear?" Hazel was thinking out loud.

"Is this part of your Irish crusade?" asked Alice.

"Of course – what else?" Hazel clasped the letter close to her heart. "This is a real opportunity for me to make a difference – if I can just get Lloyd George on side, make him change his policy on Ireland!"

"What are the chances?" whispered Alice to herself sarcastically.

"When are you meeting him?" asked John.

"Thursday afternoon," answered Hazel.

"Thursday? But we are due to be in Windsor on Thursday, looking at the horse for sale!" said Alice.

"Well, we will just have to postpone that appointment, Alice," said Hazel.

"But we can't!" cried Alice. "We've been trying to arrange this appointment for days. They won't wait any longer. If we don't go this week, they will sell the horse to somebody else."

"For goodness sake, child, I can't imagine there is that much demand for a nag in Windsor!" said Hazel.

"There is, I tell you!" Tears were coming to Alice's eyes. "I'll lose the horse for sure if we don't go."

"John, can you go with her in my place to see this damned horse?" said Hazel.

"It's impossible, I'm afraid." He looked sympathetically at Alice. "I've a commission that day, painting the French Ambassador."

"Well, there you go, we will just have to reschedule Windsor. I will speak to them myself," said Hazel.

"But –" began Alice, in her eyes a mixture of anger and upset.

"For goodness' sake, Alice!" said Hazel, brimming with frustration. "This is a meeting with the Prime Minister to try and stop the war in Ireland – can't you see it has to take precedence over the purchase of a horse? I am trying to stop innocent men, women and children being slaughtered and all you can think about is a horse! I've had enough modelling for today, John, I need a lie-down!"

John and Alice watched as Hazel swept past them out of the room.

John reached out and put an arm around Alice's shoulders. "I'm sorry, Alice. There is really nothing I can do about the French Ambassador, otherwise I'd go to Windsor with you."

"Oh, it's not your fault, John. I just don't understand this obsession she has with Irish affairs. I know you are Irish, and she sees herself as Irish by descent, but what does she hope to achieve with all this? She's not a politician, she's a wife and mother – has she forgotten that?"

"But she's happy doing this, Alice, and that really is the main thing. Don't you remember how bad she was a few short years ago – when she became depressed and couldn't get out of bed?"

Alice nodded. "I remember – she was just sad all the time."

"This gives her something to fight for, to live for – we can't take that away from her."

"I know," Alice sighed. "But what about you, John? What about Shane Leslie and the others – how can you bear watching her flirt with them so openly in front of you?"

"Well, as long as it is only flirting, what harm is there in that? He amuses her and it reminds me how lucky I am to be married to her."

"*Hmmm* – I think *she* is the one who is reminding you how lucky you are to be married to her!" said Alice cynically as she looked at the painting of Hazel's beautiful face on his canvas.

CHAPTER 5

Kitty Kiernan sat in the parlour, engrossed in a romantic novel, an open box of chocolates beside her. She loved romantic novels, liked nothing more than getting lost in a good love story. She had taken the afternoon off work and was enjoying the peace and solitude. The Kiernan house was usually a busy house with much coming and going. The only time to get some peace there was during the day when everyone was out at work, except for the two house servants they employed. The house was annexed to the Greville Arms Hotel which the family owned.

She put down her novel, stood up and walked across the large finely furnished parlour to one of the windows that looked out onto the main street of the town of Granard. It was a busy day with much activity. As the Kiernan family owned half the businesses in the town, her brother Larry would be very happy to hear the tills ringing with profit. Her father had been a very enterprising man who had come to Granard and expanded the business until he owned half the town.

Kitty often thought back to the happiness of her childhood with her close-knit family. That was before a series of tragedies struck them. There had originally been one brother and six sisters, two of them twins, but in 1907 the youngest twin died. The following year both her parents died within a couple of months of each other and then the elder twin sister the following year. The remaining family had been devastated. Kitty had been only fifteen at the time. What they went through could have destroyed them and would have destroyed many families. But Larry and the surviving sisters, Maud, Helen, Chrys and Kitty, refused to be defeated. Even though they were still very young they all went to work in the family businesses, taking responsibility for different parts. They had worked hard, and the businesses had not only survived but had become stronger and more profitable.

As Kitty looked down at the cream chiffon dress from Paris she was wearing and looked around at the expensive furniture in the parlour, she reflected that the family had enjoyed the fruits of their labour – and these would soon include the upcoming lavish wedding they would be giving their sister Helen at Vaughan's Hotel in Dublin. Some of the townspeople resented their success, but Kitty didn't care. She worked hard and was determined to enjoy the money they earned. She loved fashion and could spend hours looking through the fashion magazines sent to her from Paris and London. She had even taken control of the clothes department of the store they owned, which was also on the main street of the town, overseeing the ordering.

She sauntered back to the couch, picked up her novel and smiled to herself as she glanced at the cover before marking the page she was at and placing the book on the mantelpiece. Yes, it wouldn't be long until her sister Helen was married to a local solicitor named Paul McGovern. Chrys was engaged to Tom Magee from Belfast and everyone expected Maud to announce her engagement to Gearóid O'Sullivan soon. But what about her? When would Kitty be getting married and, more importantly, to whom? She was now twenty-seven years old – in Longford that was considered quite old for a bride. Kitty had never worried too much about the prospect before. She had always been extremely popular, with a number of suitors pursuing her. She had allowed quite a few to court her, but that was before the war of independence now raging. She smiled to herself as she remembered life before the war – an endless cycle of hunt balls, parties, tennis and days at the races. All the Kiernan girls were well known on the social circuit and all had been very popular. But the war had changed everything and brought an end to most social activity. And now here she was at a crossroads, left stranded by the conflict in Ireland. There were two men in her life, and she didn't know which one to choose.

She remembered the first day she had met Harry Boland. It was in 1918, a year before the war had broken out. He was campaigning for an election and had come to Longford with Michael Collins to campaign. Both of them had been introduced to the Kiernan family by Gearóid who had started courting Maud. They had all come to stay at the hotel during the election campaign and they had all become great friends very quickly, forming a tight group. Gearóid, Harry and Michael became regular visitors. It wasn't long until Kitty was courting Harry and they soon had become serious. But then the war had broken out and Harry had been sent to America to do fundraising for the war effort.

When Harry was first sent to New York, it was supposed to be temporary, but now it appeared to have become permanent. There was no sign of his being posted back to Ireland and she had become frustrated with the situation. Part of her was grateful he was in America and not in Ireland where he would be under constant threat of arrest or being killed like the other republican leaders. But she was twenty-seven years of age and needed to make a decision soon about who she was going to marry. She couldn't live in this limbo for evermore.

Gearóid was due down for a few days and Maud had been beside herself with excitement with the thought of seeing him again. Kitty shook her head in bewilderment as she thought about Gearóid, Harry and Michael Collins. Why couldn't they all have just had normal jobs! Helen was the clever one, Kitty thought – she had got engaged to the nice country solicitor and wasn't embroiled in this war that she and Maud had allowed their hearts to lead them into.

"Miss Kitty, yeer guest is here," said the maid.

Kitty turned around to see Gearóid standing in the doorway of the parlour.

"Gearóid!" Kitty exclaimed, hurrying excitedly over to him. "We weren't expecting you until later this evening."

"We decided to get out of the city early in case we met roadblocks and had to divert," said Gearóid, enveloping her in a big hug.

"Hello, Kitty!" said a voice in the corridor and Kitty looked over Gearóid's shoulder to see Michael Collins standing there.

"Mick!" She let go of Gearóid and embraced Michael. "What are you doing here? We didn't expect you at all!"

"I decided I needed a bit of a holiday!" he said, laughing.

"Ah, it's good to see you – both of you!" she said, hugging each of them again.

That evening there was lively conversation around the table in the cosy dining-room as the maid served a dinner of bacon, cabbage and potatoes. As Michael looked around, he felt glad to be back there. It was one of the few places he felt he could relax and unwind and forget about the war and everything else.

All the family were at the table – Kitty, Helen, Maud, Chrys and their brother Larry. Gearóid and Maud were sitting side by side, stealing looks at each other, their hands occasionally touching, so obviously in love.

Kitty was dominating the conversation, as could often happen, regaling everybody with a story about a customer in the shop who wanted to buy an umbrella for a pet donkey.

Michael thought she was very attractive, with a bright smile and mischievous eyes when she was in the right mood – as she was now. Other times her eyes could flash dangerously with temper if somebody upset her or crossed her. She was also very flirtatious.

There were a couple of others at the table that Michael didn't know. A young blond man, who had been introduced as Lionel, sat beside Kitty and appeared enraptured with her story. There were always guests at the Kiernans' – it was a very sociable house As much as Michael tried to concentrate on Kitty's story about the umbrella and the donkey, his attention was taken by the woman who sat opposite him – Helen. He tried not to be too obvious, but he couldn't help looking at her whenever he got the opportunity. She seemed to get more beautiful every time he saw her. She had soft blonde hair that was never out of place and her blue eyes were trustworthy and kind. He remembered being bowled over when he met her first by her elegance and the way she gracefully conducted herself. Harry had been smitten with Kitty and indeed Michael had at first been interested in Kitty too. They had even competed for Kitty's attention at the beginning. But then, as Michael found himself falling hopelessly in love with Helen, he had left the way open for Harry. Helen and Michael had grown close as friends, but it had been hard to form a proper relationship with her because of the war, often hard to even see her. He was very much hoping that he would get the opportunity that week to express his feelings for her and establish something between them. As he looked at Gearóid and Maud, he was filled with the envy of wanting the same in his own life.

"So, there the customer was, after purchasing the umbrella, walking down the main street in the rain – holding the umbrella over the donkey while it pissed down raining on himself!" said Kitty, causing everyone at the table to erupt in laughter.

"It must have been a very special donkey!" said Larry.

"Certainly a special owner!" said Kitty.

"I didn't realise you sold umbrellas in the store – do you sell galoshes too?" asked Lionel.

"Eh – yes, we do," said Kitty, hoping Lionel would not follow his habit that evening of missing the point and leading the conversation off into dull directions.

"That would be some sight if he had put galoshes on the donkey!" said Michael, laughing. "If the British saw it they'd be wondering what kind of a mad country they were in at all!"

"It's a country they *shouldn't* be in – *at all!*" said Gearóid, causing everyone at the table to loudly voice agreement.

"We had six British officers booked in at the hotel last week," said Helen, her soft voice carrying around the table.

Michael looked across at her, grateful to have the excuse to stare at her beautiful face.

"What were they doing here?" asked Gearóid.

"On their way to the North – they were stopping for the night until they continued their journey," said Helen. "The officer in charge was a charming fellow by the name of Rupert –"

"Rupert!" guffawed Michael.

"Yes, Rupert!" confirmed Kitty. "I put him in your usual room, Mick – I thought you'd appreciate the irony of that." She made a face over at him.

"As long as he doesn't get lost on the way back from the North and end up here again tonight!" said Michael.

"Sure, even if he did, he wouldn't have a clue what you looked like," said Gearóid.

"I could place the two of you at the same table for breakfast," said Helen, "and Rupert wouldn't have a clue he was eating his bacon and eggs across from the great Mick Collins!"

She smiled over at him and Michael found himself blushing at her compliment.

"All the hotel rooms have been recently painted a lovely ivory colour, I understand, so I'm sure they would have found the accommodation tasteful to stay in," said Lionel, causing everyone to look at him momentarily, wondering what he was talking about.

"Speaking of your anonymity, headquarters got an unusual request this week for you, Mick," said Gearóid. "Did you hear about it?"

"No. What was that?"

"It came through Shane Leslie – you know, the Irish lord who has swapped sides to ours."

"I don't care how many sides he's swapped – I'd never trust a lord!" said Michael.

"Or a lady, Mick!" said Kitty, winking over at him.

Michael burst out laughing. "Do you never change, Kitty Kiernan, with the smart remarks?"

"Rest assured, I will never change, Mick Collins!" Kitty announced proudly.

"What was the request, Gearóid?" asked Chrys, trying to bring bring the conversation back to the point.

"He put in a request from a Sir John Lavery who is coming to Ireland and wants to paint your portrait, Mick," announced Gearóid.

There was silence for a moment as Michael's face turned from confusion to amusement and then everyone burst out laughing.

"My portrait!" Michael laughed. "What the hell does he want a painting of my mug for?"

"Well, you have a very interesting face, Michael. I could see how you would be any painter's dream," said Helen with a warm smile and Michael felt himself going bright red again.

"Mick Collins – freedom fighter and model!" teased Kitty.

"A British plot, no doubt!" declared Michael. "Lure me to an artist's studio where an assassin lies in wait, at worst. Or for them finally to get what I look like captured by an artist, at best!"

"Imagine, Mick, if you agreed to the portrait and you were captured by the British due to vanity!" said Kitty.

"No fear of that, Kitty, my dear!" Michael shook his head and flicked his hair back from his forehead.

"This Sir John Lavery is a famous artist," said Gearóid. "He was the British government's official artist during the Great War and got a knighthood for his efforts. He and his Yank wife are big shots in London and are coming to Ireland to paint a bunch of famous religious leaders and whoever else they can get. He's Irish – a Protestant from the North – and sympathetic to our cause, they say."

"Sounds unlikely!" said Michael. "If he did anything official for the British government during the Great War, I wouldn't trust him as far as I could throw him, along with his Yank wife!"

"I thought the request would amuse you all the same," said Gearóid with a smile.

"It does surely!" said Michael, grabbing another potato from the bowl in front of him.

"I am quite jealous," said Helen. "I would love it if a famous artist wanted to do my portrait."

Michael smiled as his eyes met hers across the table. "Now that would be a painting worth hanging in the best art gallery in the world," he said softly.

Helen lowered her gaze to the plate in front of her as it was her turn to blush.

The others at the table fell into an uncomfortable silence. Kitty sat back and observed their guest and her sister. She wondered were the rumours about Michael being smitten with Helen true. For some reason the notion irritated her.

"My mother had her portrait painted by a French artist once," said Lionel, causing everyone to momentarily look at him again. "He said she had the most exquisite hands he had ever seen."

"More gravy anyone?" asked Kitty quickly, lifting the sauce boat up invitingly.

After dinner they retreated to the parlour where there were the usual songs and some piano-playing.

Kitty was walking around the room, filling everyone's glass from a decanter of sherry.

Michael was standing beside the fireplace, listening to Maud playing the piano.

"Another top-up?" Kitty asked him, raising the decanter.

"Only a tiny drop – I don't want a sore head in the morning," he said.

"I thought you said you were on holiday."

"I still need to be alert."

Kitty nodded her understanding.

Although whenever Michael and Gearóid came to visit they kept a low profile, only socialising in the Kiernans' private home, Kitty was sure some of townspeople must notice their comings and goings. She was sure some might remember Michael from when he was campaigning locally in the 1918 by-election, before he had to go underground. That was before the Anglo-Irish war had erupted and Michael had become a fugitive. Kitty was certain the area was staunchly pro-Independence and that, even if anybody recognised Michael, they would not betray him. And even if somebody had a mind to do it, they would be fully aware that retribution from Michael's Squad would be fast and merciless. Even so, Molly, their maid, had walked into Michael's room one morning when he was still asleep, and she told Kitty that Michael slept with his hand on the revolver that was on the side table. Also, he slept with the window open in order to make a quick getaway if the British troops arrived in. Sometimes, Kitty had to pinch herself when she heard such stories. When she was chatting to Michael as an old friend, she never thought about him being the most wanted man in the empire. Or she never thought that he could order the killing of an enemy without a second thought. All that wasn't Kitty's world and she had no interest in it. Some women might have found it all exciting and romantic, but she didn't. She had fallen for Harry, her sister Maud had fallen for Gearóid, and through this they had fallen into this world – Michael Collins' world.

"Helen?" asked Kitty, the decanter hovering over her sister's glass.

"Not much, Kitty, I have to be up early in the morning."

Kitty ignored her sister's plea and filled the glass to the top, before winking at Michael and going on back to the piano where she stood beside Lionel.

As Maud played, Kitty and Lionel sang along.

"Kitty is in good form," said Michael.

"Kitty's always in good form, except when she's not!" said Helen, causing Michael to laugh.

"Ah, it's so good to see you again, Helen. You have no idea how I've missed you, with this blasted war going on and not being able to get down here."

She smiled at him. "We've all missed you, Mick. You know you are welcome here – sure you're like one of the family."

He felt his heart pound more quickly and he put his hand up on the mantelpiece to steady himself as he searched for the right words to respond.

"Lionel is quite taken by our Kitty," she said before he could speak.

"Who is he? Where's he from and who are his family?"

"Lionel Lyster, an extremely wealthy young man by all accounts."

"Oh, I see!" said Michael, surveying Lionel with interest.

"They have been spending considerable time together recently. He's calling on her quite a bit."

"Calling on her? As in courting?" Michael was shocked.

"Nothing official, but it looks like a courtship to me!"

"But – but what about Harry?" Michael's face creased in concern.

"What about him?"

"Does Harry know about him?"

Helen shrugged her shoulders. "I don't know, Mick ... and I would prefer you didn't say anything about it to him. I don't want to be the cause of any trouble."

"Well, it looks to me that Kitty is the cause of any trouble – courting two men at the same time!"

"Harry's in New York, Mick, or Boston or Chicago or wherever the cause sends him. Kitty can't be expected to wait forever for him. She's here and Lionel's here and what is meant to be is meant to be." Helen was very much regretting saying anything about Lionel. At the end of the day, Michael did not look pleased at this betrayal of his friend – his best friend.

"Well, it's a fine way to carry on!" said Mick, knocking back his sherry.

"I think it's time I went to bed," said Helen, placing her glass on the mantelpiece.

He was alarmed to see her usually pleasant expression dimmed.

"Don't go to bed on my account," said Michael, suddenly aware he might have distressed her.

"Oh, I'm not, Mick. I do genuinely have to get to bed as I have to be up early in the morning."

"For work?"

"No, I'm going away for a few days."

"Going away!" He was horrified. "But – but – but I only came because I wanted to see you!"

Helen flushed. "But I didn't realise you were coming, otherwise I might have been able to change my plans. But, as it is, I can't change them. I'm sorry."

"Where are you going?" He looked crestfallen.

"I-I'm going to Enniskillen ... to visit Paul's family," she said.

"Paul?" he said, frowning in confusion.

"Paul McGovern – you met him a couple of times."

"The solicitor?"

"Yes." She bit her lower lip and then took a deep breath. "We're engaged, Mick ... we're going to be married. I'm going to Enniskillen to meet his family."

Michael stood there with his mouth open in shock.

Helen didn't know what to say further. She knew Michael was in love with her, but nothing had ever happened between them and she had never done anything to encourage him. And she did love him dearly as a friend.

"I hope you'll be able to come to the wedding?" she said. "It would mean a lot to me to have you there."

He continued to stare at her in shock.

She reached forward, kissed his cheek and whispered, "Goodnight, Mick."

She walked quietly from the room, leaving Michael to stare after her.

Michael did not stay up much longer after that. He grabbed the decanter the next time it did the rounds and refilled his glass a couple of times, quickly drinking the contents before going to his bedroom. Helen's news had hit him like a bolt of lightning. He had known that she had been seeing a solicitor but had no idea it had progressed to the state of an engagement. He had felt that as he and Helen had become closer that naturally the courtship with the other man would fizzle out, leaving the road clear for them. He had thought they had plenty of time to plan their lives together and to make it official. But, as he had been busy waging war against the British Empire, life had passed him by. The love of his life had passed him by. But he couldn't give up on Helen, he just couldn't let her go. He would have to speak to her that morning, before she left for Enniskillen.

The next morning at breakfast, Michael was subdued and waited anxiously for Helen as breakfast was served.

"Where's Helen?" he asked finally.

"She left first thing this morning – did she not tell you she would be gone?" said Chrys.

"Gone? Yes – yes, she did ... she said she would be going to Enniskillen." He was aghast that he had missed her. "She's gone already?"

"First thing," confirmed Kitty.

49

"It will be a bit daunting for her, meeting all of Paul's family for the first time," said Maud.

"Nothing daunts Helen, she'll take it all in her stride," said Kitty as she poured tea into her cup. She glanced over at Michael's glum face. There had been those rumours going about that Michael had feelings for Helen and he certainly acted soft around her. She had even witnessed it again at the dinner table the previous night. Helen didn't wear her heart on her sleeve, so never spoke about her personal relationships even to her sisters, leaving them all to speculate.

As breakfast ended Michael got up from the table and went and stood at the window. Gearóid and Maud had headed off already for the day, desperate to spend some time alone.

"Will you tell the new cook we'll have trout for tonight's dinner," Kitty told Molly the maid.

"Tell her yourself! She won't take any instructions from me, that one won't! If I told her to put on trout, she'd put on salmon out of spite and if I told her to put on salmon she'd put on trout!"

Kitty raised her eyes to heaven. "Alright, I'll tell her myself!"

"She's nothing but an old trout herself, if you ask me!" said Molly as she stacked plates. "I don't know where you found her, but it was a sorry day for this house when you hired that one as a cook! And you could have hired my second cousin once removed as I suggested ye did and have enjoyed proper cooking cooked by a proper cook! Trout indeed!"

She exited in a huff and suddenly there was a loud crashing sound from down the corridor. Obviously, Molly had dropped all the plates onto the floor.

"*Jesus!*" shrieked Molly in horror.

"Lord save us!" gasped Kitty, shaking her head in despair as she went and closed over the door to protect Michael from any more of Molly's unnecessary drama.

"You don't have a place for her in your army, do you, Mick? She'd scare off the British in a moment, that's for sure!"

"Can't help you with that request, I'm afraid," said Michael with a grin.

"She's half demented, I'm convinced, and she has me fully

demented listening to her every day!" said Kitty with a despairing laugh.

Michael laughed and turned to the window again.

Kitty realised Michael would be left on his own for the day, with Helen gone and Maud and Gearóid out galivanting.

"What are we doing today, Mick?" she said.

"We?" he asked, spinning around to her.

"It's my day off today from the store," she lied. "So you're in luck. A nice walk in the country? Or are you too much of a city boy now to enjoy the fresh air?"

He smiled at her. "Sounds good."

CHAPTER 6

Michael and Kitty walked down the busy main street of Granard. Michael had his hat pulled down on his forehead and kept his head lowered.

"It's Fair Day, so the town is packed," explained Kitty as they passed stalls filled with all sorts of goods for sale and pens full of livestock. "We'll be out in the country soon and you can relax then."

"The sooner the better," said Michael as a truck carrying British troops drove down the main street, causing many to start jeering and booing them.

"*Go back to your mammies!*" shouted a man as he grabbed a turnip from one of the stalls and hurled it at the truck.

"Not much pro-British sentiment around here!" smiled Kitty.

"No. The trouble is, though, that the flying turnip could have hit the head of one of the Tans and they are untrained undisciplined men who have been given free rein and they could have opened fire and turned the street into a bloodbath."

Kitty shuddered at the thought. She had read the reports of such atrocities happening in other towns and cities throughout the country, but she had never contemplated it happening on her own doorstep.

"Come on, let's get out into the open air," she said, taking his arm and quickening their pace.

"Well, my father died when I was only six and I missed him badly," said Michael as they strolled along a country road. "He was much older than my mother and so it didn't surprise anybody when he died – he was eighty-one. But I was still very young, and he was my father."

"Of course," said Kitty.

"We just were small farmers," he said and then winked down at her. "We weren't rich like the Kiernans."

"Oh, shut up! Everything my family have we worked for."

He could see that flash of temper across her face again and realised she had to endure a lot of resentment from the locals due to her family's success.

"I was told there wasn't much money to be spoiling me and so I'd better put my head down in the books and get myself a good education. And then I passed the British Civil Service exams and went to work for the Post Office in London. I learned a lot of my organisational skills there."

"To think the British Civil Service trained the man who is now threatening to bring down the empire with those organisational skills!" said Kitty.

"True for you, Kitty," said Michael, laughing. "And I went on from there and did my accountancy exams and became an accountant."

"To think you would have been a nice professional man – if you hadn't ended up a terrorist!"

"Are you taking the piss out of me?" he said, pretending to be offended.

"Would I?" she said with a smile as they sauntered over to a gate that led into a huge rolling field.

Michael opened the gate and they went in.

"What age are you now, Mick?" she asked.

"Thirty."

"Did you never want to settle down? Most fellas your age are married by now."

"Well, if this war hadn't come along – who knows? As you said, I might be an accountant living in a small country town married to a nice girl."

"That sounds like Helen and Paul!" Kitty noticed Michael's smile vanish at the mention of her sister Helen. "What's wrong, Michael?"

"Eh, nothing, nothing at all!" he said quickly, trying to disguise the fact he was still in turmoil over Helen. "It's just as you say, the fight for independence has robbed me of another life that might have been for me."

"To be honest, I don't think you could ever settle down with a nice girl in a nice job in a nice town – it's just not you, Mick."

"Why not?"

"Because you're too restless and clever and ambitious. You're a politician and one day you'll be head of our country, wait and see," said Kitty.

"I don't know about that. Dev is the one over in New York signing himself as President of Ireland. I think he thinks if he tells enough people that, they will believe him and think we already have independence! But enough about me – what about you?"

"What about me?"

"Well – for a start – who is this blond fella who was hanging on your every word last night?"

"Lionel? Oh, he's just a friend."

"I'd say he'd like to be a lot more than that!"

"Get away out of that! As I said, he's just a friend."

"A very wealthy one, from all accounts?"

"I see how you became head of Irish Intelligence! So, what if he's after me? I don't belong to anyone. I'm my own woman and can do what I want."

"I'd say Harry would have something to say about that."

"Harry is across the Atlantic Ocean and can say whatever he wants – I can't hear him from here! At the end of the day Harry left me while he went off to America to get funds to fight your blasted war and I can't sit here on the shelf with my legs dangling forever!"

Michael stopped walking and looked at her. "So you would? You'd finish with Harry and take up with this Lionel?"

She stopped and turned to him. "I don't know ... Well, he wants to marry me."

"What! Jaysus, there's more marriage proposals going on around here than on top of the Eiffel Tower! And what did you tell him?"

"Well, I said I'd have to think about it. Lionel has a lot going for him. He's a very wealthy man, from a very wealthy family – I'd want for nothing married to Lionel Lyster!"

"You were never the sort who was going to marry for money, Kitty, not with all those romantic novels you read!"

"True! But he's very kind and very sweet also, and he worships the ground I walk on. Sure what more could a girl want?"

"Love?" asked Michael.

"Maybe love is overrated. I've a friend who says love is for fools."

"He also doesn't strike me as being … how can I put this delicately …"

"Delicacy is not a word I'd ever associate with you, Mick Collins, so spit it out whatever's on your mind!" Her face had turned sour and her voice harsh.

"Well, he just doesn't strike me as being very – clever."

"You cheeky pup!" She was angered. "Lionel is one of the brightest men I know!"

"Well, if you say so – I'll have to take your word on that one!" He winked at her, causing her to go red with anger.

"I think it's time we headed back – it looks like rain!" she snapped as she began to march away.

He looked up at the clear blue skies and laughed to himself as he followed her.

"One thing for sure, Kitty, a girl like you will never be left sitting on the shelf with her legs dangling," he said earnestly as he caught up with her.

She stopped walking and looked at him, surprised by the compliment. He usually jokingly disparaged her.

"Come on, we'll head back, or we'll be late for dinner," she said and began to walk back to the road.

Everyone had gone to bed except for Michael and Kitty who were seated in the darkened parlour beside the fire. She was reading poetry by WB Yeats to him. She sat on the green velvet couch beside the oil lamp while he sat across the fire from her in an armchair. As her soft voice read out the words of Yeats' 'The Sorrow of Love' the light from the fire flickered across her fine features. Michael couldn't help being mesmerised as her velvet voice spoke the words from the poem –

"'*A girl arose that had red mournful lips... and seemed the greatness of the world in tears ... doomed like Odysseus and the labouring ships ... and proud as Priam murdered with his peers ...*'"

She looked up from the poetry book and saw a tear trickle down his cheek. She put down the book and sat forward, concerned. "Are you alright, Mick?"

He quickly rubbed his face and flicked his hair back. "Of course I am – why wouldn't I be?"

She leaned towards the oil lamp on the table beside her and adjusted the flame, bringing more light into the room.

"I thought you had gone soft on me for a moment," she tenderly mocked.

"*Pah!* It would take more than a few words of poetry to make Mick Collins soft. Maybe, now, if I waded through some of these romantic novels you read, I might be in floods of tears then – tears of laughter!"

She stood up and, laughing, said, "If you're going to start mocking my novels, then I'll go to bed!"

He grabbed her wrist as she went to walk past him. She froze at the feel of his tight grip and felt a spark. She glanced down at his hand on her wrist.

"Don't leave me yet, Kitty – stay another while – I don't want to be alone," he said softly.

"It's late, Mick, and I'm tired . . ."

He nodded, released her wrist and stood up too. "You're right. I'd better be getting to bed myself ... thanks for today ... you were the best company."

"I'm always the best company – sure isn't that why your best friend is in love with me?" she said with a smirk.

"Treat him well, Kitty, he's one of the best."

"I know that, Mick."

"Don't string him along if you plan to end up with Lionel."

"The truth is I don't know yet who I want to end up with. I have a lot of thinking to do."

"I guess it's nice to have options," said Michael with a laugh. "If you did end up with Harry then I guess he won the bet."

"What bet was this?"

"When we met you first, he and I had a bet on about who could win you over."

"Well, you didn't try too hard to win, Mick! I don't ever remember you trying to woo me in any shape or form."

"Sure how could I compete with the gifts of glass ornaments and bowls Harry kept bringing you!" Michael said, laughing out loud at the memory of Harry's seduction technique.

"*Shhhh!* You'll wake the house!" she snapped, forcing herself not to laugh at the memory of the array of ornaments Harry had given her. "Anyways – you're in no position to mock another man's courting ritual. Maybe you should copy him next time you want to woo a girl, instead of relying on your looks and charm."

"Ah, now you flatter me, Kitty!" He beamed a smile down at her.

"Go to bed, Mick. I'll see you in the morning for breakfast, if we have any plates left after our clumsy maid!"

She reached up and kissed him on the cheek before turning and walking down the corridor.

"Goodnight, Kitty!" he whispered after her.

She turned and waved before continuing to her room.

He smiled to himself as he turned and began to walk down the corridor to his room. But then he stopped and walked back to the parlour. He went and stood by the fire, staring into the glowing embers. He looked at the photographs on top of the mantelpiece and he took up the photograph of Helen that was there. He stared at it, the frame slightly shaking in his hands. She had come up in conversation earlier over dinner. The plans she had for the future with her fiancé and all the details about the forthcoming wedding. He remembered the great times he had there in that very room with her over the past couple of years. It was impossible for him to accept those times were over.

"Did you sleep well?" Kitty asked Michael as he sat down at the breakfast table the next morning with the family.

"Like a baby," said Michael.

Gearóid suddenly came quickly into the room, looking agitated. "Mick – I need to speak to you."

Michael was on his feet in a second and followed him out into the corridor.

"What's going on?"

"I was just on the telephone to one of the lads in Dublin. They found the informer – it was George!"

"George!" Michael's mouth dropped open. "I don't believe it!" George was a trusted aide in the organisation who was privy to the whereabouts of Michael and the other leaders.

"Believe it, Mick! He was on the payroll for the British and he told them you were in Sally's house that night."

"Where's the bastard now?"

"He's gone missing – he could be out of the country already."

"One of the flying columns will track him down." The flying columns – small, independent groups capable of rapid mobility – were among Michael's most effective tools.

The memory of that awful night came back to Michael. "Any word on Sally?"

"Yes, they have released her."

"Thank the Lord for that," sighed Michael with relief.

"They interrogated her, but Sally wouldn't give anything away, so they let her go in the end. It would be a different story for her if they had found you at her house."

"It would have been a different story for us all," said Michael with a grimace.

"There's more news from Dublin – three of our lads were arrested and are dead. Shot by the Black and Tans, and badly beaten before that."

"For fuck's sake!" swore Michael. "Right, we'd better get back to Dublin – cut this holiday short. Sorry, Gearóid, I know you wanted to spend more time with Maud."

"Plenty of time for that when we've won this war," said Gearóid.

"There's the spirit," said Michael, clasping his shoulder.

He went back into the dining room.

"I'm sorry, everybody, but we have to get back to Dublin."

"So soon!" cried Maud, leaping to her feet. "But you said you would be here for the rest of the week, Gearóid!"

"Can't be helped, Maud."

"For goodness' sake!"

"Come and we'll talk," said Gearóid, taking her by the arm and leading her away.

"Don't be long – that motorcar will be leaving here in five minutes with or without you!" Michael shouted after them.

"Ah Mick! Will you give them some time together – who knows when they will see each other next!" pleaded Kitty.

"I haven't got time to give!" snapped Michael angrily. "I have to get on the road and get back to work and I have no time to spare for a couple of – of – sweethearts!"

Kitty stared at him, her temper surfacing. Where had the gentle man from yesterday gone? The sensitive soul whose tears trickled down his face when she read 'The Sorrow of Love'?

"Thank you all for your hospitality and your company and see you next time!" said Michael.

He turned and strode out of the room.

"Gearóid! Will you come on!" he shouted down the corridor.

"And what am I supposed to do with all this food that has been cooked for those lads now?" demanded Molly crossly, her hands on her hips, as she looked down at the plates of bacon and sausages ready to be consumed. "I hate to see waste!"

Kitty got up from the table and, ignoring Molly, walked quickly out of the room and down the corridor into the parlour. She hurried over to the window and looked out. A minute later she saw Michael and Gearóid leave the building and walk to the automobile parked outside. They threw their suitcases in the back and Gearóid got into the driver's seat while Michael got in beside him. Michael pulled his hat down as the automobile started.

Kitty watched as they journeyed down the street and out of sight. She then turned and walked over to the couch and picked up the book of WB Yeats poems she had read from the previous night. She became angry. They had spent all that time together over the past couple of days and he hadn't even said goodbye to her. Not so much as a 'Goodbye, Kitty'! She had just been reminded why she had steered away from Mick Collins when she had met him and concentrated on steady dependable Harry Boland. Despite his charm and presence, a girl would never know where she was with Michael. One minute crying, the next shouting. Sitting down to breakfast one minute, dashing out the door to Dublin the next. How relieved she was that she had not fallen for Michael. Michael would bring no girl any happiness.

CHAPTER 7

Hazel drove her Rolls Royce through the streets of Kensington and on to Knightsbridge. Although their footman doubled as a chauffeur when required, Hazel had got used to driving herself around London during the war, when they had been left with hardly any servants due to the male servants going to the front to fight and the female servants leaving to work in munition factories. Hazel had learned to become quite self-sufficient domestically during the war.

She turned into Park Lane and parked outside Philip Sassoon's house – Number 25. Although Hazel and John were very proud of their own house at Cromwell Place, even their palatial home paled beside the splendour of Philip's four-storey mansion. Hazel had often been a guest in the house, and it was impossible not to be deeply impressed by the building which had its own ballroom and was decorated with the finest French antiques and exquisite paintings.

As she knocked on the door she reflected on the fact that Philip's mother had been a Rothschild, which explained the vast luxury on display.

Prime Minister David Lloyd George was sitting in Philip Sassoon's grand drawing room with an air of impatience.

"Is it really necessary for me to meet his woman?" he asked.

"Not really necessary, Prime Minister, but I think it may be advantageous to you in the long run. Hazel has become very well

connected and it would be better to have her as ally than a foe …
and you are doing me a personal favour meeting her – she is a good
friend of mine."

Lloyd George nodded, well aware of Philip's own reputation as
a socialite who rubbed shoulders with artists, actors, movie stars
and of course the political class he was a member of as well. Philip
looked the perfect socialite, always impeccably dressed, his sallow
skin always tanned, his hair slicked with Brylcreem, his lean tall
body kept fit from polo. He had a touch of the exotic about him,
fanned by his family's immense wealth.

"From what I know of John Lavery's wife, she is sticking her oar
into something that is none of her business."

"She wants to make a difference," said Philip.

Lloyd George raised his eyes to heaven as he took a sip of his tea.
"Don't they all? They all want to make a difference these days!"

"Winston is quite taken with her," said Philip.

"I'm not sure that is an endorsement," smirked Lloyd George.

The butler knocked and opened the door, announcing, "Lady
Lavery."

Lloyd George stood with Philip and watched as Hazel walked
confidently into the room. He immediately realised how this
woman had reached the top of London society in a few short years:
she oozed charm and beauty.

"Philip!" She greeted him with a kiss on the cheek, before
turning her dazzling smile on the Prime Minister.

"Hazel, may I introduce you to –" began Philip.

"I feel introductions are unnecessary – David, I have so looked
forward to meeting you," she said, taking his hand and shaking it
warmly. "I just know we are going to be friends."

"Yes, indeed, madam, the pleasure is all mine, I'm sure," said
Lloyd George, deciding he needed to be on his absolute guard with
this woman. She was so disarming, she could be dangerous.

"Please, have a seat, Hazel," urged Philip.

As she sat down on an armchair opposite them, she spotted one
of John's painting on the wall behind them beside a priceless
tapestry.

"I am so glad to have the opportunity to *finally* meet you!" said Hazel, observing the Prime Minister and realising he was a lot shorter than she had expected. He struck her as having crafty, cunning eyes set in a cheerful good-natured face. She suspected his right hand didn't know what his left hand was doing most of the time!

"Yes, I'm sorry it has taken this long to meet you," said Lloyd George, "but I've been busy – the Treaty of Versailles, you know." He wondered if she recognised the touch of sarcasm in his voice.

"Indeed! I am glad you mention it as I was devastated that Ireland was not included at the Treaty. An Irish delegation should have been invited to decide the country's independence, along with the other countries of Europe. Now we are left with the terrible consequences of decades of mismanagement in Ireland – the Anglo-Irish war."

Hazel was getting straight down to business.

"Lady Lavery, please –" began Lloyd George.

"Hazel, please call me Hazel," she urged.

"I have been told that you are passionate about this subject and please be assured the last thing I or the rest of the government want is this war, but we have been put in an impossible situation with these terrorists committing mindless assassinations and murders of our troops."

"Well, if the troops weren't there committing their atrocities they wouldn't be attacked, David. Why not just give the Irish their independence and let history take its natural course?"

Lloyd George shot Philip a look before responding. "My dear Hazel – it is not as simple as you seem to think. Firstly, we cannot just let Ireland sever its ties from the empire as these terrorists are insisting."

"Why not?" demanded Hazel.

"Because we can't allow a part of the whole to just cut itself off. It would set a precedent and could mean the end of the British Empire." He smiled at her to soften his words.

"All empires must eventually come to an end, David – look at the Romans or the Greeks," said Hazel.

Lloyd George's smile turned sour. "I would prefer that the British Empire did not meet its demise under my watch! I would not like to go down in history as the Prime Minister who oversaw its dismantling. Then there is the whole Northern problem – the large Protestant population who refuse to join the Catholic South in this quest for independence. We cannot just abandon those friends of ours in the North to an independent southern-controlled country which they vehemently do not want to be part of."

"But you are fighting against the tide of history," said Hazel. "You are like King Canute trying to stop the tide when nothing will stop it."

Lloyd George glanced at Philip and decided the discussion had gone on long enough. Bad enough trying to explain his actions to the leader of the opposition in the House of Commons – he really didn't need to spend any more time discussing it with an American socialite.

"Look, Hazel," he smiled warmly at her, "we all want peace in Ireland. Nobody wants this killing and slaughter to continue – we just have to find the right path to achieve that peace."

"And I hope you understand that you are on the wrong path?"

"I've taken on board everything you have said today, and you have made some very valid points."

"Really? You agree with what I'm saying?"

He nodded compassionately. "We all need to sit back and rethink things." He stood up. "But it has been an absolute pleasure to meet you, Hazel."

Hazel stood and took his hands. "I feel as though I've made a new friend."

"I feel the same way," he said, smiling at her.

After Lloyd George had left, Hazel clasped her hands together. "My goodness, Philip, it seems as if he really has had a change of heart and is ready to change policy."

"Yes – indeed," said Philip.

When she arrived back home Hazel was in a euphoric mood, believing she had received an assurance from Lloyd George that he would re-evaluate the situation in Ireland.

In John's studio she walked up to the portrait he was doing of her and began to inspect it. Although John was an artistic genius, Hazel herself had been an accomplished artist in her youth and considered herself a very able art critic. John often relied on her opinions. As she inspected this latest portrait of her, she examined the face closely. She looked thirty in the portrait. And she knew her husband was not flattering her. She looked thirty in reality as well, a good decade younger than her real age. A number of years before, when she had first arrived in London, she had begun to lie about her age whenever questioned. She liked to think this was not vanity or shallow behaviour. It was more a case of trying to remain current. She had important things to do in life, important people to influence. She had always used her charm and her looks as her main currency, and so she had to ensure that currency stayed in demand. Lying about her age helped achieve that. John had told her once that he would always see her as that young girl he met in France in 1903, seventeen years before. She had only been twenty-three at the time and John had been forty-seven. Hazel had wanted to be an artist at the time and had come to France with her mother, also called Alice, and her sister Dorothy. Her father had died six years before that, leaving the small family devastated by the loss. Alice had been determined the family would not lose their place in society and spent lavishly to ensure that. Both Hazel and Dorothy had been presented as debutantes in Chicago and sent to expensive finishing schools in New York. Both girls were expected to marry into the upper echelons of East Coast society. When Hazel met Ned Trudeau in New York on the social circuit, he certainly fitted the bill. A dashing, handsome Yale-educated doctor from a highly respected New York family, Ned was a sweet boy who fell head over heels in love with her. Hazel had been well used to men falling for her and hadn't given Ned too much thought, despite her mother's absolute approval of him.

"You won't find better than Ned, Hazel. He is everything a girl could want in a husband," said Alice.

"But I don't love him, Mama."

"For goodness' sake, Hazel. Is there a debutante in America who has actually loved the man she married? She may come to love him, but it's not that important compared to other things!"

Hazel disagreed with her mother but knew she was only trying to look after her daughter's future. She found out years later, after her mother died, that the family's financial situation had been precarious when she was trying to coerce her into a marriage with Ned. Since her father's death, his estate could not keep up with her mother's lavish spending. When Alice had sold their beautiful home on Astor Place and the family moved into an apartment at one of the city's best hotels, this was not for convenience, as her mother had claimed at the time, but because they were being forced to downsize by the banks she had begun to borrow extensively from.

Like so many of America's upper class, the Martyns also spent great swathes of time travelling in Europe. It was on one such trip in 1903 that Hazel had first met John Lavery, in Paris. John had been visiting the artists' community where she was taking classes. John said it was love at first sight for him. Hazel had never met anybody like John before. He was kind, patient, steady and a most wonderful painter. He was also widowed, twenty-four years her senior and had a young daughter with whom he spent little time as he was so consumed by his work. Hazel immediately felt this was the man she wanted to spend the rest of her life with and the two began to secretly see each other. He seemed to be able to understand her as nobody had before. He was encouraging of her art and listened to her thoughts, accepting of her. Soon they were madly in love. They kept their relationship clandestine at the beginning and as soon as Hazel told her mother about it, her mother, as expected, saw red.

"He's older than *me!*" exclaimed Alice in horror.

"Only by a year!" Hazel knew her defence on this issue was lame.

"*He's twice your age!*" Alice shouted as if Hazel could not do maths. "He's widowed with a young daughter! He's already been around the block more times than the No. 64 tram!"

"I don't care about all that, Mama! I really don't. All I know is that I love him, and I want to marry him."

"*Marry him?*" cried Alice in despair. "You could marry anybody you wanted. You're a beautiful, bright, intelligent girl – have you lost your marbles even contemplating marrying such a man?"

Before Hazel knew what was happening, she found herself on an ocean liner heading to New York. After that she kept up a secret correspondence with John, but she did not stand a chance of stopping her mother getting what she wanted. Alice reacquainted the family with the Trudeaus and, more importantly, Hazel with Ned. Hazel was subtly manipulated and coerced into a courtship. In the end she decided to stop fighting what she decided was obviously her destiny. She had been born and bred to be an East Coast society wife and there was no point in trying to fight it any further. Her heart breaking, her love for John Lavery as strong as ever, she consented to marry Ned Trudeau. Their marriage was the society event of the year and they settled down to live on New York's Park Avenue.

Within a couple of months Hazel was pregnant. Then, when she was five months pregnant, Ned came home from work at his surgery one day complaining that he was not feeling well and dropped down dead in front of her.

As Hazel stared at her own face on the canvas in John's studio, she remembered vividly the image of her young, strong, handsome husband lying dead before her. It was a terrible shock to everybody. Out of all the ironies of her life, Hazel thought the biggest was that the young, fit, dashing man her mother thought was ideal had died in front of his pregnant young wife at only twenty-nine years of age. Whereas the much older man who her mother considered totally unsuitable was still alive, in good health, had risen to the top of British society and had even been knighted and made her a 'Lady'. Hazel had learned never to take anything in life for granted.

Over the breakfast table the next morning, Hazel reached over, took the morning newspaper and opened it.

She saw the headline on the front page: LLOYD GEORGE TO SEND ANOTHER ONE THOUSAND TROOPS TO IRELAND.

"I don't believe it!" said Hazel.

"What is it?"

"*This!*" She flung the newspaper across the table at John and began to pace up and down in frustration and anger.

"He lied to me! Lloyd George sat there and said he had no wish to continue this war in Ireland and all the time he had planned to send hundreds of more troops and escalate the conflict. How could he?"

"Well, he is a politician, Hazel."

"I'll have him expelled from every drawing room in the city!" Hazel swore in anger.

CHAPTER 8

Eileen Lavery stood outside 5 Cromwell Place looking up at the building. Even though it was her family home, she did not have particularly good memories of the place.

Eileen was John's daughter from his first marriage. The marriage had not lasted long as Eileen's mother, Kathleen, had died when she was a toddler. Eileen was now twenty-seven years of age, a woman, a mother. She was not just a wife, but a divorcee who had remarried the previous year. And yet, as she looked up at 5 Cromwell Place, she felt she was regressing to being that lonely young girl again. A girl whose mother had died and whose father had left her care to family friends and boarding schools as he travelled Europe building his reputation as an artist.

She climbed the steps and knocked. A few moments later Gordon answered.

He smiled in welcome and ushered her in.

"Hello, Gordon," she said taking off her coat and handing it too him. "Is my father home?"

"Yes, he's in his studio with Lady Lavery. I'll inform them you are here."

"No need – I'll show myself up," said Eileen as she walked down the hallway towards the sweeping staircase.

Gordon hurried after her. "Please … it might be wise if I announced you as there is a photographer there from *Vogue* magazine engaged in a photographic session with Lady Lavery."

Eileen raised her eyes to heaven. "It will be fine, Gordon. I will tell them I insisted on coming up unannounced."

Gordon nodded and watched her walk on. He always thought her a handsome young woman, dark-eyed with her jet-black hair pulled back in a bun – but her face, which showed great character, was always serious – almost as if a cloud of unhappiness followed her. Although that might just be the memories stirred up when she came back to her childhood home. He knew Eileen had not had one of the happiest of childhoods.

Eileen continued up the stairs to the top of the landing and turned left. She opened the double doors leading into her father's studio. As ever the sumptuous glamour of the studio hit her. The polished teak floor, the sweeping velvet curtains, the domed glass roof. And the paintings of different celebrities adorning the walls. But the most significant presence was Hazel. Portrait after portrait of her gazed down from the walls. Other paintings of her that were not finished rested on easels or against the walls. And the woman herself was that day poised on a gold-leaf-framed, red-velvet throne as a man with an elaborate-looking camera took her photograph.

In the background, proudly looking on, was her husband.

The camera flashed and a cloud of smoke billowed from it.

"Beautiful!" declared the photographer.

Eileen coughed loudly. "Am I interrupting?"

Hazel looked over and her initial surprise turned to a smile as she got up and walked quickly across the floor with her arms outstretched.

"Eileen!" she said, embracing and kissing her.

"Hello, Hazel," Eileen said with a smile.

John approached his daughter and kissed her on the cheek. "You should have let us know you were coming, and we would have prepared something special for dinner."

"No, I'm not staying for dinner. I have to get back to Ann."

"Oh – did you not bring her?" Hazel said in disappointment.

"No, she has a cold so I thought it best to leave her at home," said Eileen. Ann was her five-month-old baby.

"Oh, what a pity!" said Hazel. "I would have loved to have seen her before we leave for Ireland."

"Ireland? You're going to Ireland?"

"Yes – did we not mention it to you before?"

"Excuse me, ladies," said John, "but we have to continue with the photographic session – we cannot waste this man's time or the magazine's."

"It's quite alright! I have all the photographs I need," said the *Vogue* photographer as he began to pack away his equipment.

"Are you sure?" asked John.

"Quite sure. Thank you for what I'm sure will be some excellent photographs."

John rang the servants' bell. "Gordon will assist with your equipment."

Hazel thanked the photographer and then led Eileen over to the couch.

"It's for *Vogue* magazine," she said as they sat down.

"Yes, Gordon did warn me," said Eileen.

Gordon arrived and John escorted him and the photographer out.

"So, Ireland?" said Eileen. "What for?"

"We are going there officially for your father to paint the Archbishop and some senior political figures. Unofficially, we are going on a fact-finding mission to see this terrible war for ourselves and report back what we see and hear."

Eileen looked confused. "Report back to whom?"

"Well, to Winston Churchill for starters – and the Prime Minister. I met him recently and, although he seems a little –" Hazel waved her hand in the air, "airy, I believe he can be influenced to our side."

Eileen looked at her stepmother as if she were mad. "And are you taking Alice?"

"No, no – she will stay."

"And who's going to look after her while you're gallivanting around Ireland?"

"Oh, I have arranged a full itinerary for her in our absence – she won't be bored!"

"I see ..."

John re-entered the studio and came to sit by them.

"Well, I fear I have had a wasted trip here," Eileen said. "I had intended to invite you all to our place for dinner next week – for you to spend some time with your grandchildren … and to have an opportunity to get to know William better."

"Oh, dear, what a pity we shall not be here," said John.

"A pity or a convenience, Papa?" asked Eileen.

"A pity, of course!" said Hazel.

"I wonder!" Eileen addressed her father. "You have made little or no effort to either meet William or your new granddaughter."

"That's not true, Eileen!" objected Hazel.

"Hazel!" snapped Eileen. "I know you are my father's biggest champion and supporter but please – *please* – allow him to speak to me himself!"

Shocked by Eileen's outburst, Hazel looked at John who nodded reassuringly at her.

She then stood and said, "I need to check on tonight's dinner arrangements. I'll let you two have some time to chat."

"Thank you," said Eileen as she watched her stepmother leave the studio and close the door behind her.

"There was no need to be rude to Hazel, Eileen. All she has ever done is try and be a friend to you."

"Indeed – who could say anything bad about Hail Saint Hazel!" Eileen's voice dripped sarcasm.

"She even arranged your first marriage for you in Tangier."

Eileen sighed loudly. "I know, and I apologise. I have no gripe against Hazel – apart from the constant adulation you have given her to the exclusion of everybody else in your life."

"Another untruth!"

"Really?" said Eileen as she waved at the numerous paintings of Hazel around the studio. "This place is like a shrine to her!"

"Well, she is a celebrity."

"She's a celebrity because you made her one!" She sighed loudly. "I try not to be jealous, Papa, I really do. But when I think of the adulation you give Hazel – and Alice, by virtue of the fact she is her daughter – and compare it to the disinterest you had for me and my mother – it hurts."

"You were just a baby when she died – what could you know about my relationship to your mother?"

"I know you never really loved her because I never once saw you mourn for her over the years."

"When you mother was diagnosed with tuberculosis, I was working on my first big commission – recording the visit of Queen Victoria to the International Exhibition, Glasgow."

"So, you put the royal family before your own family?"

"I – I couldn't turn my back on such a commission, Eileen. Not a job of that magnitude. It was out of the question. And there were doctors' bills to be paid and I was a struggling artist at the time. But I admit I could have been a better father to you."

"William is very upset that you and Hazel have not made an effort with him."

"Well – it hasn't been easy, Eileen. Your divorce and being cited as an adulteress because of your affair with him – it was a lot for us to take in."

"I would have thought with your overriding love for Hazel you might have understood how I followed my heart?" Eileen stood up abruptly. "I think I'm wasting my time here. I don't think you'll ever accept William."

He stood and embraced her. "I do love you, Eileen ... when we get back from Ireland we will spend more time with you – and with William and the children."

She nodded. "But something else always comes first with you, doesn't it, Papa?"

She walked out of the studio, followed by a silent John.

"Well?" asked Hazel after Eileen had left.

"She feels neglected," said John.

"Oh dear!" Hazel pulled a face.

"She feels we haven't accepted William."

"Well, under normal circumstances we would have welcomed him with open arms – he's going to be a Scottish lord! But the divorce was very unpleasant, and I am in the process of converting to Catholicism – the Bishop did raise an eyebrow about Eileen's divorce to me. She's just feeling a little needy. Once we get back from Ireland, we'll smother her with love and attention!"

"That's what I said to her too."

"Very good." Hazel smiled at him before walking off to the drawing room.

John stood there silently, Eileen's words whirling around his mind.

CHAPTER 9

Hazel was shocked by what she saw during their stay in Ireland. Gone was the beautiful relaxed atmosphere of the country she had loved. In its place were armed tanks, Tans everywhere and violence.

She saw their trip as a peace mission, and they had a packed itinerary meeting people. She found that John's celebrity status as an artist as ever opened doors and powerful men were willing to have meetings with them.

"Vanity!" declared Hazel. "They all want to have their portrait painted by John Lavery."

She was correct and the temptation for these men to be captured for posterity by one of the greatest artists of the day was too strong to resist. However, even that temptation was not enough to lure the republican leaders out from hiding to pose for a portrait. During their stay in Dublin, Hazel anxiously awaited news from Shane Leslie or one of their other contacts saying the rebel leaders, and particularly Michael Collins, had agreed to meet them. But there was no response.

Meanwhile Collins' infamy was growing by the day, as it seemed impossible for the British authorities to track him down.

"*'They seek him here – they seek him there!'*" said John as he read the morning newspaper headline about Michael Collins while they had breakfast in their room at the Royal Marine Hotel.

"The Irish Pimpernel!" added Hazel as she took a sip of tea and looked out at the sea view.

John began to read from the front-page article: "*British*

Auxiliaries raided a number of houses on Dublin's northside in the early hours of this morning in their search for Republican leader Michael Collins. It is understood the raids were made after a number of tip-offs. No arrests were made."

As well as forming the 'Black and Tans', the British had created another constabulary unit, the Auxiliary Division, consisting of ex-army officers. They operated in well-armed mobile units whose job was to hunt down and wipe out IRA groups in the Irish countryside.

"So Michael slipped through their fingers again," said Hazel.

"*'However,*" John continued to read from the article, "'*a number of casualties were reported after gunshots were fired. It is understood two of the cases were fatal.*'"

Hazel put down her cup of tea in horror. "In other words – innocent people were gunned down and killed in the fruitless hunt for Collins! What a mindless tragedy!"

There was a knock on the door and a porter entered the room, holding a silver tray.

"Your morning post, sir."

"Ah, thank you, young man," said John, reaching out and taking the post.

Hazel took up the newspaper and looked through it as John sorted through the envelopes he had just received.

"It is heart-breaking," said Hazel. "Six RIC officers killed in an ambush in Tipperary ... a village burned by the Auxiliaries in retaliation for the killing of a police officer in Galway ... the shooting dead of a suspected informer in Cork."

"Shocking," said John.

"It's deeply depressing," said Hazel.

"On a lighter note, my dear, here's a letter from Alice."

"Ah!" Hazel smiled and, putting down the newspaper, reached out and took the envelope addressed to her in familiar handwriting.

As John began to open his post, Hazel sat back and began to read the letter from her daughter.

"She misses us dreadfully," she said. "She sends you all the love and kisses in the world ... she even misses my singing ... and says we are to hurry home. You see, absence does make the heart grow fonder!"

Hazel laughed and looked up at John.

She saw his face had gone deathly pale and his frown nearly scared her.

"John? What's the matter?" she asked urgently.

"Nothing! Nothing at all," he said, quickly folding over a letter and putting it back into its envelope.

"What is that? Who is that letter from?"

"It's nothing!"

"John Lavery – give me that letter now!" demanded Hazel, her hand outstretched.

John reluctantly handed the letter over to her.

"It doesn't say who it's from ... the writer didn't sign it," he said.

She began to read: *People like you should be extinguished from the face of the earth. Stop interfering in something that is none of your business. Go back to London and your high-society friends and take your bitch Yankee wife with you.*

Hazel gasped and her hand shot up to cover her mouth.

She read on: *Stop interfering in Irish affairs that have nothing to do with you. Profiting from war and the killings of others is a sin.*

"Good Lord!" she said. "What a venomous correspondence! Who would write such a thing?"

"I don't know, but it's frightening that somebody could," said John, worry etched across his face.

"What is all this nonsense about profiting from the war?"

"They must think I'm getting paid for the painting of the political and religious leaders here," said John.

"So, the writer is misinformed as well as cruel and vulgar – '*bitch Yankee wife*' indeed!"

"Frightful. What should we do? We don't want to offend anybody or alienate people."

"Who are we offending or alienating? We are trying to make friends across the divide – that's all!"

"But in doing so we risk doing damage to the very cause we are espousing."

"Nonsense!" Hazel got to her feet and, clasping the letter, began to pace up and down excitedly. "Don't you see, John? This letter shows we are making progress – real progress! To receive a letter like this means that we are unsettling people and that people are taking us seriously. When people want you to go away, you know you're a force to be reckoned with! This has strengthened my determination that we should be envoys in any way we can during this dreadful, dreadful war. Now we must hurry – we have a long journey to make to Belfast to meet the Lord Mayor – a staunch Unionist, so we must be prepared for a cool reception! I must wear something bright and cheerful."

As Hazel waltzed away to her dressing room, John looked after her in awe. He wasn't sure whether his wife was brave or mad, receiving such a letter without it causing a moment of concern, but he was in awe of her either way.

Hazel and John spent the month of October continuing their tour of Ireland. As John painted important figures, Hazel made mental notes of all she saw and wrote back to political friends in London about the horrors she witnessed.

One night, when they were staying at their friend Charlie Vane-Tempest-Stewart's estate in Ulster, Hazel tossed and turned in her bed. She was having a nightmare. It was a dream she'd had before. It concerned her dead sister Dorothy. In the early part of the dream Dorothy was young and beautiful and happy, as she had been growing up. They were at their home in Astor Place in Chicago and her mother and father were still alive too and they were all so happy. But then the bright happy feeling in the dream began to fade away and suddenly her father wasn't in the dream anymore and neither was her mother, and neither was their house in Astor Place. And it was as if she wasn't in the dream herself anymore either but was just looking on at Dorothy who was very alone and very scared and very ill. In the dream Hazel was desperately trying to reach out to her sister but she was slipping away from her.

And then Hazel awoke and realised she had been crying while she slept and had dreamed. The morning light was coming through the windows and John had already got up and wasn't there. And now she was awake the tears wouldn't stop. It was like as if she was mourning her sister all over again and the pain and the grief were too much to bear. She grabbed a pillow and, hugging it, began to sob into it.

The door opened and John walked in.

He stopped abruptly as he saw Hazel in a huddle, sobbing into the pillow.

"Hazel!" he said, rushing to her. "Whatever is the matter?"

He sat on the side of the bed and reached out to her. She turned to him and he saw her face was red and her face tearstained.

"Hazel!"

She embraced him and began to sob loudly as she held him tightly.

"Oh, John, I was having the most awful dream. It was about – Dorothy." She was unable to speak as the pain of the memory of her sister overwhelmed her.

He sat soothing her and stoking her hair.

"It felt – so real," she said between sobs. "She was alive, in front of me, and I tried to reach out and help her – but I couldn't!"

John held her tightly as she continued to sob. She'd had this dream often since her sister's death. The guilt of Dorothy's death and how she had died alone and impoverished in a Chicago hospital haunted Hazel and John knew she would never escape that ghost. This was the other Hazel that nobody on the outside saw. Behind the beauty and the wit and charm was this guilt-ridden woman who could never escape what had happened to her sister.

"Oh, John, what will I do if you ever leave me?" she cried.

"But I will never leave you, Hazel. I love you and I will always be here for you."

CHAPTER 10

Kitty was sitting behind the bar in the Greville Arms hotel. Ever since the war had started, business in the evenings was slack. Before the troubles, the bar would be filled each night with drinkers. But now there wasn't much trade after a certain hour. People didn't like to be out late – they liked to be safe at home before darkness fell. Everyone lived in a climate of fear. Kitty had sent the barman home and said she would look after the bar for the rest of the evening. There had been an ambush of an army lorry twenty miles away that afternoon and so tensions were running high. She knew that the barman lived a few miles outside the town, and she didn't want him cycling back late through a rural area when all she had to do was walk down a corridor to be home.

There were only two customers, sitting at the end of the bar having a chat. It was her brother's Larry's night off and he was with them enjoying conversation that was no more controversial than the price cattle had fetched in the market that week.

Kitty sighed as she reached into her pocket and took out the envelope she had received in the post that morning. It was from Harry. She took out the letter and read it again.

My darling Kitty,

I can't tell you how happy I was when I received your letter today. Since it had been a couple of weeks since I received your last one, I feared you had forgotten about me! Or worse, had been swept away by some dashing fella the likes of whom I could not compete against.

But, with the receipt of your letter, all is well with my world again. Every letter I get from you is like a magic carpet that sweeps me from this huge lonely impersonal city and back to the loveliness of Ireland and to you, my sweet, darling Kitty. I long for when I can see you again and be with you. I had a dream the other night that I was back in Longford like before. You were there, of course, beside me and the whole gang. We were dancing and singing, and Mick had us in stitches laughing over some joke. Then I woke up and realised it was but a dream and you were an ocean away from me.

Have you seen Mick at all? I haven't heard from him in a while. I miss him and the fun we had with him. I long to get those days back, the three of us together – a trinity of fun and friendship.

Kitty stopped reading and looked up from the letter. As often over the past few of weeks since Michael had visited, her thoughts drifted to him. She hadn't heard anything from him since then, though he was mentioned in the newspapers every day, his exploits becoming more daring all the time. What savage pressure he lived under!

She had enjoyed his company so much during that last visit and had been upset that he had dashed off so quickly – but the war came before everything. As she looked down at Harry's letter, she remembered that last night with Michael when she had read poetry to him by the fire and when he had reached out and asked her to stay longer and she had run off to bed feigning tiredness. The truth was he had stirred something in her that she didn't want to acknowledge and didn't want to face. She kept thinking about the revelation that there had been a bet between him and Harry when they first met, about who would win her heart. It was flattering to hear that Michael had originally been interested in her. Initially she had suspected that, and she had always found him attractive. But it was Harry she had ended up falling for and she had ended up courting. He was more attentive, gentle, genuine and romantic than the dramatic, unpredictable, glamorous Michael – but, also, as time went on it was obvious to everyone that Michael's interest was in Helen. He had all the hallmarks of a man in love. She idly wondered how things might have worked out if Michael had pursued her. She shook her head, willing the daydream away. She had ended up courting Harry but fate had then taken him away to America. Then, to add further complication into the mix, she had a fine fellow like Lionel Lyster actively trying to woo her – and everyone told her she was mad not to accept him. Her love life was complicated enough without daydreaming about Mick Collins!

She put the letter away, then looked up and saw a young man enter the bar. She recognised him immediately as the local RIC policeman for the town, Philip Kelleher. It must have been his night off as he was wearing civilian clothes. He had been stationed in the town a few months and kept mostly to himself. He was an affable-looking young man with a very polite nature. Like everywhere else in the country, the war had stopped the police from carrying out their duties in the area. Most too frightened of being shot in retaliation, they left the policing of the country to the army and the hated Black and Tans. Although the police were Irishmen, they were being paid by the British government and this made them a target and an enemy. Many had resigned as their positions were untenable and their stations were quickly burned down by the rebels once they vacated.

Kitty had chatted to this young policeman, Philip Kelleher, a few times when he came into the bar on a night off. He was the son of a Cork doctor and had fought on the front in France during the Great War. After the war he had joined the police and been stationed in Granard. Wisely, he did not try to implement his post and was just seen as a polite figurehead around the town.

"Good evening, Miss Kiernan," said Kelleher as he approached the bar.

"Hello, constable," she said, getting off her stool.

"Quiet evening," he said, glancing around the near-empty bar.

"Isn't every evening?" She smirked at him. "What will you be having?"

"A pint of stout, please."

"Certainly."

She set about pulling him a pint and when it was ready placed it on the bar.

"Thank you," he said and paid her.

She felt sorry for him. He must be very lonely so far from home and, with the townspeople keeping a distance from him, it must be impossible for him to make friends. Even when people indulged him in polite conversations, they never lowered their barriers.

He sauntered down to the other end of the bar, to Larry and the other men.

"Do you mind if I join you, gentlemen?" he asked.

"No, be our guest," said the men, but everyone knew, including Kelleher, that the conversation would be guarded.

But Philip didn't mind – it was human contact after staring at nothing but the four walls of his barracks every day for the past week since his last day off.

Kitty sat up on the stool again and reached for the newspaper.

When the door of the bar opened again, she looked up to see two figures walk quickly in. She couldn't quite comprehend what she was seeing. The two men were wearing balaclavas over their heads. Before she had time to react, they marched quickly to the end of the bar where Larry and the others were chatting to Kelleher.

"*What the fuck?*" shouted Larry on looking up and seeing them.

One of the men took out a gun and, aiming it straight at Kelleher, shot him twice before turning and racing from the premises, his partner at his heels.

Kitty saw Kelleher slump and slide off his chair to the ground. She ran from behind the bar to where Larry had knelt down beside him.

"What – who –" The words tumbled out of her mouth.

The young man was still alive, but blood was pouring out of him. His eyes were open as he gurgled.

"*Get a doctor – and a priest – now!*" shouted Larry at the other men and they ran out of the bar.

"*Will I get anything, Larry? Will I get anything for him?*" cried Kitty. She was trembling, and her eyes filled with tears.

Larry looked up at her, his face as pale as a ghost, and just shook his head. She covered her mouth with her hand, recognising that he was indicating that the young man was beyond help.

"You're fine, Philip, there's a good man," Larry said softly as he stroked the young man's head. "You're going to be alright. Brave lad like you, sure didn't you show the Germans how brave you were at the front?"

Kitty dropped to her knees, reached for Philip's hand and held it while Larry continued stroking his head and saying comforting words.

Time passed. Kelleher stared at the ceiling and the gurgling noises became less loud.

At last the door of the bar swung open and the doctor and priest rushed in, followed by the men who had fetched them.

Kitty and Larry quickly moved out of the way as the doctor knelt down beside Kelleher. "How many bullets?" he demanded.

"Two – two shots," answered Larry.

The doctor did a quick check and then looked at the priest and shook his head. The priest got down on his knees and began to give the Last Rites.

As the doctor and priest attended to the dying man, Kitty stumbled to a table at the far side of the lounge and sat down in a chair, shaking uncontrollably.

Nothing seemed real to her as eventually the body of the young policeman was taken out of their premises and taken to the local undertaker's.

Late that night, the Kiernans sat in the parlour trying to digest what had happened.

"You hear about these atrocities, but you don't expect it to happen in your home," said Maud.

Kitty raised her eyes and said angrily, "Why not? Are we supposed to be immune because we are friends with Mick Collins and Gearóid?"

"Come now, Kitty! Admit that you would never have expected such a thing to happen here," said Maud. "Isn't that so?"

Kitty, in fact, had not. "I can't see how the killing of that young man benefits anybody," she said, not answering Maud's question.

"He was a target as long as he was wearing that uniform, Kitty – you know that as well as any of us," Larry said. "War is war – and we've been lucky so far in that it's been kept away from us until now."

"I'm glad Helen isn't here to see it," said Chrys.

Helen had gone again to visit her future in-laws in Enniskillen.

"I think you girls should go away for a while as well," said Larry.

"Go away – where? Why?" demanded Kitty.

"We won't be opening the hotel or any of the businesses tomorrow," said Larry. "There's something in the air. The Black and Tans won't take this sitting down. There will be reprisals and this place will be high on the list."

"If the police found out about our connection with Michael Collins, we would be in extreme danger," said Maud.

"It would only take one informer," said Larry. "And there's many a local who must recognise him from when he was campaigning for the election in 1918." He shook his head. "This killing of the young policeman on our premises – it's going to turn a lot of attention on us – attention we don't want."

"Well, I'm not leaving my home," said Kitty. "I won't leave my home because of fear. I won't be driven out."

CHAPTER 11

Michael sat at a desk in an office he was using in Dame Street in Dublin. Around him was gathered a group of men as he pointed to a map on the desk.

"If we can get the arms arriving here at the port at midnight, stash them in these sheds that are close by until the patrol passes at two, then move them by lorry to the Cork –"

A man came rushing into the room.

"What is it, Emmet?" asked Michael.

"There was a killing of an RIC constable in Longford last night – in the Greville Arms Hotel."

"*In* the hotel?" Michael was incredulous.

"In the bar!"

"Who the fuck is responsible for that? Who gave the order?" Michael looked accusingly at the men gathered around him as they all shook their heads in denial. "*For fuck's sake!*" He slammed his fists on the desk, causing everyone present to shudder at his temper. "Are the family alright? The family – the girls?"

"No other casualties – just the policeman," said Emmet.

"Well, that won't be the case for long. The place will go up like dropping a match in a tinder factory. Get a message down to the Kiernans to leave the area immediately. Tell them it's an order from me for their own safety."

"Yes, sir," said Emmet as he turned to leave.

Michael went to the window and looked out at the street below. He was shaking. He only hoped the family had the good sense to get out of town. Knowing Kitty, she would be obstinate and refuse to leave. He began to fear for Helen's safety. They had no idea what was coming their way. The retaliation would be quick and savage and aimed at the local civilian population. He could only hope his message would get to them on time.

It was early the next morning that the sound of gunshots echoed around the town. Kitty ran to the window of the parlour.

"*Oh no!*" she shouted.

Coming down the street was a convoy of vehicles full of Black and Tans.

The Tans were firing into houses on the main street and breaking windows.

"May the saints preserve us – what will we do?" cried Molly, shaking with fear. "They will kill us all! Kill us for sure and hang us from the treetops!"

"They will not! Keep calm!" said Kitty. "We'll get away from these windows and go to the back of the house. We'll be safe there."

Kitty ushered everyone out of the parlour and down to the kitchen at the back of the house where they locked the door and sat in silence, listening to the growing riot outside.

"*Arrrgh!*" There was a collective scream as they heard breaking glass at the front of the house.

"*Shhhh!*" whispered Kitty. "Don't make a sound!"

But the terrifying noises seemed to be getting closer.

Michael desperately tried to get information from Granard all day. But the whole area was on lockdown since the shooting of the police constable. It was crawling with Black and Tans so impossible to get information in or out.

"We do know that they are carrying out a raid on the town," said Emmet, "but hard to know how severe it is. It started early this morning."

"Well, of course it's fucking severe! They'll level the town!" Michael ran his fingers through his hair as he paced up and down. "She won't have got out in time ... she wouldn't have time to leave ... she's trapped there." He seemed to be talking to himself.

"Mick?" asked Emmet, concerned for his leader.

"We have to get to the hotel and get the Kiernan family out of there to safety. Send the Squad in!"

"Are you mad? To the Greville Arms – where the shooting took place? Sure, even if the Squad could get near the place with the amount of Black and Tans there, it would be a suicide mission!"

"Well, we can't just *leave her there*!" Michael shouted, tossing his hair back from his forehead and slamming his fist on the table.

"Leave who?" cried Emmet in confusion and desperation.

"Helen – for fuck's sake!"

As night fell, the family and the servants still cowered in the kitchen. The rioting outside had been going on all day. The hotel had come under heavy fire and they could hear Tans rampaging through the building. Outside, gunshots, screaming and shouting could be heard continuously.

Now the family and servants were praying the Rosary in whispers. By the sound of it, the Tans were in the hotel bar helping themselves to the alcohol there. By the laughing and shouting it sounded like they were having a party and the idea of the Black and Tans being high on alcohol made them even more terrifying. Kitty prayed with all her might that they wouldn't come from the hotel back into the house and find them.

It felt like the longest night of Kitty's life as the sounds of rioting from the bar, shooting and houses being ransacked went on and on.

When the sun arose the next morning, the town was quiet. Kitty and Larry cautiously left the kitchen and walked through the house to the parlour which they found empty. There was broken glass on the plush carpet from where the windows had been smashed. They carefully went to a window and looked out. The street looked as if a bomb had hit it. Broken glass everywhere, contents from houses and shops strewn everywhere, small bonfires burning all along the street. There were also Tans passed out from the night of drinking while others wearily sauntered up and down.

Kitty could see people were taking advantage of the lull and timidly coming out of their houses. However, they weren't waiting around but were leaving as quickly as they could, by foot, bicycle, horse and cart or automobile. By any means people were getting out of town before the next wave of rioting, which nobody was in any doubt would occur.

"We'll just pack what we need and leave now, while we can," said Larry.

Kitty nodded. "I'll tell the others."

Kitty did not stop praying until they were at least an hour outside Granard and she felt she was safe from immediate threat. As they approached Dublin, they veered south of the city. They were heading to the Grand Hotel in Greystones. After the ordeal they had been through, they needed peace and quiet and so wanted to stay out of the city itself and yet be close enough for Gearóid and Maud to meet. The family had often visited the little seaside town over the years and Kitty and her sisters had gone to the Loreto boarding school in nearby Bray, before spending two years at Patrick Pearse's nationalist St. Ita's College, in Ranelagh in Dublin.

Kitty thanked God that they had all got out of Granard alive and uninjured. The war had certainly not just come to their doorstep, but into their home.

All day long, in the Dame Street office, Michael anxiously awaited news from Longford. Although none of his intelligence agents had got near the town, there had been reports of fires seen in the distance and the continual sound of gunfire all day.

Gearóid had been at the office earlier and was sick with worry about Maud. Michael had tried to calm him down.

As night came and there was still no news, knowing he would be unable to sleep, Michael did not make his way to one of the safe houses but stayed in Dame Street anxiously pacing the floor. He was imagining the worst. He, more than anybody, knew what the Black and Tans were capable of doing when they ransacked a town. They got completely out of control and, mixing alcohol into the equation, they were capable of committing any atrocities against the civilian population.

Eventually, Michael put his head down on the desk and drifted off to sleep.

CHAPTER 12

"*Mick! Mick!*" came a voice.

Mick awoke with a start and saw it was Emmet.

"What's happening?" he demanded.

"News came through from Granard. The Kiernan family managed to leave the town along with most of the other townspeople."

"All of them? All the family?"

"Yeah, the brother and the sisters," confirmed Emmet.

Michael felt his body flood with relief. He sank down into the chair again and buried his face in his hands as tears threatened.

"Where are they now?" he asked, wiping his face with his hands.

"They are on their way to Greystones – to stay at the Grand Hotel."

Michael jumped up. "And the town? What condition is the town in?"

"Sure, they ransacked the whole place. Set houses on fire, looted business – the usual. They were all pissed as farts, falling around the town drunk from all the alcohol they stole from the bars and houses. That's how the townspeople managed to escape – there were no proper roadblocks in place."

"Excellent!" said Michael and his eyes narrowed as he planned. "They'll be making their way back to their barracks at some stage today or tomorrow – have a column waiting for them on the road back to the barracks – they'll be in no condition to fight back after all that drink. We'll teach them a lesson they can carry back to Mr. Lloyd were you when we needed George!"

"I'll give the order," said Emmet as he turned to leave.

"And Emmet – get me a motorcar to take me to Greystones."

"Yes, Mick," he said with a smile before leaving.

Michael slumped down in the chair again but now with relief clear on his face.

It was late afternoon by the time Michael's automobile pulled up outside the Grand Hotel, a large Victorian building close to the sea. He glanced up at its unusual exterior with gabled dormer windows on the upper floor and a long balcony on the second, then hurried inside.

"What room is Miss Helen Kiernan in?" he demanded of the man behind reception.

"We don't have a Miss Helen Kiernan staying here, sir," said the man.

"Of course you do! Look at your registration book, you eejit!"

"*Michael!*" came the call of a familiar voice and he turned to see Kitty standing at the bottom of the stairs.

"Thank God – Kitty!" he said, hurrying to her and embracing her.

She suddenly felt overcome with feelings of safety and comfort and she held on to him tightly as she started to cry.

"Oh, Michael – it was terrible," she sobbed as he soothed her and stroked her hair.

"I know," he soothed. "You're safe now, Kitty."

She wanted to stay there, forever safe in his arms.

"It's so good to see you, Mick," she whispered.

"And you – I was worried sick about you all."

"I thought they were going to burn the house down around us. They've destroyed the hotel."

"I know, I know, love," he soothed her.

"And then the poor young constable, Mick! He was a nice young man and he was shot right in front of me in our bar."

"*Kitty!*" came another voice.

Reluctantly she lifted her face from Michael's chest and turned her head to see who the speaker was.

It was Gearóid, who had just arrived at the hotel and looked equally as frantic as Michael.

"Kitty – where's Maud?"

"She's in the restaurant with Larry."

"Are you alright?" asked Gearóid.

"I'm fine – go in and find Maud, Gearóid," she urged.

As Gearóid rushed away, she gently pulled back from Michael's arms and looked up into his face. He pulled a handkerchief from his pocket and wiped away her tears. She was embarrassed, feeling that she had let her guard down in front of him – he had never seen her vulnerable before.

"Well, you are a right one, showing up when all the drama is over!" she said. "Where were you when we needed you most?"

He smiled at her apologetically and then asked anxiously, "Where's Helen? Is she inside with the others?"

"No – she's in Enniskillen. She's with Paul's family. Sure, she wasn't home at all during the whole thing."

"Oh!" said Michael. "I thought she was here! That's why ..."

They looked at each other blankly for a few moments.

"*Kitty – my darling!*" came another voice.

Kitty spun around to see Lionel had just arrived into the hotel lobby and was rushing to her.

"Lionel!" she gasped in surprise as he enveloped her in a bear hug.

"I have been sick with worry about you – literally sick! I had to stop the automobile to vomit on the side of the road!" Lionel's voice was high on drama. "I couldn't get near the town during the siege – yes – *siege* is the word I would use to describe it! And when I finally got there the hotel was destroyed and no sign of any of you!"

"How did you track me down?" Kitty said as she glanced over at Michael who now had an amused look on his face.

"Lionel," he said.

"Oh, hullo, Michael!" He turned back to Kitty. "I tracked down your servant, the insolent one – Molly – and she told me you had come here." He took her arm and began to lead her away. "I need a stiff drink after it all – hot toddies all round, I say – and you can tell me about this awful ordeal you've been subjected to by those beasts."

Kitty glanced back at Michael who saluted her and then turned and walked into the restaurant to join Gearóid and the others.

Later that evening Michael and Gearóid were sitting with the Kiernan family in the hotel lounge. Kitty sat quietly, almost embarrassed by what had happened between her and Michael earlier. Michael for his part was talking as normal, occasionally looking at her and smiling sheepishly. Gearóid was holding Maud's hand protectively while Lionel sat with an almost unconcerned look on his face.

"The best place you can be is here for now," Michael told the family. "I'll let you know when it's safe to go back to Longford."

"I'll have to try and get back as quickly as possible to secure the hotel and other premises – if they're still standing," said Larry. "But the girls can stay here for however long it takes for it to be safe again."

"It won't be safe until this damned war is over," said Kitty.

"You could always come and stay with my parents, Kitty," said Lionel. "Mother would be delighted to have you stay … and we could try out the new tennis court we've had installed." He looked out at the grey skies through the window and added, "Although it's not the best weather for tennis, I suppose."

Kitty glanced at Michael's smirking face, feeling awkward at Lionel's vacuity during such a terrible time.

"It is simply all unbelievable," said Chrys.

"You should just be glad you got out of there alive," said Gearóid.

"I had better be getting back to Dublin – work to do," said Michael, rising from his chair.

Larry stood up and shook his hand. "Thanks for coming out to see us, Mick, and making sure we are alright."

"If you need anything – anything at all – let me know," said Michael. "Goodnight, ladies."

He nodded to Kitty and Maud before turning and leaving quickly.

"It was very good of Mick to come and see how we were," said Maud.

"Good of him?" snapped Kitty. "It's the like of him and his bloody war that destroyed our business and nearly cost us our lives!"

As Kitty sat at the dressing table brushing her hair, Maud came out of the bathroom in her nightgown.

"You shouldn't have said that about Mick earlier, Kitty, not in front of Gearóid," she said.

"Why not?"

"Because it's as much Gearóid's war as Mick's – he's fighting it too – on all of our behalves, may I add!"

"I never asked anybody to fight any war on my behalf. I was quite happy with my life before this war came along – now look at us! Staying a hotel because we are too frightened to go home, if we still have a home standing!"

"It wasn't the Irish who attacked our town, it was the British. You sound like a British sympathiser!"

"I'm an Irish patriot, Maud, you know I am. But I can't stand all this murder and mayhem – the British may have attacked our town, but they didn't shoot that young constable in our bar, did they? I'm not a political person, Maud, I never was, and sometimes I don't know why I am part of this circle – Gearóid, Mick and Harry. How did this happen? I'm just a straightforward girl who likes dances and the races – I'm not a political beast. I'm no Countess Markiewicz."

"You know the reason why we are all together. I'm engaged to Gearóid, you are courting Harry and then there was whatever was going on between Mick and Helen. It was love that brought us all together."

"Yes, love might have brought us together but war is tearing us apart! Helen was the wise one, abandoning whatever was going on between her and Mick. She was safely ensconced in her nice fiancé's respectable home while the rest of us shivered in the kitchen praying for deliverance. As for Harry – what kind of courtship can you have from three thousand miles away? That's why I have made a decision – the cleverest decision of my life."

"What decision?" asked Maud, sitting down on the side of the bed and staring at her.

"This evening Lionel asked me again to marry him – and this time I said yes."

"Oh!" Maud was shocked. "And what about Harry?"

"What about him?"

"He thinks you're his girl," said Maud.

"Let him think away! If I'd got killed by the Black and Tans last night then I'd be nobody's girl! I don't want any more of this war and fighting, Maud. If I settled with Harry this would be my life forever more, right in the middle of politics and mayhem. I just want a nice quiet life with somebody like Lionel who can give me that. I'm not like you, Maud. I guess I'm much more like Helen."

"But you don't love Lionel, Kitty!"

"I'm – I'm very fond of him."

"Fond! Fond won't keep you warm at night!"

"And neither will a man who lives three thousand miles away! Or for that matter a man like Mick Collins who you'd never see because he's always on the run from an assassin's bullet! No, I've made up my mind and it's me and Lionel from now on. I just know we'll be very happy together."

Kitty turned back to the mirror and resumed brushing her hair as Maud sat staring at her in amazement.

CHAPTER 13

Although Maud's words had unnerved her, Kitty was sure she had made the right decision in accepting Lionel's marriage proposal. After the terrible things she had witnessed in their hometown, she wanted to escape the war and anybody involved in it. Lionel was her escape route and, as she had said to Maud, she was very fond of him. He was a very agreeable fellow.

As they continued their stay at the Grand Hotel, Gearóid came regularly to see Maud. Kitty kept wondering if Michael would show up with him, but he didn't come again.

A week after the ransacking of the town, the Kiernans got word from Michael that it was safe for them to return and secure their premises and home.

Kitty went home with a sense of dread. Arriving back in Granard, she saw that the town bore the scars and wounds of the ransacking. Buildings and houses were boarded up, shops still remained closed, their stock stolen by the Black and Tans. People were still very frightened, having experienced first-hand what the Tans could do. They were fearful that anything could set them off again and they could raid the town again, leaving another trail of mayhem and destruction.

As Kitty walked into the Greville Arms, her heart sank. It had been badly damaged. From windows broken to the bar being smashed, there wasn't a room left that had not been vandalised. She sat down on a windowsill and the tears fell down her face as she saw thirty years of her family's hard work destroyed in one night's reckless thuggery.

"We'll build it up again," promised Larry. "No matter how long it takes."

Kitty looked over at the spot where the young constable had been shot and where he had lain dying in their bar. She remembered the terrible look of fear on his face. She felt haunted by that night. Her thoughts drifted to Harry and she was glad that he was in America, safely far away from an assassin's bullet. But Michael wasn't in America. He was there and a target every day of his life.

As she stared down at the spot where the constable had died, she was possessed by this terrible fear for Michael – fear that he might suffer a similar fate. A tear trickled down her face as that thought consumed her with a sadness that she found unbearable.

"Are you alright, Kitty?" said a voice behind her and she turned to see Maud there.

"Oh, yes, just remembering that dreadful night. That poor young man, I wonder how his family are."

"I don't know what's happened to the world over the past six years," sighed Maud. "With the Great War and everywhere in turmoil, from Russia with its revolution to Ireland with our war. It's like the whole world has gone mad and people just kill and think nothing of it anymore – right down to here in our own home."

"Do you worry about Gearóid?" Kitty was curious about how she dealt with her fears. Somehow, they had always avoided discussing the matter. Although not as well known or as high-up and powerful as Michael, Gearóid was a national hero too. At twenty-five, he had been the youngest officer to fight at the General Post Office in the Easter Rising and he had been given the role of raising the new national flag over the GPO when independence was being declared. He was certainly a target.

"Of course I do. I'm worried sick about him all the time. I fear the day will come that I get the news he has been shot and killed. But I can't live my life in fear, and I can't run away from the man I love because of that fear. I have to get on with it, Kitty." Maud smiled at her then turned and left her alone with her thoughts.

* * *

It will be Christmas soon, Kitty thought, time to put up the Christmas tree and decorations. Time to pretend everything is still normal, as things used to be.

A flash automobile pulled up outside the building.

"Look who has arrived – your fiancé!" said Maud.

Kitty turned and saw Lionel jump out of his motorcar and walk jauntily towards the building.

"Hello!" he said as he came into the bar.

He came across to Kitty and kissed her.

"How is everyone?" he asked cheerily, as if he was oblivious to the destruction that lay around them.

"How do you think we are – coming home to this?" said Maud.

"Oh – yes – yes – of course," said Lionel, looking around for the first time and grimacing at the wreckage. "What a mess!"

Kitty stood and sighed as she rolled up her sleeves. "Well, this place won't get put right with us just staring at it. Let's make a start."

As the women got to work, Lionel stood looking on blankly.

Kitty threw her eyes to heaven, grabbed a sweeping brush and thrust it at him.

"Don't just stand there, Lionel! Start sweeping up that broken glass!"

"Oh, right, yes, of course," he said as he looked at the brush and began to haphazardly sweep.

CHAPTER 14

Once Hazel and John arrived back in London, Hazel wasted no time resuming her campaign to bring peace to Ireland. Armed now with first-hand experience of the war, she regaled all her friends and contacts with stories of the horrors of what they had seen during their visit.

Winston Churchill was often in John's studio painting while John worked beside him. Winston loved painting in the studio as it was common knowledge that it was the best in London. He also hoped that some of John's genius would rub off on his own art. More than all that, though, Winston found it therapeutic to be at the Laverys' house. However, as Hazel now took every visit as an opportunity to lecture him on Ireland, he found the visits less therapeutic than he used to.

The time seemed to fly with the lead-up to Christmas. John and Hazel threw themselves into the Christmas party circuit. Only two years after the ending of the Great War, people wanted to now forget about the horrors and devastation it had brought. The Roaring Twenties had begun, and the upper classes of London were leading the way. John and Hazel were at the heart of it. But Hazel could not stop thinking of Ireland and the ongoing war and campaigned tirelessly to bring peace to the country.

It was the night of the Marquess of Londonderry's Christmas party, to be held at his London residence on Park Lane. The Marquess, Charlie Vane-Tempest-Stewart, had been a very good friend of the Laverys for well on a decade since Hazel had first arrived in London and befriended him and his wife, Edith. Charlie had even lent John and Hazel their estate in Ulster to stay in during their recent Irish tour. Much to Edith's displeasure, Charlie had relentlessly pursued Hazel over the years, sending her expensive gifts that John had insisted be returned. Charlie was one of the richest men in Britain and his wealth came from his vast estates in Northern Ireland. A Protestant and vehemently against Irish independence, he sat on the opposite side of the political divide from the Laverys, despite their close friendship.

As Hazel sat at her dressing table in her bedroom, applying her make-up, her personal maid Florrie combed back her auburn hair.

Hazel sat back and looked at the result.

"You look amazing, my lady," said Florrie.

Hazel leaned closer to the mirror and examined her flawless skin.

"I wonder how long I've got left," she said.

"Sorry, my lady?"

"How long have I got before the ravages of time begin to appear."

Florrie giggled. "But you are only a young woman, my lady. And there is no sign of age with you. You're the most beautiful hostess in London, everyone knows that."

"Thank you, Florrie – I wasn't fishing for a compliment, just stating facts," Hazel said, fully aware she wasn't as young as everyone assumed she was. "The problem about women who are deemed beautiful is that, once they are deemed so, all everyone does is wait for the beauty to fade and disappear. It's like an ugly spectator sport the woman is meant to endure. The jealousies, the envy, the spite – everyone knows they will get their revenge in the end as time will carry out that vengeance all on its own. All they have to do is sit back and watch and wait."

"Well, I think they'll have to wait a very long time for that vengeance to be carried out on you, my lady!" said Florrie with a smile as she continued fixing her hair.

"Thank you, Florrie," said Hazel, smiling at the girl's reflection in the mirror.

John stood at the fireplace in the drawing room, looking at his watch.

"Where is your mother? We are going to be late for this damned ball!" he said.

Alice stifled a giggle. It was so rare to see John agitated that she found it highly amusing when he was.

"I shouldn't worry, John," she said. "The party won't start until Mama has arrived anyway!"

"That's not the point. Edith will be looking for excuses to berate us – your mother anyway, and I'd prefer not to give her any opportunity."

"Edith will be looking for excuses to berate Mama because she is furious that her husband has shamelessly pursued Mama for years – and he doesn't care who knows it! Including poor Edith and you!"

John looked at Alice with a mixture of concern and amusement. "I sometimes wonder if we have been responsible guardians to you, Alice. You are far too precocious and knowing of things that girls of your age shouldn't be aware of."

"I couldn't have wanted for better guardians than you and Mama, John. But let us be honest – Mama is not like other mothers. She has never held back from speaking freely in front of me on any issue or matter concerning her. I sometimes think she forgets I'm in the room, she speaks so freely!"

"Oh, she always knows when you are in the room, Alice dear, do not think otherwise. It is more that, because your father died before you were even born, her circumstances were such that she didn't have the resources to be like others. In a way you had to grow up more quickly and your mother treated you more as a friend than a daughter."

She sighed. "I sometimes think I have taken the mothering role with her!"

"Well, she does rely on you, Alice, as she relies on me," said John. "To others, outside the family, she epitomises the overconfident socialite. We know the truth."

Alice smiled at him. "I hope she never forgets how lucky she was in meeting you. And not just for her, for me too!"

He walked over to her and kissed her forehead. "You don't

know what it means to me to hear you say that ... in a way, it makes me feel better for the mistakes I made with my first family."

She looked at him speculatively. "You know, I think the reason you are agitated tonight has nothing to do with being late and everything to do with whose party it is – the Marquess of Londonderry who openly pursues Mama."

"I must admit I find Charlie's behaviour distasteful. Most of the men who flock around your mother I do not mind. Sometimes I tell myself it is almost flattering that my wife is so admired. But Charlie is far too wealthy and far too aristocratic ... he's the real deal – whereas I am just the cheapest of imitations. In the world of art, he would be described as the masterpiece, whereas I would be classed as a forgery."

"But, John – you have something that none of the rest have and they envy you it shamelessly."

"My talent?"

"No – your wife!" said Alice as she threw her hands in the air and laughed loudly.

John burst out laughing too and they hugged.

Their car pulled up outside Londonderry House, a gigantic mansion on Park Lane. Their footman, who was acting as chauffeur for the night, got out of the front of the car and opened the door, allowing Hazel and John to step out.

They made their way to the front door.

"Good evening, Sir John and Lady Lavery," the butler greeted them.

"Good evening," said Hazel as two of several footmen assisting him took their coats and scarves.

They continued into the giant foyer which was full of exquisitely dressed guests. The whole place was decked out in marvellous Christmas decorations. On either side of the splendid staircase, which was the centre point of the foyer, were giant Christmas trees. As they made their way through the crowd they were greeted warmly by different guests.

They climbed the stairs with its ornamental bannisters and

reached the first landing where Hazel spotted Charlie and his wife Edith with the Prime Minister Lloyd George and some others.

"Hazel!" cried Charlie as he broke away from the group and came to embrace her warmly.

"Dear Charlie," she said, returning his embrace.

"And John – must not forget John!" said Charlie as he shook John's hand.

He led them to join the others.

"Edith," Hazel greeted her as she kissed her cheek.

"Hazel," Edith replied, her cool blue eyes surveying Hazel's outfit.

"You know the Prime Minister and of course Philip?" checked Charlie as he gestured to Lloyd George and his private secretary who stood beside him

"Yes, of course, so good to see you again, Prime Minister." Hazel beamed a smile at Lloyd George.

"The pleasure is mine, Lady Lavery," said Lloyd George with a smile before shaking John's hand.

Hazel kissed Philip's cheek. "Philip and I are old friends," she said.

"Thank you so much for allowing us to stay at your house in Ireland, Charlie," said John.

"We were delighted to lend you the house," said Edith.

Edith had tidy, coiffured brown hair and a long serious face. John felt she looked a little washed-out standing beside Hazel.

"It is an amazing place – we enjoyed our time there immensely," said Hazel.

"A wonderful house and estate – a very peaceful setting," added John

"Which is about the only place you could call peaceful during our travels throughout Ireland!" stated Hazel.

Lloyd George looked at Philip and discreetly raised his eyes to heaven, prompting Philip to make an apologetic face.

"I have never seen anything like it!" said Hazel.

"Yes, we all read your letter in the *Times* last week, Hazel," said Charlie, trying to cut her off.

"And the week before," murmured Edith as she took a sip of her champagne.

"Towns burned, Tans drunk, civilians murdered!" said Hazel.

"Yes, well, I'm sure the Government of Ireland Act that came into law this week will bring the whole unfortunate situation to an end," said Lloyd George with a condescending smile.

"You are deluded, Prime Minister!" Hazel said loudly, causing everyone to drop their mouths open with shock. "The Government of Ireland Act is too little too late – about ten years too late! It might have worked in 1910 but it won't work in 1920! Things have moved on, events have overtaken the pace of your politics. Giving one parliament with little or no power to Belfast to satisfy the Protestants in the North and one to Dublin, again with little or no power, to the Catholics in the South will not satisfy the Irish now. Those days are gone, Prime Minister! The Irish demand full independence, a republic free of any control from the British and not this puppet parliament you aim to establish."

"I hardly think this is the time or the place, Hazel," cautioned Edith coldly.

"When is? When is ever the time – or the place? This parliament you have given permission for in Dublin will have such limited powers that in reality it will be nothing more than a glorified County Council! It will simply be ignored by the Irish and members of the Dáil who will fight on with this war until they get full independence. How many more must die until you understand this?"

"My dear Lady Lavery, as I told you last time I met you, I will never give the go-ahead for an independent Ireland. It just will not happen."

"I, as one of the biggest landowners in Ireland, say to that – *hear, hear!*" said Charlie loudly.

"But it won't work!" objected Hazel.

"I can't see why we can't make the Belfast parliament work with some good old-fashioned elbow grease, determination and gung-ho!" said Edith.

Edith's organisational skills were legendary as she had been the head of the Women Volunteers throughout Britain during the Great War, literally making sure the home fires kept burning. She was thrilled for once to have all the male company vehemently disagreeing with Hazel Lavery, as opposed to having them as usual fawning over her every word. Always a thorn in her side, particularly as it galled her that Charlie never bothered to disguise the fact he was in love with her, Edith now wondered if Hazel Lavery was on some kind of self-destructive social suicide with this Irish crusade she had embarked on. If she continued on this track Edith was sure even Winston would sever ties with her soon. That would leave her with only the company of that other extremist Shane Leslie.

"Well, you are all insane if you think the violence will stop or the fight for independence will not continue," insisted Hazel.

Charlie was becoming frustrated with her. "Hazel! What has this to do with you? You're not even Irish!"

"I am Irish-American!" Hazel retorted.

"You're only pretending to be Irish as it's chic to be Irish in London at the moment," said Charlie.

"That is not true!" said Hazel, becoming angry too. "How dare you, Charlie! I can tell you now – ask any Irishman which of us he considers more Irish – me, albeit born in Chicago – or you, born in London, educated at Eton and Sandhurst – and they will say me! Despite your owning thousands of acres of land there which they would say you stole from them in the first place!"

"*Hazel!*" hissed John, realising she had gone way too far.

Charlie was enraged as he lunged in anger towards her.

"*Charles!*" shouted Edith, causing people around to turn and stare.

Charlie pulled back, his face red from anger.

Hazel, seeing the upset she had caused, realised she had provoked him too much.

"Well – I –" She turned and smiled at Edith. "The gardens at Mount Steward were simply amazing, Edith. The gardeners tell me you are responsible for the creation of them yourself?"

"Ah – yes –" Edith looked at Charlie and then smiled at Hazel. "I am rather proud of them."

"Every morning after breakfast, we went for a walk through them – didn't we, John?"

"Yes, very pleasant," said John.

"Anyway, we had better mingle – we do not wish to be accused of being anti-social!" said Hazel.

"I do not think anyone could ever accuse you of that, Hazel dear!" scoffed Edith.

Hazel spotted an acquaintance and, waving over at him, moved away from the group, quickly followed by John.

As Edith too moved to check on her guests, Lloyd George and Philip were left alone. The Prime Minister observed Hazel as she flitted from one guest to another.

"And there, Philip, lies our biggest problem with Ireland," said Lloyd George, nodding over at Hazel.

"Hazel Lavery, Prime Minister?" asked Philip, confused.

"Not Hazel Lavery *per se* ... but her ilk, who and what she is – Irish America. If we were just dealing with the Irish alone it would be one thing, but they have millions of Irish Americans standing with them – backing them financially, politically, spiritually with their unswerving, never-ending loyalty to the Mother Country."

"True, Prime Minister," conceded Philip. "That is why De Valera has spent the last two years in America courting their support and money, as opposed to being in Ireland leading the war against us."

"Yes, he left that in the hands of Collins – the unfortunately very capable hands of Collins," sighed Lloyd George.

As Hazel mingled with the other guests, she quickly regained her composure. She worked the crowd like the expert she was. As the night wore on, she looked out for Charlie but he never seemed close by. She knew she needed to make amends. She had gone too far in questioning his Irishness. She spotted him taking a cigar from a passing waiter and sauntering over to an open French window that led out to a balcony. She waited a minute and then excused herself from the people she was talking to and followed him out. She found him looking out at the views across Hyde Park while he smoked his cigar.

"So, this is where you ran to escape me?" she said as she went to stand beside him.

He looked down at her. "A step too far, Hazel!"

"I know!" she said, raising her hands in surrender. "I shouldn't have said it! But you shouldn't have said what you said either! But – I'll admit – what I said was worse. Friends?"

"Of course … I could never stay mad at you too long. But I don't understand you anymore, Hazel. You were much more fun before you started with all this Irish political stuff."

"I can't ignore what's going on there, Charlie. And I feel it's my destiny to be involved in it."

"A bloody tedious destiny in that case!"

"I don't want to be just – fun. I want more in life. I want to be … I want to make a difference. I want my life to have meaning."

"You could have made a huge difference in my life," he said as he put his hands on her shoulders. "God – how I chased you for years!"

"Everyone thought we were having an affair," she laughed.

"Why didn't you?" he asked.

Hazel actually did find Charlie attractive with his aristocratic features and tall frame. She smiled at him as she thought of her answer.

"I'd never do that to John, Charlie. And, besides, once you had been with me, you'd tire of me quickly enough."

"Never!"

"You would! I often think, if I had been stupid enough to have affairs like the other wives with all those men who have chased me, I would have been a joke by now."

"None of those other wives have become jokes."

"I'd have lost my integrity. John is my husband and I don't need or want any other man. But I do want you as my friend," she said, leaning forward and kissing his cheek before turning and going back inside.

CHAPTER 15

It was Christmas week and Kitty and Lionel were in Dublin doing their Christmas shopping. As they walked down a crowded Grafton Street, Lionel was laden down with shopping bags and boxes.

"Gosh – it looks like we have bought all Dublin!" declared Lionel.

"We've a bit to do yet!" said Kitty as she stopped to look in a shop window.

Suddenly there was a screech of a bicycle stopping behind them and Kitty turned around to see Michael there.

"I thought it was you!" said Michael as he dismounted.

"Mick!" said Kitty as she gave him a warm hug. "Well, it's that good to see you!"

"And you, Kitty – you're a sight for sore eyes! Hello, Lionel, Happy Christmas!"

"Oh, yes – Happy Christmas," said Lionel as he struggled with the shopping to reach a hand out to shake with Michael, but he ended up dropping everything on the ground. "Oh shit!"

Michael tried to stifle a laugh as Kitty raised her eyes to heaven in embarrassment. Michael bent down and started picking up the bags and boxes with Lionel.

"Maybe if you gave Lionel a hand with all this lot, he wouldn't be so overloaded!" said Michael, handing Kitty some of the shopping.

She narrowed her eyes at him in irritation, making him stifle another laugh.

"We are just up doing a spot of Christmas shopping," explained Lionel.

"Eh, yes … so I see! You shouldn't let her use you like a donkey, Lionel." Michael clapped him on the back. "So how are ye all keeping?"

"We're fine," said Kitty. "The hotel still isn't opened, or the store. We are still trying to get everything fixed – it will take another while yet."

"*Bastards!*" muttered Michael under his breath.

"We kept expecting you to visit with Gearóid," said Kitty. "Will you get down to us over Christmas?" Michael loved Christmas and she knew it must be very lonely for him not to be able to return to his own family in Cork for the festive period. "There will be singing and dancing and enough turkey to feed an army!"

"There's nothing I'd like more than spend Christmas with you all, but it's too dangerous for me to go there so soon after the riot. There's still too high a presence of Black and Tans in the area and they'll watching your place like hawks after the young policeman was killed there."

She nodded. She knew this to be true. The Black and Tans were keeping a close eye on the Greville Arms after what had occurred there.

"Besides, there's too much going on here, with the passing of the Government of Ireland Act – and then of course De Valera is back from America tonight. I'll be seeing him first thing in the morning."

Kitty noticed that he looked apprehensive.

"What will you do for Christmas?" she asked, worried about him.

"Ah, sure, I'll be with the lads – we'll have a bit of fun tomorrow night. We're going to the Gresham for a few drinks."

"No word on Harry?" asked Kitty tentatively.

"Well, he hasn't come back with De Valera to the best of my knowledge, that's all I know." Michael bit his lower lip and then asked the question he had been burning to ask. "How's Helen?"

"Great form," said Kitty. "She won't be home for Christmas. She's spending it with Paul's family."

"Oh!" said Michael, disappointed at the news.

"Sure, it won't be long now until her wedding in the spring," said Kitty.

He nodded, trying not to show the gloom that had overcome him on hearing the wedding was still on schedule.

"Speaking of weddings," Kitty said, raising her hand in the air and showing off an engagement ring.

"*You* got engaged!" Michael nearly shouted in shock.

"I did surely!" She smiled happily.

"And – and who's the lucky fellow?" Michael asked.

Kitty blinked a few times and then nodded at Lionel. "Well, Lionel, of course!"

"Oh!" said Michael, turning and looking at Lionel whose eyes he could just see over the boxes of shopping. "Of course! Indeed – who else!"

"Well, I'd shake your hand to wish you congratulations, Lionel, but I wouldn't want to risk another avalanche of bags and boxes!"

"Yes – yes, indeed!" said Lionel as he precariously balanced the shopping.

"Well, now, that is a turn-up for the books!" said Michael, his face full of amusement as he looked at Kitty.

He was beginning to annoy her by his reaction and attitude.

"We are hoping for June or July," Kitty said, trying to sound aloof to fend off his mocking attitude.

"Indeed, best to stay away from May – as they say, '*Marry in May and rue the day!*'" Michael gave a chuckle.

"We very much hope you can come to the wedding," said Lionel. "I know what a close friend you are to the whole family."

"Well, now, that is one day I would not miss!"

"Yes, well, we'd better be going," snapped Kitty. "We still have shopping to do and we don't want to miss our train back home."

"Sure, poor Lionel won't be able to carry any more shopping, Kitty! You'll have him killed before you can get him to the altar!"

"Oh, no, it's quite alright, Michael, I have very strong arms – it's from all the tennis and rugby," said Lionel.

"Tennis – indeed!" said Michael in bemusement.

111

"As I said, we'll be off!" snapped Kitty.

"I believe Gearóid is heading down to you for the Christmas?" said Michael.

"Yes – if you can spare him?" she responded coldly.

"Ah, sure, I wouldn't want to keep him away from Maud for the Christmas. I wouldn't want to hamper *true* love!" said Michael, smiling mockingly at both of them.

"Nice to see you again, Michael," said Kitty.

"Hopefully we'll see you soon," said Lionel.

"Yes, and maybe we can plan a game of tennis," Michael suggested with a wink at Kitty.

"Yes, that would be lovely!" said Lionel.

"Happy Christmas, Michael – come along, Lionel!" said Kitty as she walked briskly away.

Michael shook his head as he watched the two of them trot down the street.

"Yes, run along, Lionel, and be a good little lapdog," Michael whispered and he chuckled to himself.

"He seems such a nice fellow," said Lionel.

Kitty sighed loudly. "Lionel! Did you not notice he was taking the piss out of us the whole time?"

"What?" Lionel asked, confused.

"I don't know which is worse – the fact that big-headed eejit was taking the piss out of you or the fact that you didn't notice he was!" she said, trying to contain her temper.

"I don't know what you're talking about," said Lionel.

"Oh Lionel, sometimes – when we are in company – sometimes I just wish you'd say nothing – nothing at all!"

CHAPTER 16

Michael had been intrigued, amused and a little worried when he bumped into Kitty and Lionel on Grafton Street. Intrigued, as he would never have put somebody as vivacious and smart as Kitty with a man as dull as Lionel. Amused, because she looked as if she was embarrassed by her own fiancé half the time. Worried that she was making the biggest mistake of her life in the hope of having a secure and stable marriage. Also worried about how Harry in America would react to the news. If Lionel hadn't been there, he would have queried her about Harry and whether he had been informed. He hoped Kitty knew what she was doing.

He was also confused and dismayed over Helen. She was spending the Christmas with Paul's family. He had been hoping to hear that the engagement had been called off. He desperately wanted to speak to her but, as he had said to Kitty, it had just been too dangerous for him to go anywhere near Granard after what had happened there. He didn't know what to do, but he wished he had told her strongly how he felt about her. He was sure that if Helen knew how he felt she wouldn't go through with her marriage to Paul.

In the early hours of the morning of Christmas Eve, Michael's driver drove him to Greystones to Éamon de Valera's house.

Michael was nervous about meeting Éamon again after his long absence in America. A lot had changed. Michael had changed. He had just been another delegate before De Valera had left. In his absence he'd had a meteoric rise, his fame and reputation now eclipsing even De Valera's. In the British press Michael had almost become an obsession as tales of his organisational brilliance, inability to be captured and aura of mystery were becoming legendary and were reported daily.

As the automobile pulled up outside the house, he looked up the pathway at the now familiar building. He had been there every week in De Valera's absence, making sure his family were alright and bringing them supplies.

He got out of the automobile and, opening the garden gate, walked up the frosty pathway and knocked on the door.

It was opened by Éamon's wife, Sinéad.

"Good morning, Mick," she smiled, beckoning him in and kissing his cheek.

He had got to know Sinéad well over the months and come to respect the discreet and sensible woman.

"He's arrived back, I take it?" asked Mick.

"He has." She spoke softly so as not to awaken the children. "He's waiting for you in the parlour."

Michael followed her down the hall.

She gently opened the door and ushered him into the small room where Éamon was sitting beside the fire.

"Well, if it isn't the Big Fella," said Éamon, standing up and shaking his hand.

Michael saw that Éamon had hardly changed at all physically during his time in America. His long face had hardly aged at all, and his intense eyes continued to shine behind his trademark round spectacles.

"Good to see you, Dev," said Michael as Sinéad closed the door, leaving them alone.

"And it's good to be back. Back in my own home. I've been living in hotel rooms for so long that I've forgotten what it feels like to be in my own bed."

"I know that feeling, Dev, only I haven't been sleeping in hotel rooms but any room, attic or hayshed I can find," said Michael with a smirk.

"Indeed, the world has become tantalised by your exploits. Even the *New York Times* delights in saluting how you have evaded the authorities 'through your wit and charm and intelligence', to quote an article I read about you last week."

Michael laughed. He thought he detected a cool mocking tone in Éamon's voice. Almost a resentment.

Éamon turned and walked to the fire and put some coal on it. "I thank you most genuinely for what you did for Sinéad and the children while I was away. Things haven't been easy for them, not having me here. But they were never short of anything, thanks to you, and I hear you took the time to play with the children and listen to them."

There didn't seem to be any resentment in Éamon's voice as he spoke these words, but Michael still sensed he was being made to feel that he had been intruding. He knew Sinéad would have only spoken highly of him and with gratitude … maybe that's not what Éamon needed to hear either. As Michael knew only too well, the heart could play cruel tricks on the mind.

"It was nothing, Dev, I did nothing special." Then he asked about the one thing that was burning him up with curiosity. "No Harry?"

"No – no Harry," confirmed Éamon.

"When he is due to come home?"

"I have no plans for Harry to return to Ireland just yet. We need a strong presence in America, more now than ever, and Harry can fulfil that role. He can be our ambassador, for want of a better word. He will continue to lobby our cause and raise the much-needed funds."

"But you have already raised nearly six million pounds," said Michael.

"A fairly decent amount of money and enough to get us up and running once we have independence. But we will need ten times that amount to rebuild the country after the destruction I've seen since I arrived back yesterday. And that's only coming from the port to here. I shudder to think what the rest of the country looks like."

Michael shrugged. "It's been total warfare, Dev."

"Well, there's a train of thought that says what is the point of having an independent country if that country has been wiped out and there's nothing standing there anymore."

Michael looked at Éamon in surprise. It was almost as if he was criticising him and how he had conducted the war in his absence. He decided not to engage him on that point.

"I can't imagine Harry was so happy about being left behind," he said instead.

"Well, no, he wasn't … he's very anxious to come home. He misses his family… and there's a young woman involved, I understand, from Longford?"

"Yes – Kitty Kiernan."

"Unfortunately, the personal life must come second while we put country first. As you are only too aware, Sinéad and the children have had to suffer long enough without me. She did come to join me for some weeks in America, as you know, but she had to come back for the children."

"Sure, they couldn't do without her, or her them."

"Yes, and the whole circus of the political and fundraising circuit in America was too much for her … she's a private woman, and she couldn't be on show like that. Perhaps this Kitty Kiernan woman is different, and Boland could send for her to join him in America?"

"I – I –" Michael didn't know what to say after just hearing she was engaged to Lionel.

"I understand he did ask her to join him when he was going there first," said Éamon.

Michael didn't know what to say. He certainly wasn't going to start talking about Kitty Kiernan with Éamon. He didn't want Harry hearing about her engagement through another source if Kitty hadn't told him herself.

"But I know what good friends you are with Harry and what a great team you make," said De Valera.

"We do," said Michael, wondering where this was heading.

"So, I have made a decision."

"What's that?"

"You are to go to America to replace me there. From now on I'll be taking over your role here in Ireland and you will be taking over mine in America."

Michael's mouth dropped open with shock.

"As I said, everyone knows what a great team you and Harry make – and I have no doubt you will take America by storm."

That evening Michael was in the Gresham Hotel where he had arranged to meet some close friends including Gearóid. He had very much looked forward to spending Christmas Eve at the hotel, having dinner and Christmas drinks. But he had been totally thrown by his meeting with De Valera.

As he sat in the plush restaurant, he told his team about De Valera's plan to send him to America.

"America! But sure, he can't do that! Who'd run everything here?" demanded Gearóid.

Michael sighed loudly. "*He* will – seemingly."

"*What?* That's nuts! He wouldn't be able to do what you do!"

"No more than I could do what he does! Could you imagine me going around posh hotels and conferences in New York and Chicago hobnobbing with high society while looking for handouts at the same time?"

There was a chorus of voices shouting "*No!*", followed by loud laughter at the thought of Michael in such a scenario.

"That's not you, Mick – dressed up in black tie watching your p's and q's!" said Emmet.

"Fuck that!" laughed Michael as he grabbed his beer and took a swig before continuing to eat his turkey dinner. "I don't mind telling ye, lads, I'm very hurt by what Dev wants to do – sending me into exile. I thought he'd want me close by him, especially after … after everything. But no, he wants me the other side of the Atlantic!"

Gearóid could see De Valera 's plan had affected Michael deeply.

"Of course, the reason he wants you gone is because he's jealous of you!" he said.

"Get away out of that!" Michael said dismissively.

"He's jealous of the power and respect you've got and he's trying to marginalise you so he can take it all back for himself!"

Michael sighed – the notion had gone through his own head which made him even sadder. He leaned towards Gearóid. "When are you heading down to Granard?"

"First thing in the morning."

"I bumped into Kitty a couple of days ago out shopping with her fiancé!"

"Oh, yes, Lionel!" Gearóid rolled his eyes.

"Bit of a turn-up for the books," said Michael. "The question I want an answer to is – does Harry know?"

"I haven't a clue, Mick. Sure, you know Kitty – if you started asking her too many personal questions you'd get a slap across the face quick enough!

Suddenly Michael spotted Auxiliaries marching into the restaurant. The others followed his gaze as the Auxies quickly secured the back entrance to the kitchens and the windows.

"Stay calm, lads, show no reaction," muttered Michael as he tried to figure out what was going on.

Once the restaurant was secured a group of Auxies marched straight to Michael's table, pointing guns.

On reaching the table the captain said, "Michael Collins, you are under arrest."

CHAPTER 17

Maud had been very concerned about Gearóid as he was supposed to be in Longford for Christmas morning. When he didn't show up Maud began to fear the worse.

"He'll be fine, Maud. He's probably been delayed by the weather," Kitty comforted her as she looked out at the wind and the rain.

"Something's happened, I know it. He was meeting Mick for dinner last night."

Kitty bit her lower lip on hearing this as her concern expanded from Gearóid to Michael. Like Maud, she started feeling sick from worry as the day moved into the evening.

"I'm sure Gearóid will be fine – he probably had a puncture," said Lionel to Kitty.

"It doesn't take a whole day to fix a bloody puncture, Lionel!" snapped Kitty.

If something had happened to Gearóid, the likelihood was something had also happened to Michael. She couldn't bear the thought of that. As she twisted her handkerchief in her hand, she felt sick at the thought but also perplexed as to why she was having this reaction.

There was a collective sigh of relief when Gearóid finally arrived in, just as it was getting dark.

"Any turkey left?" he asked with a laugh as Maud ran to hug him.

"What happened? What are you so late?" said Kitty.

"That's quite a story – I'll tell you – but, first, where's my Christmas dinner?"

Gearóid was sitting in the parlour, replete with turkey and Christmas pudding, whiskey in hand. Maud was sitting at his feet, holding his hand, the rest of the family gathered round listening to his account of what had happened the previous night.

"So, there we were, surrounded by British Tans, their guns pointing at us and them telling Michael they knew who he was and putting him under arrest – along with the rest of us, mind you!"

"And what happened?" demanded Larry.

"Mick held his cool – I don't know how but he did – and insisted he was not Michael Collins but John Grace, an accountant, with a practice in Dame Street. The Tans didn't believe him and showed him a copy of that grainy old photo of him, the really bad one that you can hardly make him out in, and insisted he was Collins. They even got him to part his hair like in the photograph to prove it was him!"

"Then what?" asked Chrys.

"Mick stuck to his guns – insisted he was John Grace, with no connection to Michael Collins, out having Christmas dinner and drinks with a few friends and they should leave him alone. I tell you – Mick was that convincing I nearly believed he wasn't Michael Collins myself!"

Everyone laughed except for Kitty who was horrified at the story.

"Finally – after much persuasion from Mick, the Tans actually believed his story and left us alone. We left the Gresham as soon as we could without arousing suspicion and headed up Vaughan's Hotel on Parnell Square, where we knew we were amongst friends and safe. And we drank whiskey into the night out of relief, celebrating at not being caught and it being Christmas as well!"

"And that is why you were late down to us then!" said Maud, slapping his arm playfully. "It was from a sore head and nothing to do with Tans nearly arresting you last night!"

"It was a lucky escape for sure! I tell you Mick should be on the stage he's such a good actor! That fella is very lucky – he has nine lives."

"Yes, well, even the luckiest of cats run out of lives!" Kitty snapped. "What were ye doing going into a place as public as the Gresham on Christmas Eve? Sure, it was asking for trouble!"

"We just wanted to celebrate Christmas," said Gearóid, surprised by her attack.

"And what, Gearóid, is there exactly to celebrate?" Kitty went on angrily. "With the country on its knees and no sign of this cursed war ending? And you and Mick running around playing Cowboys and Indians!"

"Kitty!" admonished Maud, shocked at the sister's outburst. "What is wrong with you?"

Kitty remembered herself and shook her head before saying quietly, "Nothing – nothing at all."

She turned and went to the window where she stared out at the rain lashing against the glass.

As usual in the Kiernan house nobody went to bed early on Christmas night. There was singing and piano-playing and dancing. Alcohol flowed and chocolate and fine food were served well past midnight.

Kitty was sitting on the couch, Gearóid next to her, the fire blazing beside them.

Gearóid turned to her and said, "Sorry if I upset you earlier, Kitty – talking about what happened in the Gresham Hotel last night."

"Oh, it's me who should be sorry, Gearóid. I can be so contrary at times ... I was just upset that you and Mick were nearly caught. I'm very fond of the both of ye. And Maud would be devastated if anything happened to you."

"Nothing will happen to me, Kitty, don't you fret. As for Mick – he'll soon be out of danger's way anyway, if Dev has his way."

"What do you mean?" asked Kitty, startled.

"He's being sent to America as Dev's replacement there now he's back in Ireland. He'll be working alongside Harry – the old team back together!"

"*What?*" Kitty was appalled. "When was this decided?"

"Who knows? You can never tell what's going on in Dev's mind – not like Mick who is an open book. He's not happy about it anyway, Mick. You know him – he wants to be here on the ground, one of the lads – not hosting a fundraiser at the Waldorf Astoria in Manhattan!"

Maud overheard. "Mick's going to America! They can't send him there – who will fight the war?"

"Well, if Dev has his way that's what will be happening," said Gearóid.

"Why don't we have a game of charades?" said Lionel, suddenly rising to his feet. "I'll go first!"

"*For goodness' sake, Lionel!*" Kitty suddenly burst out, causing everyone to jump. "You have the most annoying habit of interrupting what everyone else is talking about with something that is completely inconsequential!"

There were a few moments of embarrassed silence before Lionel said, "Yes, of course, sorry." He sat back down, looking glum.

"No, it's me who's sorry, Lionel," said Kitty. "I'm sorry for speaking to you so rudely."

The clock struck two and, although everyone else had gone to bed, Lionel seemed to still have the energy of a cocker spaniel as he sat on the couch talking incessantly about a holiday he had in France the previous year.

Kitty felt her eyes begin to close as she fought hard not to fall asleep. She suddenly shook her head and sat up straight to wake herself up.

"We then took a sailing boat and sailed down the Côte d'Azur …" Lionel droned on.

"Lionel!" Kitty said to halt him.

"Yes, my dear?"

"Lionel …" She reached forward and took his hand. "I am afraid I have something that I must tell you."

"Oh?"

"I – I can't marry you, Lionel," she said. "I'm truly sorry."

"Oh – I see. May I ask why?"

"It's – because, we just aren't compatible."

"But we are!"

"No, no – there's a lovely girl out there somewhere waiting for you – perhaps on a tennis court somewhere – but it's just not me. It wouldn't be fair to you to marry you. I'd only end up resenting it and not being nice to you. You don't deserve that."

She took off her engagement ring and placed it in the palm of his hand.

"Can you forgive me?" she said.

"Well, yes, what choice do I have?" he said, looking more confused than upset.

Later Kitty sat at her dressing table, staring at the mirror. She knew she had done the right thing breaking off her engagement to Lionel. A life together would make neither of them happy. He would see that himself soon enough, she was sure. She looked down at an unopened letter on her dressing table she had received from Harry before Christmas. She hadn't written to him about her engagement. She just hadn't known how to put it in writing. She wondered if Michael had written to tell him. Her thoughts drifted away from Harry and focused on Michael, remembering the fear she had felt all day that something had happened to him. The relief when Gearóid confirmed he was alright. And then to hear he might be leaving for America. It had never occurred to her that Mick would ever leave Ireland. It had occurred to her he could be shot or arrested or executed for treason by the British – but never that he would leave Ireland to go *fundraising* in America! The thought of both Harry and Michael being on the other side of the Atlantic was an irony too far. She shook her head in despair. And yet she now accepted that her fate would be tied to men like Harry and Michael. She had tried to go down the traditional route like Helen and find happiness with a nice normal man with a normal life. Unfortunately, it had bored her to tears. She just wasn't cut out to have a life like that. She was drawn to men like Harry and Michael – that she could now at least admit to herself. But she knew, deep down, it couldn't bring her happiness. She stared down at the unopened envelope on her dressing table. It had arrived the day before Christmas Eve with the usual American stamp on it. She hadn't opened it because she couldn't face reading his usual beautiful sentiments. She was too conscious of her duplicity. But now that the engagement was over, why was she still overcome with guilt as she began to open the letter? She realised it was down to her feelings for Michael.

BOOK 2

1921

CHAPTER 18

Michael and Gearóid walked briskly down the steps from a clandestine meeting of the members of the outlawed Irish parliament, the Dáil, in the Mansion House on a grey January day. Michael felt elated. The scheduled meeting had been cancelled once because of fear of a security breach. That would have been a treat for the British government, he thought – for the Auxiliaries to arrive in during a secret parliament meeting and in one swoop arrest every member of the illegal Irish government. What a field day Lloyd George and Winston Churchill would have had with that.

To Michael's delight, there had been much opposition to De Valera's plan to send him to America. He was very touched to hear deputy after deputy stand and announce that it was a ridiculous idea and the country and indeed the war could not do without Michael Collins. De Valera had accepted the decision and quietly dropped the proposal, although Michael suspected it would have angered him to be opposed and not to have conveniently got rid of him.

As he walked down the street with Gearóid, he felt he was walking on air after the show of support from his friends and colleagues.

"That showed him I couldn't be so easily disposed of!"

"Dev surely got a shock to see the level of support you have."

"Will we head to Vaughan's and have a few pints to celebrate?"

"I can't. I'm meeting Maud now – she's up from Longford with Kitty."

Michael stopped in his tracks. "Well, why didn't you say earlier?"

"I thought you had more important things on your mind with the prospect of being shipped off to New York by Dev by the end of the week!"

"Is Helen up as well?" asked Michael, excited at the thought of seeing her.

"No."

Michael's heart sank. He had written to Helen numerous times but had heard nothing back. He didn't know if she was ignoring him or just not receiving the letters.

"Well, come on! Let's go meet the girls!" he said as he hurried down the street.

Kitty and Maud were waiting outside Clery's department store on Sackville Street. Kitty was hoping that Michael would come with Gearóid to meet them.

Suddenly, to her delight, she saw Michael's large frame beside Gearóid, coming down the street.

Maud went hurrying towards Gearóid and hugged him while Kitty followed behind.

"Well, you're a sight for sore eyes," said Michael as he kissed Maud's cheek and then added "Both of ye!" before he kissed Kitty's cheek as well.

"You too, Mick," Kitty said.

"No Lionel?" asked Michael, looking around in an exaggerated fashion.

"No – no Lionel," said Kitty, before adding coolly, "We have ended our engagement."

"Oh – I see! What a shame!" he said, trying to stop himself from laughing. "Ye made a handsome pair!"

She saw red. "If you are going to take the piss out of me like you did the last time I was unfortunate enough to meet you, then I'll get the next train back to Longford now!" And she began to march down the street.

"Don't upset her, Mick!" said Maud. "She's very sensitive about it all! She feels she made a bit of a fool of herself getting engaged to poor Lionel!"

"Well, she's right – she did!" said Michael with a laugh.

"Mick!" Maud pleaded.

Michael bounded down the street after Kitty and caught up with her.

"Will you wait up, woman!"

"I think you are one of the rudest men I've ever met!" she said as she continued walking quickly along. "I don't know what has you thinking you're so great that you can mock me!"

"I'm only joking. Can you not take a joke?"

"No! You are being highly insensitive."

"I'm sorry – I truly am!" he said and grabbed her shoulder, halting her. "It's just that I couldn't take you and Lionel seriously when you said you were engaged."

"I can't see why not! He's a lovely fellow!"

"I'm sure he is! But he was not in your league, Kitty... I knew, he knew, everyone knew it – except you! I was just looking at the two of you and thinking 'What she is doing with him?'"

Despite his attitude, she was delighted to hear him say those words.

"Any woman would be lucky to have Lionel," she said in an injured tone. "He's the cream –"

"Yes – and like cream, rich and thick!" said Michael as he burst out laughing.

Her face went red from anger again and she was about to explode but then she started to laugh as well.

"What is the matter with you two?" asked Maud as she and Gearóid caught up with them and saw the two of them in convulsions of laughter.

That evening Michael and Kitty sat at a table in a restaurant off Wicklow Street. Gearóid and Maud had taken the opportunity to spend time together. Instead of Kitty going back to the hotel, she had accepted Michael's offer to go to dinner.

"So, you're not going to America?"

"No, thank God."

"You must be flattered that the delegates wouldn't hear of it."

"Much to Dev's irritation!" Michael chuckled.

"You must be relieved."

"Of course I am. Could you really see me going to posh functions in Manhattan?"

"No!" She laughed. "Although at least you'd have had your partner in crime there – Harry."

"True. Have you heard from him?"

"Yes, he writes to me all the time."

"He's mad about you."

"So he says," she said and changed the subject, deciding to keep her cards close to her chest. "And what is all this I hear – that you very nearly got yourself arrested on Christmas Eve? What kind of an eejit are you at all – that went out into the restaurant in the Gresham in full public view on such a night?"

"We asked for a private room, but there was none left, it being the night that was in it."

"So – you decided to throw caution to the wind and show off to your friends in the middle of the busiest restaurant on the busiest night of the year!" she mocked angrily. "You sure are the Big Fella!"

"Will you cut me some slack, woman! I just wanted one night out with my friends like any other man."

"But, Mick, you're not like other men. And you could have got yourself shot – not just arrested! It was careless and stupid."

"I'd nearly swear you cared!"

"I do care, you fool – would I be sitting here listening to your rubbish if I didn't?"

Michael looked at Kitty across the table with a curious look on his face.

"What's the matter with you?" she asked.

"I'm just trying to figure you out … whatever possessed you to get engaged to a man like Lionel who it was plain to see you had no feelings for?"

She looked out the window. "Oh, I long for things to be normal. I think that's why I got engaged to Lionel … to try and make life feel normal again … after the killing and riots at home."

"But they will be normal again soon, Kitty."

"How can they be, Mick? The war is just getting worse and worse and both sides are more entrenched in their fighting. The British are not going to give up, Mick. They are not just going to walk away and leave us in peace to run our own affairs."

"There's a few things coming that are going to really shake things up," he said with a gleam in his eye.

"Is there anything left to shake, Mick?" she asked incredulously.

"Is the hotel back up and running yet?" he asked.

"No, construction is still being done – and on the stores as well. I'm going on a holiday for a few weeks."

"Really, where?"

"Up to Donegal for a while and then to the Continent ... I just need a bit of time to think after everything that has happened these past few months. But I'll be back for Helen's wedding, of course."

"Yes. She's been very quiet – I haven't heard a word from her," said Michael, probing.

"Sure, she's up to her eyes arranging the wedding, Mick. You would swear it was going to be the wedding of the year!"

She saw the flash of despair in his eyes and turned her head away to look out the window onto the street again.

Three British Tans were passing. One stopped abruptly and stared in at Michael.

"There's –" began Kitty, as her heart began to beat quickly.

"I know," said Michael. "Just act normally. Laugh and joke and flirt with me."

Kitty did what she was told and threw her head back, laughing. Then she reached out and took Michael's hand and began to stroke it. He began to rub her hand as well as he pretended to flirt with her. The Tan stopped looking and he and his colleagues walked on.

"Thank goodness!" said Kitty.

"You can say that again," he said, letting go of her hand. "We better get out of here. I'll pay the bill and get you back to your hotel."

Michael stood up from the table and walked across the restaurant to reception while Kitty stroked the hand he had been holding as her eyes followed him.

CHAPTER 19

The first months of 1921 were the bloodiest yet of the war as the British government continued to pour troops into Ireland to try to restore their law and order and stamp their authority on a country that increasingly saw itself as an independent sovereign nation. The harder they tried, the harder the Irish fought back, with Michael continuing to orchestrate the military campaign. The British government and forces in Ireland still relentlessly searched for him and it had become a cause of international embarrassment for them that he continually evaded capture.

As Michael lived life on the run, his thoughts never strayed too far from Helen. She still hadn't responded to his letters and he was giving up ever hearing from her again.

Then Gearóid handed him an envelope one day.

"What's this?" asked Michael, looking down at the white embossed envelope.

"Sure, open it and find out!" said Gearóid with a laugh.

Michael tore open the envelope and saw it was an invitation to Helen's wedding at the University Chapel in Dublin, followed by a reception at Vaughan's Hotel.

His heart sank when he saw it.

"Will you be able to go?" asked Gearóid. "It could be a bit risky. They decided to have the wedding in Dublin and not at home because the hotel isn't up and running yet."

"I'll see," said Michael, tucking the envelope into his pocket.

"Well, the Kiernan family must still have plenty of money left, even after paying for all the repairs on the damage that those Black and Tans caused, to have a swanky wedding up in Dublin," said Molly as she dusted around the parlour.

Kitty was at the writing desk, writing to Harry in America.

"All you should be concerned about is whether there is enough money to pay your wages!" she retorted.

"It must be a cause of concern for you, all the same," said Molly.

"What is?"

"Miss Helen's wedding being nearly upon us. And with Miss Chrys's and Miss Maud's engagements, sure it won't be long until they traipse up the aisle as well. That will leave only you!"

Kitty pretended not to hear Molly as she continued to write her letter.

"I don't understand the young women – and the *not so young* women – anymore. There you were, engaged to the lovely Mr. Lionel, and you threw him out with the rubbish and now here you are – always the bridesmaid and never the bride!"

Kitty raised her eyes to heaven as she tried to block out Molly's talk.

"Did you never hear the saying 'Marry in haste, repent at leisure'?" she asked.

"And did *you* never hear of the saying 'A rolling stone gathers no moss'?" retorted Molly, picking up some of Kitty's books that were on the mantelpiece she was dusting, and examining them. "Of course I blame all these romantic novels – filling people's heads with rubbish. Tall, dark and handsome! Tall, dark and handsome never put bread on the table!"

"Indeed!" sighed Kitty.

"I hate that word *spinster* – but sure if it's meant to be, it's meant to be!"

"Molly!" snapped Kitty loudly. "Can't you see I am trying to write a blasted letter? How can I write it with you twittering on, talking absolute nonsense!"

"I'm sorry, I'm sure! I'll go lay the table for dinner!" Molly departed in a huff.

"Do that!" said Kitty after her. She shook her head and looked down at the letter she was writing.

Molly's words of warning echoed through her head – *a rolling stone gathers no moss.*

As she looked at the flirty, non-committal lines she had just penned to Harry, she realised she was acting more like a young girl with years to spare before having to settle down instead of a woman knocking on the door of thirty. What Molly was saying was true – people would be talking about her at Helen's wedding. The only sister not settled down – they might even describe her as a spinster! She shuddered at the thought. Maybe she was being too choosy. Maybe she would never find what she was looking for. As she picked up Harry's last letter to her, where he was declaring undying love to her, she thought she should just realise she had already found it with Harry. But then why was she still so hesitant to put anything committal in writing to him?

CHAPTER 20

The automobile was parked discreetly across the road from the Shelbourne Hotel on St Stephen's Green in Dublin. It looked just like a normal automobile with nothing different from the others that were parked along the green. Nobody passing it would suspect that the most wanted man in the British Empire sat in the back.

Michael's eyes were trained on the entrance of the hotel. He was wearing a hat and kept the collar of his coat turned up. As he looked around the area, he could see British troops at the top of Grafton Street and more at the top of Dawson Street. His driver was one of Michael's infamous Squad.

The rest of the Squad were dotted around St Stephen's Green that afternoon, fitting in with the people going about their daily business. The Squad's daily business was keeping a watchful eye on Michael, making sure he was safe. Michael smiled to himself as he watched one of his men go up to a British soldier and ask for a light for his cigarette. The soldier obliged and the Squad member thanked him before continuing down the street. And the British army thought they were in control, Michael chuckled to himself.

Michael suddenly sat up as he saw the party he had been waiting for walk down the street towards the Shelbourne Hotel. The whole Kiernan family up from Longford for the wedding of Helen the next day. They made a rowdy and glamorous party walking down the street. He spotted Gearóid holding hands with Maud amongst them. He saw Kitty laughing as she walked along, wearing a big hat.

And then he saw Helen. He stared across at her as she glided along the street, as elegant and serene as ever.

He watched them make their way up the steps to the Shelbourne Hotel, laughing and joking.

They disappeared into the hotel and Michael sat back and waited for darkness to fall. He knew what he had to do that night. It wasn't an honourable thing he planned to do, but like many things he had come to realise about the world – the end justified the means.

Darkness had fallen when a porter came to the door of the hotel and waved across at Michael who walked briskly across the road and followed him down a laneway to the back of the hotel where another porter was waiting.

"Good evening, Mr. Collins, follow me," whispered the second porter.

"Good man," said Michael, clapping him on the back, and he quickly followed him through the kitchens and along some corridors then up a back staircase until they reached the top floor. There, a chambermaid was waiting.

"She'll take you the rest of the way, Mr. Collins," said the porter.

Michael winked at him in appreciation and continued on his journey, following the young girl until they reached the door of a hotel room.

"This is it, Mr. Collins, this is the room she's staying the night in," whispered the chambermaid.

"Good girl," said Michael.

"I'll be waiting at the top of the stairs at the bottom of the corridor polishing the banisters – so when you're finished, I'll take you back down and out the way you came."

He nodded, winked at her and watched her go down to the staircase and start polishing. He smiled to himself as he thought she could be polishing there all night waiting for him as far as she knew. That was the level of dedication in the people, and that was why they were winning this war.

He steadied himself and put an ear to the door to see if he could hear anything, but it was all quiet on the other side. He steadied himself and then he knocked on the door. There was no answer and so he knocked again, louder this time. A few moments later he heard the door unlock and there she stood, looking shocked to see him there.

"*Michael!*" Helen exclaimed.

"*Shhh!*" he said, walking quickly into the room and closing the door behind him. He listened at the door for a moment and then quickly locked it.

"Michael!" Helen exclaimed again. "What on earth are you doing here?"

He turned around and looked at her. Her hair was flowing down as she was just preparing for bed, but she was still wearing an evening dress. Behind her, in the corner of the room, was a mannequin wearing a wedding dress.

Michael took in the woman's beauty for a few moments before he approached her.

"Helen ... forgive me for just landing in on you like this," he said.

"But – what are you doing here?"

"I – I'm sorry I couldn't go to the dinner tonight with ye all." He was searching for words.

"But sure, we didn't expect you, we knew it might be too risky. Can you not make the wedding tomorrow, Michael? Is this what this is about? Is it too dangerous for you to come?"

He shook his head. "It's not that, Helen ... it's more than that ... bloody hell, woman, you know what it's about!" he suddenly snapped, his patience stretched by his own procrastination.

Confusion suddenly gave way to realisation and shock on Helen's face.

Michael approached her quickly and took both her hands.

"You can't go through with this, Helen – you know how I feel about you!"

She stared into his eyes, not quite wanting to believe what was happening. She pulled her hands quickly away and turned her back to him.

"For God's sake, Michael. It's the night before my wedding! Can you not see the wedding dress in the corner of the room?"

"I can see it and it's not too late – not too late at all! It will only be too late when you are wearing that damned wedding dress walking back down the church aisle after saying 'I do'!"

She turned quickly to face him again. "Michael, I am marrying Paul in the morning! The church is booked, the priest is ready! The groom is waiting at another hotel and all the guests have gone to bed to be up bright and early tomorrow morning to be at the church on time – and to celebrate with a wonderful feast at Vaughan's Hotel after!"

He reached out and grabbed her hands with his trembling ones. "But can you not see how much I care for you – how much I want you?"

As she looked at him, she bit her lower lip. She knew very well that Michael cared for her. She had done nothing to encourage those feelings except continue to be a good friend of his. When he had finally told her how he felt, she had explained she didn't feel the same way. He had taken the rejection hard but continued to visit with Harry and Gearóid. And when she had become engaged to Paul, she had seen the hurt on his face. But this! To show up at her hotel room the night before her wedding! She had always known Michael was spontaneous, often easily led by his emotions – but this was incredible even for him!

"Did you not get the letters I sent to you this past month?"

"Yes, I got them," she said.

"I thought – I thought when I didn't hear anything back from you that the letters hadn't arrived."

"They all arrived. I didn't respond – I didn't respond as there was nothing to be said to you! Michael – I am getting married to Paul in the morning! Have you lost your mind?"

"But he won't make you happy, Helen! How could you be happy with a man like that? He is staid and boring, a small-town country solicitor. What kind of life is that for a girl like you?"

"It is exactly the kind of life I want! A stable, good man who I will always know where I will be with. Don't you understand that's the life I want, Michael? To be a small-town solicitor's wife. No more or less!"

"You'll die of boredom!" he spat. "Kitty thought she wanted the same thing with that eejit Lionel, and she came to her senses quick enough!"

"That's Kitty, not me! I'm nothing like Kitty – and Paul, for that matter, is nothing like Lionel! Kitty is searching for something she will never find – I've found exactly what I was searching for!"

"You'll die of boredom!"

She was becoming frustrated with him and his arrogance. "Better than to die by a stray bullet that was meant for you! In all honesty, what kind of a life could I have with you? Not knowing where you are sleeping from night to night as you rush from one safe house to another? Never knowing when I would see you next or if I would even see you again. Waiting for the news every day that you had been killed! What kind of a life would that be for any woman?"

He stared at her angry face and then moved away from her and went and sat down on the bed, putting his face in his hands. She suspected he was softly crying. Her heart melted and she went to him, knelt in front of him and took both his hands in hers.

He looked into her eyes.

"You're right of course. As you say, what woman would ever want the kind of life I could provide?"

"You've chosen this life, Mick. You didn't have to. But there's consequences for the life you have chosen and perhaps one of those consequences is loneliness ... but this war won't last for ever ... maybe then ..." She reached out and hugged him tightly.

He stood up. "I'd better be going."

She nodded. "Where are you staying tonight?"

"A safe house in Ranelagh."

"You'll be at the wedding tomorrow?"

He nodded and then leaned forward and kissed her cheek.

He went to the door, unlocked it and looked up and down the corridor before walking rapidly away.

Helen saw him reach the top of the stairs where a chambermaid was waiting who whisked him down a back stairs. He didn't look back once.

Michael had crept into the University Chapel the next day through a side door. Loud organ music was playing. He scanned the church which was filled with wedding guests waiting for the bride. Spotting Gearóid in the congregation, he went and sat beside him.

"You're late! I wasn't sure you would make it," whispered Gearóid.

"I said I'd be here, didn't I?" growled Michael.

"They've stepped up the military presence – there's Tans on every street corner in the city."

"I know, Gearóid!" snapped Michael before adding, "I *am* the head of Intelligence!"

"I said to Maud you'd be taking too much of a risk coming here today and you should stay away."

"Everything I do is a risk, Gearóid. Now give me some peace and let me enjoy the organ music," said Michael, looking at the groom at the top of the church waiting with his best man.

Suddenly the organ began to play the Wedding March and all the congregation stood to attention. Michael looked back down the church and saw Helen being escorted up the aisle on the arm of her brother, Maud and Kitty attending to her as bridesmaids. Helen smiled at all the familiar happy faces as she walked down the aisle. As she passed Michael, her smile faltered for a moment then returned as she continued to the altar.

Outside the church the guests were chatting in the sunshine. Michael kept apart from the crowd, feeling awkward and uncomfortable as he watched Helen with her new husband pose for the photographer.

"Hello, Big Fella!" said a familiar voice behind him and he swung around to see Kitty there.

"You should know better than to creep up on a man like that!" he snarled, before his mouth broke into a grin and they embraced each other warmly.

"You must have a guilty conscience, getting a fright so easily!"

"Isn't that a fact?" murmured Michael, looking across at Helen.

"You look very handsome in your suit, Mick. The most handsome man here."

"I'd say you've said that to every man here," mocked Michael.

"Only some of them." She leaned forward and kissed his cheek. "Good to see you, Mick."

"And you, Kitty." He looked her up and down in her bridesmaid's dress and then winked at her. "The colour white suits you!"

Kitty raised her eyes to heaven and ignored his comment. "They want everyone for a group photograph."

The smile left Michael's face as he looked over at Helen who was standing arm in arm with her husband as everyone gathered around them for the photograph.

"Ah no – I'm fine here, you go ahead," said Michael, shaking his head.

"Oh, but you have to come for the photograph, Michael. Sure, it wouldn't be the same without you!"

Michael shook his head vehemently.

Helen looked over at them and called, "Will you come on, the two of you, and hurry up! Stop gossiping and get over here – the photographer hasn't got all day!"

Michael felt relieved that Helen had addressed him in a jocular fashion, with no awkwardness after what had happened the previous night.

"Well?" asked Kitty with a smile.

Michael nodded. "Come on so."

Kitty smiled and led him over to the rest of the guests to take their positions for the photographer. As the photograph was taken, Michael looked glumly down at the ground. Kitty suspected it was because he didn't want to have his full face taken for the photograph in case it fell into British intelligence hands. Only Michael knew the truth – that it was because he felt his heart was breaking.

After the wedding breakfast in Vaughan's Hotel Michael was sitting at a table beside Gearóid and Harry as the plates were being cleared away.

"I'm meeting Dev tomorrow to discuss this plan to attack the Customs House," he said.

"If we could pull it off it would be a huge coup," Gearóid said. "Destroying the centre of British administration in Ireland."

"But at what cost to us?" cautioned Michael. "This is bringing the war away from guerrilla fighting to an outright battle. We don't have the resources to defeat the British in an outright battle. Not a hope."

The best man at the head table rose to his feet and clinked a spoon against a glass to bring silence to the room before he started his speech.

As Gearóid studied Michael, he didn't seem his usual in-control self. He looked stressed and worried. He sat in silence as the best man made his light-hearted speech praising the groom, flattering the bride, thanking the families. Michael seemed in a different world, hardly hearing the words being spoken.

After the best man's speech, the new groom Paul got to his feet. Suddenly Michael became alert, anxious to hear every word.

"Ladies and gentlemen – friends – relatives," Paul paused as he turned and looked at his new wife and her sisters sitting beside her, "and new relatives – you are all very welcome. My wife and I –" there was applause and cheers when he said this, "are delighted to share this, the happiest day of our lives, with you. I cannot tell you how happy I am to be standing here before you as the husband of Helen. What can I say about Helen that you don't already know? She is beautiful, kind, strong, loyal and now she is my wife!"

The whole room broke into loud applause. As Paul continued with his speech, Gearóid saw Michael had gone as a pale as a ghost. He was also twisting a napkin in his hands, tugging at the cotton in frustration.

The speeches over, Helen turned to Kitty who was sitting beside her at the head table.

"How's – how's Michael today?" she asked.

"He's fine." She raised her eyes to heaven. "Busy talking to Gearóid about politics, no doubt! Do they never stop talking about politics?"

"They are politicians, Kitty."

"Sometimes I wish they could just be like other men," sighed Kitty.

"I'd say they wish that themselves sometimes," said Helen as she looked down at Michael's sad pensive face. "Kitty, will you look after Mick today? I won't be able to pay much attention to him." She and Paul would spend the night at the hotel with their guests as their boat wouldn't depart until the following morning. "He seems out of sorts to me and a little lost. Sure, he was never one for big social events. Will you look after him and make sure he's alright?"

Kitty was a bit surprised by the request but shrugged. "Of course."

As the afternoon wore on into the evening, a band began to play and couples began dancing. Being a bridesmaid, Kitty had been in high demand as a partner and she found it hard to get an opportunity to spend time with Michael. Mindful of Helen's request to look after him, she had been keeping an eye on him. He seemed to be drinking a lot. Gearóid was preoccupied with Maud and so Michael didn't seem to have much company. She felt sorry for him as he sat in the corner of the banquet room on his own.

When the band finished playing, she quickly made her way from the dance floor before she could be apprehended by another partner and made her way over to Michael.

"At last!" she said as she flounced down on the chair beside him. "I have been dancing for three hours solid! I'm exhausted!"

"That's good – I thought you were going to ask me to dance for a minute, and I have two left feet," said Michael, taking a drink out of his glass of stout.

"Well, it wouldn't make you any different from the rest of the men I've been dancing with all afternoon. There aren't any champion dancers here today, I can tell you!"

Michael's eyes were fixed on Helen and Paul as they swirled around the dance floor.

"Well, I'm just back from that holiday I mentioned," said Kitty. "Five weeks. I've been to Donegal and the Continent. Sure there was no point in me hanging around Granard while the reconstruction work was going on and nothing for me to do."

"I guess not."

"But the hotel is re-opening next week and the store the week after – so I'll soon be back busy at work."

"That's good," he said, his eyes still focused on Helen.

"I got a letter from Harry only this week. He's in great form," she said.

"Is he still in love with you?" asked Michael, looking at her for the first time.

"He says he is. But a man can say many a thing."

"So can a woman – just ask Lionel!" he shot back.

She became angry. "I don't know what's wrong with you today, Mick."

"There's nothing wrong with me – sure what would be wrong with me?"

"I came over to have a chat, and you're completely distracted! They're queuing up to dance with me, so I don't know what I'm doing wasting my time sitting here talking to a – a dummy!" She stood up abruptly and went storming over to the dance floor where she grabbed the first free man she came across and began dancing with him.

Surprised by her vitriol, Michael couldn't help smiling as he watched her.

Night had fallen and yet there was no sign of the wedding party ending.

Michael had wandered out onto the patio and was looking out over the city. In the distance gunshots could be heard. He walked on into the gardens.

"I hope you are in better form than you were earlier," said a voice and he swung around to see Kitty sitting there.

"What are you doing out here?" he asked.

"Same question back to you!"

"I felt a bit lonely in the crowd," he said. "Better to be lonely on your own than lonely in a crowd, I always think."

"If you made an effort with people today you might have not felt as lonely!"

"I shouldn't have come today," he said, shaking his head.

"And let Helen down?"

"Sure what does Helen care about me? She's starting a new life today and barely said two words to me. I'm in the past as far as she is concerned."

She studied him then stood up and walked to him. "Well, I'm very glad you came today."

"Are you?" He was surprised.

"Of course. Come on and have a dance with me. You're the only man I haven't danced with today." She put her arms around him.

Soft music was flowing from the banquet hall as they swayed around the garden dancing.

As she stared into his eyes, she leant forward, and they began to kiss.

After a while he pulled back. "We shouldn't – Harry."

"Harry's not here – you are, Mick," she said, pulling him closer and kissing him again.

CHAPTER 21

Kitty stood at her bedroom window in the hotel the morning after the wedding, looking out at the gardens at the back of the hotel. She smiled to herself at the memory of Michael the previous night. She could hardly believe it had happened. That wonderful moment in the garden when they had kissed. Afterwards they had spent hours in the garden, not wanting to leave each other's company. The music had ended and the party was over inside the hotel by the time they came back inside and Michael walked her to her room before giving her a final kiss and leaving her.

There was a knock on the door and she went to answer.

It was Helen, dressed in a very elegant suit with a fur collar and a fur pillbox hat.

"Good morning, Kitty. I just came to say goodbye before Paul and I head away on our honeymoon."

Helen walked in and Kitty closed the door behind her.

"Thank you so much for all your help yesterday and in the lead-up to the wedding. You and Maud were the perfect bridesmaids." Helen smiled warmly.

"Sure, it was my pleasure – what are sisters for?" Kitty smiled back.

"The wedding was wonderful. I enjoyed every minute of it. I think everyone else did too?"

"Yes, everyone had a ball," confirmed Kitty.

"I've been looking for Maud but can't find her anywhere. She has probably gone somewhere with Gearóid. I didn't get a chance

146

to spend as much time talking to guests as I would have liked. The whole day went so quickly," Helen sighed with happiness at the memory. "I hardly said two words to Michael. Was he alright? He looked as if he was drinking a lot."

"Oh, yes – he was perfectly fine!" smiled Kitty.

Something in the way she said it set off an alarm in Helen. "Are you sure?"

Kitty smiled and nodded before looking out the window.

Helen's warm smile turned sour as a realisation dawned on her. "Oh, Kitty – please, tell me you didn't!"

"Didn't what?" asked Kitty casually as she went to the mirror and fixed her hair.

"Oh, dear God – you did! Kitty – how could you? With Michael of all people!" Helen's usual tranquil demeanour had disappeared.

"Why shouldn't I? He's a free agent, as am I."

"Why shouldn't you! There's every reason in the world for you and him not to go anywhere near each other!" Helen was appalled. "What is wrong with you? You're just out of an engagement with Lionel!"

"Lionel was a mistake, everyone knew that. It was just a reaction to what I'd been through with the riot and seeing that young policeman shot dead in front of me. Lionel was a port in a storm."

"And what are you to Michael Collins? Only one of many ports he has docked into!" said Helen.

"That's not true!"

"Yes, it is! Michael Collins is a flirtatious womaniser. He has stayed in more safe houses run by women than I have had hot dinners!"

"There's nothing going on between Mick and those women – it's part of the war!"

"He would say that! Half the intelligence operation he runs is women: cloakroom attendants, waitresses, receptionists, post-room staff – he has all these women eating out of the palm of his hand! And you – poor deluded creature that you are – have just joined those ranks!"

"You are talking nonsense!" Kitty shook her head. "If the truth

be told, I always had a soft spot for Mick. Right from the moment
I met him I was interested in him. And he was in me too! He said
he and Harry had a bet who could go out with me. But he didn't
pursue me at that time."

"And why do you suppose that was?" snapped Helen, putting
her hands on her hips.

"Oh, I know Mick was interested in you for a time, Helen. That
was plain to see, but you missed your chance with him and now
you need to let go!"

Helen's mouth dropped open in horror. "*Me* to let go!"

"Yes, whatever feelings there were between you and Mick it was
a very long time ago ... you're married to Paul now and Mick
should be allowed to get on with his own life."

Helen almost blurted out the truth about Michael coming to her
bedroom. She closed her mouth tightly to stop herself from saying
anything that she would regret. And she would regret it. Not only
would she hurt Kitty deeply but then it would get out that Michael
Collins was in her bedroom the night before her wedding. How
could she explain that to her new husband, as well as to everyone
else? But how could she stop this ridiculous situation between Kitty
and Michael from going any further? How could she get Kitty to
realise that Michael had just been on the rebound, having got a
final rejection from her and that in the midst of the raw emotion of
the wedding day, coupled with copious amount of alcohol, he had
latched on to the nearest substitute – her sister!

"And what about Harry?" she asked instead.

"What about Harry?"

"Don't you think you have messed that poor man around
enough? Between getting engaged to Lionel, without even telling
him, to now having a liaison with his best friend? It's immoral!"

"It's not immoral! It's unfortunate they are friends, but not
immoral! I care for Harry deeply, but Mick – I don't know – Mick is
–" She searched for the right words but couldn't come up with them.

"Oh, dear God," muttered Helen as she sank down on the bed,
realising Kitty had fallen in love with Michael.

There was a knock on the door. Kitty went to answer.

"Is Helen with you, Kitty?" Larry asked.

"Yes, she's here."

Larry stepped in. "Helen, Paul's waiting for you down in the lobby. The taxi is ready to take you to the port – your honeymoon awaits!"

Helen stood up reluctantly, went to Kitty and kissed her cheek, whispering, "He won't bring you any happiness."

"Come on, Kitty! Get a move on!" said Larry as Kitty stood staring after Helen. "We're all gathering to see them off!"

"I'll be right down," said Kitty, turning her back as tears sprang to her eyes.

Helen walked down the main stairs of the hotel, distracted and disturbed by the news she had just heard from Kitty. Michael and her sister were both adults and she should, as Kitty said, just back away and let them deal with it. But it just seemed wrong to her. The guests who had been staying at the hotel were gathered in the hotel lobby and clapped as she came down the stairs. She beamed at them all.

Paul was waiting for her at the bottom of the stairs and she took his arm.

"Have a wonderful honeymoon!" a voice called.

"Thank you!" said Helen as they made their way to the front door.

She spotted Michael amongst the familiar faces and her smile dropped. She needed to talk to him and now was her only opportunity. When they got back from the honeymoon, she would be going to live in Enniskillen and she might not see him for quite some time. Goodness knows what could have happened between Michael and Kitty by then.

"I just need a couple of minutes," she said to Paul, letting go of his arm.

"Helen! We have to go now! We're already running late and we'll miss the boat!"

Helen paused and then nodded, and they walked out into the sunshine.

Kitty had come down the stairs and joined the rest of the guests as they followed Helen and Paul outside. She saw Michael among the others as everyone waved and cheered and the bridal car took off. She went and stood beside him.

"How are you this morning?" she asked as she waved at the automobile.

He turned to her and smiled sheepishly. "I'm good – it was a great day yesterday."

"It certainly was ..." She gestured down the street. "Let's walk ... we need to talk."

He looked at her warily and nodded.

Kitty was mindful of Helen's departing words. She realised she needed to protect herself from being hurt and Helen had strongly said that Michael was not to be trusted.

A little way down the street she said, "Well, that was a fine way to treat your best friend. Kissing his girl when he is on the other side of the Atlantic!"

He looked at her, aghast. "So you're Harry's girl now, are you – that's not what you said last night!"

"You know Harry and I have an – understanding," she said.

"I don't know what you and Harry have – particularly after the interlude with Lionel!"

Kitty flushed. "Well, that's what that was – just an interlude!"

Michael fell silent, struggling to adjust to her about-turn.

"I suppose I got carried away in the moment last night," he said then. "The wine, the music – a beautiful woman. I felt bad this morning when I woke up ... I do feel guilty about Harry."

"So you regret it?" It was more of an accusation than a question.

"No. I don't," he confessed. "I don't regret a moment of it. In fact, it's the first time – in as long as I can remember – that I've felt happy, truly happy. Even when I was feeling guilty this morning over Harry, I had a spring in my step the likes of which I can't remember."

"I won't lie, Mick. I won't say I haven't had feelings for you this past while. And maybe if Harry wasn't in the picture ..."

"But he's not in the picture! He's in New York!"

"He's in love with me. He tells me in every letter. He asks me to go to live with him in America. But it wouldn't be the life for me, running around city after city."

"That's beside the point! There's no point in stringing Harry along if you are not in love with him, Kitty. It's not fair on him."

"So now you have Harry's best interest at heart? After last night?" she asked scathingly.

"I'd lay down my life for Harry," said Michael.

"While you steal his girl at the same time?"

"I told you before that Harry and I had a bet when we first met you about who could win you and we agreed there would be no hard feelings whoever you chose – if you chose either of us!"

"But that was a long time ago, Mick. Harry would be shocked to find out you have re-entered the race at this stage in the game."

"Harry is like me – we are practical about these things – all's fair in love and war!" said Michael.

"*Love*, is it?" She stopped and looked at him, eyebrows raised.

He halted. "I have to go. I have a meeting with Dev."

"Alright," she sighed.

They stood awkwardly, looking at each other.

"So, where do we go from here?" she asked.

"I'll write to you and I'll see you soon," he said, bending down and kissing her.

He then turned and she watched him striding back to the hotel, his eyes constantly surveying his surroundings. She bit her lip, Helen's words of warning screaming through her head. But she knew she wouldn't be able to help herself from running when he called.

CHAPTER 22

In May that year the decision was taken to stage a full-on military attack and occupation of the Custom House Building, the administrative headquarters of British rule in Ireland. The resulting battle saw the burning and destruction of the building. Michael had opposed a direct attack, fearing the casualties that would be suffered. The burning of the building was a massive propaganda boost for the Irish as all the British administrative records for running the country were destroyed. The government no longer had the means to collect taxes – even if they found a tax collector brave enough to do his job.

Harry Boland looked at the subtitle of the article of the *New York Times* which read 'Priceless Records Lost', referring to the fact that records dating back to the 1600s had been destroyed, including countless birth, marriage and death records from all over the country. Harry fully appreciated the blow the attack dealt to the British government's reputation and esteem around the world, but there had been five casualties on the IRA side and up to a hundred of their best men captured. It had been a victory but at what cost? Meanwhile the world looked on with increasing condemnation of the violence widespread through Ireland.

In Granard, the hotel and stores reopened and the Kiernan family returned to work and life as normal, or as normal as it could be during the war. Kitty waited for the post anxiously every day. Some days there would be a letter from Michael and some days one from

Harry. Harry's letters were always romantic and full of declarations of love. Michael's letters were always more reticent – it was harder for Kitty to figure out what he was thinking and more importantly what he thought of her. When they got together, she immediately felt the attraction. She tried to travel up to Dublin whenever she got the opportunity and whenever Michael was free. But they often ended up arguing, often over silly unimportant things. He stood up to her, she realised. He didn't let her always get her own way. He had a powerful and strong personality and wasn't afraid to display it. It made her crave him all the more.

One Saturday afternoon she met him on Grafton Street. She had been doing some shopping.

"Do you ever get sick of shopping?" he asked as he looked down at the hatbox she was carrying.

"No! If I went around in dowdy clothes, you'd have something else to say then." She held out the hatbox to him. "Will you carry this for me?"

He looked at her incredulously. "Well, blast you anyway, woman! I will not carry your hatbox for you! If you bought it then you can carry it!"

He went off marching down the street and she rushed to keep up with him.

"Some gentleman you are!"

"You had your chance to marry a donkey when you were engaged to Lionel! You can carry your own shopping ... what would it do to my reputation if I was seen carrying a hatbox!"

"If Harry was here, he'd be delighted to carry it for me."

Michael stopped walking abruptly, turned to her and put his hands on his hips.

"Would he indeed? Then he's the bigger eejit, isn't he?"

They glared at each other and then burst out laughing.

"Come on and we'll get some dinner," he said, putting an arm around her waist, and they walked off down the street.

CHAPTER 23

Hazel Lavery was hosting a drinks party in her drawing room at 5 Cromwell Place. She had invited an interesting collection of people from George Bernard Shaw to the writer J.M. Barrie to Winston's new private secretary Eddie Marsh who also was the agent for the deceased war poet Rupert Brooks. And, of course, Winston and Clementine Churchill were present too. As she looked around at everyone mixing freely, she thought that this was what she loved – bringing clever, intelligent but diverse people together.

She stood at the drinks cabinet making cocktails.

"Now, Gordon – hand me the vermouth," she instructed. The butler gave her the bottle and she lashed a good part into the cocktail shaker.

"Careful, Hazel – we don't want to be inebriated before ten!" cried a guest.

"Why not? We don't have prohibition here – thank God!" she said as she took a bottle of angostura and added a splash into her concoction. "I have to say, out of all the things that the country of my birth has done, bringing in prohibition last year was by far the most stupid!"

"*Hear, hear, Hazel!*" shouted Winston in agreement and raised his whiskey glass.

"Friends of mine in Newport have told me that they stocked their wine cellars to the hilt before prohibition came in last year. But *now* their cellars are running dangerously low and they simply do not know what they are going to do when they run out, which they are bound to do in the not-too-distant future!"

"Doesn't bear thinking about!" shuddered a guest as he protectively held his cocktail glass close to him.

"I've told them all that there is only one solution," said Hazel as she began to furiously jiggle the silver cocktail shaker. "Leave America and come live here and join the party in London!"

"And tell them to bring their fortunes with them – the exchequer could do with the revenue!" said Winston.

"Maybe if you lowered the taxes a little you might entice some of our wealthy back from their exile on the Riviera, Winston!" retorted Hazel.

"We will know all about taxes should the day ever arrive that we get a Labour government!" said Winston, causing a collective groan of fear and dread amongst the well-heeled guests in the room.

"I'm not too sure – I think their leader Ramsey MacDonald is rather attractive. I think he would make the most interesting of dinner guests," said Hazel.

"Hazel!" tutted Clementine. "I honestly do think there is nobody you would not fraternise with. The more controversial the better! Labour leaders and all!"

"Well, life would be very boring if we only did what we were meant to do!" said Hazel, filling Clementine's glass. "Winston, can I tempt you?" She shook the shaker in her hand.

"No, I am quite happy with my whiskey and soda, Hazel. I shall leave this new fashion of cocktails alone – I daresay it's not for me."

"Well, you never know until you try," said Hazel.

"I have some interesting news for you," said Winston, lowering his voice, taking her by the arm and drawing her away from the others.

"Yes?" she asked, her eyes wide with excitement. She knew by his tone he was going to share political news with her, and she loved when he treated her as his confidante.

"Lloyd George is going to give the order that British troops are to stop all reprisals in Ireland," he said.

Hazel nearly dropped her cocktail shaker as she covered her mouth in excitement.

"Was it the Pope's plea?" she asked.

"General international condemnation has somewhat forced our hand on the matter," informed Winston. "The colonies – South Africa and India – are pleading for the war to stop and the whole matter is in danger of destabilising the empire. If we can't be seen to bring order in Ireland, then how can we elsewhere? Then there is America, of course." He grimaced. "We need favourable terms for our war loans from Congress in Washington and no chance of that while the war is still raging in Ireland."

"I see," said Hazel, digesting it all.

"Of course, His Majesty the King as well is insistent something must be done to stop the bloodshed," said Winston.

"His Majesty is such a *good* man," stressed Hazel.

"All in all – there has been a cross section of pressure that has forced the government's hand."

"And what is it hoped will happen now?" said Hazel excitedly.

"We are to extend the hand of friendship – ask for a truce on both sides – and ask the Irish for talks to find a permanent solution."

"A truce!" said Hazel, deep in thought as she considered where all this could lead. "And what if they don't agree – the Irish?"

"Well, in that case we will have been seen by the international community to have done our best and the Irish will have been exposed as being impossible to deal with and we will bring martial law throughout the whole country and – whatever it takes – we will impose law and order on Ireland." He looked at her pointedly and then moved away to chat to other guests.

A few moments later, as he engaged another guest in conversation, he glanced back at Hazel who was standing stationary where he had left her, deep in thought, clutching her cocktail shaker tightly.

He loved Hazel deeply as a friend but was also aware that she was not known for her discretion. By telling Hazel private British policy on this matter he was sure it would get back to sources on the Irish side. She would do his work for him without his ever having to say a word, which he would not be allowed to do. The Irish needed to know the consequences of rejecting this one-off offer of peace and Winston was sure Hazel was just the woman to let them know that.

That night, after all the guests had left, Hazel paced up and down the drawing room excitedly as John stood by the fireplace.

"This is the best news we could have hoped for! A chance for peace – real lasting peace in Ireland. This could be the one opportunity we get for peace for a generation. If it's not grabbed in both hands by the Irish now, then all could be lost!"

"Let us hope the Irish leaders seize the opportunity," said John as he took a sip from his gin and tonic.

"We can't leave anything to hope, John! First thing tomorrow I must meet with Shane Leslie. We must make sure word gets through to all his connections with the rebels that the British are not joking and, if they reject this offer of peace, they will be playing into British hands and allowing them to obliterate Ireland!"

"Shane Leslie!" grumbled John under his breath.

"And you must play your part, John Lavery! Start writing letters to all the people you have painted on the Irish side so far, to impress on them to embrace this offer with both hands!"

CHAPTER 24

Michael sat in the parlour of De Valera's house in Greystones.

"So, after two years of suppression, murder, looting, burning – the British government now offer the Irish people an olive branch," said Éamon.

"Can we trust them?" asked Michael.

"Of course we can't trust them. But it shows how we have affected them, brought the mighty empire to its knees."

"My intelligence people report back that this is a ploy. It will be seen as an act of goodwill by the international community and, if we reject it, the British will have a licence to crush us and blame us at the same time."

"They haven't crushed us yet, having thrown everything they could at us," said Éamon.

"But how much further can we continue? We don't have the arms, the rifles, the men, to keep up the fight for much longer."

"They don't know that," said Éamon.

"They have infinite resources compared to us," said Michael.

Éamon sat with his hands together in a spire-like pose in front of his face as he thought.

"We must accept this truce and at least give peace a chance," said Éamon. "But I will not go to Lloyd George with cap in hand as a beggar. I will not be grateful for any crumbs he throws us if, as surely will happen, an invitation to talk to him follows this truce. We will have demands attached to this truce."

"So will they," said Michael.

* * *

As Michael left the De Valera house, he was cautiously optimistic. He had been living in a war for so long it had become almost inconceivable that there could be any kind of truce. But he knew they were seriously low on arms and had lost a large number of men in the attack on the Customs House. He wasn't sure the country could take much more fighting. What's more, he himself craved a normal life. He was tired of living from day to day, never knowing where he would be sleeping that night.

Since he had started courting Kitty, it had opened up a new world for him. A world of normality, or a glimpse of what a normal life could be like. He often didn't know what to make of her. She could be laughing one minute and shouting the next. She never praised him or said anything loving to him. But then he didn't either. He never had with women. With all the women he had met and courted, there had always been a kind of challenging going on. They would try to bring him down a peg or two and he and they sparred off each other. Kitty was the ultimate sparring partner. Helen had been a bit different. She had said kind words to him and words of praise that nobody had ever said to him before. He didn't want to mess up with Kitty as he had with Helen. He wanted peace so he could have a chance at a normal life.

He went straight to the Grand Hotel in the village where Kitty was waiting for him, having made the trip up from Granard. As he bounded up the steps of the hotel, he found himself excited at the thought of seeing her.

She was waiting in the hotel bar. "You're late!"

He raised his eyes to heaven. "Sorry – I should have cut my meeting discussing the upcoming truce with Dev short and told him I had to go – that Kitty Kiernan was waiting in the bar up the road!"

"Truce?" Her ears pricked up at the mention of the word. "Oh, Mick – is there going to be a truce!"

"That's what they're saying! The Brits are holding out the olive branch."

"Well, I hope you grab it!" she gasped, full of excitement.

"The decision isn't mine – but if we can agree to each other's demands, we might have a truce."

"Oh Mick!" She flung her arms around him and hugged him tightly. "I can scarcely believe it! That we could finally have peace and life could go back to how it was – before all this war started."

"That seems so long ago, I can hardly remember what peace feels like," he said.

"But think what this would mean for you, Mick. No more running around, no more hiding, no more living life on the run."

"If the truce did come, it might mean Harry could come home from America," said Michael.

She blinked a few times at the thought.

"You've told him nothing – about us?" Michal asked.

"No – I keep putting it off," she said. "I'm a coward, I know that. But every time I sit down to put pen to paper, I don't know what to say to him. We've never talked about the future, Mick. You've never told me what you want or expect from me. This could be just a dalliance for you, as far as I know."

"It's not a dalliance."

"Then what is it – exactly? With Harry, I know exactly where I am – with you I don't."

"But how can I plan for the future – how can I commit to anything when I'm not even sure where I'll be sleeping tonight?" He thought of Helen's words to him. "Somebody once said to me no woman could put up with what I am offering – this life of instability."

She sighed. "And yet I'm still here – trying to see into the future – trying to see if there is any way this could work."

He reached out and took her hand. "All we can do is live for the moment, Kitty – there's no other way for me to live, at least until this war is over. Hopefully now with a truce ..."

She couldn't hide the worry and concern spread across her face.

CHAPTER 25

The British government and the Irish, after much deliberation, finally declared a truce on the eleventh of July 1921.

The demands on both sides were agreed to. Most importantly, all British Tans and Auxiliaries were to be confined to barracks while all attacks on British personnel by the Irish were to cease.

Michael was not included in the delegation that was to travel to London on the fourteenth of July – it was to be headed by De Valera.

John could hardly remember a time that he had seen Hazel so elated and full of optimism. The truce in Ireland had thrilled her and now she was hoping and praying that the oncoming talks between the British and Irish sides would bring about permanent peace.

He glanced up from his book and over at his wife. She was still lost in thought, her expression changing from worry to excitement.

"John!" she said, suddenly rising quickly to her feet, her hands clasped together.

"Yes, my dear?"

"I have been thinking – about the upcoming peace conference – this is the perfect opportunity to paint the Irish leaders we have been so anxious to capture on canvas for our Irish collection."

He put down his book and looked at her. "I sincerely doubt they would have time to sit for a painting with such important negotiations being conducted, Hazel."

"But don't you see? That is exactly why they must pose for

161

paintings – not just the Irish side but the British as well – to capture this momentous occasion for posterity."

"The Irish wouldn't want their images captured in such a permanent and exact way – they are fugitives –"

"*Were* fugitives, John, past tense. They are now politicians – representatives of a free and independent Ireland."

"I doubt the British press and a great swathe of the British public will view them as such. To them they are still murdering thugs."

"Regardless of all that, this needs to be captured on canvas – the cornerstone of our Irish collection! And who better to do it than you? You were awarded a knighthood by the government for documenting the Great War on canvas. This is just an extension of your work as a political and social documenter."

He thought for a while. "Yes, I can see the importance such paintings will have in the future. If they agree . . ."

"Oh, they will agree, leave that to me! I'll get Winston on side straight away – as a committed artist he will understand the importance of the paintings and, of course, as part of the British delegation he no doubt will revel in his own portrait being part of the collection. I will also personally write to all the delegates, including Éamon de Valera in Dublin – Shane will get the letter to him."

"We don't have much time to lose," said John. "I would say the conference will be starting within days."

She nodded in agreement before throwing her hands in the air. "John, I have had a splendid idea!"

"Another one?" He almost feared to hear it.

"What do we do best, John?" she asked excitedly.

He shrugged. "Paint?"

"Yes, but also – we host! We are famous for being the best hosts in London. I suggest – I propose – that we offer 5 Cromwell Place as a home from home to the Irish delegation – a place where they can come and unwind and relax after a hard day's work at the conference table."

He looked at her in horror. "Have you lost your mind, Hazel?"

"No – I have not lost my mind, John Lavery. In fact, I have never thought with such clarity in all my life! It makes perfect sense. Not only we will offer our home as an open house to the Irish, but invite the British delegation here as well. A place where both sides can get to know each other informally and socially away from the conference table." She was relishing the prospect of it.

"Good Lord, Hazel, these men are sworn enemies! They are not going to politely have tea and crumpet in our drawing room and discuss cricket!" He wanted to burst out laughing but didn't for fear of upsetting or hurting her.

"Why not? Why not drink tea and discuss cricket? Though I doubt the Irish side will be too interested in that particular subject. They need to stop seeing each other as ogres and start seeing each other as people. I am *convinced* that the solution to the problem of Ireland rests in talk and not guns. This is a once-in-a-generation opportunity to bring the sides together and for them to really talk to each other and get to know each other – once that happens they will begin to see the others' point of view and compromise will follow – I am sure of it! They won't get a chance to do that over a conference table, but they will here."

"With you as intermediary?"

"Why not?" she said with a smile.

"Placing yourself, ourselves, at the very heart of the peace conference – of Irish political affairs?"

"It is my dearest wish!"

"But, Hazel, you have not thought this through. You will be attracting far more than just controversy – indeed far more than just scandal – you will be attracting venom and hatred from many people in this country if you invite these men who many people view, as I said, as murdering thugs into our home."

"I do not care for people's thoughts, John – I only care to do the right thing, and to help with this peace as much as I can. I know people think my involvement in Irish affairs is merely a fad of mine, a passing hobby, but it means everything to me and I don't care what I risk to achieve what I want to achieve with it."

"You may find your role as a society hostess destroyed if you go ahead with this plan of yours. There might not be a drawing room in London that receives you after you have received the likes of De Valera in yours."

"Let them punish me if they will, I do not care ... perhaps I have too much confidence in my own position in society but I believe that I will not be boycotted."

"My God, you are determined, come what may!" said John, admiring her now.

"I most certainly am, John. Besides," she said with a sudden mischievous smile, "I have a feeling, and I am rarely wrong on these things – that the Irish delegation are going to cause so much intrigue and attract so much attention that other society hostesses, rather than shunning me, will in actuality be quite envious once I have given them my seal of approval!"

To John's astonishment, Hazel's plan was not dismissed by either the British or the Irish delegations as agreements came in from most of the major players including Lloyd George, Winston and De Valera to have their portraits painted.

Of course it was Michael Collins that everybody wanted to see, and indeed who John most wanted to paint, but the surprising news came that he would not be part of the Irish delegation coming to London. Collins was to remain an elusive figure, John thought. Maybe it was a clever ploy, for the unknown quantity often carried more respect than the known. Perhaps if Collins had come to London, the disappointment of the world to see him as a mere mortal would be too great. As it was, he would remain a giant in people's imaginations.

The peace conference was to start the week of July 14th. De Valera and his delegation left Kingstown Harbour in Dublin and, arriving in Britain, got the train to London. Film crews followed their journey and even more were awaiting their arrival at Euston Station. Hazel and John were at Euston, together with hundreds of others, as well as the international press. The majority of the people were Irish sympathisers and cheered De Valera as he was given a police escort to an awaiting automobile. The delegation had declined the government's hospitality and decided to stay at the Grosvenor Hotel instead.

"I hardly thought there were that many Irish living in London!" Hazel shouted to be heard over the cheering crowds around them.

"They're not just the Irish," said John, surveying the crowd. "There are plenty of trade unionists here, as well as pacifists and even a large amount of communists. The war in Ireland has attracted a most remarkable alliance of people you would not usually group together."

"Including the odd American society hostess!" smirked Hazel, striking a pose in her fur stole.

"Indeed!" said John.

"How things change!" said Hazel. "A couple of weeks ago those same policemen would have arrested De Valera if they got near him – now they are escorting him as a VIP."

"And things could change back just as easily. The same police who are escorting them today could arrest them next week. Despite the assurances and truce, I doubt the Irish can quite relax while they are on British soil."

"Well, they will be able to relax at our house, I'll make sure of that," said Hazel.

John glanced at her and smiled. Although the parties had accepted the invitation to be painted, there had been no official acceptance of Hazel's offer of hospitality. John was sure neither party quite knew what to make of the offer – or what to make of Hazel either.

"Portrait! Dev has agreed to have his portrait painted!" exclaimed Michael and he shook with laughter as he sat behind his desk.

"Yes, Sir John Lavery is going to do all their portraits," said the intelligence man who had presented a report to him.

"I suppose we can add vanity to Dev's other attributes in that case," said Michael as he quickly read the report his intelligence had gathered on the Laverys. "This is very odd. Hazel Lavery is an Irish sympathiser but she's great friends with Churchill? She knows half the cabinet and is a good friend of Sir Philip Sassoon – what kind of a name is that? – Lloyd George's private secretary."

"Well, she's a society hostess."

"And she even has had private meetings with Lloyd George!" said Michael, his face clouding with worry. "And she wants everyone to go around to her house and be friends over tea? And our lads are all going in to get their portraits done there? Have they all lost their minds? Has Dev lost his mind? It could be like walking into the lion's den."

He couldn't make sense of it. Was it possible that their vaunted Irish allegiance was a front?

"Get her watched and her letters looked at. I want a full report on this woman before any of our lads step into 5 Cromwell Place."

Hazel was in the Café Royal, about to have afternoon tea with Charlie Vane-Tempest-Stewart. A waitress began to set the table, unloading china, cutlery and napkins from a trolley.

"You look very happy, Hazel," said Charlie as he smiled across at her.

"I am in particularly good form!"

"And what has you in such good form?"

"Why, the arrival of Éamon de Valera and his cabinet in London for the peace talks of course. Have you seen the newspapers today? Mr. De Valera and his friends are on all the front pages – he has come to London for peace – to find a lasting peace."

Charlie frowned as Hazel reached into her handbag and took out a copy of that morning's *Daily Mail*. She unfolded the front page where there was a large photograph of Éamon de Valera taken with the other delegates at the Grosvenor Hotel under the headline 'I WANT PEACE.'

"What De Valera says and what he means are two entirely different matters, I should imagine."

"Nonsense, Charlie!" she said, putting the newspaper away again. "He wouldn't be here if he didn't want peace. And the newspapers report that the ceasefire is continuing to hold in Ireland."

"We shall see," he said.

"They are all coming around to our house to have their portraits done," said Hazel gleefully.

"They are *what*?" questioned Charlie, his voice rising.

"We want to capture this for history – the British cabinet portraits are to be painted as well," said Hazel, preparing herself for the full wrath of Charlie's temper which was about to come her way.

"I just can't believe you! Hazel – you have crossed the line of decency! How can you allow those murderers into your home? What do you hope to achieve except a disgusting notoriety?" Charlie's face was red with anger.

"I am not looking for notoriety – you take that back, Londonderry!"

The waitress nervously began to unload a silver teapot with accompanying milk, sugar and strainer.

"Hazel, I am one of your oldest and dearest friends in London but if you persist in this ridiculous pursuit of republican politics, of which you know nothing, then you are putting our friendship at risk!"

"You are just being a bully, Charlie! A horrible and uncompromising bully! You can't dictate what I believe in politically and you cannot dictate who I receive in my house ... this *bullying* is exactly what I am talking about with the British establishment in Ireland. You expect everyone in Ireland to just blindly accept your will and cannot take it when the Irish fight back! You cannot take it that I am not on your side, Charlie, and you are now using threats to end our friendship if I don't bow to your will!"

"Hazel!" pleaded Charlie, trying to calm her down as people from the other tables were staring.

The waitress was hovering over her trolley, waiting to unload the three-tiered silver stand laden with sandwiches, scones and cakes.

"I will not be bullied by you, Charlie – not one little bit! If that means our friendship must come to an end – so be it! As dear as you are to me, I have no doubt life will continue without you. But I can assure you that it will be *you* who'll be the loser in the long run. For there are many titled aristocrats in London who I can replace you with at my dinner table, but there are not nearly as many entertaining, witty and intelligent American women in London who can replace me! And if you can find one then please introduce me to her as I would love to make her acquaintance!"

As the two of them stared at each other in silent anger, the waitress seized her opportunity and placed the three-tiered stand on the table between the opponents.

"Shall I pour the tea, Lady Lavery?" she asked then.

Hazel tore eyes away from Charlie and glanced at the afternoon tea and its accoutrements.

"No, that will be all, thank you," she said.

The waitress made a little curtsey and hastily departed with her trolley.

The other diners began to talk again as Hazel picked up the teapot and poured the tea.

"I didn't realise you were quite so passionate about it all," said Charlie quietly, embarrassed by the scene that had just played out in public.

"It means the world to me," said Hazel.

"Well, we will just have to agree to differ," said Charlie. "I was wrong to threaten to end our friendship ... I could never do that – you mean far too much to me."

She nodded. "And the last thing I want is to fall out with you, Charlie. But I will not be attacked for my beliefs."

The waitress wheeled the trolley into the kitchen.

"May I take my tea break now?" she asked her supervisor.

At the woman's nod she walked quickly through the kitchen, out to a corridor and on to a quiet corner at the back of a stairs.

She glanced around and then sat down on one of the bottom steps. She took out her notebook and pen and began to write down the whole conversation and scene she had just witnessed between Lady Lavery and the Marquess of Londonderry. She would have the report despatched back to Dublin Intelligence that evening and in Mick Collins' hands by the next day.

* * *

At the sorting office in the post office in Kensington a line of postal workers sat at a long bench, working diligently on sorting the stacks of letter before them. A young woman called Rose, as she sorted through the post for Cromwell Place, kept a keen eye out for post addressed to Lady Hazel Lavery. Once she spotted what she was looking for, she swiped the letters and stashed them under her apron, confident nobody had seen.

When it came to lunchtime, Rose stood up along with the rest of her co-workers.

"Are you coming to the new café around the corner for lunch, Rose? I hear you can get a bun for free with your sandwich and tea there," said a colleague.

"I can't today, Sylvia – I have to run an errand for my mother."

Rose waved Sylvia and the rest of her friends off outside the sorting office. She waited until the girls had turned the corner and then she hurried back into the building, down a corridor and into an empty office, locking the door behind her. She put the kettle on the stove to boil then took out the Lavery letters and placed them on a desk. Once the kettle was boiling, she held the letters over the steam and began to unseal them. She would have all the letters read and documented, resealed into their envelopes and back on the sorting desk by the time the girls got back from their sandwich, tea and free bun at the café.

Michael sat behind his desk in Harcourt Street, having studied all the information his intelligence had gathered to date on the Laverys.

"Well?" asked Gearóid who was sitting across the desk from him.

"Nobody has managed to get anything damning about the Laverys. They seem innocent enough, though slightly perplexing," said Michael, scratching his head.

"The Yank probably has too much time on her hands and nothing to do with it," Gearóid suggested.

"She has a young daughter and a famous husband, that should keep her busy enough," said Michael. "Anyway, from reports on her conversations at restaurants by our girls and boys working on the ground and our team reading through her post, she seems to be a genuine supporter of an Irish Republic. However, she could be just a very good actress. Her husband is a Protestant from Northern Ireland and so their natural allegiance shouldn't be with us. There is nothing to stop Dev from visiting their house and getting his portrait painted – but advise him to tread with extreme care and we'll keep Hazel Lavery under careful surveillance."

"Right," agreed Gearóid.

"On to more important things – the news from London is not positive," said Michael. "The meetings are mostly between Dev and Lloyd George and Lloyd George is refusing to budge an inch. He says all that is on offer from their side is to give Ireland dominion status like South Africa or Canada and for us to remain in the empire."

Gearóid laughed derisively. "In that case we'll fight on! They have more to lose than we have – did they not learn anything from the last two years? We're not asking for independence – we're taking it!"

"Gearóid – what are we to fight on with? Three thousand rifles and a couple of thousand men? We're on our knees and the country is on its knees and can't take a continuation of this war."

They fell silent, pondering on the situation.

"I wonder," said Gearóid at length, "if Dev will be home for Tom Barry's wedding next month?"

"If things don't pick up in London, he may be home next week!" said Michael.

"The venue will be at Vaughan's Hotel," said Gearóid. "It's hard to believe, isn't it, that we can all go and celebrate Tom's wedding in the open – like normal people – and not be looking over our shoulders like fugitives."

"For the moment," said Michael, with no joyful anticipation on his face.

Michael looked so troubled these days that Gearóid suspected his unease was not all down to the political situation. It must also be due to his personal life. Gearóid was as surprised as everyone when it became known that Michael had been seeing Kitty over the past few months. He knew they had grown close, but it was a very delicate situation that had arisen. Obviously, as he himself was great friends with Michael and also related to him, there was nothing he would like more than that his future sister-in-law should marry Michael. But he didn't want to see Harry Boland hurt either and everyone knew how much Harry was in love with Kitty. As for Kitty, Gearóid had tried to prise out of Maud what her intentions were but it was like getting blood out of a stone. According to Maud, Kitty was confused, indecisive and exhausted from the whole situation. Gearóid just hoped she made a decision soon, as the last thing the Republican movement needed at this critical stage was a falling-out over a woman. Gearóid was certain it would not be long until Harry returned to Ireland, now the truce had been declared, and the truth about Kitty and Michael would then emerge.

Hazel gazed at Éamon de Valera as he sat for his portrait in their studio.

"It's such an honour for us to have you here," said Hazel.

"So you've already said – several times," said Éamon.

"We want you to treat our house as your house – avail of it any time you want," Hazel urged.

"Thank you, but the Grosvenor Hotel supplies us with all our needs," said Éamon.

John and Hazel exchanged looks. The legendary De Valera was proving to be a bit of a disappointment to Hazel. He seemed a little bored and uncomfortable to be there. She had hoped to become his friend but had to admit that even her charms were lost on him.

CHAPTER 26

Like everyone else in Ireland, Kitty could scarcely believe it when the truce was declared. After two long vicious years of war, people had forgotten what peace felt like. Slowly at first, people tentatively came out on the streets, looking around for Black and Tans or Auxiliaries, but realising they had gone. Frightened that the truce would break quickly, the men who had been in hiding, fighting the war, crept home to their wives and families. As days passed and the truce held, people began to go out in the evening. The bars and restaurants began to fill up again and courting couples queued to go to the new cinema houses that had been opening up. Dance halls began to open again, and stadiums began to stage sporting events without the fear of an attack or massacre by the Black and Tans.

And then, in the glorious weather of that July, the whole country exploded in euphoric joy, not just that people could go about their lives as normal again but because they saw the truce as victory. After centuries they had finally got rid of foreign rule.

For Michael, he felt he could breathe again for the first time in years. But he still didn't let his guard down. He continued to nervously watch out for suspicious-looking people. Kitty was so excited about the truce that he felt he could not burst her bubble by letting her know that the news from London was not good. Lloyd George and the British were not compromising and were absolutely ruling out giving Ireland independence. After De Valera and the Irish returned to Dublin in mid-July, Lloyd George sent his official proposal on the twentieth. The proposal was just short of an insult to Irish Republicans and Michael could not see how it would be accepted.

Now with the British troops confined to their barracks, Michael was free to travel home to Cork to see his family without restrictions. And free to travel to Longford to see Kitty. On one such visit he drove the automobile through the country roads at high speed, Kitty beside him. The joy on the people's faces they passed touched his heart. But he feared it would be short-lived and the truce would collapse.

"Slow down, you'll end up crashing!" begged Kitty, but she was laughing.

Every automobile they passed was travelling too fast for the country roads, almost as if the drivers were drunk on the euphoria of peace. The automobiles were mostly driven by dashing young men with fashionably dressed young female passengers, heading off to tennis matches or horse shows or races or any one of the multitude of social events happening after years of suspension. It was as if the country had been transformed by the truce and the advent of peace.

"*We won the war! We won the war!*" shouted an intoxicated young woman who was swinging a bottle of champagne in the passenger seat of a passing car.

"She looks like the only thing she ever won was a drinking competition!" said Michael, causing Kitty to burst out laughing.

The Irish demand for complete independence was outright rejected by Lloyd George and his government. As July slipped into August, the British proposal was hotly debated by the provisional Irish government in Dublin before it was officially turned down on the tenth of August. As Ireland continued to bask in the long hot summer of peace, nobody wanted to see a return to the war and frantic diplomacy was being carried out between London and Dublin to try and organise a new set of negotiations and maintain the fragile truce that was in place.

Tom Barry's wedding on the twenty-second of August brought a welcome respite in the midst of this political intensity. As Tom was one of the leaders of the Republican movement, the elite of the Republican membership and the provisional government were all there.

"It's a wonderful day," said Gearóid as he and Michael arrived at the church. "Here we are, free to do as we want. Like a normal group of friends celebrating a friend's wedding."

"We may as well enjoy it as it might not last for long," said Michael.

They entered the church and took their seats, nodding to all the familiar faces in the congregation.

"I don't believe it! Look who it is!" Gearóid hissed to Michael.

Michael turned to where he was indicating and saw Harry Boland sitting across the aisle from him.

"Did you know Harry was coming back from America?" Gearóid whispered.

"No – I hadn't a clue."

Harry smiled over warmly at them and waved. Michael gave a salute to him.

As the organ music began to play and the bride began her advance up the aisle, Michael's face clouded over as he thought of Kitty.

After the marriage ceremony the congregation filed out into the church yard. Attention was lavished on the bride and groom but many of the guests descended on Harry, thrilled to see their friend back and congratulating him on the tremendous job he had done in America.

"Six million pounds raised! Well done!" shouted a man as he clapped Harry on the back.

"Well, Dev had a hand in it too!" said Harry, nodding over to Éamon who was standing nearby.

But there was only one person Harry was interested in seeing as he cut his way through the fawning crowd to Michael.

"Well – Big Fella! Where's my greeting?" he demanded with his arms outstretched.

Harry hadn't changed a bit since his time in America. His face had lost none of its friendly honesty – there was kindness in his eyes and always a ready smile on his lips.

"I thought you'd have a Yank accent by now, the amount of time you've been over there!" teased Michael.

"I can have any accent that the audience requires when I'm making speeches, as long as there's big enough donations afterwards! Come here to me!" said Harry, pulling Michael into a bear hug. "Sure it's great to see you, Mick. I can't tell you how much I've missed you."

"Me too," said Michael, but as he hugged Harry tightly his smile dropped.

At Vaughan's Hotel, the photographer lined up all the guests in the back garden for the official photograph.

"For fuck's sake!" Gearóid whispered to Michael. "What the British government wouldn't have paid for this photograph a couple of months ago. An up-to-date photograph of all the Republican leaders!"

"If we don't get back into negotiations with London quickly then this photograph might be valuable to them again in the near future! I'm keeping my head down for the camera in any case!"

"Doesn't she make a beautiful bride?" smiled Harry as Tom's new wife Leslie chatted to the guests in the garden.

"She does surely," agreed Michael.

"And a brave one. She was one of the last women to leave the GPO the week of the Easter Rising," said Harry, full of admiration.

"I know – wasn't I there, Harry?"

"True!" laughed Harry. "I'm so used to talking to Americans, explaining over and over again who everyone is to them!"

Michael felt incredibly awkward. He and Kitty usually tried to avoid talking about Harry – it was like the elephant in the room everyone was ignoring. But there was no ignoring him now.

"Kitty wrote that Helen had got married," said Harry. "I was sorry to have missed the wedding."

"Yes, it was a fine day."

Harry placed a hand on Michael's shoulder. "It must have been hard for you – I know you had a great respect for her. But, sure, there's plenty more fish in the sea, as my mother says! I can't wait to see Kitty!"

"She has no idea you're home?"

"No, I'm going to surprise her!" laughed Harry.

"I see."

"You've seen a bit of her over the past year, I understand? She always writes about you and says you've been in contact."

"Yes, well, I tried to keep . . ." Michael searched for the right words to say but couldn't find any. He felt the truth needed to be told to Harry quickly, but it needed to come from Kitty. He would have to continue the charade until he had a chance to speak to her and decide how to tackle the situation.

"Thanks, Mick, for all you've done for her. I worried about her when I was away all the time and it just made me more relaxed, knowing you were here to make sure she was alright."

"Well – eh – least I could do, Harry." Michael went red with embarrassment.

Éamon came up to them. "If we can drag ourselves away from the festivities of the day – Michael, Harry – I need to speak to you."

"There's a room upstairs we can use," said Michael, grateful of the distraction as he silently cursed Kitty for not being more assertive with Harry and explaining to him where he stood – where they all stood.

Harry had heard a lot about Vaughan's Hotel when he was in America. It had been one of Michael's principal hiding places, a place where he was always protected by the staff and management. As Michael led them into a room and locked the door behind him, Harry realised he had the run of the whole building. Michael seemed to have had the run of everything and everyone during his absence, Harry thought, feeling slightly envious that he had been side-lined in America for so long.

"Sorry to drag you away from the day's celebrations but we have business to discuss," said Éamon. "Since we turned down the British proposals after the negotiation I attended, Lloyd George wants us to go to London to try again. Harry, I'll be sending you over to Lloyd George with our reply to the invitation."

"Right," nodded Harry.

Michael was a little surprised that Harry was being chosen to go and realised how much Éamon had come to rely on him while in America.

"In my reply to Lloyd George I will sign myself as the leader of a free and independent Ireland," declared Éamon.

"You can't do that, Dev!" stated Michael. "You will immediately get their backs up if you write that down on paper and they won't meet you. A free and independent Ireland is what we are fighting for, but it's not what we have yet and to declare we have is just a farce!"

"I don't agree," said Éamon coldly. "I want to address Lloyd George as leader of one sovereign nation to another."

"But isn't that what the whole war is about?" said Michael, allowing himself a snigger. "Trying to become a sovereign nation and them not allowing us. If you put that in writing to Lloyd George you're risking the truce collapsing!"

"We are not going to be cowards at this late stage. I've made my mind up and that is what I am going to write in the correspondence to Lloyd George."

Michael shrugged, realising the decision rested with De Valera.

Later, in the function room, Michael watched as Harry continued to be given a hero's welcome by everyone.

Gearóid came up to Michael. "That's a turn-up for the books, Harry being home."

"Yes," Michael grunted.

"I take it he knows nothing – about you and Kitty?"

"No." Michael sighed and shook his head.

"Well, don't you think it would be wise to get things sorted with Kitty – before all this blows up in everyone's face?"

"Yep." Michael nodded.

"Look, I'm going to visit Maud tomorrow for a couple of days. Why don't you come down as well and you and Kitty can decide what ye're going to do and what's best for the both of ye and for Harry?"

Michael thought for a while and then nodded. "What time are we leaving?"

CHAPTER 27

Michael and Gearóid walked through the reception of the Greville Arms and saw the bar was packed with customers. It had been Fair Day and instead of all the farmers heading home straight after the fair as they had been doing during the war, many had headed straight for the bar to celebrate the day's business.

Gearóid stood at the doorway of the bar with his hands on his hips, smiling as he looked at them.

"What are you smiling at?" Michael asked.

"Normalcy! I'm smiling at the normalcy of it all!"

Michael hit his arm. "Come on, you big eejit!"

"Are Miss Kitty and Miss Maud in the house?" Gearóid asked the girl on reception.

"Miss Maud is out but Miss Kitty is there alright in the parlour," said the girl.

"I'm dreading all this," said Michael to Gearóid. "I don't know how Kitty will take it that Harry is back – or what she's going to do about it!"

"It will be fine," Gearóid assured him as they walked down the corridor and into the parlour.

Michael stood stock still. Kitty was seated on the couch and Harry was standing over her.

"Harry!" said Gearóid, getting just as much a shock as Michael had.

Harry turned around and looked equally shocked to see them.

"What are ye doing here?" he asked.

178

"Er," Gearóid thought quickly as Kitty and Michael looked too stunned to come up with an excuse, "I had arranged to come down to see Maud and talked Michael into coming down with me."

"Eh, yes, last-minute decision," said Michael.

"Well, if I knew you were coming down, we could have all come down together!" said Harry with a big smile as he came and shook both their hands and clapped them on the backs.

Michael looked at Kitty nervously. She looked as pale as a ghost.

"I thought you were being sent off to meet Lloyd George by Dev?" said Mick.

"Well, I'm due to go, but Dev is still deciding what to write in the bloody response. And I just couldn't wait any longer. I had to get down here to see Kitty." He swung around to look at her. "The old gang all back together, Kitty – just like the good old days!"

"I'll tell you I wasn't sure who was more glad to see the back of the other most – me or the Yanks!" said Harry.

He was sitting beside Kitty and across the dining-room table from Michael, Gearóid and Maud. Larry was at the head of the table and Chrys was at the end.

There was an air of unease which a beaming Harry was oblivious to.

"God, there's nothing like good old-fashioned homemade Irish food!" he said as he looked up from his roast chicken dinner and smiled at Michael and Kitty. "Seriously, I've had enough of America to last me a lifetime. I mean it's all very exciting and fast and big at the beginning. But after a while it became wearying. And all those fundraising events! Having to smile all the time – sure Dev couldn't smile to save his life half the time! Which meant I had to smile enough for the two of us!"

"It's no pressure for you to smile, Harry – sure there's always a smile on your face." Maud spoke quietly and allowed herself a fleeting look at Michael who was staring at Kitty from across the table.

"Thanks, Maud! Gee – thanks!" said Harry, mimicking an American accent. "Well, I'm smiling now – now that I'm back. But

I feel as if I've missed so much while I was away."

"Sure mostly it wasn't good, Harry, with the war. You didn't miss anything good," said Gearóid.

"I know that. But other things – like Helen's wedding. I really felt it that day, not being able to attend."

Kitty and Michael exchanged guilty looks at the memory of their romance starting that day.

"And just this! Missing all you guys – my friends." He turned to Kitty and said seriously, "And of course you, Kitty – my Kitty."

"But why didn't you tell us that you were coming home, Harry?" asked Maud.

"Because I wanted to surprise Kitty!"

"Well, you certainly did that – you nearly gave me a heart attack!" said Kitty.

"But, sure, isn't life full of surprises? Here's another one with Mick Collins down for the weekend as well! The best greeting party I could have wanted – my two favourite people in the world." Harry smiled from one to the other.

"So – you're finished with America now, Harry?" asked Maud, trying to distract him from that subject.

"Sure, with the truce now my role in America is over and I can get back to my life and the ones I love," he said as he clasped Kitty's hand in both of his and stroked it fondly, "the *one* I love."

Michael bit his lower lip as he looked on, beginning to tremble at the sight of the two of them together.

Kitty gently released her hand from Harry's and said, "More wine?"

"I will surely!" he said, raising his crystal glass, and she refilled it. "That's another thing I won't be sorry to see the back of – prohibition!"

"No fear that will ever be introduced here!" Michael managed to joke.

Harry raised his glass. "I want to propose a toast."

The others raised their glasses and waited.

"To friends," said Harry. "To the best kind of friends – old friends!"

* * *

Molly had led Harry off to show him to his room for the night and Michael watched as Kitty cleared the plates in the dining room.

"What are you doing?" he hissed as he stood up.

"Clearing the plates! What does it look like?" she spat back, glaring at him. "Why didn't you tell me Harry was home?"

"I only found out yesterday! At the wedding. I came down straight away today to tell you – but he got here first!"

"You could have sent me a bloody telegram to warn me! You're supposed to be the head of Irish Intelligence – I'm sure you could have got a message to me if you'd tried hard enough! I nearly dropped dead on the spot when he walked in the door!"

"And what would I say in the telegram?" He pulled a sarcastic face. "Your lover is back?"

She slammed the plates down hard on the table and spat, "Damn you, Mick!"

"You got yourself into this mess! You've been leading him on. Why didn't you tell him about us?"

"It's none of your business whether I tell Harry or not!" she hissed. "And what's this *us* business? You don't own me, Mick! Nobody owns me."

"But you're being unfair to him by not telling him about what has been going on between us – and you're being unfair to me too! For fuck's sake!" He flicked his hair back off his forehead.

"My usual room, nothing changed!" said Harry as he happily walked in.

Kitty turned and smiled falsely at him as she picked up the stack of plates and saucers again.

"I'll just drop these down to the kitchen." She smiled at Harry as she passed him. "You two head down to the parlour and join the others – fix yourselves a drink."

"We will surely!" said Harry as he threw an arm around Michael and led him down the corridor.

In the parlour he went over to the drinks cabinet and began to fix them two whiskies. "How I dreamed of being back here so many times when I was in America," he said. "Dev had said you were coming over to America to join me – then, when I heard nothing further on it, I thought the plan had been dropped. I didn't think you could be spared from over here anyway – but I still hoped you would be coming over to me – the old team back together."

"It would have been an adventure alright," said Michael, taking the glass of whiskey from him. "Though maybe we're getting too old for adventures."

"Never too old for adventures!" said Harry, clinking his glass against Michael's. He beamed a smile over at Gearóid and Maud who were seated on the couch. "As for you two – have you fixed a date yet?"

"Not yet," said Maud. "It's been hard to plan anything with Gearóid's involvement in the war. But we're hoping for next year."

Harry leaned forward and lowered his voice. "Well, I'm hoping me and Kitty won't be too far behind you! Who knows – we might end up having a double wedding!"

Michael swilled the whiskey around his mouth.

"Wouldn't that be nice?" whispered Maud, glaring at Michael.

Michael raised his glass and downed the contents in one go.

CHAPTER 28

Kitty hardly said anything for the rest of the evening. She observed Michael didn't say much either. But that was alright because Harry, brimming over with excitement that he was home, had enough talk for all of them. She carefully observed him and could see he did not suspect anything had been going on. He thought that everything was the exact same as he had left it. Never in his wildest dreams would he have suspected anything had been going on between his girlfriend and his best friend. And now here he was beside her and she was desperately trying to work out how she felt about him. As she listened to him and watched him, she saw how she had fallen for him. But as she watched Michael, she felt her heart was torn in two.

At last Michael rose to go to bed. She could tell Harry had been giving him signals to leave them alone. Harry must have thought that Michael was short on the uptake, it took him that long to leave.

"Goodnight, Harry – goodnight, Kitty," said Michael.

"Night, Mick," she said and avoided eye contact with him, as she had countless times that night.

"Goodnight, Mick," said Harry.

"We'll be off too," said Maud, standing and gesturing to Gearóid who hastily stood up too.

"Goodnight, Maud – Gearóid." Kitty nodded at them.

"Goodnight," said Maud, staring meaningfully at Kitty.

As Michael made his way through the house up to his room, he could hear Harry's laughter echoing behind him. In his room, he closed the door behind him and sank down to the ground, sinking his face in his hands.

It was breaking his heart, thinking of them together downstairs. Had she forgotten about him now that Harry was back? Had he just been an amusement to fill in time for her while her true love Harry was away? He felt himself being consumed by jealousy. It was exactly like the feeling he had with Helen before, a feeling he was being rejected, that he was being passed over for somebody else. That Kitty, like Helen before her, did not understand him or could never be his soulmate. But he was also overcome with a dreadful guilt about Harry.

Maud and Gearóid spoke in whispers as they walked down the corridor.

"What the fuck is she playing at?" demanded Gearóid.

"I don't know – heavens knows!" said Maud, throwing her hands in the air.

"She has the two of them sleeping under the same roof – with Harry, the poor eejit, having no idea what's been going on!"

"I despair of her! It's like she's lost her mind!"

"Well, she's your sister!"

"And Mick is your cousin! He's not an innocent party in all this, you know!" Maud shot back.

"A simple decision is all she needs to make. Can she not just follow her heart?"

"I think that's what she's so very frightened of doing," sighed Maud.

Harry held Kitty's hand tightly as they sat on the couch, the oil lamp casting shadows around the room.

"You don't know how much I dreamed of this in America. Just to be here with you, holding your hand," said Harry.

"Did you not hold anyone else's hand while you were over there?" she asked, already knowing the answer would be a resounding no.

"Apart from Dev's – no!"

She allowed herself to smile at his humour. "Harry – it seems a very long time since you were here ... a lot changed during that time ... I've changed."

"You haven't changed one little bit – you are the exact same," he said.

"But I *have* changed – in here," she said, placing her hand on her heart. "There's no easy way to say this so I'll just come out and say it. I tried to write it to you many times, but every time I did, I received a letter from you saying how much you loved me and I couldn't bear to say it."

"Say what?"

"I- I -I met somebody else."

He blinked a few times in disbelief.

"I know I should have written to tell you ... but I didn't want to upset you when you were so far from home ... besides, I think I was too cowardly to tell you. I tried to put pen to paper many times and the letters always ended up in the fire."

"When you say you met somebody ... you mean ..."

"Romantically."

"But you're my girl. Everyone knows that," he said with a half-smile.

She pulled back her hand and stood up. "For goodness' sake, Harry, I'm not your girl, or anybody's girl ... I'm a woman and I don't belong to anybody. I never committed to you – not fully."

"But I asked you to come to America with me –"

"And I didn't go!"

"No, but you said you'd wait –"

"And I waited and I waited and I waited – and I know this isn't what you wanted to hear after just arriving back from America – but you don't know what it has been like here with the war. The attack on the town here and seeing that young policeman killed in front of me ... I know I'm making excuses but we've all been living on borrowed time here, that's what it felt like ... and we had to live for the moment."

"Live for the moment." He repeated the words as if they were incomprehensible to him.

"I tried everything to resist the other man but I have to be honest with you, Harry ... I can't lie anymore and I have strong feelings for him."

"And who is he – this man?" Harry asked astounded.

Her mouth opened and then she shut it tightly again.

"Kitty – who is he?" persisted Harry.

"It's – it's ..." As she looked at him, she decided she could not tell him. Not while Michael was under the same roof. There was no accounting how Harry might react and she didn't want a fight breaking out or worse.

"It's of no consequence who it is."

"Well, I most certainly think it matters a lot. Tell me who he is, Kitty – I at least deserve to know that."

"It's ... Mick," whispered Kitty as her eyes filled with tears.

His face dropped in confusion as he stared at her.

"Mick? You mean our Mick? Mick Collins?"

She nodded.

"For fuck's sake, Kitty, you must be joking! You and Mick! As if that could ever be! Sure you'd kill each other after the first day of courting!"

"It's true, Harry, it's been going on a few months. I told you we have been in constant contact and that he has been down here and I've been to Dublin."

"But, sure, I asked him to keep an eye on you ... you must be misunderstanding the situation ... I *told* him to spend time with you, to take care of you ... he was doing that for *me*, Kitty!"

"Harry, I know ... that's how it began ... but then we discovered we had feelings for each other. There is no misunderstanding. I'm sorry."

Harry stared into the fire, trying to process this. Then he spoke quietly. "I thought he was just ... I thought he was just being a friend ... not a traitor."

"I know it's hard for you not to think the worst of us. I should have said it to you ... he urged me to ... but I was too much of a coward. And then there was the possibility that it might fizzle out and go nowhere, so ..."

"So you decided to keep me warm on the stove – just in case." His voice dripped cynicism.

"Oh God, Harry, I didn't want this to happen – I tried everything to stop it from happening!"

"You can't have tried that hard!"

"I'm despicable," she whispered under her breath.

He stood up and stayed standing, staring into the fireplace.

"Harry?" she prodded.

He then walked out of the room without another word. She sat there, terrified that he had gone up to Michael's room to have it out with him. But there were no words, no shouting, just silence through the house. Harry had gone to his own room. As she sat there on her own, she put her face into her hands and wept.

CHAPTER 29

The next morning Kitty sat uncomfortably across the table from Michael at breakfast. As the rest of the family chatted about the continuing truce, she and Michael sat in silence, waiting for Harry to appear.

"Where's Harry? The breakfast will have gone cold if he doesn't come soon," said Maud, reaching over for more bacon and sausages. "Did you sit up late last night?" She looked meaningfully at Kitty.

"No, not at all," Kitty said, glancing at Michael. "Molly, will you go knock on his door – he must be sleeping in."

"Sure Mr. Boland is gone, Miss Kitty," answered the maid.

"Gone? What do you mean?" demanded Kitty.

"I don't know. But sure I saw him leave at the crack of dawn this morning when I was getting up myself to clean the ashes out of the fireplaces. Yes, the crack of dawn I was up emptying those ashes – like I am every morning while ye are still all getting yeer beauty sleep! And setting those fires so as to have the place nice and warm for ye when ye choose to rise and then –"

"Did you speak to him, Molly?" Maud cut in.

"No, sure there I was cleaning out those ashes –"

"Molly! Did he have his suitcase with him?" Maud asked.

"How would I notice that? There I was struggling with those ashes –"

"Why didn't you tell us before that he had left?" snapped Kitty.

"Because you didn't ask!" huffed Molly as she picked up the teapot and waltzed out of the room.

"Pity the Black and Tans didn't get her while they were at it!" said Gearóid.

"*Gearóid!*" Maud chastised him.

Kitty looked at Michael across the table, both their faces solemn and confused.

After breakfast Michael beckoned Kitty into the parlour and closed over the door behind her.

"What the fuck happened last night?" he hissed.

"I told him! I told him everything, Mick ... I told him all about us."

"Oh, for fuck's sake!" said Michael, rubbing his face ferociously with his hands.

"Isn't that what you wanted me to do?"

"Yes, but not while I was here!"

"I was at the end of the line – I couldn't keep deceiving him."

"I know ... I know ... and?" Michael was almost too afraid to ask.

"He couldn't believe it. Said he thought you were taking care of me ... as a friend ... for him. Then he just stood up and left the room, without another word, not a single word."

Michael shook his head in incredulity. "It was a shock to him. So that's it? That's the end of it – he's just going to give up on you without any fuss or nonsense?"

"I don't know ... I don't know anything anymore." She shook her head sadly as she thought of Harry's crushed face.

Harry's disappearance that morning cast a shadow over Michael. Guilt and confusion hung heavy over him. It would have been better if Harry had exploded in anger, attacked him, punched him – done *something*! But to say nothing and then just disappear confounded Michael's guilt. He was obviously so disgusted, he couldn't even bear to see him again.

The truth was Harry had not returned to Dublin. He had not been able to sleep that night when he had gone to his room and spent the

189

whole night deep in thought. Finally, with the sun coming up, and not able to bear staring at the four walls of the bedroom anymore, he got up and left the house and set off walking from the town far into the country. He retraced the walks he had taken during all the times he had been down courting Kitty. He walked up to a small hill and sat at the top of it, watching the morning sun continue to rise. Michael and Kitty's relationship was an awful shock to him. Never in a million years would he have suspected such a thing could happen.

Last night he could have flown up to Michael's room and flattened him with a punch. But what good would that have done? Hitting somebody that he cared for deeply would have achieved nothing. Nor would it make Kitty feel any less strongly about Michael or more strongly about him. If anything, it would be counterproductive and turn Kitty away from him. To react in any way hostile or aggressive at this point would lose Kitty for good.

One thing Harry knew was that he had fallen in love with Kitty Kiernan – hook, line and sinker. She was all he had thought about in America and all he wanted to get back to. He needed her in his life, he wanted her in his life. Michael Collins was no more than a passing fancy with her. Harry had seen it loads of times with Michael and women in the past. They thought they had fallen in love with him. They were seduced by the looks and the charm and the humour and gregarious personality. But once they got over all that and saw the man behind it, they realised it was all style and no substance. Sure, Michael Collins couldn't even sit still for thirty seconds without having to jump up and run off somewhere – what woman could put up with that? Kitty had been blinded by the man's glamour, not to mention his reputation that had grown over the past couple of years. Sure when she met Mick at first, when he was more of a nobody back then, she didn't have much time for him.

He would just have to woo Kitty again. He had done it before and he could do it again, he just knew he could.

"He wouldn't have done anything stupid, would he?" asked Kitty as she paced up and down in front of the fireplace in the parlour.

She was alone with Michael. It was now late afternoon.

"What do you mean by something *stupid*?" he asked.

"I don't know!" she said.

Suddenly the door opened and in walked Harry, smiling broadly, carrying a turkey.

"Harry! Where have you been?" demanded Kitty, hurrying to him.

"Oh, I just had a few things to do. And I got this for tonight's dinner!" he said, holding up the turkey proudly.

"How – how are you?" Michael said, almost afraid to ask.

"Top of the world!" Harry declared.

Kitty stared at Harry, trying to understand what was going on.

"Will you do me a favour, Mick? Take this turkey down to the kitchen and give it to the cook to start preparing for dinner – will you do that for me?"

Michael's mouth dropped open and he looked at Kitty, who nodded at him to do as he was asked. Michael went to Harry and took the turkey. He glanced at the two of them and then left the room.

Harry closed the door and then turned to look at Kitty.

She was trembling slightly and fearful of what he was going to do and how he was going to react.

"I've been so worried about you, Harry. When you just left last night without saying a word and then were nowhere to be found this morning."

"I just went for a walk, to clear my head. Went to all the places we used to go – do you remember them?"

She nodded. "Of course. Harry ... I know you'll never be able to forgive me for what I've done – with your best friend as well."

He smiled gently as he walked towards her and took her hand softly in his.

"Oh, my darling Kitty – there's only one person to blame for all this and that's me."

"You?" She blinked a few times.

"Sure. I have been selfish and neglectful. What was I thinking? Leaving a young woman as beautiful and as intelligent as you on

191

her own for all this time? Sure of course some vagabond was going to sweep in and try to steal you!" He caressed her hand. "I should have at least tried to come back and see you more often. It's been a whole year since I was back – and such a year, as you say, with the war raging around you. You must have been terrified."

"It – it – was very scary," she muttered, not sure how she felt about Harry's reaction. She was overcome with relief he wasn't angry or shouting the house down or, worse, killing Michael. But as she saw his kind and considerate face, showing nothing but compassion for her, she remembered why she had fallen for him in the first place.

"But I'm back now, Kitty, and you don't have to worry about anything anymore. I'm here to protect you." He leaned forward and enveloped her in a hug.

"Wasn't that the best turkey ever!" said Harry as they finished eating dinner that night.

Michael looked on in a state of confusion. Kitty and Harry had spent hours in the parlour talking and when they finally emerged Harry was smiling like the Cheshire Cat while Kitty looked a little shell-shocked.

"The best," said Maud who like everyone else was totally confused.

Harry was sitting beside Kitty and was behaving as if nothing had happened. He was treating Kitty as his fiancée almost. He kept referring to Kitty and himself as 'we'.

Gearóid and Maud tried to keep the conversation light.

"What was Tom Barry's bride like on her wedding day?" questioned Maud.

"She looked gorgeous," said Gearóid.

"And what was the wedding dress like?"

"White," answered Gearóid.

Maud raised her eyes to heaven. "Well, of course it was white! What else was it like?"

"Long," said Gearóid. "White and long!"

"You are useless!" snapped Maud as she looked from Harry to

Michael. "I guess you two took about as much interest in the wedding dress as Gearóid?"

"You'd be right there!" laughed Harry.

"I tell you one thing that made me laugh," said Gearóid. "When the photographer was taking the group photograph of us all, Dev positioned himself between the bride and groom for the photograph!"

"Good old Dev! Has to be in the middle of everything!" Michael said with a laugh.

"Well," said Harry coolly, "I guess Dev isn't the only one who has tried to come between a couple in love."

Everyone at the table fell into an awkward silence and Michael's face went red.

"Shall we retire to the parlour?" said Maud, quickly standing up.

For the rest of the night Harry never left Kitty's side. And he certainly did not allow Michael to get near her.

When Michael got any opportunity he would look at Kitty and make a gesture of confusion to her. But all she did was shrug back at him.

CHAPTER 30

The next morning, Gearóid and Michael were due to go back to Dublin after breakfast.

"I might hitch a ride with you men, if you don't mind," said Harry. "I have to meet Dev this afternoon."

"Of course," said Michael, wondering if Harry was making sure that he wasn't left behind with Kitty.

After breakfast was finished, Michael watched Harry whisper something to Kitty and she nodded before getting up and following him out of the room.

Harry closed the parlour door behind them. Kitty walked over to the fireplace and turned to face him.

He walked over to her and put his arms around her. "I love you, you do believe that, don't you?"

She nodded. "Yes, I do believe you."

"I have to go to Scotland to meet Lloyd George, Kitty. But as soon as I get back I'll come down and see you again. I want to plan our future. Now I'm back, I want us to get on with our lives. We've wasted enough time and, let's face it, we aren't getting any younger."

"But I need time, Harry. There are things to consider –"

There was a knock on the door and Gearóid popped his head in. "Harry, we have to leave now if you are coming with us. Dev will be waiting."

"Of course – I'm coming now," he said and smiled at Kitty

before leaning forward and kissing her. "I'll see you when I get back from Scotland."

"Have a safe trip," she whispered.

He turned and walked out of the room. Kitty put her fingers to her temples and began to massage them.

When she heard the automobile start outside, she went over to the window and looked down at the street below. Gearóid was in the driver's seat, with Harry in the back. Michael was getting into the front passenger seat when he turned and looked up at the building. He spotted Kitty in the window. They stared at each other for a few moments before Michael got into the automobile and she watched them drive away down the street and out of view.

"What on earth is going on?" demanded Maud, coming into the parlour.

"Please don't start, Maud, I'm getting a headache."

"Damn your headache, Kitty! It's about time you sorted your life out! Gearóid is horrified by it all – Mick and Harry under the same roof – both courting the same girl!"

"Well – poor Gearóid!" Kitty's voice dripped sarcasm.

"I thought the whole Lionel situation was bad enough – but this! Harry thinks he's practically engaged to you!"

"Well, I didn't see Mick trying to say anything otherwise – did you? He just sat there the whole time looking on, without saying a word. He didn't even say goodbye this morning!"

"Mick was looking on as he was as confused as the rest of us and didn't want to make a bigger eejit of himself than he already has! As for 'looking on', as you put it, he was looking on consumed with jealousy, if you ask me!"

Kitty felt a little excited at this. "I didn't see any jealousy in Mick."

"Then you are blind. It was plain to see he was burning up with jealousy."

Kitty walked over to the couch and sat down. "If only I could believe that, Maud. If only he told me how he felt, what his intentions are ... I would know where I was. But it's like I'm hitting my head off a brick wall with him."

"Have you said this to him?" asked Maud.

"No, we don't have that kind of relationship – we have banter and rows and tease each other."

"Well, perhaps if you tried being honest with him, he could be honest back."

"Honest? The honest truth is that I'm mad about him – totally, crazily in love with him," said Kitty.

Maud's eyes opened wide in surprise.

"Why do you think I finished with Lionel?" said Kitty. "Why do you think I'm on such tenterhooks all the time? If the truth be told, I've been crazy about him since the beginning – but I didn't think he was interested in me."

"And what about Harry?"

"Sure I love Harry, who wouldn't? But it's a different kind of love. I'm at a crossroads, Maud, and I don't know what to do … on one side I have Mick, who I am mad about, but everyone and my own instincts tell me not to trust him and that he will not settle down … on the other side I have Harry, who will offer me the happy loving life that everyone deserves … and he will probably be my last chance of getting it."

"Oh, Kitty!" sighed Maud as she came to her sister, sat down beside her and put her arm around her to comfort her.

As Gearóid drove through the country roads back to Dublin, the conversation alternated between talking about the banal to lapsing into long silences. Gearóid felt if he had a knife he could cut the air it was that thick and so unlike the usual closeness and camaraderie that had always existed between Michael and Harry.

During another long bout of silence, Michael suddenly said, "Pull over the car."

"What?" asked Gearóid confused.

"Just pull over the car now to side of the road," ordered Michael.

Gearóid, like everyone, had been so used to living under the fear of attack during the war that he suddenly panicked, thinking that Michael had spotted some threat. He pulled over.

"What is it?" asked Gearóid, looking anxiously around.

"Gearóid – go for a walk," ordered Michael.

"A walk! We are in the middle of nowhere ... where to?" cried Gearóid as he looked around the open countryside.

"I couldn't give a fuck!" snarled Michael, pushing him out of the automobile. "Give Harry and me some space and don't come back until you hear me calling you!"

"Oh!" said Gearóid, suddenly becoming aware of what was going on. He quickly started to stroll off down the road.

Michael got out of the automobile and said to Harry, "We need to talk!"

"We are going to be late meeting Dev! We've no time to spare for chats on the side of the road."

"Fuck Dev! We are going to have this out!" said Michael.

Harry got out of the back of the automobile.

"I understand Kitty has – finally – told you what's been going on?" said Michael.

"Well, she told me ... she said you two had got ... close."

"Yes! So why are you pretending nothing has happened?" demanded Michael, getting angrier.

Suddenly Harry's calm demeanour evaporated. "Well, how the fuck do you expect me to act?"

"I don't know! Angry – sad – furious – give me a punch in the face – but not to fucking pretend nothing has happened!"

"Well, of course I'm fucking angry – more *dismayed* – that you went after my girl as soon as my back was turned!"

"Harry ..."

Michael had rehearsed many things to say but now, face to face with Harry, none of them felt right.

"Harry, there is no explanation for how things happened between Kitty and ... and me."

"Yes, it's all a bit of a mystery to be sure!" Harry's voice dripped sarcasm.

"I always liked Kitty, you know that. Sure we started off on an even playing field when we both went in pursuit of her. I was as interested in her as you were."

"Yes, but that was a long time ago. Then you were smitten with Helen, don't deny it – so what's Kitty – the consolation prize?"

Michael's forehead creased with hurt and his eyes filled with tears. "That's fucking low!"

"Low? You accuse me of being low?" Harry looked at him with contempt. "I wonder what Helen makes of all this?"

"Helen's married. I'd say she doesn't think anything of it one way or the other."

"I wouldn't be too sure of that – I'd say she thinks it's as bizarre as I do – there's you jumping from one sister to the other and then there's Kitty jumping from one friend to the other! Hard to keep up with the antics going on around here – and they think they're a wild bunch in Manhattan! You lot could teach them a thing or two!"

"Neither of us ever wanted to hurt you – sure both Kitty and I think the world of you, you know that."

"I do surely!"

Michael's face crumpled. "The look of hatred on your face ... I never thought I'd see you looking like that at me! And I have nobody to blame but myself."

He went and sat down at the side of the road on the grass verge, his head lowered.

Harry sighed loudly and went over to sit beside him. He put his arm around him. "Oh, you big eejit ... what a mess you got us all into ... I don't hate you, Mick, sure that would be impossible for me to do."

"I'd have never intentionally hurt you, Harry. Kitty and I just fell in love."

Harry looked alarmed. "Love? That isn't love, what you and Kitty have ... I have no doubt in my mind that she is in love with me and that she will decide to marry me as was the plan all along before you."

Michael looked at him, stunned. "But Kitty and I –"

"Are over. Sure, how could a lady like Kitty Kiernan ever be happy with you, Mick? Look at yourself, running around cracking jokes one minute, crying your heart out the next. Kissing babies one minute, ordering the killing of British Tans the next. She'd never know where she was with you. She'd never be happy with you."

Harry's words reminded Michael of what Helen had said to him when he had pleaded with her to leave her fiancé for him. And now he was being told the same thing about Kitty.

"I don't say these things to be cruel to you, Mick, but for you to understand. There's somebody out there for you, I'm sure there must be, somebody the same as you who gets overly excited about things – *everything* – as you do. But that's not Kitty. For Kitty, you are like one of those characters in those romantic novels she is always reading. But sure that's not real life, that's escapism. And Kitty is realising that now before she gets in any deeper with you. As for you, you just want what is unobtainable. You were like that with Helen and you are like that with Kitty. You've built her up into something she's not as well, just because you see me and other men desperate to marry her ... but that's not where love comes from, Mick. Love doesn't come from envy, it comes from the heart."

Harry's words were like slaps across the face to Michael and, despite feeling crushed by both Harry's words and his own guilt, something was stirring deep inside of him. A defiance, a will to battle and to fight for what he wanted.

"Well, Harry, you know me very well," said Michael. "And you might be describing me very well. But, if you know me, then you know I'm a fighter. I'll never give in and I'll never walk away. So we'll see who Kitty chooses – it's her choice at the end of the day." He put his hand out for Harry to shake.

Harry looked at his hand and then reached forward and shook it. "And let's make our own truce and our own treaty ... whoever Kitty chooses, we will remain the best of friends."

"Agreed," said Michael.

CHAPTER 31

After the departure of Michael and Harry, Kitty decided she needed a break away from everything, not least Maud's constant questioning. She went to Donegal for a few days' holiday. Her friends there knew nothing about her relationship with either Michael or Harry so she could just relax.

As August slipped into September, she took long walks along the coast and the cliffs on her own. She could at last allow herself to think as she walked along with just the seagulls crying as they soared in the blue sky above her. She stood looking out at the ocean at the top of a cliff. Across that ocean lay America where Harry had been and where he had invited her to go with him. But she had said no at the time and that she would wait for him. She doubted she would have been able to say no to Michael if he had proposed such a thing. And there laid her answer, she thought. She loved Michael, and she would be just settling for Harry. But unless she could get Michael to commit, and if she lost Harry in the meantime, she could be left with nothing.

When she arrived back in Longford, there was a stack of letters from Harry waiting for her. As she riffled through them she saw that he was professing undying love for her, planning their life together, assuring her that he would make her the happiest woman in the world. He reminded her that he was going on official business to Scotland to meet the British prime minister and that as soon as he was back in Ireland he would visit her.

* * *

Once Harry returned from Scotland, he was summoned to meet De Valera. The trip had not gone smoothly. Harry had been given strict instructions to hand the correspondence to Lloyd George and then leave. However, Lloyd George had requested him to stay while he read it. As expected, once Lloyd George had seen De Valera refer to himself as the president of a free and independent Ireland, he had erupted in anger and the mission to secure a new round of treaty talks nearly collapsed before agreement to start it began. Harry, with some frantic diplomatic skills, had managed to finally smooth the matter over and now the new round of talks was due to start the following month, in October, in London.

As Harry walked into the De Valera 's study, Éamon did not look to be in a good mood.

"So – we are all set for the next round of negotiations, Éamon," said Harry once they had sat down. "Hopefully better luck this time!"

"Indeed," said Éamon, frowning. "Harry, when I sent you to Scotland I distinctly told you, without any fear of misunderstanding, to deliver my reply to Lloyd George and to leave immediately – did I not?"

"Yes," Harry said with a nod.

"You deliberately disobeyed my order. When Lloyd George asked you to stay until he had read my correspondence, you stayed – and thus nearly created a diplomatic incident."

"With respect, Éamon, I don't think it was me staying for tea and sandwiches that created the diplomatic incident but what you had written in your letter – declaring yourself president of a free and independent Ireland. We all knew Lloyd George would go mad when he read that – and I thought I'd better stay to try and smooth things over – which I did successfully."

"I fully expected Lloyd George's reaction and you undermined me by disobeying my order."

"I apologise if I did. But at least we are on course now for the next round of negotiations. I would like to request to travel to London to be part of our delegation."

Éamon waved his hand dismissively in the air. "That won't be happening."

"Why not?" said Harry.

"I have other plans for you."

"Which are?"

"You are to return to America to continue the excellent work you have been doing there."

"*America!*" Harry nearly jumped out of his seat in shock.

"Yes, you are to return by the end of this month, early next month at the latest."

"But – but I can't!"

"You can and you will," said Éamon.

"But you don't understand – I'm finished with America! I've spent the last three years there and I don't want to go back! I want to be home here in Ireland building our new country."

"You can best build our new country in America. It is a great privilege I am offering you – you will effectively be our first ambassador to America, with a very substantial salary."

"Fuck that! So I am to be the first ambassador and you the first president of a country that doesn't exist yet and may never do if these next set of negotiations fall through like the last!"

"Careful, Harry," warned Éamon.

Harry shook his head. "This is all because I disobeyed you in Scotland, isn't it?"

"The matter is no longer up for discussion," said Éamon.

"Dev – Éamon – please, you don't understand. I just can't go back – I have to be home – there's a woman, you see – Kitty, I told you about her – I just can't leave her again!"

"Take her with you then," said Éamon. "As your wife, of course."

"It's not that simple –"

"If she loves you, she'll go with you, Harry … it is simple … we all have to make personal sacrifices. I had to leave my wife and children as you know for my time in America. We just have to get on with it."

202

"Éamon – please!"

"Harry, please don't embarrass either of us by continuing with this display – it's hardly fitting for our first ambassador to America."

Harry turned and stared out the window in despair.

Michael made his way up the garden path to the De Valera home in Greystones and was surprised to see Harry coming out the front door. Harry looked angry and depressed as if there was a heavy cloud hanging over him.

"Harry! How was Scotland?"

"Fine," Harry said, avoiding eye contact.

"Is everything alright?"

"I'll talk to you later," said Harry, brushing past him.

Michael watched him leave, wondering was it Kitty or Dev who had put him in such a foul mood. He continued through the open door into the house and on to Éamon's study.

"What's the problem with Harry today?" he asked when they had settled down to talk.

"He didn't take the news he is being sent back to Washington very well."

"He's going back to America?" asked Michael, shocked.

"Mmmm ..."

"For how long?"

"For good."

Michael stared past Éamon almost in a trance, as a million thoughts went through his head. He had heard there had been some problem over in Scotland with the delivery of the letter to Lloyd George and that De Valera was not impressed. Obviously Éamon was taking his revenge by sending Harry into exile. Not just a lesson to Harry but a warning to the others not to contradict his orders.

As Éamon talked on, Michael was not listening as his thoughts were consumed by how this left the situation with Kitty. This now put a short timeframe on everything, and he feared he could lose Kitty for good if she was suddenly pushed into a situation. On the other hand, if Harry had to leave without anything being resolved, that would leave the field open for himself again.

"So – you will be travelling to London with the delegation," Éamon was saying

Michael was jolted out of his trance. "What are you talking about?"

"Were you not listening to a word I was saying? For the next treaty negotiation, I will not be going to London. You will be going in my place."

"*Me!*" shouted Michael at the top of his voice. "Forget it! I'm not going to London – no fucking way!"

"You have no choice, Michael. I need somebody of your calibre there."

"But, sure, why aren't you going yourself? Nobody is of your calibre – and certainly not me!"

"You flatter me and undermine yourself, Michael. I have every confidence in you that you can handle the negotiation with aplomb."

"Aplomb! But sure, I'm a soldier not a politician. I wouldn't know how to handle it – how to handle Lloyd George or Winston Churchill or any of them!" Michael was horrified by the prospect.

"You will have the others there supporting you – Arthur Griffith, Erskine Childers – all experienced men to assist and guide you."

"But – I can't do it, Éamon. I just can't. Apart from anything else, I'd be out in public view after all these years of hiding."

"The war is hopefully over for good and there will never be a need for you to hide again. I've made up my mind, Michael, and you may as well get used to the fact that you will be going to London. You will be part of the delegation and you will bring home a permanent peace and an independent republic of Ireland with you."

CHAPTER 32

Kitty stared at Harry in disbelief. They were seated in the parlour of the Kiernan house.

"But he can't do that – can he? Send you back to America?"

"He can and he will and I'm to leave very soon," he said.

"I – I don't know what to say. You've hardly been home for a month and now you're being sent off again." She shook her head in bewilderment and dismay.

He sat down quickly beside her. "But it doesn't change anything, Kitty."

"But of course it does, it changes everything."

"Not at all. I am being given a huge salary and a wonderful job as ambassador and –"

"In America!" she said.

"But we could be so happy there." He reached forward and grabbed her hands. "Oh, Kitty, if you saw it there you would love it – the stores are enormous, the buildings so tall, the automobiles so big and fast. We would be going to receptions all the time and parties and fundraisers – the Yanks would love you and together we could own the world."

"I don't know if I want to own the world." She pulled her hand back and gestured around the room. "This is my world, Harry, not the Waldorf Astoria Hotel."

"I won't be able to make it without you, Kitty. We can't let it happen again – being apart. Look what happened last time – we mightn't survive another parting."

"Well, clearly we wouldn't survive another parting," she muttered.

"That's why you have to come with me. Please, Kitty, I'm begging you – I'm no good without you – you just have to come with me. Do you understand, Kitty? I'm asking you to marry me."

As she looked into his face, she didn't know whether to hug him or run away from him. Her emotions were a mixture of pity and caring for him and being frightened of the intensity of his love.

"Does Mick know you're to go?" she asked.

"I presume he does," said Harry.

"Has he no say in this?"

"No – he has no say in anything anymore, now that Dev is back and running things. In fact, Mick is ordered to go to London in Éamon's place to lead the delegation for the treaty talks."

"*Mick* is! But sure that would be Mick's idea of hell – he wouldn't be able for all that!"

"Of course he isn't able for it – he's not like me, a natural-born politician," said Harry, seeing the opportunity to come out from under Michael's shadow. "But Dev is giving him no choice."

"But why is Dev doing that? Why isn't he going himself?"

"Who knows? No one holds his card closer to his chest than Dev."

"And why choose Mick of all people?"

"I don't know ... when he has experienced men like Childers and Griffith. It's a puzzle."

They fell silent for a while, Harry contemplating De Valera's machinations, Kitty focusing on her own situation.

At last Kitty spoke. "Harry?"

He looked at her intently.

"It's a huge thing you're asking of me, Harry. Not just marriage, but to leave my family and my friends and my whole life to start a new life abroad so far away from home ... it's terrifying."

"But you aren't saying no?" Harry's face ignited in hope.

"I'm saying I have to think about it, Harry."

"Of course!" He nodded, delighted he was not hearing a rejection. "It's your decision what you want to do. No matter what you decide, I know we'll always be friends – you, me, Mick – all of us together." He smiled at her and, taking her hands again, he clasped them in his.

Maud and Kitty were walking through the countryside as Kitty relayed to her the news about Harry's proposal, his imminent departure for America and Mick being sent to London in De Valera's place.

Maud was astonished. "And what does Mick have to say about it all?" she asked.

"I haven't heard from him. I imagine he is beside himself with worry over the talks in London."

"But what about you, Kitty – what about you and him?"

"He hasn't ever said he wanted to marry me – or anyone for that matter. I could be on a wild goose chase with him and let my real chance of happiness slip by with Harry."

"Well, why don't you confront Mick and then you'll know where you stand?"

"That wouldn't work with Mick. He needs to be in control all the time. Look, he knows where I am if he wants me – he knows Harry wants to marry me – so he had better act quickly if he doesn't want to lose me."

"My God!" Maud halted abruptly and, taking Kitty by the arms, pulled her around to face her. "You're laying a trap for Mick! You are trying to use Harry to force Mick's hand!"

"I'm not being that calculating, Maud. I haven't created this situation. If Mick wants me, I'm here for the taking ... if he does nothing, I'll know where I stand."

"If you love Mick, Kitty, you're playing a risky game. You could lose him altogether."

"I never had him altogether in the first place," Kitty said, and her thoughts drifted to Helen. "But I do know Mick doesn't want what he can get easily – he wants what he thinks he can't have."

As Kitty turned and continued to stroll down the country road, Maud stared after her, shaking her head in disbelief.

CHAPTER 33

The days and weeks of September sped by as Michael prepared to go to London. At the meetings of the Irish cabinet with De Valera, he felt overwhelmed. He had spent his life for so long in the shadows that he felt terrified at the thought of being in the full glare of everyone from the press to the government ministers to Lloyd George. Even with the truce, Michael steadfastly kept a low profile in Dublin, but he would be completely exposed in London. He tried to get De Valera to change his mind but there was no moving him. In the same way there was no moving him to change his mind about sending Harry back to America.

With everything going on, Michael had no time to visit Kitty or to think about what to do regarding her. But he had concluded that time wouldn't permit anything dramatic to happen between Harry and Kitty, his rival would be soon across the ocean again and things would have a chance to return to the way they were.

Michael saw Harry regularly at meetings but with the heated and frenzied political climate their communications did not have an opportunity to stretch to Kitty.

The date for Harry's departure by liner from Queenstown in County Cork was fixed for the first of October and there was a huge going-away party organised for him on the twenty-ninth of September in the Gresham Hotel.

"Let's keep to the terms of our own treaty tonight, Harry," said Michael as the two of them walked in the front door of the hotel and saw all their old friends and comrades there.

"What's that, Mick?"

Michael slapped his hand on Harry's back. "Let's not discuss politics tonight!"

"Agreed!"

It was a wild night.

"Just like old times!" shouted Harry across the dance floor to Michael as they swung around with their dance partners to the lively Irish accordion music.

"Indeed it is!" shouted Michael as he swirled the girl he was dancing with around the floor.

The old times, the times that both Harry and Michael were thinking of, were the early years in Longford when they first met the Kiernans – when they first met Kitty. When they never dreamed how things would develop.

It was after four and, apart from a few people who had passed out from booze, only Harry and Michael were still up as they lay stretched out on sofas, drinking beers.

Harry was wondering if he should go to bed at all as he planned to leave for Cork by train early the next morning, in order to give himself plenty of time in case of mishaps.

"I'm just thinking of last Christmas Eve," said Michael. "When I was nearly arrested here while I ate my dinner. I don't know how I got away with claiming to be an accountant!"

"And this time next week you will be meeting Prime Minister Lloyd George while I'll be in Washington," said Harry.

"I wish you weren't going," sighed Michael.

"So, do I! But that's what is to be. By Dev's dictate."

There was an elephant in the room and neither of them wanted to address it but finally Michael raised the courage and said, "How did Kitty take it? Your heading back to the States?"

Harry looked over at Michael and bit his lower lip. "She wasn't happy at first."

"It will be hard for you – leaving her again."

Harry looked at Michael and realised he thought that, with him returning to the States, he would now have a clear run with Kitty.

"She's coming over to me, Mick," he suddenly announced, sitting up.

"What?"

"I went down to see her and proposed marriage – and she accepted."

Michael sat up and silently stared at him.

"I'm sorry, Mick. I know it must come as a bit of a shock for you."

"Well, I'm disappointed for myself – but I'm happy for you, Harry, truly happy for you and Kitty." He reached his glass out to Harry.

Harry reached forward and clinked his glass against Michael's.

"No hard feelings?" asked Harry.

"No – I guess the best man won," said Michael and he managed to smile.

By the time Michael finally made his way up to his room in the Gresham it was five in the morning. He lay on the bed as he thought of Harry and Kitty's engagement. As the hours ticked by, he felt a loss. The loss of a life that he would now never know with Kitty – a life that had been held so tantalisingly close to him. And he felt he was losing much more than that ... not just Kitty, but Harry as well leaving for America. He felt the friendship was ending and all the good times they'd had with Kitty and Helen and Gearóid and Chrys – that the gang would now be pulled in so many different directions and life would never be the same again.

He suddenly jumped up, put on his coat, ran out of the hotel and grabbed a taxicab.

"Kingsbridge Station!" he shouted at the taxi driver.

Michael arrived at the station and waited at the entrance to the platform. It was seven thirty in the morning and he saw Harry arrive, walking quickly through the station carrying his suitcase.

"What are you doing here?" asked Harry, shocked to see him again.

"Sure, I couldn't let you go back to America without waving you off," said Michael.

"Thanks, Mick," said Harry, feeling moved, as they walked down the platform. The train was due to go to Cork, where Harry would get the liner.

"I suddenly had a thought that things will never be the same again," said Michael as they reached Harry's carriage.

"Things are never the same, Mick – every day brings a new change. Our mistake is when we think we can ever keep things the same." He climbed into the carriage and put his head out the window.

"And don't worry about anything here," said Michael. "As I said, I'm truly happy about you and Kitty."

"You're not too heartbroken?"

"I'll live!" called Michael as the train began to pull away from the station.

Harry waved out the window until the train gathered speed and Michael became a small speck on the platform. He then sat down, feeling scared at the lies he had told. But he had to tell them, he had to scare Michael away from Kitty. This was the only way he knew how.

CHAPTER 34

Kitty sat in the parlour looking through her post for that morning. She opened a letter and, not recognising the handwriting, turned the page to see who the writer was. It was Harry's mother. She had never met the woman or his family and was curious as to why she was writing to her. Her eyes widened as she continued to read the letter. To her shock, Harry's mother was under the impression that she had become engaged to her son! As Kitty read on her mouth dropped open as Harry's mother wished them all the luck in the world for their forthcoming wedded life together and said she was so looking forward to having her as a daughter-in-law.

Having finished reading the letter, Kitty crumpled the paper up in her fist.

Maud walked into the room. She had just returned from Dublin where she had been visiting Gearóid.

"I swear that train service is getting slower," she declared. "We had a delay for an hour on the line. I mean, they had excuses for the delays when the war was raging – what's their excuse now?" She stopped and stared at her sister. "Is everything alright, Kitty?"

"Did you see Mick in Dublin?"

"No. He's very busy arranging to go to London next week for the treaty negotiations," said Maud.

"Next week! But he might be gone for months … I need to see him urgently," said Kitty, standing and beginning to pace up and down frantically. "Can you get Gearóid to arrange for Mick to see me – it's urgent!"

"I'll try – but he's the busiest man in Ireland right now."

"He's always the busiest man in Ireland! Tell Gearóid to tell him it's a matter of life or death if he has to!"

The arrangements for the delegates going to London were being carried out at a frantic pace. The delegates were going to stay at Hans Place, but Michael insisted he wanted his own building for himself and his team and it was arranged for him and his people to stay at 15 Cadogan Place in Chelsea. The building was rented by the Irish government.

"I could be over there months with these fucking negotiations!" he declared to Gearóid who had just arrived. "I want my own place and to be with my own people, not having to watch my p's and q's all the time with the likes of Griffith and Childers!"

Gearóid laughed. "Don't blame you!"

"I don't want them carrying stories back to Dev and the others about me either," Michael confided. "I want to be able to have a bit of peace with people I can trust."

"Of course you do," agreed Gearóid. "But, listen, Mick, I have a message from Kitty for you – through Maud."

"Right – what is it?"

"She wants you to meet her."

"Meet her! But I'm going to London the day after tomorrow with the delegation!"

"Kitty says it's urgent. In fact, she called it 'a matter of life or death'."

"What? What's happened? What's it about?"

"Something about Harry. That's all Maud would say."

Michael stared, alarmed.

"Very well," he said at last. "I'll not be heading over with the delegates on Saturday – I'll need another couple of days in Ireland."

"What? But you can't do that, Mick! The British government is waiting!" Gearóid was shocked.

"The negotiations aren't starting until Tuesday – I'll travel over on the Monday."

"That's leaving everything to the very last minute!" Gearóid pointed out.

"It will have to fucking do! I have to meet Kitty."

Kitty could barely contain her nerves as she waited to hear back from Dublin. It was just her and Maud having breakfast that morning.

"Are you sure Gearóid delivered my message?" Kitty asked.

"For goodness' sake, Kitty!" said an exasperated Maud. "How many times do I have to say – yes! He did. Yesterday."

Molly came in and flung the morning's newspaper on the table.

Kitty picked it up and looked at the front page which was dominated by how the Irish delegation would be travelling to London the next morning.

"If you ask me – it's a waste of time!" declared Molly. "The British government will make mincemeat of our lads! Sure, how could our lads talk to the likes of Lloyd George and Churchill! They don't stand a chance! Sure, I've seen one or two of them sitting around this very table – they wouldn't inspire much confidence as the saviour of the nation!"

"Thank you, Molly – but we are not asking you!" snapped Maud.

Molly huffed and walked out of the room.

"She's getting worse!" declared Maud.

As Kitty studied the newspaper article, which was all about how Michael would be leading the delegation, she said, "What planet am I on? Thinking that Mick would drop all this to come and see me! I've lost him for good. I thought if I played it cool and Mick saw Harry chasing me, then he would come chasing me as well. Now I've lost him forever."

Tears trickled down her face as Maud reached over and comforted her.

Molly came sauntering into the room and announced, "Telegram!"

She flung it on the table beside the newspaper and walked out.

Kitty reached out, took the telegram and opened it.

"It's from Mick," she whispered. "He wants to see me."

CHAPTER 35

As time was so short and there was so much for Mick to still do before his departure for London, he could not travel to Longford. And as there was a frenzy of excitement with the newspapers trying to locate Michael before his departure to London, they decided to avoid Dublin. They hastily telegrammed each other, arranging to meet at the Grand Hotel in Greystones.

As Kitty travelled on the train, she remembered the last time she was there. It was just after the raid by the Black and Tans and the whole family had taken refuge there. Now she was travelling back nearly a year later, to try and save her life from imploding.

She booked into the hotel, changed into one of her most flattering dresses and waited for him in the hotel reception.

As the hours ticked by she became overcome with worry that he would not show.

"More tea, miss?" asked the waiter as he went to fill her cup and found the pot empty.

"No, I'm fine," she said, her voice nearly a whisper.

Suddenly the hotel front door swung open and Michael stormed in and looked around. Kitty rose to her feet. He looked at her and, hurrying to her, enveloped her in a hug.

That evening they walked along the beach. There was a chill in the air, and she wrapped her fur-lined coat close around her.

"I didn't think you'd come. I thought you'd have to be in London tomorrow," she said.

"I managed to wrangle another couple of days," said Michael. "What's this all about, Kitty? Why did you need to see me so urgently? What's this 'matter of life or death'?"

She stopped walking abruptly and turned to him. "I'm not engaged to Harry!" she said.

"What?"

"Did he tell you I was?"

"Yes! He told me the last night in Dublin that you were engaged," Michael stated as he stood, hands on hips, in front of her.

"Harry seems to have told everybody that we are engaged – but we aren't! I swear to you it's not true. It's wishful thinking on his part."

"Did he propose to you?"

"Yes, he did – but I didn't say yes."

"But you didn't tell him no either? Am I right?"

"I told him I needed to think about it," said Kitty.

"But what is there to think about?" demanded Michael, his temper rising. "You either want to marry him or you don't! We have an expression at home – piss or get off the pot!"

"But don't you see – can't you understand – I've been waiting for you! I've been waiting for you to say something – to tell me you love me – to tell me you want to marry me – to tell me something – *anything*!"

"Me? But, sure, since Harry came back, I've been made feel not welcome – that I was intruding on the two of you."

"Not by me! By Harry – maybe," said Kitty.

"He's my best friend and I didn't want to upset him if I thought there was no future between us two," Michael said.

"And if you did think there was a future – what then?" she demanded.

He stared at her and then blurted out. "Then – then I'd walk through fire for us to be together."

She blinked a few times and then went to him and held him. "Oh, Mick – that's all I needed to know. That you cared – I don't want anyone or anything else but you. Don't you know, I'm madly in love with you."

He held her tightly and kissed her.

That night, Kitty lay in Michael's arms on the couch beside the roaring fire in her room.

"I wish you had been a little more honest with me along the way – it might have saved us all time and heartache," said Michael.

"Well, how many hints did you need? When I broke off with Lionel and went running after you – wasn't that reason enough to think I might be in love with you?"

"All you ever did was mock me," said Michael with a laugh. "How was I supposed to know you cared?"

"You gave as good as you got, you big eejit! Besides – you were always so big-headed and full of yourself, I was too frightened to show how I felt in case it went to your head and you had no time for me anymore."

"You've been playing a lot of games," he said.

"And then I realised I nearly lost you for good."

"I'm so scared going to London. Having you here, waiting for me, will make me feel as if I'll be able to do my job there."

"I'll be here waiting for you, Mick – nothing will ever get in my way again." She sat up, her face growing anxious. "But what about Harry?"

"He'll be alright – he'll have all the women in America to choose from." Michael tried to make a joke of it.

"He did say that no matter who I chose it would never affect his friendship with either you or me," she said, her voice filled with hope that this might be true.

"Well, if Harry said it, he meant it," said Michael and then his eyes got a faraway look as he stared into the fire. "I wonder can you ever really be happy if your happiness is the cause of another person's misery?"

The next day Kitty sat brushing her hair at her dressing table in the hotel. She bit her lower lip as she thought of the previous night and how she had finally secured her relationship with Michael. She felt elated but terrified. Terrified that after coming so far she could lose him. She checked her appearance in the mirror and then left the room.

Downstairs, Michael was waiting for her in the restaurant for lunch, studying the menu, a bottle of red wine open before him.

"You look lovely," he said as she sat down.

A waiter approached. "Are you ready to order, sir?"

"Well, I'll be having the beef, but the lady needs some time to look over the menu." Michael looked at Kitty.

"The beef is fine for me as well," she said, smiling at him.

The waiter poured them each a glass of red wine before leaving.

"How long do we have?" asked Kitty.

"I should be getting back to Dublin before dark."

"How long will you be in London for?"

"Who can tell?" He shrugged.

"But it could be months. It might be months until I see you again . . . I can't go through this again, Mick. The way I did with Harry when he went to America. I can't live in this – limbo."

"But sure London isn't like America. If it drags out, you can visit easily and I can come back to see you."

"In the middle of negotiations with Lloyd George?" she asked sceptically. "I've spent too long waiting for men – waiting for Harry and for you – I just can't go through the waiting game any longer!"

"Well, don't wait then!" he said as his smile turned to a frown.

Her heart jumped with fear thinking she had pushed him too far. That she had pushed him away.

"What do you mean?" she asked, terrified of his answer.

"Marry me ... then you don't have to wait."

Her eyes widened in shock. "You're asking me ...?"

"I am asking you to marry me."

She jumped out of her chair, embraced him and kissed him. "Yes."

Michael had arranged for an automobile to take Kitty back to Longford that evening. As they stood in the forecourt of the hotel, another automobile was waiting to take Michael back to Dublin.

"I'll write to you every day," he said.

"Will you, Mick? Promise me? Even if you're so busy you can only write a short note – that will do me, just to know you are alright."

"But of course I'll be alright – aren't I the luckiest man, getting engaged to the most beautiful girl in the world?" He smiled at her.

"It's I am the lucky one," she said as she put her arms around him and kissed him.

"I'd better go. They'll be waiting for me in Dublin."

She nodded and whispered, "I love you, Mick."

"And I you." He smiled at her as he helped her into the back of the automobile and closed the door.

As the driver started the engine and they drove out of the forecourt, Kitty looked back at Michael standing there waving at her. She waved back at him until they turned the corner onto the open road.

She felt happier than she ever had in life. But she couldn't stop a feeling of terror overtaking her. She fought the overwhelming desire to tell the driver to turn back so she could beg Michael not to go to London.

CHAPTER 36

On the Monday, Michael and his party left Dublin for London. There was a large group of people travelling with him, from a publicity department to his squad of bodyguards to his assistants.

When they arrived in England they were met by a police escort who took them to a private train supplied by the British government to take them to London.

"If you need anything, then just call for us," said their constable. "We'll be in the front carriage."

"Thank you."

Michael watched them walk away before turning to Emmet and saying, "Keep two men posted at the door to our carriage – just in case."

The train began to depart from the station.

"We should have checked the train to make sure there isn't a bomb on it planted by Lloyd George," said Michael, only half in jest as he looked around the luxurious carriage.

"I wouldn't put anything past them," said his assistant Emmet.

"The British government would never do that," said their recently hired head of publicity, Malcom. "It would be a worldwide publicity disaster if anything happened to any of the Irish delegates while under the protection of the British government."

"Still, we are to remain on guard at all times." Michael pulled back his jacket to show the gun he had inside. "We could be a target for anyone from a disgruntled British soldier who served in Ireland to a lunatic released from an asylum. We have been this country's enemy for a long time and that still makes us targets – truce or no truce – particularly me as the press has focused on my part in waging the war."

"Speaking of the other delegates," said Emmet, "rumours have been circulating that some of them are angry that you are bringing such a large contingent of people and that you have chosen to stay in a separate house in Chelsea, apart from the main headquarters of the Irish delegation."

"I couldn't give a fuck if they are angry or not!" snarled Michael. "I don't want to even be fucking here – so I'll bloody well come on my own terms!"

Michael sat back and stared out at the countryside as it whizzed past.

The truth was he needed all these people, the people he relied on, who he had come to trust with his life over the years. He needed them around him to even be on that train. He was terrified of what lay ahead of him in London and he had no confidence that he would be capable of negotiating this treaty. The only thing that kept him strong was the thought of Kitty. They had agreed to keep their engagement secret. But he had to keep kicking himself to believe it. He was engaged to Kitty – he could soon begin to start living his life like normal people did.

As the train pulled into Euston Station the British police officers who had been travelling on the train entered Michael's carriage.

"We have a police protection unit waiting to escort you to Chelsea, Mr. Collins. Perhaps my men can work with –" the chief officer glanced disparagingly at Michael's squad of bodyguards lounging around the carriage, "with yours."

"It will be our pleasure!" called one of the bodyguards with a note of sarcasm in his voice.

As Michael looked out at the platform he saw it was thronged with people.

"We will have to move you quickly through the crowd, Mr. Collins, for your own safety," said the police officer.

When the train became stationary, he opened the carriage door.

Looking out at the sea of faces, Michael said "Who are all these people? What are they waiting for?"

"You! They're waiting for you, Mick!" said Malcom, whose face always seemed agitated, his demeanour always stressed, his attire always immaculate.

Michael was stunned at the size of the crowd.

"That's him! That must be Michael Collins!" screamed a woman and the gigantic crowd began to cheer and push forward.

Michael's bodyguards and the police quickly took control of the situation and he found himself being manoeuvred through the crowd.

People were calling his name and surging forward to try and touch him. The press was there in force and they struggled to get near him.

"How does it feel to be in London, Michael?" called a journalist.

"Bless you, Michael!" came a scream from the crowd.

As they approached the car, a pack of journalists were waiting there. Michael was pushed into the automobile by the policemen and his head of publicity got in beside him.

"Get me the fuck out of here!" Michael shouted at the police driver.

As the automobile started moving through the crowd people were jostling to get a view of him inside.

"You can't blame them, Mick," said Malcom. "You've been an enigma for years – a name they couldn't put a face to and suddenly here you are in full view."

"I spent years trying to hide my face and now they've all seen me," said Michael in despair.

"And the whole nation will see you tomorrow. You'll be on the front page of every newspaper."

"Did they give the other delegates this reception when they arrived?"

"No, but you're the one they wanted to see. You know, everyone expected to see some kind of monster and instead they got a matinee idol. You're going to be a star, Michael Collins."

Michael shook his head grimly. "It's a long way from Cork."

As the cavalcade of automobiles arrived at Cadogan Place in Chelsea, Michael was shocked to see another huge crowd gathered outside the house they were to stay in. The house, 15 Cadogan Gardens, was one in a row of very large five-storey buildings.

"I don't like all this," said Joe Dolan, one of Michael's bodyguards who sat beside him in the vehicle. "This is a massive security risk – there could be any number of assassins in that crowd."

Michael understood Joe's concerns. As one of Michael's infamous Squad, he had spent the last years protecting and making sure he was hidden from view and danger. To a man like Joe, what was happening in London went against everything he had been trained to do over the past number of years.

"We all need to calm down," said Malcolm. "For God's sake, don't get trigger-happy and end up shooting a journalist – we don't want a major diplomatic incident before we even sit down at the negotiating table!"

"Where did you find this prick?" Joe whispered to Michael, causing him to burst out laughing.

The automobile pulled up outside the house and the police who had been waiting there quickly pushed through the throng to open the car door. As Michael got out, he saw somebody had painted the words 'Collins the Murderer' across the pavement.

"Michael – give us a few words! Do you expect the talks to go well?" cried one of the newspapermen.

"It's best you give them a quote – otherwise they'll hang around the house for the rest of the day and night," whispered Malcom.

Michael nodded and, drawing a deep breath, turned on the steps leading into the house and faced the people. He raised a hand and the crowd fell silent in an instant.

"Thank you! This is what we've been fighting for!"

He stood there looking staring at this strange new world as the crowd erupted into full-throated cheering.

"Well, at least it's big enough anyway," said Michael as he looked around the spacious house.

"I apologise for the words painted on the footpath – we'll have them cleaned off at once," said the police officer.

"Pity you couldn't have cleaned them off before we arrived – some welcome!" snapped Joe.

The police officer ignored him. "If there is nothing else, I shall leave you in peace. My men will be positioned at the front of the house for your security. If you need anything, please let them know."

Once he had left, Michael said to Joe, "Search the whole house – make sure it's safe."

"Yes, Mick," said Joe. He and the other bodyguards dispersed around the house.

Michael wandered around from room to room.

"All clear!" announced Joe, finding Michael in a bedroom on the top floor.

Michael jumped in the air and landed on the beautiful big bed.

"I'll take this room!" he announced.

"Ah, you've taken the best views!" complained Joe, looking out the window.

Michael got off the bed and went over to the writing desk. He ran a finger over the beautiful writing paper waiting there. It would be from here he would write his letters to Kitty every evening.

"Let's see what there is to eat," he said.

As they scanned the larder Michael looked miserable.

"Eggs! And bread!" he said, disgusted. "That's all that's here!"

"Gone-off bread at that!" complained Kathleen, one of the secretaries, as she inspected it.

"Lloyd George supplies us with a police escort and doesn't think we might be starving when we arrive!" said Michael.

"Probably a British ploy – starve us so we are weak when the negotiations start tomorrow!" said Liam, one of the other bodyguards.

"Right!" said Michael, pulling up a chair and sitting down at the kitchen table. "Kathleen – take a note!"

Kathleen sat down at the table with her notebook and pen and waited anxiously to take dictation for Michael as she had done countless times before. All of Michael's party had gathered in the kitchen at this stage.

"One slab of beef – two turkeys – six chickens – potatoes, bags and bags of potatoes – vegetables, turnips, cauliflower, parsnips ..." Michael started laughing as he clapped his hands together. "One thing, lads, we won't arrive weak from hunger at Downing Street in the morning. What else do we need – wine, twelve bottles – beer, six crates – what else, lads?"

"Whiskey!" called one.

"Brandy!" cried another.

Kathleen stopped writing for a second, put up her hand and said, "Chocolate?"

All the bodyguards roared together. "*Yes – chocolate!*"

"Write it all down, Kathleen!" ordered Michael. "You'll just about make Harrods if you're quick. The police outside can give you a police escort up to Knightsbridge and bring back the shopping with you!"

"Well, they did say ask if we needed anything!" said Joe, bursting out laughing.

"I beg your pardon – Harrods? Is all this not going to cost a fortune?" said Malcom.

"Of course it is – but, as Ireland's Minister of Finance, I authorise payment," announced Michael.

"I'm not sure if the rest of the delegates staying at Hans Place would approve of the extravagance," said Malcom.

"That's their business – what to approve or not to approve of. I can guarantee you Lloyd George is dining on the best tonight – and so will we."

CHAPTER 37

The next morning Michael was in the drawing room in Cadogan Gardens riffling through paperwork with Kathleen and the other secretaries, preparing for the day ahead at Downing Street. The rest of the delegation in Hans Place would be collecting them on their way.

"Have you got that last memo from Dev, Kathleen?" asked Michael.

"Yes, it's filed in this briefcase," she confirmed.

Malcom came into the room with a load of newspapers under his arm.

He flung them down on the table in front of Michael.

"I just went down to the newspaper stand in Sloane Square – you got all the front pages – *The Times, Daily Mail, Daily Express* – the lot!"

Michael reached out for the newspapers and began to unfold them, his heart beating quickly as he saw his photograph on the front pages.

"For fuck's sake!" whispered Michael.

"You're famous, Mick!" said Kathleen excitedly.

"I never expected – never wanted this," mumbled Michael.

As he looked around at his excited secretaries, typists and bodyguards poring over the newspapers, he knew they couldn't understand the turmoil this was causing for him. They were the people he was closest to in the world, friendships forged through the fighting of a war over the past few years. But he still couldn't confide in them his feelings on feeling totally exposed and vulnerable with this publicity. It was because he was their leader – they expected him to be strong and belligerent – he couldn't let that image ever slip in front of them. If they ever saw him as vulnerable and weak, then they too would feel vulnerable and weak and the cause would be lost.

"Will you clear this shite away from me!" he said, sweeping the newspapers on the floor. "I have to get my notes ready to meet Lloyd George and I have no time to be admiring myself in newspapers!"

Everyone in the room erupted in laughter as they promptly continued with their work.

"*They're here!*" shouted Joe, looking out the window.

"Right!" nodded Michael, standing up and going to look out the window. A row of automobiles was waiting there. "I'm to travel in the first car with Griffith and Childers. Joe, Liam, Kathleen – there's room for the three of ye in the last automobile. The rest of ye remain here."

Michael bit his lower lip as he saw there was a large crowd gathered outside again and the press were waiting.

He went to the front door and breathed in deeply.

"Best of luck, Mick!" said one of the typists as she leaned up and kissed his cheek. "We're all depending on you – we all believe in you."

"Thanks, Mary," he whispered and winked at her before nodding at Joe to open the door.

Michael walked confidently down the steps.

"*There he is!*" shouted a journalist and there was a rush towards him.

The police were either side of him as he strode confidently towards the first car in the procession. A woman suddenly broke free of the crowd and raced to him – flinging her arms around him, she kissed him.

Michael looked at her, startled, as the police manhandled her away and ushered him into the front automobile.

Arthur Griffith and Erskine Childers were seated inside, Arthur looking every bit the statesman with his large moustache and spectacles and sincere face. Although he was only fifty, he seemed older than his years, and Michael worried that the strain over the past few years had taken its toll on his health. Erskine always seemed to have a permanent pained look on his stern face. Today his sharp features were set in an uncompromising expression.

"Good morning, Michael, so glad you could join us!" said Arthur with a bemused air.

"This place is a bloody circus!" said Michael as the automobile drove away with the crowd rushing after them.

As the cavalcade of automobiles made its way through London to Downing Street, the footpaths along the way were teeming with well-wishers. Michael looked out the window in awe at everyone from schoolchildren to adults clapping and cheering or waving Irish flags or banners. Priests and nuns were praying along the route while choirs sang.

"Where have all these people come from?" gasped Michael.

"Most of them are Irish, I would say," said Arthur, looking out at them.

"Or communists!" joked Erskine.

"Is there anyone left in Ireland or are they all here for the day!" exclaimed Michael. "We can't let them down this time ... we just can't. We have to bring an everlasting peace."

"Well, it takes two sides to make an everlasting peace, Michael," said Erskine.

"Well, give them a wave, Michael – that's what they want from you!" urged Arthur.

Michael looked at Arthur, startled, but nervously waved out the window to the crowd's delight and applause.

The cavalcade arrived into Downing Street which was teeming with police.

"Best foot forward!" said Michael as their automobile pulled up in front of 10 Downing Street and a policeman opened the door. Michael got out and looked up at the building. Then he strode across the pavement to the front door.

CHAPTER 38

Hazel sat in the drawing room with Alice, looking at Michael's photograph in the newspapers.

"He's very handsome," commented Alice.

"Isn't he just?" agreed Hazel, studying the photograph up close. "He would make a wonderful subject for John to paint."

"He still hasn't agreed?"

"No. I am up against a brick wall every time I reach out to him and Erskine Childers." She picked up a copy of Erskine Childers' novel *The Riddle of The Sands* on the table beside her. "I wouldn't mind but I've read Childers' novel again – for the tenth time! And I keep gushing in my letters to him about how much I enjoy his writing – but still no response! You'd think he would at least have the respect to reply as one artist to another!"

"Well, never mind Erskine Childers, Mama – it's Collins who is the prize!"

"Well, I give up on him!" Hazel threw her hands up in the air. "I think I've tried everything. I wrote again yesterday to his accommodation in Cadogan Gardens but expect no reply. All I can say is he is a very rude man!"

Alice giggled at her mother taking offence at a man's rudeness when half of the country was describing him as a murderer.

Hazel set her mouth in a tight thin line. "But I will not give up, Alice. I have one last trick up my sleeve. He had a sister living in Kensington as I recall. As often is the case – the best way to a man is through a woman!"

* * *

That evening Michael sat at the writing desk in his bedroom at Cadogan Gardens writing a letter to Kitty.

... so, when we went through the front door at Downing Street, there were all these formal-looking staff there looking at us as if we fell down from another planet. After some small talk we were shown upstairs into this big boardroom. And waiting there was the Prime Minister and the others – Churchill, Birkenhead and the rest. So, we Irish were at one end of the room and they on the other and nobody was saying anything. We just stared uncomfortably at each other – enemies facing each other. Then Lloyd George took control and, breaking the impasse, he walked across the room with his hand outstretched and shook all our hands. Then we all sat down and started setting out our stall. It feels very strange being here. I feel like a fish out of water. I wish I was with you walking the fields around your home place.

Suddenly there was a shout from downstairs. "*Mick!*"

Michael got up and went to the door and opened it. "*What is it?*"

"*Dinner's served – come down while it's hot!*"

"*I'll be right down!*" Michael shouted back and then he went to the desk and finished off the letter, signed his name and placed the letter in an envelope.

He then came bounding out of the room, down the flights of stairs and into the dining room where everyone was in great form, sitting down to a turkey dinner.

"Will you get that in the post tomorrow, please?" said Michael, handing the letter to Kathleen.

"I will surely," nodded Kathleen, taking the envelope. "Incidentally, another request has come from the artist John Lavery to paint your portrait."

"Oh, tell him to fuck off! As if I have time for a portrait!"

"Well, you will be the only one in the delegation not to accept –

except for Erskine Childers who says he will not have any fraternisation with the enemy while he's here!"

"Is John Lavery the enemy?" Michael asked. "I thought we had given him and his wife security clearance?"

"As a British lord, Lavery is deemed the enemy in Erskine's mind," Kathleen said with a smile.

Michael raised his eyes to heaven. "Move up, will you?" he said, grabbing a chair and making room for himself. He looked at the beautiful display of food on the table and the happy faces around it.

"This is a bit like a holiday, Mick!" said one of the typists.

"Well," said Michael, clapping his hands together and then taking a knife to the turkey, "we may as well enjoy ourselves since we are here!"

That night the drink flowed as a party started up. Accordions and a fiddle came out and they all danced around the drawing room.

As Michael opened another bottle of whiskey, Malcom said despairingly, "How are you going to have a clear head to negotiate in the morning with the Prime Minister?"

"I tell you, the last thing you need is a clear head when you're talking with that man!" joked Michael as he downed another glass.

CHAPTER 39

Those first few days in London passed in a spin for Michael. The negotiations with the British cabinet were slow, bogged down in detail with neither side willing to budge an inch. Michael quickly realised why the original negotiations with De Valera had collapsed so quickly. When he wasn't at Downing Street, he remained in the safety of the house in Cadogan Gardens. He was too intimidated to even step outside the door as journalists were waiting there to pounce on him.

His sister Hannie visited often and that evening she was laying out his clothes for the next morning.

Michael was at the writing desk, writing to Kitty.

"You could do with buying a couple of new suits," Hannie said.

"*Hmmm* – least of my worries," grumbled Michael.

"You can't let the side down, Michael. You don't want to be seen in the same suit too many times. You have to –"

"Put my best foot forward. I know!"

"Is it Kitty you are writing to?"

"I am – if you would ever give me a bit of peace to concentrate!"

"So, when will we get to meet the future Mrs. Michael Collins?"

"We just want to keep it private for now. There's too much going on. And there's Harry to consider – we want to tell him in person and not have him read it in a newspaper."

"The whole scenario is rather complicated, but she sounds like a lovely girl anyway! Oh, by the way – I got this letter in the post from Lady Lavery."

She laid an envelope on the desk in front of him.

"*What?*"

"Yes, she tracked down my address. She met you years ago when you were working for the Post Office here and going to the theatre with the Solicitor to the Post Office, Crompton Llewelyn Davies, and his wife Moya. She remembered you had a sister living in Kensington. She wants you to pose for a painting to be part of this Irish collection they're working on."

"Oh, I know, I know! She's managed to inveigle all the others – except Childers – into posing. She's very persistent, I must say – coming at me now through you!" He took out the letter and scanned it.

"She's a great lady, very connected – she's always in the magazines. She knows everyone in society and is offering her home once again to you and the delegates as a home from home."

"Sure, I have a home from home here in Cadogan Gardens with all my best friends and people around me here – and you. Why would I want to be going to –" he picked up the letter and peered at the address, "5 Cromwell Place to be amongst posh strangers?"

"Well, I think you should at least consider allowing them to paint your portrait, Michael. It's not every day you get the chance to have your portrait done by a world-famous artist. Mam and Dad would have loved it – they would have been so proud to have their son painted by one such as John Lavery." She bent down and kissed his head before turning to go. "I'll be off now. Will you try and get an early night? I'm hearing stories there's wild parties going on here every night!"

"They're lying!" Michael called after her, laughing loudly.

"*Hummh!*" Hannie grunted as she left.

Michael sat back, took up Lady Lavery's letter and began to read through it properly.

CHAPTER 40

The doorbell sounded through 5 Cromwell Place as Gordon hurried up from the kitchen downstairs, putting on his blazer. He quickly smoothed his hair as he passed the huge mirror in the hall – then he unbolted the front door and opened it.

"Good afternoon, sir – may I help you?"

Gordon observed a large automobile in which three unsavoury and suspicious-looking men sat staring up at the house.

"Is Sir John Lavery home?"

"Who may I say is calling?"

"Who is it, Gordon?" came a soft female voice.

Hazel Lavery came walking down the wide staircase at the back of the hall.

"*Michael Collins!*" she cried, her voice filled with delighted surprise as she walked to the front door and gently pushed Gordon aside.

As Hazel and Michael stared at each other, Gordon didn't know what to do or say.

"Shall I inform Sir John that Mr. Collins is here, my lady?" he asked.

"Yes – yes," said Hazel, waving him away with her hand.

Gordon bowed and left.

"Do you remember me?" Hazel asked, staring into Michael's face.

"Yes – yes, I do now," Michael said, nodding. Indeed he remembered the stunning woman who used always be centre-stage among the theatre crowd he used to occasionally meet. Of course she hadn't been 'Lady Lavery' then, so he had never imagined it was the same woman. What perplexed him was how she remembered him, a post office clerk from many years before.

"Do come in!" said Hazel, stepping aside and beckoning him in.

Michael paused, turned to his men waiting in the automobile and nodded to them. He entered the house and Hazel closed the door. He glanced down the huge hallway with the impressive stairs and the balcony that stretched around the landing upstairs.

"I had nearly given up on your ever agreeing to come," said Hazel.

He turned to her and said, "I'm sorry for ignoring the invitation before – it's just been very hectic since I arrived. It's been like stepping into a circus."

"Or a zoo!" She smiled sympathetically at him.

He smiled back. "That's probably a better analogy. And I'm the caged animal they all have come to see."

"You poor thing, I can't imagine how unsettling it is for you," she said.

Her face creased with such genuine concern that he didn't know how to react. He was so used to dealing with sarcasm and wisecracks at best, aggression at worst, that genuine kindness from a stranger felt uncomfortable.

They stared, each studying the other intently.

Suddenly there was a click of heels and John was hurrying down the staircase, fastening his cufflinks.

"I could scarcely believe it when Gordon informed me you were here," he said as he hurried down the hallway to them with an outstretched hand. "My dear fellow, it is a pleasure and an honour to meet you."

Michael reached out and they shook hands.

"What kind of hostess am I, leaving you standing in the hallway?" said Hazel. "Gordon, will you bring tea to the drawing room for Mr. Collins, please?"

"That won't be necessary – I'm afraid I don't have that much time," said Michael. He turned to John. "You said you needed just three hours to do the portrait?"

"Ah, yes – if that is all your schedule allows then I can have the portrait mostly completed in that time."

"Mostly?" asked Michael.

"Well, yes – later I can work on anything further that needs to be done."

Michael stood awkwardly in the hallway, as if undecided.

"Did you want to sit now?" John asked.

"Yes, if that's alright."

"Certainly. Shall we make our way to the studio?"

Michael nodded and followed him down the hallway and up the staircase as Hazel walked alongside him.

"How are you finding Cadogan Gardens?" she asked.

"Very nice," nodded Michael. "Roomy."

"They are splendid buildings there," said Hazel.

Even as seasoned a hostess as Hazel was finding Michael hard work. Having been struck initially by his aura and presence, she realised he was very uncomfortable to be there, and his eyes kept darting around nervously checking out the building.

They reached the top of the stairs and crossed over the landing and into the studio. Michael was taken aback with the room's size and grandeur and marvelled at the glass ceiling. As he walked around the room, he stopped to admire a huge painting of Hazel dressed in a cream gown.

"If you could sit there, please," asked John, pointing to a chair.

Michael turned and walked to the chair. He was going to sit but then stopped and moved the chair to a different position.

"If you don't mind, I'd prefer this angle," he said.

"Well, the light isn't as good ..." said John, perplexed. Then he realised that Michael had moved the chair to face the door. He didn't want to have his back to it. "But that position is fine – whatever you are most comfortable with ... although, please do try to relax, Mr. Collins. I have entertained prime ministers, royalty and film stars here and am glad to say I have not lost a single one to an assassin yet!"

236

"There's always a first time!" said Michael as he sat down.

As he sat, Hazel saw the nozzle of a handgun in the inside pocket of his jacket.

John went and set up the canvas as Michael shifted uncomfortably in the chair.

John nodded at Hazel. This was her cue to leave.

"I just have to catch up with my post – if you need anything, please let me know." She smiled at Michael.

"Thank you," said Michael.

Hazel turned and, as she passed John, smiled encouragingly at him.

Once out on the landing, she closed the double doors to the studio behind her and leaned against them. Out of all the guests they'd had there, she could hardly believe she had Michael Collins. He had such incredible magnetism that she felt relieved to be out of the room – and yet at the same time she wanted to turn and rush straight back in again. She walked slowly across to the drawing room.

Hazel looked at the clock. They had been in the studio for two hours and there had not been a peep. She had kept expecting them to call for tea and refreshments, as always happened during one of John's sittings, but this time the call never came. Finally, she quickly got to her feet. She couldn't wait any more.

She swung open the drawing-room doors and quickly walked to the studio. Knocking on the door, she opened it and entered.

Michael was still on the chair, fidgeting and moving around. He looked even more uncomfortable than when she had left him. She walked across the room to the canvas John was working on. When she reached it, she got a shock as there was hardly any work done.

She looked at John for an explanation, but he just shrugged.

"He won't sit still for a minute," he muttered.

"Oh dear," she murmured.

She went over to Michael who was at that point straining his neck to look out a window, then pulled up a chair and sat next to him.

"How are you finding the sitting, Michael?" she asked.

"Terrible! British intelligence could use this as a new form of torture – they would crack our men every time!"

Hazel laughed loudly. "It's really not that bad," she said. "It's like anything – you just need to know how."

"Easy for you to say – how many portraits and magazines have you sat for?" He gestured to the many paintings of Hazel dotted around the studio.

"Quite a few, I will admit. Well, it's always a bit daunting to sit for a portrait as in doing so we are exposing ourselves. We are showing a part of us that we never show the world. The artist is capturing our soul almost … and not many of us feel comfortable with that. You are moving around today a lot because you are resisting your soul being laid bare … but there is nothing to fear, Michael. Just relax and it will be a wonderful experience for you, I promise you."

"And how do you – relax?"

"When I first started sitting for my portrait I used to think back to when I was a child … I used to lose myself in memories of when I grew up in Chicago … I used to think of my parents and my sister and suddenly I'd forget I was in a studio." As she spoke, her eyes misted over. "I'd think of the happy times we all had together … my parents were always so busy and the house was full of people … they were important socialites … often they would be out late at night and wouldn't be home until way past our bedtimes. Sometimes I would wake and hear my sister, Dorothy, crying … she would call for Mama or Papa, but they wouldn't be home yet. And I would get up and tiptoe past our governess's room and into Dorothy's room and get into her bed …" Hazel's eyes welled up with tears as she continued to speak, "and I would take Dorothy in my arms, like this," she cradled her arms together, "and I would sing her a lullaby as I gently rocked her until she fell asleep in my arms."

Michael looked at Hazel in astonishment, engrossed by her story, as a tear slipped down her cheek. He sat absolutely still, his own eyes welling up as he fought the overriding desire to reach out to the beautiful woman and comfort her. He could see there was a terrible pain there and he wanted to know what it was and comfort her.

As Michael sat absolutely still, John quickly sketched on the canvas.

Hazel led Michael down the staircase once the sitting was over. They had left John in the studio where he continued to feverishly work on the portrait.

"Are you sure you can't be tempted to stay for tea – or even dinner?" she offered.

"No, thank you. I'd better be getting back. Besides, my lads have been sitting outside for hours – they will be going mad with boredom!"

"I see."

They reached the bottom of the stairs and walked across the hallway to the front door where they halted and faced each other.

"So that is now all the Irish delegates caught on canvas," said Hazel. "Apart from the continued exception of Mr. Erskine Childers!"

"Ah, I think you'll never get him in here – he would not succumb – not even to the great charms of Lady Lavery!" Michael's voice dripped sarcasm.

But the sarcasm was lost on Hazel. "Oh dear! Such a pity!" she said.

He looked at her, puzzled. He usually used wit and sarcasm with women, and found they enjoyed giving as good as they got. But Hazel seemed not to work like that.

"Childers has sworn off fraternising with the enemy," said Michael.

"Well, I am not the enemy," said Hazel, looking hurt. "I'm his friend, if he let me be. I'm friend to all of you – if you could just understand that I want to help – and I am in a position to help. The Irish cause is very dear to me – it means everything to me."

"It's just hard to understand a great lady like you, with no real connections to modern Ireland, wanting to identify herself so much with us ... I don't say that to be cruel or rude, but just to try to understand."

"Yes, I do identify with you – I have even converted to Catholicism. Michael, Ireland runs through my veins as much as yours – I won't be shut out or worn down or frightened off. I'm in it for the long haul."

He stared at her with a sense of awe and wonder.

"So, if you need anything – anything at all – you come here to me," she said. "You know where I am now."

"Thank you," he said, opening the door. He paused. "You've converted to Catholicism, you say. You know, I'm not very religious, but I promised a priest before I left Dublin that I would attend Mass every morning and pray for success. I go to the Brompton Oratory – just up the road from here – for eight o'clock Mass. Do you ever go there?"

"Yes, I do – it's such a wonderful church."

"Well, I might see you there," he said with a grin as he walked out.

She watched him hurry out and into the waiting automobile. Then suddenly they were gone.

She turned around and closed the door then leaned against it, her mind spinning.

She had been mesmerised by Michael. Shocked by the power his presence exerted on her.

He had sat for his portrait now and she should draw a line under it and him. But she knew she couldn't – his magnetism was too powerful.

All that evening Michael couldn't get Hazel out of his head. The way she had walked down the staircase when he saw her first with the light from the window at the top of the landing streaming down around her. She had looked magical. Her beauty had stunned him, and almost frightened him. Her confidence and allure and the way she had told the story from her childhood ... He had never given Lady Lavery a thought previously, except to wonder was she a British spy. Now he realised what all the fuss was about and why she had London society at her feet.

He sat at the bureau in his bedroom, writing a letter to Kitty. He described having his portrait done that day. He smiled to himself as he knew that would entertain Kitty much more than any descriptions of the events that were unfolding in Downing Street each day during the negotiations.

He put down his pen and looked out the window as his thoughts switched back to Hazel.

"*Mick – dinner is served!*" came a shout from downstairs.

"*Coming!*" he replied.

He smiled to himself. He expected it to be another evening and night of high jinks. The fun they were all having at Cadogan Gardens was immense and he was so glad he had insisted on his own house for his own people. He could only imagine the austere and dutiful atmosphere up at Hans Place where the other delegates were staying. His staff, his people, worked bloody hard, were dedicated to the cause, were completely trustworthy and loyal, and deserved to have time in the evenings when they could unwind and enjoy themselves. He had ordered several more hampers from Harrods that day.

CHAPTER 41

Hazel attended Mass next morning at the Brompton Oratory. She entered the magnificent church, chose a pew and kept alert, looking to see if Michael would attend. To her delight she saw him arrive in just before the priest came out on the altar. He sat across the aisle from her, spotted her and gave a small wave over. She smiled and gave a discreet wave back as the organ music began to play.

As the Mass ended and the priest left the altar, Hazel stepped out onto the aisle and waited for Michael to join her.

"What an amazing church and wonderful Mass," he said.

"I find it so," she replied.

They walked down the aisle and out onto the street.

"What time are you in Downing Street today?" she asked.

"Eleven. Can I offer you a lift home?" He pointed to his automobile which had two of his bodyguards waiting inside.

"It's only a few minutes' walk and it's such a nice morning I thought I'd stroll back," she said. "Would you like to join me – if you have time?"

"Yes, I would, thank you," he said, and signalled to the driver to follow them at a distance.

They walked on side by side.

"How is the portrait?" asked Michael.

"Excellent! John is very pleased with it, he says."

Michael was wearing a trilby hat and kept his head down as his eyes darted from right to left.

"You should not be scared of your fame, Michael," she said.

"It's not fame I'm afraid of but an assassin's bullet!"

"Yes, it must be very unsettling. You are in a unique position of being loved by so many and hated by so many as well."

"Unique isn't the word I'd use for it!" smirked Michael.

"But I do also think you are frightened of the fame that you have found – or rather the fame that has found you. But it is an asset and you should use it."

"How?"

"Fame is power. I should know, I've had it long enough. It has brought me to where I want to go, given me access to people and places ... and your fame will do the same for you, if you use it correctly and wisely."

"I don't think fame is an asset – it's a curse. Having people chase you around all the time – it's awful!"

"It's just very intense and new for you. But it's power, Michael, never underestimate that. Everyone wants to know you and know about you – that's a huge advantage in dealing with Lloyd George and the British delegation."

"In what way?"

"Each headline and article that appears of you in a newspaper adds to your power. They can't ignore you, not when you command that much attention. It's your currency and only a few people have the ability to get it. I've had it myself for many years and you have it now. Use it wisely."

"I could be on the front page of the newspapers every day of my life and Lloyd George wouldn't respect me. Every time I walk in to meet them, I feel their eyes on me, Churchill and Birkenhead, looking down on me – seeing me as a peasant boy."

"Winston and Birkenhead are aristocrats who see you as a murderer and the enemy – they always will, unless they get to know you personally and you can prove otherwise. Lloyd George has a lot more in common with you than you might think. His father died when he was young, like yours, and he was brought up by a widowed mother like you. He is Welsh, a fellow Celt, who worked up the ladder like you. He was even involved in having the Welsh get Home Rule when he was younger. He's more a kindred spirit of yours than you think, Michael!"

"I never looked at it like that. I just see this bunch of toffs looking down on me."

"You must never let them see or sense that. If they sense that, they will smell blood. These are incredibly experienced negotiators. Lloyd George is fresh from the Versailles Treaty for goodness' sake! They will try and take advantage of your youth and relative inexperience. But they are also frightened of you, Michael. You cracked British Intelligence and reduced it to a laughingstock. They know how intelligent you are – and you should never stop reminding them of your intelligence either!"

They turned into Cromwell Place from Brompton Road.

"Ah, here we are – home! Won't you come in for breakfast?" she asked.

"No, I'd better be on my way – but, thank you, Hazel. Thank you for the advice."

"It's my pleasure," she said, smiling at him.

He turned and signalled. His automobile zoomed up beside him and he jumped into the back.

He smiled and waved at Hazel as she stood at her front door and rang the bell.

All Hazel could do for the rest of the day was think about Michael. She had actively pursued him for so long that it seemed surreal that she had finally managed to have captured him for the portrait. Like everyone else she had built up this impression of what Michael would be like. The most surprising thing was that at the back of her mind she had expected to be disappointed when she had finally got to meet him. He had been built up to be such an enigma that he could hardly be anything but a disappointment. The fact that not only was he not a disappointment but surpassed even the wildest exaggerations of her imagination left Hazel feeling intoxicated and exhilarated.

Hazel looked in awe at John's portrait of Michael in his studio.

"Well – is it a good likeness?" he asked.

"You know it is," whispered Hazel. "It's wonderful. It captures him perfectly – the determination, the vision, the sincerity mixed with the slightest tinge of vulnerability."

"I am just glad the fellow managed to sit still long enough for me to paint him! Imagine, having finally got Collins into my studio I was unable to paint him as he had ants in his pants!"

"I believe it is just his nature. He was the same when I walked back with him from Mass this morning. It's only to be expected when he has been living as a fugitive for so long."

"You met him at Mass this morning?"

"Yes, at the Brompton Oratory. I think I shall attend tomorrow morning as well."

John shook his head in amusement. "This newfound religious zeal has nothing to do with your determination to be the first hostess in London to land Mr. Collins as a dinner guest?"

"Well, the competition is intense out there, John! A girl's got to do what a girl's got to do! I've even heard Edith wants to meet him now!"

"*Paah!* Edith may want but it will be over Charlie's dead body that a Fenian will ever get over the threshold of Londonderry House!"

"You might be surprised, John!"

CHAPTER 42

The next morning Hazel sat in a pew before Mass at the Brompton Oratory, anxiously looking out for Michael. She couldn't see him and, as the priest walked on to the altar and the congregation stood, she felt her heart sink in disappointment. Suddenly a large figure stepped into the pew and she looked up to see Michael there standing beside her. They exchanged warm smiles and blessed themselves as the Mass began.

Afterwards, Michael walked Hazel back to Cromwell Place again.

"It is like we are at an impasse with the negotiations," he said. "Lloyd George is very good at making you feel he is giving you what you want when in fact he is giving you the crumbs off the table and keeping everything for himself!"

"Yes, well, that's why they call him the Welsh Wizard. His skills in negotiation are extremely well honed after Versailles and I imagine he thinks of the Irish delegation as easy pickings after what he had to deal with there. When I first met him I came away from the meeting under the impression he had agreed with everything I said, only to find out a couple days later that he was only pacifying me and didn't agree with me at all!"

"So how do you deal with somebody like that?" questioned Michael, his own mind searching for an answer.

"My impression of Lloyd George is that he is pragmatic. He wants peace in Ireland, but he told me that he cannot give Ireland independence because it would mark the beginning of the end of the empire. Full Irish independence then is something he just cannot possibly give."

"And anything less is not acceptable to us," sighed Michael.

"Hence the impasse!" said Hazel as they reached her front door. "Won't you come and see the portrait – it's almost finished now."

Michael glanced back at Joe trailing them in the automobile and nodded. "I'd love to see it."

Michael looked at his portrait in amazement. "I think you're flattering me, Sir John!"

"If anything, it doesn't do you justice!" said Hazel.

"Now *you're* flattering me!" said Michael.

"I'm very pleased with it," said John. "And please dispense with the formalities – my name is John."

"Alright – John," agreed Michael.

"We are just about to have breakfast – won't you join us?" urged Hazel, an almost pleading look on her face.

He glanced at his watch. "I'd love to. But my men, they haven't eaten yet."

"Gordon will make sure they are all taken care of, I can assure you!" gushed Hazel.

As Hazel, John and Michael sat having a breakfast of scrambled eggs and bacon, Michael looked around at the splendid room which was on the ground floor with views to the street in front as well as the gardens to the rear. But he was wishing he was back in the Kiernan house having a slap-up breakfast with Kitty and her family. Where he could be himself and relax and have a laugh at their daft maid Molly.

"More tea?" asked Hazel, not waiting for the answer as she filled his cup. "As I've said before, please feel free to come here any time to have your breakfast, lunch or dinner."

"We have an excellent cook who likes to be kept busy so, as Hazel says, please do avail!" said John.

"I imagine you haven't been taking care of yourself since arriving in London," said Hazel. "With your busy schedule, you've probably been skipping mealtimes."

As Michael thought of the constant bills arriving from Harrods, he smiled to himself, thinking nothing could be further from the truth.

"You are very kind," he said, smiling at both of them.

"I've been thinking about the impasse you speak of," said Hazel. "I honestly don't think it will be broken over the conference table at Downing Street. It is too formal, too intimidating for both sides. I'm going to suggest a dinner party here and invite you all – although I'd say I won't get Lloyd George to attend – he'll be too wary of how it might look. But I am sure I can get Winston and Lord Birkenhead – and certainly Winston's secretary Eddie Marsh and Lloyd George's private secretary Philip Sassoon – both dear friends of mine. The private secretaries are often the eyes and ears of their bosses – they hold great sway."

"I'm not very good at big social occasions," Michael said. "I wouldn't know what to say to such people socially."

"Michael!" Hazel reached out and put her hand on his for a second, causing both of them to be startled by the touch. "This is my very point! How can you expect to strike a deal and find common ground if both sides are not prepared to get to know each other – as men – as people!"

"Hazel is right," said John. "And we could pepper the guest list with some leading figures from the arts. J.M. Barrie and George Bernard Shaw if they available, amongst others. What do you think, Michael?"

"That would be interesting," he said, brightening. "I admire both of them."

"Excellent."

"You are a statesman now, Michael – and a very important one," said Hazel. "You can't hide away and be socially shy or awkward. Let us be honest, Arthur Griffith is supposed to be chairman of the Irish delegation, but he is tired and older. It is you who need to take command and who everyone expects to take command. You are a future leader – Prime Minister, President, call it what you will – of Ireland once independence is achieved."

"President!" Michael looked at her, shocked. "It's Dev is

President, Hazel! I'm just the military, a soldier!"

"You forget I have met De Valera last summer and I can assure you, Michael, you stand head and shoulders over him as a future leader. Now accept your destiny and begin to prepare for it!" She slammed her fist on the table.

Michael looked at her in shock. He didn't know if she was deluded, insincere or prophetic. However, her words and the way she delivered them were making him excited. He was seeing himself in a new light. While he looked at Hazel as she continued to speak in an animated fashion about him, her eyes widening in excitement, her hands dancing in the air, he felt hugely flattered that a woman as beautiful, connected and intelligent as her would think so highly of him.

She clicked her fingers as she pointed at his suit. "Clothes!"

He looked down at his suit. "What about them?"

"Your suits are perfectly adequate. But do you want to be – perfectly adequate? As an international statesman, you should be arriving in Downing Street in top tailored suits."

"That is what Lloyd George and Winston will be wearing," John said.

"I shall take you to Bond Street shopping," said Hazel.

"*Clothes maketh the man!*" said John.

"My sister Hannie was suggesting the same thing," said Michael as he looked down at his suit.

"A wise woman!" remarked Hazel.

"I wonder, Hazel, if I could ask a favour of you?" said Michael.

"Anything!"

"I wonder could you take a look through all of these and see what's what?" He reached into his inside pocket, took out a stack of cards and handed them to her. "I was going to give them to one of my secretaries to go through – but, sure, they would only know as much about London society as I do!"

Hazel riffled through the cards. "Invitations to openings, galas, dinner parties ..." She pulled a card from the bunch. "Cordelia Wrighton! An invitation to her house for a dinner party!"

"Yes – do you know her?"

"Of course I do – as does half the regiment of the Grenadier Guards! No, no, no to Cordelia! That is not an association you want to make, I can assure you! Cordelia would do anything to get her face in the newspaper. She has about as much interest in Irish affairs as I have in learning Swahili!"

Michael burst out laughing.

"Leave Cordelia and these others to me – I will see you right, rest assured!" said Hazel.

Hazel stood at the front door and waved Michael off. She closed the door behind her and slowly walked down the hallway. John came out of the dining room.

"When he reached into his inside jacket pocket, I froze for a moment, thinking he was reaching for a gun and might shoot us!" said John. "I was relieved when he just produced those invitation cards!"

"*Tut-tut*, John!" Hazel was not amused by his comment.

"You love it, don't you?" he said, smiling at her.

"Love what?"

"Taking a cause or a politician under your wing. It reminds me of when I get a new subject to paint – it kind of takes one over." He laughed as he headed up the stairs to his studio.

Hazel bit her lower lip as she admitted to herself that Michael was far more than a 'new subject'. She could not understand the feelings he was stirring in her, but she could not wait to go to the Brompton Oratory the next morning to see him at Mass again.

Later that morning, when Michael arrived at Downing Street, his thoughts were preoccupied not with the treaty but with Hazel. He had never met somebody who believed in him so much before. He couldn't imagine Kitty speaking to him like that – she would be too conscious of giving him a big head. But here in London, like a fish out of water, he was in no danger of getting a big head. He hadn't realised it before, but he desperately needed support and unconditional encouragement such as Hazel was giving him.

As he stepped out of the automobile and saw the crowd of people and journalists waiting there for him as usual, he didn't scurry into No. 10 as he always had before. He took his time. He smiled at them. He held his head high and even flicked back his hair as he had always done at home but had forgotten how to do in London. Waving at the press, he headed indoors.

"Absolutely not!" Winston Churchill said in a dismissive and angry fashion, causing the other diners in the restaurant at Claridge's hotel to look over at the table where Winston was dining with Hazel.

"But why ever not, Winston?" asked Hazel.

"Because I have no desire to break bread with a man who has ordered the killing of countless of our proud army. I would choke on my pudding!"

"I don't think there is anything to be proud of about the Black and Tans, Winston! A ragbag of rejects and ex-prisoners you cobbled together and let loose on Ireland. It's an insult to the brave British army who won the Great War to be associated with them!"

"This is utterly untrue! I am shocked to hear you parrot that unfounded rumour! The so-called 'Black and Tans' are ex-army veterans who themselves fought in the Great War. And I am very surprised at you, Lady Lavery, the wife of a knight of this realm, having Michael Collins and the rest to dinner at such a salubrious salon as yours!"

"I don't know why you are surprised – we've already had them all to have their portraits painted and I have given them an open invitation since the negotiations began."

"You are playing with fire, Hazel," Winston warned.

"Well, then so is your private secretary as he has accepted my invitation."

"Eddie! Eddie Marsh is going to this – this – debacle?" Winston was outraged.

"He most certainly is. And don't you dare try to intimidate him or force him to decline at this stage, or you will have me to answer to. You are behind the times, Winston. Dinner with Michael Collins is a hot ticket."

"You can say that again!" snapped Winston.

"Half the society ladies in London have pleaded with him to attend their events – including a royal." "I've always been of the opinion that half the society ladies in London are quite mad – you have just confirmed my long-held suspicions!"

"Be serious, Winston, for a moment. You've met Michael Collins quite a few times now at the conference table – what is your opinion of him?"

"Well, he's just a – an intelligent, I'll give him that – passionate – ambitious – peasant boy!"

"Winston! Michael is so much more than that, and you know it! He's the acting Minister for Finance in Ireland. And he brought the British empire to its knees!"

"In my opinion, he's a lout. He has no breeding, he is emotional –"

"Emotional?"

"Yes, very emotional … at the conference table, he gets too worked up. Too emotional!"

"Well, he's not a cold fish like the rest of you! And that's his strength, Winston. Can't you see how the public can't get enough of him? He's got quality – and if you don't see that soon and embrace it, then all will be lost with your treaty!"

"He might not be a cold fish, but he is a fish out of water. He's dangerous, Hazel. He's like a bomb ready to go off – and anybody who is standing too close will get caught in that explosion. And it will explode one day, Hazel, make no mistake about that. You have been warned."

Hazel was sitting at the desk in her living room as she went through the invitations for the party. Gordon stood waiting.

"I think that is everyone – a nice eclectic mix. I always find the best ingredient for a successful night is to have as varied an invitation list as a menu! Speaking of which – Cook is fully versed?"

"Yes, my lady – all is in hand," Gordon confirmed.

"Good. I know we are well used to entertaining, Gordon, but I cannot stress how important it is that everything is perfect for this night."

"Have no doubt it will be perfect, my lady."

"Gosh, is that the time?" she said, looking up at the clock and spinning out of her chair. "I'm meeting Michael at Savile Row in half an hour!"

Hazel sat in the elegant tailor's establishment in Savile Row as Michael was measured for suits and the staff displayed different materials.

"Oh, yes, that's perfect," said Hazel as she reached over and felt one cloth. "Don't you think, Michael?"

"It all looks a bit the same to me – black is black no matter how you look at it!"

"But it's the quality of the tailoring and material that matters, Michael. Having said that, I get your point." She turned to the store manager. "Can we see something in pinstripe and navy and black tie as well. And the black tie *must* be ready by Friday."

"Very good, Lady Lavery. We shall be back with a selection shortly," said the manager as he and his staff scurried off to search for different materials.

Michael sat down on the armchair beside Hazel.

"You will look dashing – dashing, I tell you!" said Hazel.

"I'll take your word for it," Michael said, raising his eyes to heaven.

She leaned towards him conspiratorially. "Unfortunately, I could not get Winston to agree to come to the dinner, try as I did. Same for Lloyd George, though I never thought he would come anyway, but their private secretaries and a lot of their cohorts will be there – so these are the men – and women – that you need to impress. Winston and Birkenhead have huge prejudices against you, seeing you as little more than a terrorist despite the publicity you are receiving in London."

"Or because of it!" retorted Michael.

She leaned even closer and lowered her voice. "I've heard back – through my sources – that they see you as being somewhat emotional at the conference table."

"Emotional?" He was shocked.

"Shouting one minute, nearly crying the next," she explained.

"That's me! I don't pretend to be a cold fish – I wear my heart on my sleeve!"

"Darling, treaty negotiations are not the place to wear your heart on your sleeve. It's a place where you should keep your cards close to your chest. It all adds up to you not being seen as a safe pair of hands for a new republic to be left in. If you want to convince the British that Ireland can stand on its own two feet as an independent and sovereign nation, then you need to come across as capable of leading that nation without falling apart!"

Michael stared at the wall in front of him as he thought hard.

"This party is a perfect opportunity to show your warmth and strength – to show the real wonderful you," she said as she reached forward and squeezed his hand.

"Don't forget – Friday morning is the latest for the delivery for that black-tie suit!" said Hazel as she and Michael left the store.

"It will be ready, Lady Lavery," promised the manager.

Joe and Liam were waiting in the automobile outside the store. Parked in front of them was Hazel's luxury Armstrong Siddeley automobile.

As she made her way to her vehicle Michael gave a long low whistle.

"Is this yours?" he asked, circling the car as he inspected it.

"It sure is," she said as she got into the driver's seat.

"Where's your chauffeur?"

"I rarely use one. I am quite capable of driving myself – even in high heels!"

Michael burst out laughing.

"Hop in and I'll give you a lift back," she said.

"But what about the lads?"

"They can follow us!"

"I'm getting a lift back with the lady, lads. You can do what you want!" Michael shouted back at them before jumping into the passenger seat.

"Hold on tight!" advised Hazel as they took off down the street.

CHAPTER 43

It was the night of the party and Michael had changed into his black-tie suit. He sat at his bureau to quickly write a letter to Kitty. He managed to write just a few lines before realising he would be late if he didn't leave. He signed off the letter and stuffed it in an envelope before sliding it into his inside pocket, hurrying out of the room and downstairs.

"Is it Rudolph Valentino?" called one of the bodyguards.

"No, more like Douglas Fairbanks Junior!" called another.

"Is that a fact?" said Michael. It was hard to know if he was angry or not. "We'll see who'll be laughing in a minute!"

Suddenly he jumped on one of the bodyguards and wrestled him to the floor.

"You'll ruin your suit, Mick!" cried Kathleen.

"Sorry, sorry!" pleaded the bodyguard, laughing.

Michael released him and stood up.

"You look great, Mick. Do us proud!" Kathleen whispered to him.

"Thanks, Kathleen." He pulled out the envelope. "Get this in the post in the morning, please."

"Alright," she said, taking the envelope.

The bodyguards who Michael had been jesting with a couple of minutes before were suddenly serious as they escorted him out of the building and into the automobile to take him to Cromwell Place.

Kitty glanced down at the envelope, already knowing what

255

address would be on it: *Miss Kitty Kiernan, The Greville Arms Hotel, Longford, County Longford, Ireland.*

Hardly one day had gone by without Michael posting a letter to this woman. And as Kathleen sorted his post each day, she knew he received a letter each day from the same writer. She knew, or strongly suspected this writer was Michael's sweetheart, but for such an emotionally open man, he never talked about it and Kathleen suspected that the love story between Mick and this woman was not that straightforward.

Kathleen had heard the others in the house begin to gossip about this woman, Lady Lavery, as well. They said Michael met her at Mass each morning and that he had become a regular visitor to her home. One of the bodyguards said she was stunningly beautiful and she seemed to have cast a spell over Michael. Kathleen didn't know what was going on, but she hoped Michael knew what he was doing.

The drawing room at Cromwell Place was filled with elegant guests. But out of all the well-known and famous faces that had gathered there, there was only one person who everybody was interested in meeting and that was Michael Collins.

Hazel led Michael around the drawing room and introduced him.

"Michael, this is James, better known as J.M. Barrie, creator of Peter Pan. I take it you know it was the nephew of your acquaintance Crompton Llewelyn Davies who inspired the character of Peter?"

"I am so pleased to meet you, Michael. I've been following your adventures in the press since you arrived in London," said James, shaking his hand.

"Adventures? You make me sound like Peter Pan myself!" said Michael, causing those around him to laugh.

"Now *your* adventures, Michael, are something I would very dearly like to hear first-hand!" said James.

"Do not tell him a word, Michael!" ordered Hazel good-naturedly. "Unless you want to end up being cast as a hero in one of his books!"

"As long as I'm cast as a hero, then I don't mind. It's being continually cast as a villain that I object to," said Michael and again the crowd around him burst out laughing.

John circulated amongst the guests as well, entering into small talk with them.

"I hear your portrait of Mr. Collins is outstanding," said Thelma, their well-heeled neighbour at Cromwell Place.

"Thank you, Thelma," said John. "I was just grateful to have the opportunity to paint it."

Thelma watched Hazel and Michael intently as they mingled with the guests.

"They do make a handsome couple, don't they?" she said, her eyes narrowing.

John blinked a few times as he looked across at Hazel and Michael.

"I do admire you, John, I really do," said Thelma.

"In what way, Thelma?"

"Your tolerance ... the never-ever-ending amount of men Hazel continues to parade in front of you – and they get younger and more attractive all the time!"

Thelma put down her empty glass on a console table and walked away, leaving John staring at Hazel as she laughed with Michael.

Gordon went hurrying from the drawing room and down the hallway where he encountered two footmen carrying trays of food aloft.

"As soon as you have served those, get more champagne opened and start refilling glasses!" he ordered, his face stressed.

"Yes, sir!" said the footmen as they hurried into the drawing room.

"Michael, try this beluga caviar!" said Hazel as she scooped some up and handed it to him.

"Do you like beluga caviar, Michael?" asked a guest.

Michael took the caviar and ate it before saying, "I do now!" causing everyone to laugh.

Hazel left Michael's side and went over to Shane Leslie who

was busy helping himself to lobster though his eyes never left Michael.

"Well, Shane – what do you think?" asked Hazel leaning against a sideboard and crossing her arms as she too observed Michael entertain her guests.

"I think he is charming – absolutely charming!" said Shane.

"Isn't he just?" said Hazel, her eyes twinkling as she stared at Michael.

"And I must say, with no doubt a little instruction from you, he has taken to socialising with the crème de la crème like a fish to water," said Shane.

"This is how we win peace, Shane."

"Through caviar and champagne?" he said sarcastically.

"Through getting to know the other side and not seeing them as ogres ... alas, I could not convince Winston to come, or Birkenhead for that matter ... and as for Lloyd George!" Hazel rolled her eyes.

"Well, I have no doubt there are enough of their friends here to report back every detail – and, I daresay, although they would never admit it even to themselves, they will be a tad jealous they missed the night. I, for one, cannot wait to tell cousin Winston about everything!" He smirked at her.

"Dear Shane, what would I do without you?" She kissed his cheek.

He moved closer to her and put a hand on her shoulder. "Let's leave this lot for a while, Hazel, and find a private corner."

His hand moved down her back.

"Shane! You are incorrigible – don't you ever give up!" she said as she moved away. "I'd better get back to my guest of honour."

"Oh, that's what he is now, is he?" said Shane, allowing the jealousy to show on his face. "I wonder, if dear Mr. Collins placed his hand on your behind, would you be quite so quick to remove it?"

Hazel rolled her eyes again. "Maybe a little less of the champagne for now, Shane? And more of the caviar. You'll thank me in the morning for that advice."

He watched as she walked away from him through the crowd, making a beeline for Michael. He grabbed another glass of champagne from a passing footman as he watched Michael and Hazel laughing together.

After a while, Hazel felt guilty that she might have been neglecting the other Irish delegates and forced herself to leave Michael's side and go chat to them.

Thelma then managed to join the group of people surrounding Michael and gently elbowed the others around him away until she had cornered him in a one-to-one conversation.

"Of course I've always had a keen interest in Irish affairs," she said. "We were once due to go on holiday to Killarney. But – alas – then the troubles broke out, so we had to go to Normandy instead."

"Really?" said Michael as he watched Hazel deep in conversation with Arthur Griffith.

To Thelma's frustration, no matter how much she tried to use her beguiling beauty, she kept losing Michael's attention as his eyes kept wandering in Hazel's direction.

"She's not as young as she looks, you know," she eventually said out of frustration.

"I'm sorry?" asked Michael, his eyes darting back to her.

"Hazel! I have it on very good authority from a friend in Chicago who knew her as a child that she is – in fact – past forty!"

Michael blinked several times. He was not sure if he was more shocked by this revelation of Hazel's supposed age, as she did indeed look closer to thirty, or by Thelma's glorious act of bitchy betrayal of her hostess.

"Also – this 'quotation' that is always being bandied about – that she was known as *the most beautiful girl in the Midwest* is poppycock! I have it on, again, good authority, that Hazel invented the compliment about herself!"

Michael's mouth dropped open. He was indeed more shocked by Thelma's bitchy betrayal than any revelations about Hazel.

Thelma moved closer to him, took a card from her purse and discreetly placed it in his pocket as she whispered, "I, however, am genuinely your own age. My address is on the card, I live just across the road. My husband is never home between three and six. I am home every day at that time. If you should ever be passing …" She licked her red-glossed lips before turning and meandering through the crowd.

Michael watched her walk away, stunned.

"She's quite simply amazing, isn't she?" said a voice beside him and he turned to see the speaker was Shane Leslie.

"Thelma?" Michael asked in confusion.

"No! Of course not! I am referring to Hazel," said Shane as he nodded across the room to Hazel who had a circle of men, including the Irish delegates, gathered around her hanging on her every word.

"Eh – yes, Hazel is a wonderful lady," Michael agreed.

"Have you and her –" Shane winked at him, "yet?"

"What are you talking about?" demanded Michael.

"Oh, come on, I'm sure even a good Catholic boy like you couldn't resist that particular temptation. And you wouldn't be the first – or I daresay the last!"

"I think you've been drinking too much," said Michael, his voice low and menacing.

"She has a notorious reputation. She's a maneater. She collects men like others collect hats. Don't flatter yourself, dear boy – you are only the latest in a long line. To be discarded once the new fashion comes in with the next season. This season it is you, next season it will be some young writer from the sticks or artist from the provinces that she feels the need to take under her wing and propel to the top of society and then take the credit for having discovered them." He saw Michael's face fill with anger and started to laugh. "Oh, dear boy, surely you didn't think you might be something special to her? You are merely this year's fashion accessory!"

Michael's fists began to tighten as he felt his anger rise. Then he suddenly remembered Hazel's words of advice. That Churchill had described him as too passionate, too temperamental. If he allowed himself to explode in anger here, he would destroy his reputation for good in front of London society and more importantly the British cabinet when they heard reports.

He forced himself to calm down. Then he leaned close to Shane and whispered to him with a smile, "Have you ever shared her bed?"

Shane looked surprised by the question. "No – no, I haven't."

"I thought as much. Sounds like a lot of jealousy and sour grapes from you if she chose all these others over you. And they say hell hath no fury like a *woman* scorned!" Michael gave a loud bellowing laugh before he clapped Shane on the back and quickly left his side to go mingle with the other guests.

The party continued until the early hours of the morning. Finally, Hazel waved off the last of the guests and closed the front door behind them. Only Michael remained – he was in the drawing room speaking with John.

"Gordon, there is no need for you to stay up," she said. "I'm sure you're exhausted after the night."

"But what about Mr. Collins, my lady?"

"I think I'll be able to show him to the door myself," said Hazel.

"My lady, if it's all the same to you, I would prefer to remain up until the gentleman has left the premises."

Hazel turned and looked at him in surprise, realising that Gordon was afraid of having Michael in the house.

"You believe too much what they write in the newspapers, Gordon – I really do insist you retire to bed! There is no need for you to remain up."

"But –"

"Mr. Collins is a friend, Gordon, and I expect you and all the other staff to extend the same courtesy to him as you do to all our other guests."

"Very good, my lady."

She watched him turn and walk down the stairs to the basement. She shook her head in puzzlement. How was she expected to lead the British establishment to accept Michael when her own servants did not?

Once she reached the top of the stairs, she turned to the right and went down the corridor into the drawing room where Michael was sitting on one couch and John on another.

"What a night!" Hazel declared as she walked over to the drinks table. "Whiskey, everybody?"

"Not for me, Hazel! I'm exhausted!" said John.

She poured two tumblers of whiskies. Handing one to Michael, she sat down on the other couch beside John.

"You poor thing – you do look exhausted," she said to him.

"I am, rather. I might trot off to bed – if no one objects?"

"Of course not!" said Hazel as she kissed his forehead.

John rose and Michael jumped to his feet.

"It's probably time I was on my way as well," said Michael. "I don't want to outstay my welcome."

"No, no! You sit down," said John, putting a hand on Michael's shoulder. "Hazel is a very late-to-bed person, so she will be glad of the company no doubt."

"John's right," she smiled. "Early to bed and early to rise was never my motto! I'm often not seen out of my bedroom until after noon!"

Michael thought her comment curious as she had been at eight o'clock Mass each morning that week.

"Goodnight, Michael," said John with a smile.

"Goodnight, sir," nodded Michael.

"Poor John!" sighed Hazel once he had left them alone. "I really don't know how he puts up with me! He's not one of life's great socialisers and he has earned the reputation of being a socialite simply by virtue of being married to me!"

"John doesn't enjoy all the partying?" Michael was incredulous, given the couple's reputation.

"Not really. If it was up to him, he would prefer a much quieter life. He's often been known to nod off at parties."

"Why does he go to them and host them then?"

"Well, he tolerates a lot of it because of me. But, as well as that, he's far from stupid and realises that the networking done at them is essential to his work as a celebrity portraitist, and a part of him enjoys the mixing with the upper crust and being part of the establishment."

"The upper crust!" Michael grunted dismissively.

"Michael – you were wonderful tonight! You carried yourself like a true statesman. I was very proud. And Winston and Lloyd George will be impressed when they hear it all reported back, I can assure you."

"Maybe they were impressed by me – but I wasn't impressed by some of them," he said, reaching into his pocket and taking out the card with Thelma's address on it and throwing it into the fire.

"Did someone upset you?" she asked, sitting forward, full of concern.

"It's not that they upset me, but I didn't like what some of them were saying," he said.

"About what?" she pushed.

"All I'll say is – some of those people here tonight aren't as good friends to you as you may think they are!"

Her face relaxed as it dawned on her what had occurred, and she sat back laughing.

"What's so funny?" he asked.

"Oh, Michael – don't let the idle gossip worry you – I can assure you I never have!"

"You would if they knew what they were saying about you!" he said.

"But I do know what they say about me – and I couldn't care less! Let me guess – that I have slept with half of London? That I am a scarlet woman that no man is safe around? That I use and abuse and move on to my next prey?" She hooted with laughter again. "Michael, not that it is anyone's business, but I assure you none of it is true. Secondly, you have to understand how British high society works in order to survive it."

"What's there to understand?"

"It's not just commonplace but expected that husbands and wives have affairs. So many take lovers, it is the norm! And as long as nobody ever does anything too public, conceives an obviously illegitimate child or ends up in the divorce courts over a scandal – then a blind eye is turned to it all! People just assume that I am like the rest. The fact I get so much attention and am pursued by so many bloody husbands, they can't bear to think that I never have!"

"But – but – does it not bother you them telling all those lies about you?"

"Not a jot! It's all a game, Michael, and I'm trying to teach you the rules."

"Well, we don't play games like that where I come from!" But as he thought of the tangled relationships he and Kitty had had, he realised that was not the truth.

"I doubt that is true, Michael," she said with a smile.

"Maybe not," he conceded. "But does it not bother John what they say about his wife?"

"I don't think so. He never has said it does. He knows it's part of the territory and besides," she said with a chuckle, "I think he feels a sense of pride that so many are interested in his wife."

"If you were my wife, I wouldn't stand for it for a moment!" he said, his face reddening with anger. "I'd sort out anyone who said anything about you in one minute flat!"

Hazel stared across at him and felt her own face blush with excitement and delight at his words.

They stared at each other as the shadows of the flames from the fire danced on the walls around the room.

"And I'd be very proud to have you defend my honour," she said softly and smiled at him.

Michael took his glass of whiskey and drained it.

"That Shane Leslie gets on my nerves!" he said. "I know he's a big supporter of us and has powerful friends, but he's no gentleman!"

"I think Shane would be insulted if anyone ever did refer to him as a gentleman! Shane is fine, Michael, a good friend. I know he's been in love with me for years, however conceited I may sound saying that."

"I know, I could tell!"

"He thinks one day we will become lovers. But he is deluded. I will never be with him. If I did such a thing, I would no longer have the power I have – the mystery would be over and my power along with it. But I've fought too long and too hard to be with John to ever risk my marriage for a fling with the likes of Shane Leslie."

He stared at her, his admiration of her growing even more.

"I'd better go – the lads will be exhausted waiting out in the car for me," he said, getting up.

"I'll walk you down," she said.

They walked in silence out of the room and down the stairs until they reached the front door. She unbolted it and, as Michael stood in the doorway, Joe and Liam jumped out of the automobile. Liam stood scanning the street up and down while Joe opened the back door of the car for him.

"I'm glad tomorrow is Saturday, with no negotiations," Michael said.

"Yes – a day off for you."

"Mass in the morning at the Brompton Oratory? Or will you still be in your bed?"

"Well, it's Sunday so let's go to a later Mass – if that suits?"

He laughed. "Yes, indeed it does."

She smiled. "I'll meet you there at eleven. There will be a Solemn Mass with full ceremonial grandeur – and the most marvellous choir and organ music."

"I look forward to it," he said and kissed her on the cheek before turning and walking quickly out to the waiting automobile.

Hazel closed the door and bolted it. She sauntered down the hallway to the staircase where she leaned against the banister and stood for a while in deep thought.

CHAPTER 44

The following week John was sitting at the dining-room table having breakfast alone as he sorted through his morning's post. He looked at his watch and saw it was quite late and there was no sign of Hazel returning yet from Mass at the Brompton Oratory.

"Did Lady Lavery say she had any plans this morning other than going to Mass, Gordon?" he asked as the butler refilled his teacup.

"My lady didn't say – she was in rather a rush out the door, sir."

"Yes, who would have thought when she became a Catholic that she would have embraced the religion to such a fervent extent!" said John with a knowing smile to himself.

"Ah, I believe this is Lady Lavery arriving back now, sir," said Gordon, looking out the window.

John turned and, looking through the window, saw Hazel's automobile parked outside and Hazel emerging from the driver's seat.

"I shall go and meet her ladyship," said Gordon as he left the room.

John continued to read his post.

A couple of minutes later, Hazel came rushing in.

"Sorry I'm so late, John. I ended up giving Michael a lift to Downing Street for the treaty talks today after Mass." She sat down at the table and poured herself some tea.

"So, you are now Michael's chauffeur? Does he not have his

own automobile and drivers at hand, as well as the whole British police force at his beck and call to take him anywhere he desires?"

"Yes, he does. But, you know, they can't guide him as I can. They would not give him the pep talk he needs going in for a full day's negotiation with Lloyd George and Winston."

"Well, I hope Michael appreciates all you do for him is all I can say."

"I don't do what I do for gratitude, John. I do it for peace in Ireland. The talks are reaching a critical phase and I'm afraid to say they are proceeding very badly. I'm terrified they will collapse again as they did in July when De Valera was over – and this time there will be no stopping a return to war."

"Meanwhile we are attracting some more unfavourable attention due to our association with Michael and the Irish delegation," he said, handing her over a stack of letters that had arrived in that morning's post.

She opened a few and scanned through them, then read from one aloud: "'You should be utterly ashamed of yourself for your collaboration with a bunch of crooks and murderers ... to welcome a man like Collins with British blood on his hands into your home makes you as guilty as he is ... I used to be an admirer of yours, Sir John Lavery, until I discovered your wife's preoccupation with the murdering Collins ...'" She shook her head in exasperation. "Honestly, do these people have nothing better to do than spread this negativity!"

"People's emotions are running very high, Hazel. And we are in the eye of the storm. I wonder would it be wiser to step back from it all – we have Alice to consider."

"No, John! We can't abandon Michael and the others at this stage! We have to fight on! We have to!" She got up, gathered the letters and walking over to the fireplace threw them in. She lit a match and set them alight. "That is what we do with negativity! Small-minded people who have nothing to do and all day to do it!"

"As you wish," said John. "I had better go. I'm expecting the Swedish prince at noon for his sitting. I must prepare the studio for his arrival."

"Yes – do that!" she said as she waved him away and began to go through her own post which Gordon had left on the table for her.

John was perplexed by Hazel. Usually, if she got wind of a Swedish prince coming to the house, she would be making plans to meet him and prepare lunch for him. Now, she couldn't care less about a Swedish Prince as all her thoughts and energy were consumed by the Irish Prince. As John walked up the stairs to his studio, he felt sure he could tell Hazel that the President of America and the King of England were both coming for lunch and it would not matter in the least to her as all her attention was taken up by Michael.

In the dining room Hazel opened a letter. She didn't recognise the writing and when she looked at the bottom of the letter, she saw it was anonymous.

> *Lady Lavery,*
>
> *Your continued association with Collins is putting your life in danger. This is a final warning to stop meddling in Irish affairs and mind your own business. Fuck off back to America, you Yankee bitch, or else ...*

Hazel immediately stopped reading, not wanted to sully her mind with any further filth. She thought about what she needed to do. She should really show this to John and inform the police about it. Although she had received poison pen letters before, since she had become involved in Irish affairs, she had never received a death threat. But she knew if John saw the letter he would become even more upset about her involvement in the peace process. Nothing could get in her way now of making sure peace came to Ireland, not even a threat to her own safety.

CHAPTER 45

The next couple of weeks passed by like a whirlwind for Michael. He quickly fell into a pattern of meeting Hazel in the morning at Mass and then she would drive him to Downing Street. There would follow a day of excruciating negotiations with the British. Then in the evenings Michael would return to Cadogan Gardens where he would write a quick letter to Kitty before going to Cromwell Place. They would spend the evening there at a social event Hazel had organised or, alternatively, they would head out to the West End to a party being held by one of Hazel's society friends or an evening at the theatre or a restaurant. Often John would accompany them, but equally as often he would not. It was as Hazel had said: John was not a natural socialite and was content to slip into the background and let Hazel take centre stage. However, the British press and public's fascination with Michael did not diminish and he found he too was centre stage wherever they went. He had followed Hazel's guidance and after some time embraced the attention. To his surprise he found at times he enjoyed it.

It was the opening night of a show in the West End. The playwright was a good friend of Hazel's and was anxious that Michael should attend it and the party afterwards.

As they finished the day of frustrating negotiations, Michael left the conference room with the other delegates.

Arthur Griffith sighed loudly as they made their way down the stairs.

"I do not know how we will break this stalemate," he said.

"Tomorrow is Saturday – I suggest we meet first thing in the morning at Hans Place to discuss strategy," said Michael. "I'll be there after eight o'clock Mass." He looked at his watch, anxious that he would not be late meeting Hazel for the theatre.

"Yes, perhaps things may be more positive after a good night's sleep," said Arthur.

"I imagine Michael has anything but a good night's sleep in mind," said Erskine Childers. "What's your social diary tonight, Michael?"

Sensing the mood darken, Arthur moved on quickly to join the other delegates ahead of them.

"And what's that supposed to mean, Childers?" demanded Michael.

"Well, one would imagine that you have forgotten the reason for your being in London. We are here to negotiate the independence of our country, not to become 'Playboys of the Western World'! I can't keep up with the whirl of social events you are attending as reported in the newspapers!"

"Well, you more than anyone should know not to believe what you read in the newspapers!"

"Very true – but I think in this case the British press are reporting things accurately."

Michael felt his temper rise. One hand on a hip with his other hand outstretched, he pointed back to the conference room they just left. "Nobody fights as hard as I do in there! I put every part of my being in there every minute of every hour, fighting for our country! You or anybody else can't say anything different! I'm hoarse from the horse-trading I'm doing. So, what if I go to a few events at night? *So fucking what?* It keeps me sane!"

"You're getting too close to the enemy, Michael," Erskine said in a low voice. "You are keeping some strange bedfellows for an Irish patriot and it will come back to haunt you. Have you asked yourself how well you know this Hazel Lavery? She could be a British spy, reporting everything back while you, the head of our Intelligence, is taken in by a pretty face!"

As Michael struggled to control his emotions and marshal his thoughts, Erskine walked off to the join the rest of the delegates.

Michael rushed back to Cadogan Gardens and quickly wrote a letter to Kitty before getting ready for the night out at the theatre. Erskine's words had upset him and cast a shadow on the night.

The horn of an automobile blew a few times outside. Michael glanced out his window and saw Hazel's automobile waiting downstairs.

He hurried down and, shouting goodbye to the others, hurried out to the waiting car.

For once Michael was not accompanied by his cohort of bodyguards. Princess Mary, the King's only daughter, was expected to attend and Hazel felt showing up with Michael's usual bodyguards might not be seen as diplomatically correct.

Hazel was not driving herself and, as they made their way to the theatre on Shaftsbury Avenue, she chatted away about her friend the playwright.

"Although he is keen to meet you, I daresay he is after the free publicity your attendance will bring!" she said.

"How do I look?" she asked as she checked her appearance in her mirror.

He studied her in her glittering white gown and white fur coat.

"You look beautiful, Hazel," he said quietly.

"Thank you." She snapped her mirror shut and turned to him. "I must say I am glad we got that black-tie suit for you – you've got plenty of wear out of it!"

He smiled and shrugged, before frowning. "Maybe too much wear ..."

"Michael, is everything alright – you seem very quiet tonight? Did the negotiations today go badly?"

He raised his eyes to heaven. "They go badly every day! Nothing new there. It's just something Childers said to me when I was leaving Downing Street."

"Yes?"

"He said I was fraternising with the enemy and letting the side down."

"Meaning me – I take it?"

"You amongst others. He criticised my lifestyle over here. Implied I was being seduced by London society and all its glamour."

"Well, you wouldn't be the first!" Hazel tried to make light of it.

"I'm just worried about how all this is playing out back home. I don't want to be seen as a traitor or falling down on my duties."

"Michael!" Hazel reached over and took his hand. "Nobody has thrown themselves into this role, which you never asked for, more energetically than you. You are forging bridges that Britain and Ireland can build on in the future when independence is achieved. You have told me that Childers is one of the chief obstacles to making progress with the treaty. That he resolutely refuses to budge or even discuss compromises. A treaty is about finding a compromise that works for both sides – not just sitting there being obstinate. That attitude ends in war!"

He nodded. "He is very obstinate on a daily basis."

"But do you see how important it is for you to recognise that? You are looking at it from the other point of view – as I am sure Winston and the more reasonable men on the British side are doing too. None of the other delegates have criticised you, have they?"

"No."

"Well, that says it all! We will just have to park Mr. Childers as a lost cause. I certainly wouldn't allow him to ruin a night at the theatre if I were you!" She smiled at him and he smiled back.

The play was a hit and Hazel and Michael rose to their feet and applauded with the rest of the audience when the curtains came down. Afterwards they made their way to Claridge's where the after party was.

"Lord Felladale, I never had you down as a theatre-goer," said Hazel as she led Michael around. "You were always too immersed in hunting, shooting and fishing on your country estate to sit in a theatre for a couple of hours."

"My dear Lady Lavery, nothing would have given me greater pleasure than to be on my estate hunting, shooting or fishing! However, my dear wife insisted I attend tonight. She is a friend of the playwright."

"Indeed – aren't we all!"

Lord Felladale's eyes switched from Hazel to Michael.

"Lord Felladale, may I introduce you to Mr. Michael Collins," said Hazel.

"How do you do?" said Lord Felladale, shaking Michael's hand.

"Pleased to meet you, sir. Like you, I might have preferred not to be cooped up in a theatre tonight. Those seats were a bit too small for me!"

"Yes, I imagine it was rather uncomfortable for you – you are a rather big fellow."

"That is indeed my nickname!"

"Watch out – here comes Princess Mary!" whispered Felladale, stepping aside as Princess Mary swept up to Hazel and Michael.

"Your Royal Highness!" greeted Hazel with an exaggerated courtesy.

CHAPTER 46

One evening in Cadogan Gardens Michael could hear the others downstairs playing music and making much merriment. They had called up to him a few times to come down. But he was in no mood to join them. He realised how much he had changed since he had arrived a few short weeks ago. At the beginning of their stay, he wouldn't have dreamt of not being downstairs with the rest of them, having a party. Now, he felt he couldn't quite fit in and would have nothing to contribute to them enjoying themselves. He was laden down with pressure from the negotiations. It had been another intense day. Even as he stretched out on his bed, reading the letter from Kitty that had arrived that morning, it did not lift his spirits. A couple of months ago he would have given anything to hear her declaring undying love in a letter but now he couldn't even concentrate on her words. Kitty was due to visit London with Maud in a few days' time. They had been arranging the visit for the past few weeks. She wrote she could not wait to see him and was counting the minutes and seconds. He also couldn't wait to see her. He felt he had lost his way in London and needed to see her. He jumped up off the bed and made his way downstairs. He glanced into the drawing room where the party was in full swing, slipped down the corridor and out the back door.

Seeing there was nobody about, he made his way down to Sloane Square and continued walking through the dark November evening to the bottom of the Kings Road before taking the turn to Kensington.

He soon arrived at 5 Cromwell Place and pulled the doorbell.

"Mr. Collins! I don't think we were expecting you?" said Gordon on answering the door.

"Is Lady Lavery home?"

"I'm afraid she is not as neither is Sir John. They are out to dinner."

"Oh!" Michael's face dropped with disappointment.

"I'm not sure how long they will be – but would you care to wait for them?"

"Yes, if I could," said Michael, stepping inside and taking off his coat. "Hazel said I could use the library here if I needed to?"

"Of course. If you would follow me, sir," said Gordon.

It was after one in the morning by the time Hazel and John arrived home.

"Did you have a good evening, sir, madam?" asked Gordon, taking their coats in the hallway.

"Yes, very good, Gordon," said John. "Although Londonderry's cook isn't a patch on our own."

"Delighted to hear it, sir. Em … Mr. Collins is here."

"Michael! Where?" asked Hazel.

"I showed him into the library as he wanted to do some research. He arrived earlier looking for you and I suggested he should wait. I didn't realise you would be so late, or I would have told him –"

Hazel didn't wait hear any more as she dashed down the hallway and up the stairs, leaving John and Gordon to stare after her.

She raced down a corridor until she reached the library. She was overcome with a feeling of joy that Michael was there and had come to seek her out. At the same time she was frustrated that she had missed an evening of his company which she had wasted listening to Charlie and Edith.

She flung open the library door, calling, "Michael!"

To her surprise, she found the room was in darkness apart from the coals glowing in the fireplace. Michael was stretched out on the couch while several books were open on the floor beside him.

"Michael?" she asked gently as she approached, but she saw he was fast asleep. She looked down at the books he had been reading and, picking them up, she saw they were all political books about the systems of government in places like Canada, Australia and New Zealand. She put them on the table before turning and leaving.

She returned five minutes later carrying a large blanket. She knelt beside Michael and covered him with the blanket. He stirred in his sleep and opened his eyes.

"Hazel," he whispered.

"It's alright, Michael. You go back to sleep. I've just put a blanket over you. You'll be safe and warm here and I'll be upstairs if you need anything."

He closed his eyes again and drifted off to sleep. She remained kneeling there, studying his face in the firelight. She could hardly tear herself away from him but knew John would be waiting. She leaned forward and kissed his forehead before rising and going to the door. She took another look at him before forcing herself to leave.

CHAPTER 47

As the train pulled into Euston Station, Kitty had her head out the window, her eyes searching the platform.

"Can you see him?" asked Maud, pushing her sister out of the way and sticking her head out.

"I'd be more capable of seeing him if you moved out of my way!" said Kitty, pulling Maud back and pushing her head out the window again.

As the train pulled to a halt, they grabbed their bags, opened the door and stepped onto the platform.

"I hope he hasn't forgotten to meet us!" said Maud as they pushed through the crowded platform.

"Hardly! I'm supposed to be his fiancée!" snapped Kitty.

"*Kitty*!" came a shout and she turned around to see Michael standing there.

She stared at him for a moment, hardly believing it was him and she was there in London with him. She pushed past the people, ran into his open arms and kissed him.

"Well, there's a welcome a fella doesn't get every day!" he said, kissing her back.

"I hope not from any other girl anyway!" said Kitty, kissing him again.

"I feel like a gooseberry!" Maud said.

"Ah, Maud, come here to me," said Michael as he went to Maud and hugged her.

"Ah, you look great, Mick!" said Maud. "Doesn't he look

great, Kitty?"

"You surely do! Where did all this come from?" she asked, running a finger down his fine suit.

"Savile Row," he said as he took both their cases and they began to walk quickly down the platform.

"Savile Row, no less!" said Kitty.

"Well, when you are meeting the Prime Minister of England every day, you have to look your finest and be fashionable," said Maud.

"Fashion! Sure, what do I know about fashion! If I hadn't Hazel there deciding, I'd be still there in the shop scratching my head wondering what to buy!"

Maud glanced at Kitty, but her face did not reveal her feelings.

"Lucky you had Hazel so," Kitty then said with a smirk, "or who'd be here to collect us from the train station while you decided what shirt to buy?"

Emmet and Joe were waiting in the front of the automobile.

"Here are the girls, lads! If you thought the parties were wild at Cadogan Gardens up until now, wait until you see these two let their hair down!" said Michael as he opened the back door.

"Shut up, you big lump!" said Kitty as she laughed and got into the back of the automobile. "Hello, lads!"

"And that's Park Avenue," said Michael, pointing to the street as they passed it. "That's where Lloyd George's private secretary Sir Philip Sassoon lives in a mansion that is about the size of Grafton Street."

"Sassoon? What kind of a name is that? Is he foreign?" asked Maud.

"No – he's as English as they come!" laughed Michael.

"He must be related to the war poet," said Kitty. "You know, Siegfried Sassoon?"

"Cousins, I believe – and I hear he's from the Rothschild family – you know, the big bankers. Anyway, whoever he is related to, he's a very nice fella," Michael adopted a posh English accent, "or *fellow* as they say here! And that's Harrods, the world-famous store."

"I don't care what else I do in London, I will not be happy until I get into that store and take a look around," said Maud, salivating at the sight of it as they drove by.

"You'll do more than that. I'll get Kathleen to bring both of ye up here for a shopping trip and ye can buy whatever ye want on me!"

"Oh, thank you, Mick!" cried Maud, kissing his cheek.

"We should come to London more often, Maud!" said Kitty, winking over at her. "We'd end up being the best-dressed girls in Ireland!"

"And this is Chelsea," said Michael. "It's around here a lot of the posh people live – the lords and ladies."

"Is this where Lord and Lady Lavery live?" asked Kitty, looking out at the big houses.

"No – they are up the road in South Kensington. But it's not that far away, A short walk. Ah – here we are – Cadogan Gardens."

As they approached the house, Kitty saw several police officers outside and a group of men.

"Who are these people?" she asked.

"Newspaper men and their photographers," answered Michael.

"Newspaper men!" exclaimed Kitty. "What are they doing here?"

"They're nearly always around, looking for a story," said Michael.

"Looking for a story! But sure, there's no story about us – we're just two country girls over for the weekend!" said Maud with a laugh.

But as the automobile parked at the side of the road in front of the house, Kitty realised she was very much a story. The press there would go crazy with excitement if they knew she was Michael's fiancée. She did not want people to find this out through a story run in the press. More particularly, she didn't want Harry and his family discovering by accident she was engaged to Michael.

"I wish you'd warned me these were camped outside the house, Mick," she said.

"Just keep your head down and head straight to the front door," said Michael as he pushed the door open.

Kitty got out of the automobile and, as the newspapermen rushed towards them, she shielded her face and raced to the door.

Inside, she wondered if she would be sorry she had come.

Everyone in the house at Cadogan Gardens went out of their way to make Kitty and Maud feel welcome. They were given a beautiful bedroom each on the top floor.

Kitty immediately sensed the loyalty they all had for Michael. As she watched their interaction, she would go so far as to say the *love* they had for him.

On that first night they all stayed in and had a wonderful dinner of venison. The drink flowed and the chat and laughter never stopped through dinner. As Kitty sat beside Michael at the top of the table, she watched the jokes and jibes flying between him and the others. As much as she too enjoyed it, she longed to be on her own with Michael, but she couldn't see much chance of that yet, with the house full of people. And with police and newspapermen outside, they couldn't even go for a walk.

After dinner, out came the accordions and fiddle and the dancing started.

"I'd say whoever designed and built this drawing room, they never thought it would witness a céilí!" said Kitty as Michael swung her around to the music.

"Ah, it's great to have you here, Kitty," he said. "I can hardly believe it."

The party went on until the early hours of the morning and they all went to bed at four, exhausted.

The next morning, Kitty got up late. She knocked on Maud's door but, realising she was still asleep, she made her way downstairs.

The scene on the ground floor was very different from the previous night. All signs of the party had disappeared. The men were all gone and only the girls were there, busy typing away on the typewriters on the dining-room table.

"How's the head this morning?" asked Kathleen, smiling at her.

"Not as bad as Maud's, I'll bet!"

"Come on down to the kitchen and I'll get you some breakfast," Kathleen said, getting up and beckoning to Kitty.

"Where's Mick?" asked Kitty as they left the room.

"Oh, sure, he was up at the crack of dawn. He was out the door at seven thirty to make eight o'clock Mass at the Brompton Oratory – he goes there most mornings." They entered the kitchen. "Bacon, eggs, sausages?"

"Yes, please," said Kitty, sitting at the huge kitchen table. "Can I help?"

"No, not at all – I'm well used to cooking in this kitchen by this stage."

Kitty watched as Kathleen busied herself at the stove with the frying pan.

"What time will Mick be back?" she asked then.

"Probably not till this evening, Kitty. He usually meets Lady Lavery at Mass and has breakfast with her before she drives him directly to Downing Street for the negotiations."

"Oh – I see," said Kitty, digesting the information.

"Don't worry – you won't be bored!" smiled Kathleen. "Mick has left instructions and money and I am to take you and Maud out shopping for the day and buy you whatever dresses you want – he even said I was to buy myself one while I was at it!"

"That would be Mick. He has a big heart," said Kitty.

"Ah, the biggest!" said Kathleen. "Kitty, I'm so glad to have met you at last. I've been posting letters to 'Miss Kitty Kieran, The Greville Arms Hotel' nearly every day since we arrived here! I was dying to know what you were like! Easily known Mick would get only the best!"

Kitty felt overcome by her kind words and that somebody actually knew or had realised that she and Mick were in a serious relationship and that it wasn't some guilty secret.

"Thank you, Kathleen," she whispered.

"It's all a bit daunting over here, but don't let it worry you too much. And don't worry about any of those Englishwomen who are swarming around Mick – take it from me, he only has eyes for you!"

As Kitty sat there, she knew Kathleen's words were meant to comfort her, but her last reassurance had only confused her.

281

CHAPTER 48

Kitty and Maud had spent a whirlwind of a day in the West End as Kathleen showed them around.

"I feel there isn't a shop left in the city we haven't gone to!" said Maud as the three women walked down Regent Street carrying many shopping bags.

"I don't know how you spend every day over here, Kathleen, without running out to look at the latest fashions!" said Kitty.

"Today's a treat for me, girls – usually all I get to see is my typewriter!" said Kathleen. "We'd better get back to Cadogan Gardens now as Mick is taking both of you out for dinner tonight and we don't want to keep him waiting."

"Mick will wait until we're ready!" said Kitty with a wink at Maud.

As they headed down Piccadilly Circus, Kathleen was intrigued by the two young women, particularly Kitty. They were obviously from an affluent background, were well educated and very glamorous. After their initial intimidation at being in a city which was so big and so unlike their small town, they took to the place like ducks to water. They seemed to have plenty of money to spend and London suited people like that very well! But Kathleen knew that Maud was engaged to Gearóid O'Sullivan and that things were very serious between Kitty and Michael. And this perplexed her because neither of the women had mentioned the treaty or politics for the whole day. As it was all anyone spoke about at Cadogan Gardens, it was strange to encounter two people who didn't have the same level of obsession as everyone else. Kathleen wondered if the girls were just being discreet, but she strongly suspected that was not the case. What perplexed her was how a relationship with someone like Michael, who lived and breathed politics, would work out for someone like Kitty who clearly did not.

That evening, Kitty spent a couple of hours getting ready. She was wearing a dress and hat that she had bought that day and she checked her appearance in the mirror for the hundredth time. There was a knock on the door and Maud walked in.

"Will you come on, Kitty! Mick says they won't hold the reservation for us at the restaurant if we're too late!"

"Ah, I'm sure they'd hold it for the great Michael Collins!" said Kitty, turning from the mirror and facing Maud. "How do I look?"

"You look gorgeous, Kitty. He's a lucky man – now, will you come on!"

Maud grabbed Kitty by the hand and dragged her out of the room. The two women giggled as they made their way down to the hall where Michael was pacing up and down, looking at his watch.

Hearing the giggling, Michael turned around. "Will you come on!"

He stopped short when he saw the two women on the bottom step.

"Well, don't you look beautiful!" he said as he stared at them.

"You're not too bad yourself!" said Kitty, admiring the suit he was wearing – no doubt chosen by Hazel Lavery on Savile Row.

"Are we worth the wait?" asked Kitty as she posed with her hand behind her head.

"You are – and longer!" he said.

As the girls put on their coats, Kathleen and the others came into the hall to see them off.

"Paint the town red, Mick!" called one of them as Mick offered an arm to each sister and proudly walked them out the front door.

Once they were out in the cool evening air, reality hit Kitty when the newspaper men came rushing to them. She hid her face as they hurried to the automobile parked outside where Emmet and Joe were waiting.

"*Who are these women, Mick?*" shouted a newspaper man. "*Are they your sisters?*"

"*Girlfriends?*" shouted another.

"How can you live under this scrutiny?" demanded Kitty as they drove away, stressed by the attention which she had only experienced for one day.

"Sure, didn't I live under far worse conditions when I was being hunted day and night by the police and army?" said Michael. "What's a few newspapermen compared to that?"

Kitty nodded but wondered if that was bravado. Michael was a naturally shy person and, in a way, living on the run with nobody knowing what he looked like suited his personality. Being here in London, exposed every day, must be torture for him she imagined.

Emmet pulled the automobile up outside a swanky restaurant in Knightsbridge, got out and opened the back door.

"Thank you, Jeeves!" said Kitty in a fake upper-class accent as he helped her out of the vehicle.

"You are welcome, my lady!" he said, winking at her.

They made their way up the steps of the restaurant.

"Your people are a lovely bunch!" Kitty said.

"I knew they'd all love you!" said Michael.

"Sure, what's not to love?" she said, doing a small twirl as they entered the restaurant.

The staff took their coats, then the manager led them into the restaurant.

The restaurant was very ornate, with gold-framed mirrors on the walls and a decorated ceiling. As they walked through it, Kitty became aware that people were looking at them. Then the diners started whispering and talking as a ripple of excitement ran though the room. She felt very uncomfortable as they reached their table.

One of the waiters pulled a chair out for her. She sat down and glanced around at the staring and talking faces.

"What is wrong with them all?" Kitty hissed to Michael.

"They're fine, just ignore them – you'll get used to it after a while," he said as he took a menu from another waiter.

"I could never get used to this!" snapped Kitty.

"Pretend they're not there!" urged Maud.

"Sure!" said Kitty sarcastically as she looked at a matronly woman who had taken out her opera glasses and was looking at her directly through them.

"Could they not have put us in a more private place, somewhere in a corner out of public view?" asked Kitty.

"I'll ask them to move us," said Michael, standing up.

"No!" snapped Kitty, catching his arm and pulling him back down on his chair. "It will only make it worse if we move at this stage!"

She began to try and concentrate on the menu the waiter had given her.

"So, I turned to Churchill and I said 'Will you stop beating around the bush and tell me what's on your mind?'!" said Michael as they started on a dessert of ice cream and cake.

"What did he say?" asked Maud.

"Churchill looked at me and said, 'Young man, you should learn some manners and patience!' And I said to him, 'I'll show you manners if you show me patience!'"

Maud burst out laughing.

Kitty bit her lower lip. The whole evening had passed mainly talking about the treaty. They had barely discussed home or anything else – even Maud and Gearóid's forthcoming wedding didn't get a look in. And all the time they were being rudely stared at by fellow diners.

"Then Lloyd George turns to me and says –"

"For goodness' sake, Mick, will you give it a rest!" snapped Kitty.

"Kitty!" cried Maud.

"Give what a rest?" asked Michael, shocked by her outburst.

"Lloyd George, Churchill, Birkenhead, and Lord and Lady Lavery! I'm sick of hearing about them all and I've only just arrived in this bloody city!"

He looked at her, not sure how to respond.

Suddenly an elderly man came up to the table.

"Excuse me – you are him, are you not? You are Michael Collins?" he asked.

Michael responded, "Yes, yes, I am."

The man's expression suddenly turned to cold anger. "I just want to tell you that if I were twenty years younger I would challenge you to a duel! You murderous scoundrel! I could hardly finish my venison knowing you were in the same room!"

With that, he turned and marched away.

The manager came rushing over. "I am so sorry, Mr. Collins! I cannot apologise enough for that!"

"It's fine, it's not your fault," said Michael.

"Let's just go, Mick! Let's get the bill and get out of here!" Kitty pleaded to him in a whisper.

"The bill, please," said Michael to the manager.

"Of course, Mr. Collins," he said and he rushed away.

They sat mostly in silence on the drive to Cadogan Gardens, with only Maud trying to lighten the mood by occasionally speaking.

Late though it was, there was one journalist still outside the house.

"Lord save us!" said Kitty as she passed him on the way to the front door. "Would you not get yourself home out of the cold and into a warm bed!"

"Can't, miss. My editor says I have to stay here for the whole night in case I miss anything."

"The only thing you'll miss tonight is a good night's sleep in a bed!" said Kitty as she went in the front door.

The others were still up partying in the drawing room.

Kitty walked straight across to the stairs.

"Kitty! Where are you going?" asked Michael.

"To bed, Mick – I'm very tired. I'll see you tomorrow."

He watched her walk up the stairs.

Maud shrugged. "She's exhausted, Mick. And I think all this is a bit too much for her. She wasn't expecting it to be as invasive and all-consuming as it is," she said, before she turned and went into the drawing room to join the party.

"Are you alright, Mick? How was the restaurant?" asked Kathleen, coming up from the kitchen.

"Bit of a disaster ... no privacy," sighed Michael. "Do me a favour, Kathleen. There's some poor sod who's been told he has to stay outside the house for the night by his editor. Will you bring him out some hot tea and something to eat?"

"I will, surely, Mick. And why don't you get yourself off to bed – you look as if you could do with an early night, for once."

He nodded and, sighing, climbed the stairs to his room.

CHAPTER 49

Kitty slept well that night. She fell into a deep slumber as soon as her head hit the pillow.

The next morning, she got up late. As she thought about the previous night, she didn't know how to deal with Michael that day. Should she apologise or should she be angry? Her overriding emotion since she had arrived in London was disappointment.

She felt they were all living under tremendous pressure. There were always policemen outside and often newspaper men. She saw that Michael's bodyguards had guns on them at all times. Mixed with this was the terrible pressure everyone was under to bring back a treaty and peace to Ireland. Kitty felt sometimes you could cut the atmosphere with a knife.

There was a gentle knock on her door.

"Come in!" she called, and Michael came into the room looking sheepish.

"Did you sleep well?" he asked.

"I did actually," she answered.

"I was wondering if the two of us could go off today – just the two of us – and spend some time together?"

"Do you not have to meet Lloyd George and the rest of them?"

"It's Saturday – we have no meeting scheduled for today."

She sighed. "But where could we go without being disturbed by some stranger? We can't even leave the house without a journalist being there or people staring."

"We can leave the back way – there will be no journalists there.

288

Make our way through the back alleys ... I've often done it, if I need to go for a walk alone. We'll make our way to a pub I know. There's just a few old fellas drinking there, they won't even spot us."

She managed to smile and nod.

"I shouldn't have come to London," she said as they sat in a quiet corner of the pub.

They had slipped out the back of the house undetected. And the pub was in a quiet corner of Chelsea.

"Of course you were right to come!" he protested.

"No, Mick! You're too busy with affairs of state to be entertaining me. I never realised you were living under such pressure here."

"But I wrote to you ever day saying what it was like!"

"But seeing is believing! And there's something else, Mick – you're enjoying it! You are enjoying all this attention and pageantry and that's the biggest shock to me!"

"I am not enjoying it! I never wanted to come here – I was forced to come," he said.

"But you've settled into this role so well," she said, "more than I could ever have imagined."

"I've had to adapt to survive. I had to! I'm representing Ireland and I have to put my best foot forward."

"I just – I just don't know where it leaves us," she said.

"Leaves us? It leaves us where we were – unchanged."

"But is there room for me in this new life of yours?"

"You're my fiancée. You're going to be my wife, for fuck's sake!"

"I don't feel like your fiancée over here." She looked down at her fingers as she spoke. "Nobody knows we are engaged. I feel like a nobody, or a floozie who just dropped by."

He couldn't help from laughing as he reached over and took her hands in his.

"You know we decided the time wasn't right to announce the engagement, not until the treaty is done and I'm back in Ireland ...

and there's Harry to consider. We have to tell him in person and he won't be back till Christmas – but that's not that long away."

"I know," she whispered, suddenly feeling as if everything was right and safe as he held her hands. "I've missed you, Mick. I've missed you so much. I love you very much."

He blinked a few times as Kitty was never somebody who wore her heart on her sleeve. She was much more prone to show her feelings through a joke or a well-placed putdown than an open display of emotion.

"And sure, you're my world, Kitty. Don't you know that?"

"I hope I am. I just don't know if I can compete with all these new people in your life."

"But there's no competition. You've already won the race," he said as he pulled her close.

They spent the rest of the day in the pub and, as evening came, they left and went to a small quiet hotel and had dinner there.

As they talked for hours, Kitty felt as close as she could be to Michael. Politics were left aside as they spoke about each other and plans for the future. As the night drew in, they still sat at the table in the hotel restaurant which was empty by then.

"I guess we'd better make a move back to Cadogan Gardens," he said eventually.

"I don't want to go back there, Mick, not tonight," she said.

"Not go back?"

"No. There will just be another party there and more shouting and laughing and dancing … I just want to be with you … let's stay here …"

"But they'll be closing up soon," he said, looking around at the empty restaurant.

"Not right here, Mick, for goodness' sake! No … we can get a room here for the night. That's what I want, Mick. I didn't come all the way to London to be in fancy restaurants or to go shopping or to party in Cadogan Gardens. I came to be with you." She reached out and held his hand across the table.

"Are you sure?" he asked incredulously.

She nodded.

* * *

The porter showed them to a bedroom.

"Anything else, sir?"

"No, thank you," said Michael and the porter left.

Kitty went over to the window and looked out at the rooftops across Chelsea.

He came and stood behind her.

"I love you, Kitty," he whispered.

She turned around and took his face in her hands. He bent his head and kissed her before they went and lay down on the bed.

The next morning Kitty awoke in Michael's arms.

She gently nudged him awake.

He opened his eyes and smiled at her.

"I look forward to waking up to your face every morning," he said.

She smiled and kissed him before her smile turned into a frown. "I want to run away with you."

"Run away?" he asked.

"Just to go – away – from here. Leave all this treaty and politics behind. Have we not sacrificed enough of our lives already?"

"I know, I know – but let's hope it will soon be all over, my love."

"No – I'm serious, Mick. I want us to run away."

"Kitty! I'm part of the delegation. I can't just – run away from my responsibilities."

"You would if you loved me," she said. "If you put me first for once."

"I do put you first, Kitty, but you're asking the impossible!"

"I'm asking to be able to marry the man I love and not have to share him with the world – is that too much to ask?"

"On this occasion, yes," he said.

She turned from him and got out of bed. "We had better get back to Cadogan Gardens before they miss us. Maud will be terrified something has happened if she wakes and finds my room not slept in. And I have to protect my reputation from the rest of them."

"Kitty!" Michael called after her as she walked into the bathroom and closed the door.

CHAPTER 50

The next couple of days passed quickly for Michael and Kitty. Sometimes they managed to forget everything and enjoy the time they had together. But then the pressure of the situation would re-emerge and result in them have an argument where one or the other would storm off.

"I just don't know what's wrong with us, Maud," Kitty confided. "I know from the start we always used to spar with each other, but this is different. This feels serious."

"Kitty, he is under terrible pressure with the negotiations – he is unable to remove his mind from the conference table. Look, you're both in a unique set of circumstances and pressures. But you'll come through it stronger than ever."

"I hope so, Maud. Because I've put my whole life into this. If something goes wrong between us now, I don't think I'll be able to recover."

On the evening they were departing for Dublin, Michael took them to Euston Station.

Maud said her goodbyes and got onto the train carriage, leaving Michael and Kitty on the platform.

"I'll write to you – every day, as before," she promised.

"And I to you," he said.

"What's going to happen now? When will you be home next?"

"It's impossible to say." He shrugged his shoulders.

She hid her frustration and embraced him.

The train whistle blew, and he led her to the carriage and helped her in before closing the door.

As the train took off, she leaned out the window.

"I'll write to you," she called as she waved goodbye.

Winston Churchill watched Hazel's face, animated as she paced up and down Philip Sassoon's opulent drawing room. Philip was hosting an impromptu meeting that rainy late-November afternoon. Lloyd George and Lord Birkenhead were in attendance. Although Lloyd George had resisted Hazel Lavery's interference in government affairs, he had to admit she had become a useful source of information since she had formed a close friendship with most of the Irish delegation, particularly Michael Collins.

"The reality is, it will soon be December and the Irish delegates will be returning home to spend Christmas in Ireland," said Hazel.

"Really? I thought they would all have been spending Christmas dinner around your table at Cromwell Place, Lady Lavery," Birkenhead mocked. "Raising a toast to the Old Country!"

"The question is," Hazel continued, ignoring Birkenhead's sarcasm, "if the impasse has not been broken by then, will they return in the New Year? Why should they return if they feel no progress can be made? You have a very small window of opportunity here to close this deal and sign a treaty. Otherwise I fear all will be lost!"

"And is this opinion coming from you, Lady Lavery – or Michael Collins?" asked Birkenhead. "We would like to be clear about the source of this information."

"Even a child would understand that what I am saying is true, Lord Birkenhead!" snapped Hazel.

"Unfortunately, Hazel is right," said Winston. "I can't see how the negotiations can continue into the New Year if nothing has been achieved by Christmas. We would just be going around in circles."

"Michael and the others are under increasing pressure," said Hazel. "De Valera and the parliament in Dublin insist on either closing a deal or going home."

"I wish people would stop calling that kangaroo debating society in Dublin a parliament!" snapped Lloyd George angrily. "It has no international recognition as of yet! And never will if we don't sign this damned treaty!"

"The way I look at it," said Hazel, "is that to break this impasse you need to remove a couple of the more serious obstacles – for example, Mr. Childers – from the negotiations. Prime Minister, Winston, Lord Birkenhead – come to Cromwell Place and meet Michael and discuss things as men and not as politicians. You will be able to speak candidly there, without having everything documented and recorded. You will have the freedom to speak as you find."

They all sat in silence for a while.

"What is this? Another impasse?" Hazel eventually said with a laugh.

"Well," Winston mused, "Hazel might have a point. My own private secretary, Eddie Marsh, has told me that when he has met Collins at Hazel's he has found him to be very easy to deal with and talk to – not always the case at Downing Street, I think you'll agree!"

"Well, there is nothing to lose at this stage," said Lloyd George. "I shan't go myself, that wouldn't look right ... but Winston, Lord Birkenhead, as friends of Lady Lavery there is nothing to stop you attending Lady Lavery's salon on a social visit – and if Mr. Collins happens to be there at the same time ..."

"*Bravo!*" exclaimed Hazel, clapping her hands together.

"We shall leave the arrangements in your capable hands, Hazel," said Winston.

"Excellent!" Hazel said. "And before I rush off – I have to collect Michael as we have been invited to a poetry recital this evening – if I could remind you that you have committed to be painted by John as part of the Irish Collection to mark this treaty."

"If there ever is a treaty to mark!" scoffed Birkenhead.

"Please put it in your diaries to attend John's studio – he is a very patient man but even he has his limits!"

Hazel threw on her fur coat, bid everyone goodbye and rushed out the door.

"John Lavery is a very patient man indeed!" said Lloyd George. "I imagine life is never dull with Hazel as a wife."

"That is unquestionable!" chuckled Winston.

"I still wonder what she wants out of all this," mused Lloyd George. "I would hazard a guess that she would have been angling for a knighthood for services to the Crown – but they already have that!"

"Hazel is just a very kind and remarkable lady," said Winston.

"Not a vain attention-seeker then?" said Birkenhead with a smirk. "Poetry recital indeed!"

CHAPTER 51

The following day Michael and Hazel went to the Victoria and Albert Museum which was across the road from Cromwell Place, a short walk from the Lavery house. They had passed it walking back from Mass each morning and Michael had expressed an interest in visiting it.

As they wandered around the museum, Michael marvelled at how relaxed he was in Hazel's company. They had become so close over the weeks that he couldn't imagine a time he had not known her. Under all the terrible pressure he was under with the negotiations, he felt he could trust her completely.

Afterwards, they went for a stroll through the vast grounds of the museum.

Hazel tightened her fur coat around her to keep out the chill. "So, on Saturday night Winston and Lord Birkenhead will arrive at seven for dinner at our house. I suggest that you are there early – it will put you in a stronger position if you are there first to greet them – instead of the other way round."

"You think of everything, Hazel," he said, smiling at her.

"I have invited Winston's secretary also – you've met Eddie a few times socially – he can help smooth over any awkwardness."

"And there will be awkwardness. Yesterday, when we were finishing up the day's negotiation, Birkenhead and I were nearly shouting at each other," said Michael.

"I want you all to leave that negativity behind and embrace the opportunity to make friendships. Ireland and Britain need to be friends – we are close neighbours and could be close allies – let's start building bridges."

Michael spotted a bench and went and sat down on it, beckoning to Hazel to sit beside him.

"I don't know how I can ever repay you for all you've done for us – for me – since we arrived in London," he said.

"I don't want repayment, Michael – I just want peace in Ireland!"

He studied her fascinating face. "You're an enigma."

"Me? An enigma?" she hooted, laughing. "Everyone will tell you I'm the very opposite of an enigma – I'm an open book!"

"I don't buy that. Behind the jolliness and the flamboyance – who is the real Hazel? Why have you thrown yourself so much into Irish politics?"

"Things haven't always been smooth for me, Michael. It was hard for me when my first husband Ned died. I was pregnant at the time and it was a shock."

"Of course it was."

"The trouble was, I never really loved Ned, not really. He loved me and he was without question the match I was expected to make. But I'd already met John by then and fallen in love with him. But my mother insisted he was not suitable … he was that much older than me, a widower with a daughter. She absolutely forbade a marriage to John and then marched me up the aisle with Ned."

"Could you not have said no? If you didn't love Ned and were truly in love with John, why didn't you follow your heart?"

"I was too frightened to. I was too frightened to go against my mother's wishes. And she had been recently widowed at the time – I didn't want to cause her any more upset."

Michael gave a small laugh. "Strange, isn't it?"

"What is?"

"How people think they know what's best. There was your mother thinking John wasn't good enough for you and here you are still married years later – he's now Sir John and you have become a titled lady through the marriage and risen to the top of British society."

"I often think exactly that!" nodded Hazel. "John would have had more than any of my mother's expectations if she could have seen into the future. Mama got it very wrong – as mamas tend to do!"

"That still doesn't explain why you are so involved in Irish affairs," said Michael.

"So – Ned died, suddenly and shockingly – fell dead in front of me when I was five months pregnant with Alice. He was only twenty-nine years of age. Eventually, after a decent period of mourning, I married John, and Alice and I moved to London. Soon after the marriage my mother died – it was hard, but it hit my sister particularly hard. I had only one sibling – Dorothy."

Michael remembered that Hazel had talked about her sister when he met her first, when he was sitting for the portrait and Hazel had spoken to him about her sister to try and calm his nerves.

"Had?" questioned Michael.

"She died, Michael. She died a number of years ago." A shadow passed over her face.

"Was it sudden?" he asked.

"It was unexpected, but in a way it shouldn't have been. It was an unnecessary waste of a life."

"How do you mean?"

"Dorothy had been very cosseted as she was brought up – as had I. After our father died, my mother continued living a very lavish lifestyle and, when she died, to everyone's horror there was very little money left. I had moved to London and started my new life with John. Dorothy, as she didn't have anybody left in America, came to London and tried to live here ... but she couldn't settle. She didn't get on with John ... and she and I didn't get on while she stayed here. Dorothy was very demanding, and she wasn't very well. She was plagued with insecurities. She used to fast – long bouts of fasting where she hardly ate anything. Well, it all played havoc with her health which was seriously damaged. When she moved back to Chicago ..." Hazel sank her face into her hands, "I was relieved. I felt she couldn't fit in here and I was so taken up with my own new life with John at the time that I felt I had no time to give her. That I couldn't give her the help she needed. Eventually we got news Dorothy had become quite unwell and we travelled back to the States to help her. But when we arrived, it was too late ..." Tears were falling down Hazel's face. "She had died. I got such a shock ... I never expected ... I just thought it was the latest drama in a long line of dramas with her. She had died alone in a public hospital with no family or friends around her."

"Oh, Hazel!" Michael was overcome with compassion.

Hazel quickly wiped her tears away. "The press was merciless. They wrote many things about me – that I was a cruel and neglectful sister who had put ambition before caring for my own family."

"I'm so sorry, Hazel." Michael's own eyes began welling up.

"They were right of course, the newspapers –"

"No!" insisted Michael. "She was a grown woman! An adult – what could you have done?"

"I could have been there for her. I could have helped her, but I was too preoccupied with myself – with my life, my marriage, my everything. I can never forgive myself for abandoning her. I will never forgive myself."

"But you can't carry the burden for the rest of your life!"

"Yes, I can. It's my burden to carry ... a few years after her death, during the Great War, John and I were in a car crash. We weren't seriously hurt, but it was an awful shock. While I was recuperating I fell into the most terrible depression. Just everything seemed to hit me all at once. Being widowed at a young age, my parents' death and then most of all what had happened to Dorothy. It was as if for the previous few years I had been rushing around from party to party, portrait-painting to portrait-painting, social column to social column, trying to – block out – the past. And suddenly when I was recuperating, I had time on my hands to face the past. It hit me so bad I could hardly get out of bed – I couldn't see any point to the future."

As Michael listened intently, he could not imagine Hazel as

being anything but vivacious and lively and optimistic. He couldn't imagine her ever having a depressed day in her life. He suddenly put an arm around her.

She melted into his arms and allowed herself to be enveloped in a hug as she held on to him tightly.

"It went on for weeks and months. John was despairing – he thought I'd end up like Dorothy. John was covering the Roger Casement trial in London, sketching the daily events for the government and press. And he would come home every evening and talk about what had happened in court that day. It was just after the Easter Rising and so the newspapers were full of it all and John spoke so passionately about the case that I became intrigued. Why had this man, with his immense international reputation as a humanitarian and his knighthood, risked it all to smuggle arms from Germany into Ireland? It was the first thing that had interested me in months. I do, of course, have Irish ancestry myself. One day, I got up and went into the court with John to witness the proceedings myself. From that day I was hooked – was hooked as I learned about the Irish fight for independence and the part Casement had played. When they hanged him, an Irishman, as a traitor to 'his country' – that is, England – I made up my mind to fight for Irish independence. I became obsessed with the Irish question."

"And here you are now," said Michael as he held her tightly and stroked her hair.

"In the arms of Michael Collins!" She managed to laugh as she wiped away her tears. "You see, it's not you who owe me anything, Michael. It's you and the Irish I owe everything to – you gave me back a purpose in life."

CHAPTER 52

The Lavery household was a sea of activity the day of the dinner party. Gordon and his staff were rushing around, making sure everything was in place. Hazel oversaw all the details, checking and double-checking the settings at the dinner table and going through the house with a fine-tooth comb to ensure all was perfect.

"For goodness' sake, Hazel," said John as he walked through the hallway and saw her arranging a display of flowers in a vase. "You are making the servants very nervous with all your fussing. I heard one of the kitchen maids had to take to the bed with a migraine, she was so stressed. It is just another dinner party, the same as countless others we have hosted in the past."

"You're quite wrong, John Lavery! This is one of the most important dinner parties every hosted in London. I do not exaggerate – it could mean the difference between war and peace!"

"Yes, dear!" He rolled his eyes as he passed her and continued up the stairs to his studio.

As advised, Michael arrived early and had a drink in the drawing room with Hazel and John before the others arrived.

"And do not spend the whole night just talking politics," Hazel told him. "Ask them personal questions, get to know them. Dear Winston is incredibly witty when you get to know him."

"I haven't seen much evidence of it in Downing Street so far," said Michael, downing his whiskey in one.

The footman who was standing by the drinks cabinet hurried over with a decanter and refilled Michael's glass.

The doorbell rang, sending a shrill through the house. Hazel raced across to one of the windows and looked down on the street below to see a fleet of automobiles parked outside.

"They're here! Everyone to their places!" Hazel pulled Michael up from his armchair, took the glass from his hand and placed him in an imposing position in front of the fireplace.

Then she quickly beckoned John to stand beside her, facing the double doors leading into the room.

"And smile, everybody!" she commanded as she heard Gordon lead the party down the corridor towards them.

There was a knock, then Gordon pushed open the double doors and announced:

"Mr. Winston Churchill ... Lord Birkenhead ... Sir Philip Sassoon ... and Mr. Eddie Marsh."

"Welcome, everybody!" Hazel smilingly approached the men and greeted each of them with a warm kiss.

"A pleasure to be here, Hazel," said Winston, giving Michael a wary look.

John moved forward and shook hands with the men.

"And, of course," said Hazel, "you all know Michael."

"Oh, yes, we all know Michael," said Birkenhead with a note of despair.

"Excellent! Gordon, drinks for everyone!" She sashayed over to the drinks cabinet where Gordon stood at the ready and whispered, "Keep the alcohol flowing, Gordon – all night!"

Conversation flowed smoothly over dinner as Gordon and the footmen served the main course of roast pork with crackling, roast potatoes, various vegetables and a delicious gravy and apple sauce.

Winston observed Michael throughout the night, trying to learn more about him than what he had seen at Downing Street. He saw that Michael had an element of social awkwardness and was still not very comfortable being in their company. But he was far more assured than when he had first arrived in London. As Winston observed the close rapport between the Irishman and Hazel, he was certain she was the main reason behind the transformation. By the time the dessert of rhubarb tart smothered in custard had been consumed, he and Michael were even on first-name basis.

"I hear you attended a poetry recital recently, Michael?" said Winston.

"I did – part of the Bloomsbury set, I believe they are called."

Birkenhead grimaced. "That crowd of communists! Where was this recital?"

"Why – here in Cromwell Place, Lord Birkenhead. In the drawing room!" said Hazel.

"Of course! Where else? Is there a rich man, poor man, beggar man or thief that has not passed over the threshold into your salon, Lady Lavery?" asked Birkenhead.

"Not a one! And there have been plenty of tinkers, tailors, soldiers and spies as well!" said Hazel, causing everyone to erupt with laughter.

"I certainly believe that spies have," said Birkenhead, causing the laughter to end and be replaced with an uncomfortable silence.

Hazel suddenly stood up. "Shall we retire to the drawing room? You can have your port and smoke there in comfort."

"We have fought for our independence for hundreds of years. We are a separate nation and a separate people. We deserved to take our place among the nations of the world," said Michael, speaking passionately in the drawing room,

"*Hear, hear!*" said Hazel.

"Nobody is denying you are a proud nation, but you can be that within the empire," said Winston.

"And you must understand that Northern Ireland now has its own parliament and will not be ruled from Dublin," added Birkenhead.

"But these are deal-breakers as far as we are concerned. I can't go back to the Irish people, after all these years of bloodshed, without bringing back a republic," said Michael.

"The reality is Ireland has become ungovernable by the

British," said Hazel. "You need the Dublin parliament to bring order to the country."

"Hazel, as it we keep reiterating – it is not a parliament – it is an illegal assembly," said Winston.

"Well, whatever it is – you need it to restore order!" retorted Hazel.

"And you need Washington to continue loaning you money," said Michael. "If you don't settle the Irish question favourably, they'll call in your war loans."

"Nonsense!" dismissed Birkenhead.

"Really?" said Michael. "There are demonstrations in New York and Washington calling on the US government to do that right now."

"If the treaty negotiations collapse and war resumes in Ireland," said Hazel, "the British government will condemn itself in front of world opinion – do you really want that?"

Winston suddenly stood up and began to pace up and down, cigar in hand. "You are deluded if you think Ireland will be granted independence by Lloyd George. He has said it over and over again. It would be seen as marking the beginning of the end of the empire and he will not allow it. You need to be practical and see things as they are. The fact is, if the Irish do not change their stance and the negotiations collapse resulting in a return to war, then the Lloyd George government will most likely collapse along with the treaty."

"That will result in the Conservatives coming into power with their leader Bonner as Prime Minister – and that will change everything," said Birkenhead. "Bonner will never give you even dominion status. It will be a return to war for sure."

Hazel and Michael exchanged worried looks.

"As bad as he is, we want to deal with Lloyd George rather than Bonner," said Michael.

"I shall take that as a compliment to my boss, shall I?" said Philip Sassoon.

"For fuck's sake!" said Michael, jumping to his feet and pacing up and down angrily.

"I would say we are the lesser of two evils," said Winston. "So, start compromising!"

Michael stood in front of the fire with his hands on his hips, his expression angry from frustration.

Hazel was trying to indicate discreetly to him to calm down – this was what Winston said about him being temperamental.

"I don't understand what is wrong with you people!" said Michael, his voice loud and angry. "Why the fuck do you want to be in a place that clearly and utterly doesn't want you? It's like being a guest at a party you aren't invited to!"

Hazel rose and went to stand by Michael. She placed a hand on his arm. "Calm down, Michael!" she urged.

"Yes, listen to your girlfriend, Michael, and calm down!" said Birkenhead.

Michael swung around, glared at Birkenhead and demanded, "What did you say?"

"I suggested calming down!" said Birkenhead.

"No – before that – what did you call Hazel?" Michael marched over to him menacingly.

"Oh, for goodness' sake – I was just making a joke to try and lighten the mood!"

"So, your idea of a joke is to insult your hostess who has gone to so much trouble for you here tonight?" Michael's voice was low and angry.

Hazel went to him. "Michael – it really doesn't matter."

"It does to me. We don't disrespect women where I come from."

She spoke softly. "He didn't mean anything by it, Michael. Please forget it and don't create a scene."

Michael looked at her pleading face and then turned and walked back to the fireplace.

Birkenhead looked relieved that he had backed away.

"Tell me more about this dominion status – how independent would we be?" asked Michael, as he flicked his hair off his forehead.

CHAPTER 53

The dinner party marked the beginning of numerous unofficial meetings at 5 Cromwell Place. On the other occasions Arthur Griffith and the other Irish delegates accompanied Michael.

"All except Childers! He still won't step over my threshold!" lamented Hazel over the breakfast table one morning as she prepared to host another luncheon for the delegates.

"He is certainly a man of principle – one must admire how he never varies from his position," said John as he began to open his post. "Ah! Another portrait commission!"

"Who is it this time?"

"The Duke of Arthington ... I must say our involvement in the peace treaty has not affected my commissions as I had feared – I am busier than ever!"

"Of course you are! We are being seen as political heavyweights and 5 Cromwell Place is now seen as the most important salon in London!"

John opened another letter and sighed. "Not in all quarters, I'm afraid ... another hate letter."

"Don't even read it!" said Hazel, reaching over and snatching it from his hand. Crumpling it up, she threw it into the fireplace.

"I have heard that our association with Michael is not stirring up controversy only in London," said John.

"What do you mean?"

"I understand eyebrows are being raised in Ireland about his close association with us and others in British high society. It has

307

all come as a surprise as he is the last man they ever expected to forge such alliances and friendships."

"Well, they like many others have underestimated Michael. He is an exceptional man with exceptional abilities. The Irish are very lucky to have him representing them here in London."

John was struck by the adoration she clearly felt for Michael which she did not in any way try to disguise.

"But we have to think of Michael, Hazel. He is our friend and we do not want to be the cause of any unnecessary embarrassment for him."

"Embarrassment!" Hazel became angry. "How on earth could we possibly be a cause of embarrassment for Michael!"

"He is discussing extremely important details of the treaty with you, instead of exclusively with his fellow delegates. Can't you see how that could look compromising for him?"

"Not in the least! I am Michael's confidante – what of it?" She shrugged. "He trusts me and needs a guiding hand from someone who has his and Ireland's best interests at heart. You've seen him, John, when he arrives here in the evening or late at night ... he's exhausted! We are his only oasis – the only place he can relax and be himself. I don't apologise for providing that oasis for him!" Hazel's eyes became misty as she spoke.

"But –"

"I don't want to hear another word on the matter, John Lavery! I have a luncheon to organise – monkfish with sage and cranberry I think is called for today. I must go and discuss with Cook."

She stood up and marched out of the room.

As November came to a close, the winter weather set in.

Hazel and Michael were returning from a night at the theatre as a flurry of snow was falling. Hazel's footman drove them through the Kensington Streets.

"I have heard that tomorrow is going to be a crucial day." Hazel kept her voice to a whisper even though glass separated them from the driver.

Michael was used to receiving information from Hazel. He was never quite sure who she heard the information from, whether it was Winston or Eddie Marsh or Philip Sassoon or even Lloyd George himself. But he found she was never wrong. *Forewarned is forearmed* had become Hazel's motto.

"In what way crucial?" asked Michael.

"The British are going to present their final deal and an ultimatum."

"A good ultimatum or a bad ultimatum?" asked Michael.

"Ultimatums are bad by definition, Michael. And I have heard that when Lloyd George says this is his final offer, he won't be bluffing."

The automobile pulled up outside 5 Cromwell Place. Michael stared out the window, lost in thought at this news.

"Nightcap?" suggested Hazel.

"Yes, alright."

The footman got out and opened the door. Michael stepped out and then assisted Hazel down the step onto the pavement. He put his arm around her as they dashed through the snow and up to the front door.

Michael kept his arm around her, trying to block out the snow and she nestled into him to keep warm. Finally, Gordon opened the door.

"It is freezing!" said Hazel as she stepped into the hallway and shook the snow off her coat and hair.

"It certainly is, my lady. I kept the fire in your own sitting room lit in case you might not be retiring to bed early," said Gordon.

"Good man! We shall go there for our nightcap. Has Sir John gone to bed, Gordon?" She handed her fur coat to him.

"He has indeed, my lady, this past hour," said Gordon, taking Michael's coat, scarf and hat. "Will there be anything else, my lady?"

"No, we can look after ourselves, thank you, Gordon," said Hazel as she and Michael began to walk up the stairs.

"Very good, my lady," said Gordon, doubt sounding in his voice.

"I don't think he actually approves of you yet!" Hazel whispered, causing herself and Michael to erupt in giggles as they reached the landing.

They turned down the corridor and walked past the main drawing room to Hazel's sitting room which was at the end of the corridor.

"Excellent!" said Hazel as they entered the room and saw the blazing fire in the hearth.

"Whiskey?"

"Yes, please."

She went to her drinks cabinet as Michael went to warm himself at the fire. He rubbed his hands together and held them close to the dancing flames.

She waltzed over to him and handed him a crystal glass of whiskey.

"So, what is this ultimatum, I wonder?" he said as he walked over to one of the windows behind Hazel's desk and looked out at the snow falling. The street down below was now covered in a veil of snow.

"*That* I couldn't find out," she said as she sat down by the fire with her own drink. "But be very careful how you react – as I said, they will not be bluffing."

Michael turned from the window and looked down at Hazel's desk, deep in thought. He suddenly reached down and took up a letter that was resting there.

"What is this?" he demanded as he quickly read through the letter.

Hazel's closed her eyes in irritation. She had received another death-threat in the post that day. In her haste to get to the theatre, she had neglected to either lock it away or burn it.

"It's nothing, Michael – nothing at all!"

"This isn't nothing – this is a vicious death threat!" he said, shaking the letter in the air. "Anonymous! Who would write such a disgusting thing?"

"I don't know, and I really don't care who writes them."

"Them! You mean there have been others?" Michael was horrified.

"One or two."

"What does John make of them?" asked Michael.

"He doesn't know, I haven't shown them to him. He gets letters as well, hate mail, but no death threats like the ones I get. I don't want to worry him."

"And what do the police say?"

"I haven't told them."

"Hazel!"

"I do not take the letters seriously and I believe to make a fuss of them is only giving the writer what he or she wants. They are best ignored. Besides, if I did go to the police, I'd hazard a guess they'd say I had invited trouble by inviting the people who murdered their colleagues in Ireland into my house in the first place. To conclude – I don't think I'd get much sympathy from them!"

"No – no, I don't suppose you would, when you put it like that," he said, putting the letter back on the desk. "But you should have told me. I had no idea – it never occurred to me – that your association with me would be putting you in such peril."

"A crank letter is not being put in peril, Michael! I am made of sterner stuff than that."

"Regardless – I can't come here anymore," he stated.

"*What*?" cried Hazel as she quickly put her glass on a table and hurried over to him.

"None of us, none of the Irish delegates can. It's too risky. If anything should happen to you, I would never forgive myself."

"But you can't just leave me! Not now – not after we have come so far!" She was horrified.

"What choice do I have? It's for your own safety."

Her eyes filled with tears. "But you can't just walk out of my life – don't you see – don't you understand – you've become the most important thing in it!"

"I know the Irish situation means so much to you, but you have to think of your own safety, Hazel."

"It's not just the Irish situation, Michael! It's you! *You* have become the most important thing in my life. I didn't want to, I don't want to – but can't you see that I have fallen in love with you?" Tears sprang from her eyes and rolled down her cheeks.

They stood staring at each other in silence until Hazel tore herself away and walked to the couch. She sat down, quickly drying her eyes.

"I fear I have just made a terrible fool of myself," she said.

"No, no, of course not," he said, walking towards her slowly.

"I believe I have. Strange, how with the amount of men who have declared undying love to me over the years, I choose to say it to the one man who doesn't feel the same way."

"It's not that I don't have – feelings – for you. I'm very flattered – what man wouldn't be? But you're married – not just married but married to a great man. And I'm engaged to be married."

"Yes," she said under her breath.

"I know I don't talk about Kitty much with you – we're too busy talking about the treaty. But it's been a long journey for Kitty and me to get to where we are – there's been a lot of hurt caused along the way – not just to us, but to other people so we can be together. I can't and don't want to throw that away." He sat down beside her and faced her. "You can understand that, can't you?"

"Of course," she nodded.

"And from what you told me the journey for you and John to be together has been even more arduous ... would you really throw that away?"

"No ... of course not. I'm being rather silly," she sighed. "I just can't help how I feel ... I'll get over it, I know I will ... but it will take some time. I just have never had such strong feelings before. How ridiculous of me to lose my head at this stage of my life – I really must be getting old!"

"No, no, Hazel, you're not being silly. I feel very strongly about you too. If there weren't so many obstacles in the way, who knows what other destiny there might have been for us?"

"Now I fear you are just being kind to try and save my damaged pride," she said, smiling at him.

She took out a handkerchief and began to dab her eyes. He

took the handkerchief from her and wiped her eyes for her. She nestled into him as he put his arms around her. Then they stretched out on the couch, holding each other tightly until they fell asleep.

Hazel stirred in her sleep and woke up. She blinked a few times before sitting up. She was still on the couch in her sitting room. A blanket had been put over her but there was no sign of Michael. She saw it was still dark outside and the flurry of snow was still coming down. She got up and went to the window.

She could see Michael's frame down in the street, his back to her as he walked away. She watched him until he disappeared from sight. Turning, she went back to the couch and sank down on it, staring into the embers of the fire. What had she done? Why had she said what she had said? What had she expected him to do? Why was she risking everything over a stupid infatuation? But the overwhelming feeling she had was loss. She felt she had frightened Michael away from her – from their friendship. And the feeling of loss was overpowering.

CHAPTER 54

Michael was not at Mass at the Brompton Oratory the following morning. Hazel waited in their normal pew for him to arrive, but he didn't. Afterwards she walked back to Cromwell Place on her own. She felt despondent. She knew he had a very heavy day ahead of him as she had been the one to inform him the British were going to present their final proposal that day. He also had got home very late after their time together. All this meant there were many reasons why he would not be at Mass that morning. But she knew deep down that normally he would have seized the opportunity to get her counsel before facing such an important day at Downing Street.

She waited anxiously all that day and evening for a visit from Michael but there was none.

Gordon brought the evening newspaper to her as she and John sat in the drawing room. She read the headline: IRISH DELEGATION TO RETURN TO DUBLIN TO PRESENT BRITISH FINAL PROPOSAL

Hazel felt strangely isolated as she read through the article. She had been such a central figure in the talks for so long, a go-between, a confidante to the players, that it felt wrong to be reading the day's events in the newspaper like everyone else.

"Are you alright, Hazel?" John asked.

"Yes, fine – just a little tired and worried about what's happened in Downing Street today," she said. "It says here that the Irish delegation is to return to Dublin to present the British final proposal. Look." She handed the paper to him and he scanned the article.

"So Michael probably won't be joining us for dinner tonight?" he said.

"Probably not."

"Well, it will be nice to have the house to ourselves for a change," he said.

"Yes," she said and managed to smile at him.

It was well after lunch the next day when Hazel awoke and rose from her bed. She sat at her huge dressing table looking at her reflection in the mirror. She was overcome with insecurities. She had been parading around London for so long as a famous beauty that she realised that she had become somewhat deluded. Allowing herself to fall in love with a man ten years younger than her and expecting him to reciprocate that love was ridiculous. She was so used to men pursuing her that this feeling of rejection was unfamiliar and painful. She knew that sounded vain, but she didn't care. And it was only going to get worse as she got older. When her looks and youth continued to fade away – who would pay her attention then? How could she cope without the spotlight when it was all she had ever been used to? She wondered was Michael a desperate middle-aged woman's last attempt to hang on to her youth, to convince herself of her attractiveness. She sighed loudly and began to brush her hair.

She spent the day wandering around Knightsbridge, desperately trying to fill her mind so as not to think of Michael. She visited art galleries and museums. She went to the boutiques and Harrods. There was an eerie fog descended on the city and a December chill in the air. Even the stores with their Christmas trees and decorations did not give any illusion of warmth. As she wandered about there was a strange feeling in the city, almost as if everyone was on tenterhooks, fearing that war in Ireland could soon erupt again.

As the evening drew in, Hazel couldn't stand the suspense anymore and got a taxi up to Park Avenue to visit Philip Sassoon.

315

"What a pleasant surprise, Hazel!" Philip greeted her as she was shown into his opulent drawing room.

"I hope you don't mind – I was passing and thought I'd drop in," she said.

"Not at all!" he said as he bade her sit down. He was sure she had come armed with information from Collins and the Irish delegation that Lloyd George could use to gauge their mindset.

"So how did yesterday go?" Hazel asked.

"Well – we presented our proposal. Michael looked as if he was going to explode in anger."

"Oh dear!"

"He looked so angry and frustrated and desperate! First, he demanded more concessions, then he almost begged for them! What has he told you?"

"Well – I haven't seen him, and I understand they have returned to Ireland?"

"Yes, they have gone back to discuss it with De Valera et al!" said Philip, very surprised that Hazel had not been in contact with Michael. "Did you tell Michael that Lloyd George was not bluffing – that the final proposal meant it really was the final proposal?"

"Yes."

"And how did he react?"

Hazel's temper suddenly gave way and she snapped, "He reacted in anger and temper. How else should one react when they are being bullied and trapped in a corner?"

Philip was taken aback to see Hazel lose control. He had never imagined she could ever be anything but calm, charming and good-natured.

"I apologise, Philip," she said. "I guess we are all a little tense over the deadline."

"Yes. The whole city is tense. It might be a good idea to be a little careful, Hazel. If there is a return to war in Ireland, I imagine there will be some heavy anti-Irish sentiment, which may be directed at you because of your involvement with Collins et al."

Hazel nodded before standing. "I'd better get back home."

"But will you not stay for tea or indeed dinner?"

"I had better not, Philip. I have been out most of the day and John will be wondering where I have got to." She embraced and kissed him, saying, "Dear Philip!"

As Hazel was shown through the sumptuous house, she was reminded of all the parties she had been invited to there over the years. She wondered, if the war did break out again in Ireland, would she become a social pariah?

Philip said goodbye to her at the front door, kissing her cheek.

It was dark now and the fog that had been hovering all day was now thick and heavy. Philip glanced out at the street where there was little visibility.

"Your automobile?" he enquired.

She pointed. "Just there," she said with a wave and set off down the street.

She pulled her coat around her as she walked down Park Avenue. Philip had assumed she had her automobile with her, otherwise he would have insisted his chauffeur drive her home. But she hadn't wanted to put upon him – bad enough to arrive uninvited and then lose her temper with him. She had thought she would be able to get a taxicab without a problem, but as she walked along the footpath the fog was so thick it was impossible to distinguish any taxi that may have been passing. She headed down to Knightsbridge on her way to Kensington. Every so often she would see the lamps of an approaching automobile and would try to see if it was a taxi but to no avail. The fog was so bad there was very little traffic or people out. She continued through the maze of streets. She could hear laughter somewhere and shouting.

And then she became aware there were footsteps behind her. She stopped and tried to peer back into the fog, but she couldn't see anyone. But the footsteps had stopped once she had stopped. She began walking and the footsteps started again. She began to feel very nervous. And she remembered Philip's words that she could be a target if the war broke out again. She then thought of all the letters she had received – the hate mail and the death threats. She speeded up her walking and the pace behind her quickened too. She turned the corner into another street and suddenly three men stepped out in front of her, causing her to gasp in shock.

"What do you want?" she demanded as she shook with nerves.

She could see they were roughly dressed. One took out a torch and flashed it in her face.

"I'm just on my way home, I don't live far," she said.

In the light of the torch she saw that one of the other men was holding a handgun.

"Get home quickly," one of them said before they slipped away into the fog as quickly as they had emerged from it.

She took several deep breaths and then hurried along. The footsteps that had been following her had stopped and she realised that whoever the three men were had scared whoever it was away. She turned the corner into Cromwell Place and raced down the street and up to the front door of her house where she pulled the doorbell loudly over and over again until Gordon opened the door.

She raced in and slammed the door behind her.

"Are you alright, my lady?"

She nodded quickly as she struggled to get her breathing back to normal.

"Can I get you anything?" asked Gordon.

She shook her head. "Is John home?"

"No, my lady, he hasn't returned from the commission he went out to do today."

She nodded and then quickly walked down the hallway and up the stairs. She hurried into the drawing room where she poured herself a large whiskey and drank half of it quickly. She wondered who the people in the street had been. Who had been following her and who were the three men who had stepped out carrying guns? She realised that she was a person of interest to everybody from the British Intelligence to Irish terrorists. The people she had encountered that night could have been either, neither or both. She took her drink to the couch and sat, trying to calm down.

She got up and went over the windows and peered out to see if anybody was outside, but the fog was too thick to see.

Gordon knocked on the door and came in.

"Is John home yet?" she asked.

"Not yet, my lady."

"Has he the automobile with him?"

"Yes, and Tim is driving him."

She was relieved to hear this.

He handed her an envelope.

"What is this?" she asked.

"It was delivered by a girl this morning. She didn't say who she was but had an Irish accent."

Hazel examined the handwriting on the envelope and recognised it as Michael's.

"Thank you," she said, waving him away.

As Gordon retreated from the room, Hazel went to the couch and sat down before quickly tearing the envelope open.

She straightened out the paper and read.

Dearest Hazel,

I'm writing this quickly before I leave for Dublin. I was so sorry to leave you the other night after the wonderful evening we had at the theatre. You were a beautiful vision as I left you. I should be in Dublin no more than a couple of days before returning to London early next week. Whatever the next few days will bring, let us hope and pray we all make the right decisions. I apologise that I did not have time to come and see you before I left London but will call as soon as time allows when I get back. I feel strong knowing you are there waiting for me, my champion and supporter – I can never thank you enough for everything,

M.

Hazel stared at the letter and was overcome with a feeling of relief.

"He hasn't abandoned me," she whispered, holding the letter close to her heart.

CHAPTER 55

It was not just Hazel who was on tenterhooks for that weekend but the whole of London, waiting for the Irish delegation to arrive back with their answer to the final proposal. Hazel could only imagine the pressure Michael was under and longed to be with him to offer support.

On Monday, December 4th, the Irish delegates arrived back in London.

Every time somebody called to the house, Hazel's heart jumped, thinking it might be Michael, but he didn't come. She kept in contact with all her friends throughout the day and heard that evening that there had been a private meeting between Lloyd George and Michael that afternoon in the home of Philip Sassoon.

"It's a pity I didn't just happen to be passing at the time and call in!" lamented Hazel.

"You would hardly be allowed into a private meeting between the Prime Minister and the leader of the Irish delegation, Hazel, at this stage of the game," John said.

"You'd be surprised what I can wrangle myself into, John Lavery! It goes to show how the British see Michael as the one to convince. If they get Michael on side, the others are sure to follow – even Childers!"

"He has metamorphosed into a leader," agreed John. "Does he appreciate that you are the reason for that?"

"I don't want appreciation, John – I just want –" Hazel stopped herself as she thought how to finish the sentence. What did she want? What did she really want?

The next day the fog still swirled around London, creeping like a menace around the elegant buildings of Kensington, seeping along every street and into every crevice.

Hazel stood looking out at Cromwell Place through one of the front windows as the afternoon darkened into evening. There seemed to be people hovering around outside in the street. It was hard to see them plainly as the fog swirled around the lampposts. She wasn't sure if she was being paranoid, or if it was the general tension in the city, but there seemed to be unusual activity outside.

The doorbell rang and she tried to look down at the front door to view who it was, but was unable to see.

She waited for Gordon's arrival with either a guest or a message.

The door opened and Gordon walked in, announcing, "Mr. Collins, my lady."

Hazel could hardly believe it as Michael's large frame came through the doorway.

"*Michael!*" she exclaimed. "Thank you, Gordon, you may leave us."

Gordon retreated from the room and closed the doors. Hazel and Michael stared at each other for a short while before she rushed to him and threw her arms around him. She felt his arms glide around her and hug her tightly back.

Michael sat on the couch with Hazel beside him, John sitting opposite them on an armchair. Hazel had never seen him so angry or upset.

"I am being bullied," he declared. "Lloyd George at the meeting today gave me an ultimatum. He said we either accept his final proposal or it's all-out war. That he would flood Ireland with British forces and bring the whole force of the empire down on the country! Martial law. He said we have until ten o'clock tonight to decide."

"He's certainly trying to force your hand!" said John. "Could he be bluffing?"

"He's not bluffing, John," said Hazel. "I have had it confirmed by every source I have that this is the final proposal and the treaty can go no further. But this! To give you so little time to make such a momentous decision!"

"I'm outraged!" Michael got up and, red in the face, began to stomp up and down, clasping his fist in his hand. "The British troops are back on the streets of Dublin! I saw them myself at the weekend – walking around and stopping people, looking for identity papers. Letting their presence be known. Showing us their power."

"But that's in breach of the terms of the truce!" said Hazel.

"They are letting us know they are getting into position if the treaty isn't passed and the truce collapses. It's the same here. Scotland Yard are teeming around the city watching us all the time. There's a load of them positioned outside my headquarters in Cadogan Place and the other delegates' at Hans Place." He went to the window and looked out at the fog. "They are even out there in Cromwell Place. I spotted them on my way in. They are watching us right now."

"How dreadful!" declared Hazel, all her worst suspicions confirmed. She went over to the windows and hastily closed the curtains.

"Who knows what tomorrow will bring if we don't sign tonight," said Michael. "I and the other delegates may be not be permitted to leave London and could be arrested on the spot!"

"They couldn't do that!" said Hazel, horrified.

"Why not?" said Mick. "If war is declared tonight, are they really going to let the leaders to travel back to Dublin to wage a war against them?"

"It would be impossible for you to wage another war like you did the last one, Michael," warned John. "Nobody knew what you looked like before – now everyone in the world knows. You'd be a sitting target."

"What of your meeting yesterday – with Lloyd George at

Philip's house? Did you sense anything else about the lie of the land?" asked Hazel.

"No – he said the same thing – just not in such stark terms as today," said Michael.

"They've lost their patience," said John.

"*They've* lost their patience – what about *me? What about my fucking patience*!" He exploded in anger.

"Perhaps if I spoke to Winston or Philip, I might be able to find out more," said Hazel.

"There isn't time," snapped Michael.

"And I doubt they would have anything else to say," she admitted. "As horrible as it is for me to say, Michael, I believe this is it! I think you either sign their damned treaty or sink Ireland into another war which will make the last one look like child's play."

"But I can't. It won't be accepted back home – they want full independence. I can't go back and say I haven't signed up to that and they are still subjects of the King and have to swear an oath of allegiance. Or that I have signed away the jurisdiction of the North to Belfast."

He slumped down on the couch and his extreme anger crumpled as he sank his face into his hands. Hazel went and sat beside him. She nodded at John who, heeding the request, got up. Putting a parting comforting hand on Michael's shoulder, he left them alone.

"Michael – Michael – look at me," Hazel said, taking his hands and forcing his tear-filled eyes to look at her. "I don't see how you have a choice in this matter anymore. If you don't sign the treaty you will be plunging Ireland back into years of bloodshed. The Irish people don't want that and are unable to fight it. You have said yourself that your resources, your arms are very low. If the full might of the British army comes down on you, then you will be crushed in days and the country will be under military dictatorship for years to come. This way – if you sign the treaty – well, it's not perfect, but it's a start. Ireland will have power over its own affairs and be somewhat autonomous – something it has not had and has fought for down the centuries. Take what is on offer now and you can take the rest later. Ireland will gain full independence in time – in the meantime take this offer. You will be hailed a hero in Dublin for avoiding any more bloodshed and war."

He shook his head and said mournfully, "Why have I been left with this decision?"

She took his face in her hands and spoke with determination. "Because you are a great man and maybe the only one capable of making this decision – the right decision."

The day passed slowly by. John mostly left Hazel and Michael alone, coming occasionally to the door of the drawing room to listen and try to get a sense of what was occurring inside. Sometimes he heard long stretches of silence. Other times Michael could be heard shouting and Hazel trying to calm him down. At times there was even sobbing coming from the room.

John spent most of the time in his studio, working on his next portrait.

"Sir, my lady has requested that you should go to the drawing room," said Gordon.

John quickly put down his brush and left the studio.

When he entered the drawing room, he saw Michael standing at the fireplace, his head hung. Hazel, meanwhile, had changed into an elaborate gown and was wearing her best coat.

"Dare I ask – has a decision been made?" asked John.

"Michael, after much soul-searching, has decided to accept the final proposal from Lloyd George."

"I see," said John, walking over to Michael and placing a hand on his shoulder "This is brave deed."

"I have decided to … give in," Michael said the words sadly.

"Not 'give in', Michael! Compromise!" said Hazel. "You have decided to *compromise* which is what negotiating is all about."

"There hasn't been much compromising from the British during these 'negotiations'," said Michael.

"When one person is holding a gun to your head, then perhaps they are in the stronger negotiating position," said John, trying to keep as much kindness in his voice as possible.

"Well – we must go! We don't have much time to lose," said Hazel, hastily putting on her gloves.

"Go? Go where?" asked John.

"Downing Street, of course! Via Hans Place – for Michael to tell the other delegates of his decision first. I shall drive him."

"You! But it's getting late, Hazel. Did Michael's driver not come with him here?"

"Yes, they're sitting outside being watched by Scotland Yard as we speak, no doubt! They can follow us in their automobile. Come along, Michael. That deadline is looming! We don't want war to be declared by accident because we got delayed in traffic!"

She sashayed towards the door and Michael followed.

In the hall below, John took Hazel's arm and pulled her aside.

"Hazel, don't you think the people he should have been discussing this with are the other delegates in Hans Place?"

"He has been discussing it with them until he is blue in the face! They could not reach a decision. They can no longer see the wood from the trees. That is why he came to me – to get some clear concise advice."

"I hope you do not get the blame if all this turns sour, as I imagine – Ireland being Ireland – it most likely will!"

"Don't fret, John, I know what I'm doing," she said, leaning towards him and kissing his cheek. "I won't be long – but don't wait up, just in case."

As Hazel quickly made her way with Michael out to her car, she felt elated and excited. Yes, peace was coming to Ireland, finally, after all this time. And she was going to Downing Street to be part of this historic event. But, most of all, as she sat beside Michael in her automobile, she felt elated that he was still in her life. That she had not frightened him away. And that it had been her he had turned to in his most desperate hour. In the hour when he needed somebody to trust, he had turned to her.

CHAPTER 56

Th doorbell shrilled through 5 Cromwell Place.

"Good Lord – who is that at this unearthly hour?" said John, sitting up in bed. "What time is it?"

Hazel quickly looked at her watch and saw it was five thirty in the morning. She was filled with panic and fear that something had got wrong with the treaty. Had Michael and the others backed out at the last minute? Had war in fact been declared? Was this the army come to arrest her and John? She jumped out of bed and tied her silk dressing gown around her. Not waiting for John, she scurried from the bedroom, down the corridor and down the stairs.

She could hear voices down in the hallway.

"Who is it, Gordon?" she called out.

"It's Mr. Collins, my lady," answered an exhausted Gordon, thinking that if he worked as the head doorman at Claridge's Hotel he would not have seen as much traffic as he had answering the door at 5 Cromwell Place over the past few weeks.

"Michael!" she gasped.

He had stepped into the hall and stood there, looking dejected.

"What's the matter?" she asked.

"It's signed, Hazel, I signed the wretched thing," he whispered.

"And the others?"

"They signed – they all signed."

"Tea, my lady?" asked Gordon through bleary eyes.

"No – no – you go back to bed, Gordon."

"As you wish, my lady," said Gordon as he shuffled off to bed.

"Oh Michael!" Hazel said, embracing him.

As John came down the stairs, he saw Hazel and Michael, their arms wrapped around each other as she comforted him. His mouth opened to say something, but instead he closed it again and retreated back upstairs.

The hours slipped by in the drawing room at 5 Cromwell Place as Michael recounted everything that had happened at Downing Street.

"I'm sure it is a huge relief to Winston, Lloyd George and the others," said Hazel.

"Not all of them," sighed Michael. "Birkenhead said that he had probably just signed his political death warrant ... and I replied that I had probably just signed my actual death warrant."

Hazel recoiled in horror. "Michael! Do not say such a thing!"

"Why not? It's probably true ... there will be people in Ireland who will never accept this and who will they blame? Me!"

"But the majority, Michael, the majority will applaud and thank you for it. The troops in Dublin will be off the streets today – when only yesterday they were on a war footing."

"I should never have come to London. I should never have been sent and I should have refused to come and bugger the consequences! I am not a politician, I am a soldier – and this was a job for a politician."

"You might not have been a politician, but you are certainly one now. And you must now rely on all your political skills to get this treaty accepted at home and passed by the Dublin government."

He looked into her eyes. "The only reason I am glad I came to London is because otherwise I would never have met you."

She blinked a few times. "Don't tease me, Michael. Although I daresay I deserve it after the number of men I have teased over the years. But if you think anything of me, then don't tease me. Not after the last few days I've had. I thought you would never speak to me again after I ... said what I said. I went through such pain, thinking I had offended you."

"Offended me? How could you ever think I was offended? I was flattered and humbled that a woman as beautiful and elegant and wise as you could consider me anything other than a country hick over to the big city making a big fool of himself!"

She reached forward and pushed back a lock of his hair from his forehead. "It's I who made a fool of myself – allowing myself to fall for somebody – somebody unobtainable. But now I have accepted there can be nothing between us and I am happy with my love for you ... unrequited love is the best kind of love, because you don't expect anything in return."

They stared at each other and only the sound of the door opening broke their gaze as Hazel quickly sat back.

"I thought it might be you, Michael," said John, coming in. "You look shattered, you poor chap."

"I am fairly shattered, John. It's been one hell of a night."

Hazel stood up and tightened the belt of her dressing gown around her. "I must change. Goodness me – I am now receiving guests in night attire – whatever next!" She went over to the bell-pull and tugged it. "You need to rest for a few hours, Michael. I'll have Gordon run a bath for you and after you need some sleep. Later we'll have something to eat."

"Thank you, Hazel – thank you both!" he said and managed to smile at them.

"I can't believe you are going back home tomorrow," said Hazel.

It was evening time and she was walking Michael down the stairs to the front door. He was going back to Cadogan Gardens to spend the night before returning with the rest of the delegation to Dublin the next day.

"It will be very strange to think you aren't just up the road from me to drop in to whenever I want," he said.

"Kitty will be glad to have you home," she said.

"Yes. She's not one for this political world though. She gets bored if I talk too much about it."

"Wise girl!" said Hazel with a smile.

He looked around the spacious ornate hallway. "When we first came to London you said you wanted us to treat your house as a home from home. Well, that's exactly what it became for me. A home. And I've haven't had a home for a very long time. Fighting the war, sleeping in a different place each night. I'd forgotten what a home felt like – but I know now it feels like here."

"I'm very touched that you think that," she said.

"I don't even have a home to go back to in Dublin. I'll be living life on the go again – more hotel rooms – though thankfully not in a war situation."

"Thanks to you! Our home is your home, Michael, you will always be welcome here ... although I daresay you will have your own home soon once you marry Kitty."

He thought it odd she was mentioning Kitty so much. She had never mentioned Kitty much before – now it was as if she was bringing the curtain down on their liaison and reminding herself he was engaged.

"Will you write to me?" she asked.

He gave a big laugh. "All the time! Lady Lavery, I will need you to be my eyes and ears in London. You will be like my ambassador – the only one I can trust over here."

She wasn't sure if his words were hollow, but it gave her a great sense of relief to hear them – that she wouldn't be seeing the last of him.

They reached the door and he embraced her and hugged her tightly. She kissed his cheek and, when he pulled away, opened the door.

He stepped out into the evening.

She closed the door, bolted it and walked down the large empty hallway feeling lost and alone.

CHAPTER 57

In the days after the Anglo-Irish Treaty was signed and Michael left London, Hazel felt a wave of sadness envelop her. She had been so busy over the previous months, being at the heart of the Irish delegation and the treaty negotiations, that now it was over she felt somewhat empty. But she knew what she missed most was Michael. It was as if there was a big hole in her life now that he was no longer there. She remembered his parting words to her, that he would be relying on her all the more now that he wasn't in London, but she wondered how true that was. He would return to his life in Ireland and would soon be married to Kitty and she would just be a distant memory to him. She understood that she must return to her life too, as painful as that might be. But she couldn't allow herself to fall into a depression. She wondered if she would ever hear from Michael or see him again.

It would soon be Christmas and she was being inundated with invitations as the party season began. She sat at her writing desk in her sitting room, looking at the stack of envelopes sitting in front of her ready to be opened and read. Sighing, she took them up and began to sift through them. She suddenly stopped when she recognised the handwriting on the front of one of the envelopes as Michael's and saw the postmark was Dublin.

Her hands began to slightly shake as she held the envelope and then she ripped it open and unfolded the letter inside.

The Gresham Hotel
Sackville Street
Dublin

Dearest Hazel,

So, I have arrived 'home'. Home for now being the Gresham Hotel. Even though it's been only a few short days since I left London, it seems an eternity since I was there and with you. After I left you that last day in London, I returned to Cadogan Place and we all packed to return home. Well, Hazel, you should have seen the crowds that were there to wave us off from Euston Station. It made the welcoming reception when we arrived in October look small! It gladdened my heart to see the goodwill from the people and the support for the treaty we had just signed. I can confide only to you how uncertain I felt travelling back to Ireland, fearing the reaction in Dublin would be nothing so great as the one we left in London.

When we arrived in Dublin, at Kingstown Harbour, there was a military welcome for us from our men. It raised my spirits to see them and when I asked one of my lieutenants if he supported the Treaty, he told me that if it was good enough for Mick Collins then it was good enough for him! Such loyalty from the men as I saluted them that day in Kingstown. If the Treaty had failed and there had been a return to war, it would have been these men whose lives would have been on the line fighting the British Auxiliaries. We travelled into Dublin and that was when the mood turned uglier. I quickly gathered that a great many people did not support the Treaty.

I met with De Valera that night and he was devastated. He sat with his face in his hands, saying we should have never accepted the terms and he could not accept the Treaty and would be strongly opposed to it being ratified through the Dublin parliament. Oh, Hazel, when I heard that my heart sank. The next day, as I'm sure you know, De Valera released a statement to the press strongly rejecting the Treaty and urging the people to do the same. Since then, I have been fighting tooth and nail to get support of as many deputies in the Dublin government as possible to ratify the Treaty in order for it to be accepted.

The main debate and vote will take place after Christmas, in January. You must tell Churchill not to despair. I am confident I will get the Treaty passed. He or the British government must not do or say anything at this stage to inflame Irish passions. Make him aware, Hazel, as only you can, what a delicate situation we are in. I and the other signees of the Treaty now rely on Lloyd George and Churchill to step back and trust us to pass the Treaty at home. It is a very delicate situation with even whispers that the end result could be civil war here. Pray it is not so.

I wish you were here with me, Hazel. I miss our time together. I miss the support and love you always gave me. I am staying at the Gresham Hotel for now, occasionally staying with friends for a night. I miss the comradeship of everyone at the house at Cadogan Gardens and I miss being able to go up to you whenever I could.

I haven't had time to even visit Kitty in Longford and I will not have the time to get down over Christmas either as we prepare to debate the Treaty in January. As I look around my hotel room, I'm still waiting to have my 'home' – the nearest I've ever had being still your home.

With fondest love and best wishes,
Michael

As Hazel read and reread the letter, she was overcome with emotion and wished as much as he did that she was beside him to encourage him and keep him strong during this difficult time. She quickly grabbed a sheet of paper and a fountain pen and began to write back to him.

My dearest Michael,

I really can't express how happy I was to get your letter today. Rest assured, my love, that I miss you in equal measure. But remember I am here for you, thinking of you, supporting you at all times. Whenever you feel down or under pressure, know I am on your side and always have your best interests at heart. Regarding De Valera, he may well disapprove of a treaty that he could not offer an alternative to! How easy it is to be critical of others' hard work, when he sat on the fence looking on while the work was being done! Now is the time to remain strong, my darling. In the face of the inevitable criticism, it is vital you remain strong and committed to the treaty you have signed.

Hazel paused and reread what she had just written. She had to write the most positive, supportive letter Michael had ever received. During his time of need, he had turned to her and she must not let him down.

CHAPTER 58

Kitty hurried up the steps and into the Gresham Hotel. She didn't know what she felt most – fear or excitement. The hotel was already decked out in Christmas decorations with a huge Christmas tree in the lobby.

"Can I help you, madam?" came a voice behind her and when she swung around she saw it was Michael.

"Oh, Mick!" she exclaimed, throwing herself into his arms and hugging him tightly.

They found a quiet corner in the restaurant and had lunch.

"Ah, it's good to see you, Kitty. It's just wonderful you are here!"

"I thought you might have got down to Longford by now," she said.

"It's been impossible with everything that's been going on. After all our hard work, I have to get this treaty ratified by the Dáil – otherwise we're back to where we started. Doesn't bear fucking thinking about!"

"I know – you've said all that in your letters. I still hoped I'd walk into the parlour one day and you'd surprise me and be standing there, the way you used to."

He reached out and stroked her hand. "Nothing would have given me more pleasure."

"I thought, now you have come back and the damned treaty is signed, we could start living a normal life. But here's you living in a hotel and most of our relationship still being conducted by post." She glanced around the restaurant. "We're still not officially engaged, as nobody outside our families knows."

"But sure we decided we'd wait until Harry is home in January and tell him first," said Michael.

"But will he be home in January or will there be another delay?"

"He has to come home to vote on the Treaty in the Dáil."

"He'll be on your side, I take it?"

"Of course – he's my best and oldest friend and he'll know this is right for the country."

"Maud says that Gearóid is shocked you signed the Treaty. He thinks it will lead to civil war."

Michael's face went red as he tried to control the anger that was threatening to erupt. "Well, it's just as well Gearóid isn't a deputy in the Dáil whose vote we would be relying on to get the Treaty ratified, isn't it?"

"No need to get angry, Mick," she cautioned.

He ran his fingers through his hair and managed to calm down. "I'm sorry. I'm just under such pressure."

She sighed loudly. "You're always under 'such pressure', Mick. I don't have that long. I have to catch the train back to Longford."

"Will you not stay until tomorrow?" he asked.

"In your hotel room?" She raised an eyebrow. "I don't think so, Mick. We're not married yet and I feel as if we compromised ourselves in London. In fact, I regret so much going to London at all."

He looked upset as he stared at the tablecloth. "Maybe you regret getting engaged to me as well?"

She reached over and took both his hands in hers. "No! Mick, that is the one thing I do not regret out of everything. I love you with all my heart and soul. And I want you, so much – so very much. And I know we can make each other happy. You make me very happy all the time. I just want you all the time and sharing you with the world is hard."

"But you knew all this when we started. Long before we became engaged."

"I know. Isn't that why I tried to keep away from you for so long? That and the fact that I wasn't sure if you had real feelings for me."

"But you know now? You know how much I return your love?"

She nodded and whispered, "Of course."

CHAPTER 59

The Churchills' chauffeur parked outside 5 Cromwell Place and, getting out, opened the back door to let Winston and Clementine out. It was late evening and it was snowing heavily. It was Christmas week and they were attending the Laverys' traditional drinks party.

Clementine pulled her coat collar tight around her neck as they carefully walked through the snow and up to the front door.

They pulled the doorbell and Gordon opened the door.

"Good evening, Gordon, and Happy Christmas," said Clementine, stepping quickly into the warm hallway.

"Good evening, Lady Churchill," he said.

"What ghastly weather, Gordon," said Winston as he shook the snow off his coat onto the tiled floor.

"Indeed, it is, sir," said Gordon, taking both their coats.

"Are we late?" asked Clementine.

"Not at all. The party is – as the Americans would say – just getting into the swing."

"I must say it's nice to be in this house without the usual array of Irish revolutionaries in attendance!" said Winston.

"Oh, I don't know," asked Clementine. "I'm very upset I didn't get an opportunity to meet Mr. Collins. Is he as dashing as they say he is, Gordon?"

"I am sure I am not in a position to judge such things ... but I daresay he could be described as having a certain ... magnetism," said Gordon.

"Well put, Gordon!" laughed Winston. "I must admit myself I was impressed by the fellow by the end of it all."

"Who'd ever have thought!" smirked Clementine. "He certainly must have a degree of 'magnetism' for you to say that, Winston."

"Well, he'll need all the 'magnetism' he has to get that treaty through his damned parliament. Enough of this idle chatter, Clementine, or we shall miss the main event!" They quickly made their way down the hallway and up the stairs to the drawing room where the party was taking place.

In the drawing room, the atmosphere was very lively as everyone chatted and laughed. Soon Clementine was deep in conversation with Thelma beside the Christmas tree that stretched to the ceiling.

"I don't mind telling you, Clementine, that you would not believe the comings and goings in this house over the past few months – if walls could speak!" said Thelma.

"Really?"

"As you know I live just across the road and so was privy to all that was going on. There were times I felt quite unsafe, there were that many unsavoury characters hanging around."

"How unfortunate!"

"Yes, there used to be this gang of men who would just sit in an automobile outside the Lavery house whenever the Irish – delegation, for want of a better word, were here. They just sat there watching everything – very intimidating!"

"I can imagine," Clementine sympathised.

"Then there were other men lurking around watching the men who were sitting in the automobile. I presume they were British Intelligence or Scotland Yard."

"It's sounds all very *Riddle of the Sands* – though I believe that book's author, Mr. Childers, was one of the few who didn't visit here," said Clementine.

"I really wouldn't know. I wouldn't know one from the other – they all looked the same to me – apart from Michael Collins, of course – I recognised him from the newspapers."

"And I believe you met him at a party here as well?" said

Clementine knowingly.

"*Hmmm* ... I will tell you something, Clementine, Michael Collins was in this house so much I don't know why he didn't just move in!"

"Yes, I believe he and Hazel became very close."

"There's a surprise with her reputation!" said Thelma, laughing.

"What are you insinuating, Thelma?"

"Well, she's slept with half of London, so she may as well start with Ireland now too!"

"Well, when you put two very attractive people like Hazel and Mr. Collins in the same company for long, rumours are bound to fly, they always do. And let's face it, Thelma, Hazel is still the most attractive woman around, bar none."

Clementine smiled sweetly at Thelma and then quickly moved on to talk to other guests.

Hazel was in a deep conversation with Winston and Shane Leslie in the corner of the room.

"Michael says that he is confident that he will get the Treaty ratified and we must bear with him," said Hazel.

"Without De Valera's support? I really am not so sure, Hazel," lamented Winston.

"He says he can get the numbers to get it through the Dáil," she said. "He is pleading that the British do or say nothing to jeopardise that vote in January."

"Well, we want to help the lad get it through at all costs. But there's unease in our ranks, Hazel. Some Conservative MPs are shouting for the Treaty to be torn up and these attacks that are resumed on British forces over there must stop!"

"I know, Winston, but these are Anti-Treaty people behind the attacks trying to provoke trouble in Ireland and looking for a reaction from you. We must not give it!"

Winston sighed heavily.

"She's right, dear cousin – we must stand with Michael and the others now we have made the pact with them," urged Shane.

"Come with me, both of you," commanded Hazel as she beckoned them to follow her out of the room.

They walked down the hallway outside to her sitting room. She opened the door and led them in, turning on the lights.

She went to her desk, opened a drawer, took out some letters and riffled through them until she found what she wanted.

She handed Winston a letter.

"What is this?" he asked.

"It's my last letter from Michael. Read it for yourself, see his own words ... and you will see how much he is trying to make this work and how much you can trust him."

Winston sat down on the couch and began to read.

"See? See how he tries?" said Hazel.

"I almost feel sorry for him," said Winston, as he continued to read.

Shane meanwhile discreetly took up some of the other letters from the desk and began to read through them.

Finally, Winston stood up and handed back the letter.

"I shall do my best in Westminster for him," said Winston. "But you are to tell him he must do his best for us too! Tell him to do all he can to rein in the attacks on British soldiers and buildings there and to try to stop the attacks on the Protestant big houses as well. I know none of it is his doing, but he is getting tarred by the same brush and the British public's patience is all but worn out!"

"I'll write to him tomorrow and tell him. Thank you, Winston."

As Winston left the room to return to the party in the drawing room, Hazel turned to see Shane reading her letters from Michael.

"Shane! They are personal!"

"Sure – that's why you left them on the table for me to read!" he said with a laugh.

"You really are bold, Shane!" she said, taking the letters and putting them back in the drawer.

"Are you having an affair with him, Hazel?"

"With who? Michael?" She laughed loudly. "Of course not!"

"Well, you act as if you are and he writes as if he is!"

"He does no such thing!"

"Those letters are full of the sort of maudlin sentimentality that should be reserved for rather dim schoolboys!" said Shane. "*Dearest Hazel ... I miss you like winter misses the sun ... I long to be back in the warm bosom of 5 Cromwell Place*' – 'warm bosom' indeed!"

"Shane! He writes as one friend to another, that is all!"

"He writes as one lover to another! Seriously, Hazel! Has it come to this? After rejecting the likes of me and Lord Londonderry for years you finally jump into bed with a barely literate soldier!" Shane was amazed and horrified.

"I haven't jumped into bed with anyone, apart from my husband. But I do take great offense that you describe Michael as illiterate, or merely a soldier. It is not true!"

He sat on the side of the desk. "Do you know what I think? I think Michael Collins has captured your heart. I think he has replaced me and Londonderry and all the rest of the boys in London who have been chasing you and you have been manipulating for years. You've barely contacted me since Collins came on the scene –"

"Not true!"

"And when you do it's only in relation to a matter involving Collins! Londonderry told me the same thing!"

"You are jealous, Shane. Envious of Michael."

"More confounded than jealous, Hazel! Confounded as to what exactly you can possibly see in a man like that!" He jumped off the desk and stormed out of the room. She watched him go and then went to the drawer and locked it.

"What do I see in a man like Michael?" she whispered to herself as she looked at the snow fall against the window

Kitty had been bitterly disappointed that Michael did not make it to spend Christmas with them in Longford. She knew he had said he wouldn't be able to come, but she still half expected for him to show up to her surprise and delight. On Christmas night, after the festivities of the day, the family and friends had retired to the parlour where the usual fun and games were taking place. Kitty watched, barely participating. She realised she had entered the life she had always demanded of herself to reject. Even after the end of the war, the truce and the Treaty signed – here she was on her own on Christmas Day. Michael seemed more preoccupied with outside events than ever. She knew, if she had any sense, she still had time to run away from this situation. But she was too much in love with Michael to do that. She would take him on whatever terms she must. She idly took up a copy of *Vogue* magazine and began to leaf though it and came to an abrupt halt when she saw a photo of Lady Hazel Lavery. There were numerous photographs of Hazel taken in her Kensington mansion accompanied by an interview where she discussed her plans for Christmas – that appeared to consist of much partying and socialising. She scrutinised Hazel's beautiful face. Up to a few months ago she had barely ever heard of Hazel Lavery. But since Michael had entered Hazel's circle, Kitty felt she could hardly open a magazine or a newspaper but there would be some photograph or article on her. As she studied the photograph of the Laverys' ornate and sumptuous drawing room, she still found it hard to imagine her Michael being in such an environment or to understand how he could ever be comfortable there. But she had to accept he had, and he was. And she needed to understand this change in him for their life together to work.

BOOK 3

1922

CHAPTER 60

As 1922 began, the debate for ratification of the Treaty reached fever pitch in the Dáil. As it was the week to vote, all the deputies were present and the atmosphere electric. Harry Boland swaggered into the government building, fresh back from America, and took his seat to listen to the debate that was raging. He looked across the floor and saw Michael sitting opposite him. Suddenly Michael spotted him and a big smile curved across his face as he saluted him.

Harry smiled warmly and saluted him before both men switched their attention back to the emotive debating and speeches taking place.

Countess Markiewicz had the floor. A hero of the 1916 Rising, the first female to be elected not only to the Irish parliament but also to Westminster (though she refused to take her seat in the British parliament), the Countess was an adored heroine of the Irish revolution.

And as she spoke that day, she lambasted Michael, rejecting the treaty and bringing his character into question.

"I have heard stories of the comings and goings in Deputy Collins' quarters in London. I have heard of the rather large drinks bill from Harrods ... rather large food bills from Fortnum and Masons ... rather large confectionary bills from Selfridges. One would wonder, under the circumstances of such a large amount of alcohol consumption, was the Deputy in a sober state of mind when signing the Anglo-Irish Treaty?"

Deputies on both sides of the debate roared approval or disapproval.

Michael sat with his lips tight, legs crossed, and arms folded. He remembered Hazel's words. He must not show temper but show statesmanship.

"As for the company Deputy Collins kept on his adventure in London ... one can only say such company was at best ill-advised and at worst outrageous! I understand that Deputy Collins is now such a mainstay of London high society that the wedding of the King's only daughter, Princess Mary, is to be called off and Princess Mary is to be married instead to Michael Collins who will be appointed the first Governor of Ireland!"

The roars of the deputies turned into shouting and thumping as shock overcame the house, not only at the accusation but at the Countess's bravery to make such an outlandish claim.

Michael got to his feet and waited patiently for silence before speaking.

"I know nothing of the lady the Countess is referring to, apart from being aware she is engaged to some gentleman. As such the deputy's accusation may cause the lady some distress ... as it may cause pain to the lady who is betrothed to me."

The chamber again erupted in chanting and shouting as Michael retook his seat.

"Did he just announce he was engaged?" said one deputy to another.

"He did indeed! He kept that quiet!"

"And who is the woman he is engaged to? Now that we can safely say it's not Princess Mary!" chuckled the first deputy.

As Michael folded his arms and looked across the chamber, he saw that Harry was staring at him without any expression on his face.

After the session, Michael waded through the deputies who were applauding him and clapping his back and made his way to Harry.

"Harry!" said Michael as he reached him. "Well, it's grand to see you!"

"You too, Mick!"

"Well – come here!" said Michael, reaching for him and hugging him.

Harry allowed himself to be hugged before pulling back.

"So – you're engaged to be married?" he said.

"I am, Harry," said Michael, becoming serious. "To Kitty."

Harry nodded as they looked at each other in silence.

"I hope you both will be very happy," said Harry as he offered a hand for Michael to shake.

Michael grabbed his hand and shook it warmly.

Then Harry turned and walked away into the crowd of deputies.

Michael rushed back to his office. He had learned enough in London about how rumours and gossip spread like lightning to realise news of his engagement would have wings. He needed to warn Kitty that the truth was out.

"*Kathleen!*" he shouted, running into his office where he hastily began to write a note to Kitty, explaining that he had announced their engagement that day in the Dáil without mentioning her name, having been forced to show his hand due to the accusation of an engagement to Princess Mary.

"Yes, Mick?" said Kathleen, rushing into his office.

"Send this express post to Kitty without any delay," said Michael, handing her the envelope. "It's urgent."

"Right away," said Kathleen who turned to rush away, but then paused. "Oh, and Mick – congratulations on the engagement – Kitty is a lovely girl!"

Michael's mouth dropped open. He watched Kathleen disappear out the door, wondering how she had found out about the announcement in the Dáil before he had even arrived back at his own office!

CHAPTER 61

"Post, Miss Kitty," said Molly coming into the parlour.

"Thank you, Molly," said Kitty.

"And the plumbing is broken again!" announced Molly as she flounced out.

Kitty raised her eyes to heaven and quickly singled out an envelope with Michael's writing that had come express post.

She tore it open and read the contents. Her mouth dropped open.

"What is this?" she whispered to herself. "Accusations he was engaged to Princess Mary! So he had to announce our engagement!"

Kitty looked up in shock. She had never in her wildest dreams ever have thought that their engagement would be announced as part of the Treaty debate in the Dáil in Dublin! Was ever an engagement announced in such a bizarre way before? Michael hadn't mentioned her name, but she wondered how long it would now take for it to become known. She felt strangely exposed and vulnerable. She felt at the same time relieved and happy the engagement had at last become official – but what a way for it to happen? No happy family announcement with family and friends. No opening of a bottle of champagne and a toast to the happy couple as she and Michael gazed into each other's eyes lovingly. No – an accusation he was to run off with the King's daughter and a defence that he was already engaged to another! She shook her head in dismay as she got up to find Maud to discuss this latest chain of events. She dropped the rest of the post in her haste and, bending down to pick the envelopes up, she spotted another familiar handwriting on the front of another envelope.

She took the envelope and held it with trembling hands. It was Harry's handwriting. She opened the envelope and read the note inside.

Kitty,

I want to congratulate you. M told me of your engagement, and I wish you long life and happiness,

Ever Yours,

Harry Boland.

She read the note again and again. She felt relieved that Harry now knew of the engagement. But what a change in his writing style. Gone was the flowery verse, the close sentiments, and they were replaced with a cool, professional almost curt note. This wasn't the Harry she knew. And yet here he was, ever the gentleman, acknowledging the engagement and wishing her well. His heart must be breaking, she thought, as she sat down on the couch holding the letter close to her and letting the tears fall down her face.

"Michael has announced you are engaged, and you must not let him down!" urged Maud. "Gearóid says Mick is under terrible pressure trying to get the Treaty passed in Dublin and he's been accused of all sorts – fraternising with the enemy and insinuations that he was a traitor to the Irish. He needs your support now more than ever!"

"And I will not let him down, Maud, but I just wish he had let me know it was to be announced and given me some time to prepare."

"Well, he kept your identity secret."

Kitty hooted with laughter. "For how long? News like that doesn't remain secret for long!"

There was a knock on the parlour door and the receptionist from the hotel walked in.

"Sorry to disturb, Miss Kitty, but all these telegrams arrived into the reception for you," said the girl, handing them to Kitty with a smile before turning and leaving.

"What are all these?" asked Kitty as she riffled through them.

"Well?" asked Maud.

"Oh, good lord!" said Kitty as she sank into the couch. "They are all from newspapers and magazines looking to do interviews with me!"

Maud grabbed some of them and began to riffle through them. "This is from the *London Times* … this from the *New York Times* … international press as well as Irish!"

"What will I do?" asked Kitty, suddenly feeling terrified and exposed.

Maud sat down beside her. "As I was just saying to you – you must not let Michael down! Michael is now an international figure and people want to know about you as his fiancée. You've nothing to hide and nothing to be ashamed about, Kitty! Let them come and meet you and do Michael proud!"

Kitty's hands were shaking at the thought but as she glanced over at the table and saw a photograph of Hazel Lavery on the front cover of *Tatler*, her mind became steely about what she needed to do.

Kitty took a look at herself in her full-length mirror before turning to Maud.

"How do I look?" she asked.

"Just beautiful, Kitty," said Maud.

Kitty was dressed in an elegant long dress in black satin with a beaded bodice and narrow shoulder straps, high-heeled black shoes and black stockings. Maud thought she wouldn't look out of place in a high-society party in Long Island.

In the parlour, invited members of the press waited anxiously. After receiving all the telegrams, Kitty and Maud had contacted the editors of the newspapers, inviting them to Granard to meet and photograph Kitty.

As she held Maud's hand walking down the hallway to the parlour, Kitty realised her life was about to change and nothing would ever be the same again.

CHAPTER 62

After days of ruthless debate, the time for talk was coming to an end and the time for the vote was fast approaching. As Michael made his way into the chamber, he felt weary. He had endured days of attacks on his character – being called everything from a traitor to a mindless drunk who didn't know what he had been doing in London when he signed the treaty. What was most hurtful were the attacks from his friends.

That morning, he was getting extra looks of curiosity. The press had made its way down to Longford and photographed Kitty in her parlour. She looked beautiful, relaxed and cheerful as she sat on the couch posing for the photographs. He was overcome with pride on seeing her. He knew she would not have wanted that level of attention but was doing it to support him and to let him know she was with him and capable and able for the life they would have together when they were married.

As everyone took their seats in the chambers, Michael wondered how Harry felt on seeing the photographs of Kitty in the newspapers. He could only imagine it would have hurt him deeply.

As the debating got under way, Harry rose to his feet to make his speech to the house. Michael thought it curious that Harry had waited until nearly the final hour before the vote to voice his opinion.

"Fellow deputies, I have listened with great interest and sometimes great pain to the debate since returning from America," he said to a hushed chamber. "I can only say that listening to Deputy Collins and the way he has vigorously defended his treaty makes me very sad ... as I wish, with all my heart, he had shown the same level of fight and passion in his dealings with Lloyd George. If he had, I believe we would not be in this mess today – for I cannot and will not support this treaty which is an insult to our people who have fought so hard and deserve their independence."

As the deputies in the chamber went wild with shouts of approval and disapproval, Michael stared down at the floor before slowly raising his eyes to look over at Harry who was staring right back at him, both men with tears in their eyes.

On the afternoon of the seventh of January 1922, the vote was taken with 64 deputies voting in favour and 57 against. The Anglo-Irish Treaty was ratified with a majority of seven votes. Éamon de Valera, who had fought tooth and nail for the Treaty to fail, then resigned as president along with his supporters. Arthur Griffith was elected president in his place. Michael was given several portfolios in the new government, including the role of chief contact and negotiator with the British government as Ireland established itself as a Free State within the British empire.

As Michael left the chamber that evening, the new Irish government was already in disarray as a severe split had emerged with Michael and the Pro-Treaty deputies on one side and the Anti-Treaty ones, led by De Valera, on the other – and those refused even to sit from then on in the new parliament. As Michael left the chamber, most deputies looked to be in tears or close to tears. But out on the street large crowds had gathered and cheered Michael as he made his way back to the Gresham.

That night in his room at the hotel he felt exhausted and emotionally drained as he sat at his desk and wrote a quick note to Kitty.

My Dearest Kitty,

I am writing you this quick note before I collapse into bed as I am exhausted. The pressure from the other side is dreadful. If you can please come and see me as soon as you can,

    M.

Michael called the bellboy and gave him the letter to post and then went to the bed and stretched out on it. He knew he should be celebrating – the treaty had been passed and now Ireland could start getting back to normal with a new government in place in Dublin. But he knew it would not end there – De Valera and his supporters would not accept the Treaty and Michael was terrified where that would lead to. He dearly wished Hazel was there to discuss the implications of everything with him. He wished he was in Cromwell Place. As he lay there he thought about Harry and the look of anguish on his face. Could they ever be friends again?

CHAPTER 63

"Well, finally we get to paint you, Prime Minister!" exclaimed Hazel as Lloyd George sat for John in the studio at Cromwell Place.

"Well, I had thought up to now there was no point that I, or any other of the British cabinet, should pose for Sir John's Irish Collection – to celebrate the Irish Treaty if there was nothing in fact to celebrate!"

"Indeed, but we must not be lax, Prime Minister," said Hazel. "We must give Michael as much support as possible to ensure success. I received a letter from him, only this morning, that he fears the walkout by De Valera and the others may result in a civil war."

Lloyd George raised his eyes to heaven. "Well, Mr. Collins will have to make sure there isn't one!"

"Easier said than done! He needs your assurance, Prime Minister, that you will not interfere with the new Irish constitution – and that you will ratify the treaty in Westminster without delay."

"Well, it would be out of the question that the Irish just draft their constitution without British input or approval. They could put anything in it – and more than likely would put anything in it!"

"Prime Minister!" snapped Hazel angrily. "Michael has put his reputation, career and even his life on the line here! There is a real fear the fledging Dublin parliament will collapse under the weight of opposition from De Valera et al! With De Valera gone out of official politics, Michael Collins is the most prominent Irish politician. Arthur Griffith may be the new President, but as you saw when he was here for the negotiations, he is tired and old. The success of the treaty – of Ireland – now rests squarely on Michael's shoulders – and if you know what's good for you, you had better do everything in your power to lighten that load!"

Lloyd George looked at her in shock. He had never seen the usually refined and jovial Hazel Lavery in such a temper before.

"I shall bear all that in mind when he comes to London and I meet him next week," he said.

"Good! And we are having a drinks party on the Friday – Michael is the guest of honour – we will expect you to attend."

"Hazel, dear," said John, frustrated, as he stood paintbrush in hand, "you are distracting the subject too much ... if we could have some quiet, please?"

"Yes, of course," said Hazel. "I must send a letter to Michael by return post anyway."

Lloyd George looked at Hazel in astonishment as she marched out of the room.

"Prime Minister – if I could be so bold as to ask you to adopt your original pose?" said John, smiling patiently.

"Yes, of course," said Lloyd George as he began to pose again.

A thick blanket of snow lay on Dublin's Sackville Street as the taxicab manoeuvred down the thoroughfare and the snow continued to fall. It pulled up outside the Gresham Hotel and a porter rushed out and opened the back door of the vehicle, holding up an umbrella for Kitty as he escorted her into the hotel. The taxi driver brought in her suitcase and she paid him.

"Mr. Collins asked for you to be brought straight up to his room when you arrive, Miss Kiernan," said the porter.

"Lead the way so!" said Kitty as she followed him up the main staircase of the plush hotel.

They continued up the stairs to the top floor where the porter stopped at a door.

"You can put it down here." Kitty pointed at the suitcase.

She smiled at the porter, tipped him, and waited until he left before knocking at the door.

"*Come in!*" came a growl from inside.

She picked up her case and opened the door.

Michael was sitting at the bureau with his back to her while the snow fell against the long windows on either side of him.

"Leave it on the table," instructed Michael.

She smiled, realising that he thought she was one of the hotel staff bringing something she had ordered.

"Leave what exactly?" she asked.

He spun around, delight and surprise on his face. "Kitty!"

He rushed to her and embraced her.

As he kissed her, her fragrance enveloped him, and he never wanted to let her go.

"Oh, I've missed you," he whispered into her ear.

She pulled back and looked at him smiling, before her smile faded. "You look exhausted, Michael."

"I am exhausted, Kitty," he sighed, letting her go and scratching his head. "It's been a draining few weeks."

She led him to the couch by the hand and they sat down.

"I wasn't sure you'd come," he said.

"Of course I came when you asked me to."

He looked out at the falling snow. "Or that you'd be held up with the weather."

"No – nothing could stop me!" She laughed but he didn't join in. "I see you got the Treaty passed," she said then.

He nodded. "But at what cost? Half of my friends will never speak to me again … they see me as a traitor."

"What about Harry? I got a note from him – congratulating me on the engagement. Did he say anything to you?"

"Not about the engagement. But he had plenty to say in the chamber about me as a politician, basically calling me a disgrace." Michael's face was a mixture of hurt and anger. "He has rejected the Treaty."

"*Oh, no!*" Kitty was shocked. "Do you think – do you think that he criticised you – because of our engagement?" She was almost afraid to ask.

"I cannot believe a politician as dedicated as Harry could be influenced by the affairs of the heart – can you?" Now it was Michael's turn to almost be afraid to ask.

"He must be broken-hearted, is all I can say. He was full sure he and I would be married. It must be a terrible blow ... who knows how anyone would react under such circumstances?"

He looked at her, alarmed. "You don't regret any of it, do you? The engagement, I mean?"

"Of course not!"

"It just sounds as if you have regret in your voice," he said.

"Mick, I love you! I want to dedicate my life to you, to loving you and to be everything a wife should be to a husband – I just didn't realise it would cause so much pain for others, for Harry."

"Well, let us try to put all that aside just for the moment – I have to go to London next week."

"London!" She let go of his hands and stood up abruptly in shock.

"Yes, a meeting Lloyd George and Churchill."

"What for?" She was horrified.

"Ah, Kitty! There's no point in me going through the political reasons for my visit – you just wouldn't be interested! Suffice it to say, since the walkout by Dev and the others, my new role encompasses being the chief liaison and negotiator with London. I am to be Ireland's official envoy."

"I cannot believe this!"

"I'm the best placed for the role. And I may as well be honest with you, Kitty, I also have been appointed to travel around Ireland giving speeches and meeting everyone at county level to explain and convince the people to make the Treaty a success."

"You! Giving public speeches! The man who spent the last number of years hiding in the shadows is now the foghorn for this blasted new country we find ourselves living in!"

"Foghorn!" Michael repeated the insult incredulously. "You have a vicious tongue on you, Kitty Kiernan, that's for sure!"

"And between you going back and forth to London like the mailboat and up and down Ireland like a travelling salesman, when – pray tell – will we ever see each other and actually get married?"

"All the time! Whenever I'm not in London or travelling around the country!"

"Glad you can fit me into your diary!" she snapped.

"There's nothing stopping you travelling with me," he said.

"Attending political rallies in the rain and the snow! No! If my fragile patience didn't break, then my fragile health would. I'm not a Countess Markievicz or a Lady Lavery – I'm not the political animal you are, Mick, and I never will be!"

"I don't want you to change, Kitty. I love you for who you are."

"So, is this our life?" she said as she walked around the suite. "A series of hotel rooms – never having a home of our own?"

"I thought of all people that would suit you, being a hotelier," he said, causing her mouth to drop open at his cheekiness.

He grinned at her and despite herself she started to laugh.

He got up and held her.

She thumped his shoulder. "To think I could be happily married to Lionel by now!"

"Ah, I'm sure he's still waiting for you in the wings – if you hurry you might catch him! If you can get past the queue of women no doubt wanting him!"

She thumped his shoulder again.

There was a knock on the door.

"That will be the sandwiches I ordered – I hope you're hungry as I ordered a mountain of them!"

He went to the door and let the porter in.

As the trolley was wheeled in and Michael chatted to the porter, Kitty sauntered around the room. She stopped at the writing desk and saw the letter he had been writing when she had arrived.

Dearest Hazel,

Snow fell all last night and today, leaving the air as cold as the hearts of the friends and colleagues who have turned their backs on me. I wish you were here so I could tell you how bad and depressed I feel. How I long for your comforting words and sweet smile. How I long to be alone with you in your sitting room as we used to be ...

Kitty saw the letter was several pages long.

"Tea's up!" said Michael and she quickly turned around to see him pouring the tea.

"Is anything the matter?" he asked, looking at her.

"No! No, nothing at all." She forced a smile and quickly walked towards him.

CHAPTER 64

Hazel stood at the window in her sitting room looking impatiently out. She kept looking at her watch and was nearly shaking with excitement. Michael was due to arrive from Dublin and he had written that he was coming straight to see her once he arrived in the city.

She saw an automobile pull up outside and her heart leapt as she saw Michael get out. She turned and ran out of the room and down the corridor. By the time the doorbell rang, she was already racing down the stairs.

"It's alright, Gordon – I'll get it!" she called as she raced across the hallway and swung open the door.

Michael was standing there.

"Michael!" she whispered as he came in and she slammed the door shut.

They stared at each other a moment before falling into each other's arms.

He sat on the couch in her sitting room with his legs stretched out as she sat beside him, holding his hand.

"That last day in the chamber, the day of the vote – the things they said about me. Cathal Brugha said I had courted publicity, portrayed myself as a romantic figure, basically accused me of being a spy and a traitor."

"You must ignore all that, Michael! When the Treaty was passed and you came out on the streets, the people cheered you – did they not?"

360

"Yes, they did," he conceded.

"Well, that is all that matters! To hell with the detractors! You have brought peace to Ireland and you are loved for that, Michael."

He smiled at her. "Why do I always feel strong when you are by my side? I feel I can do anything when you are beside me."

"That is because you can do anything!"

They fell silent, staring into the fire.

"I see you announced your engagement to Kitty," she said then.

"Yes, my hand was forced in the chamber when they made that accusation about me and Princess Mary ... I wrote to you about that."

"What nonsense! More likely that I would run off with the Pope!" she said, causing Michael to roar with laughter. "Don't let these things worry you, Michael. As you know I have been putting up with lurid accusations for years – it's the price we pay for being attractive!"

Michael threw back his head and roared with the laughter again. "Oh, my darling Hazel, I haven't laughed like that in weeks – you make me feel young."

"That's because you are young ... we both are ..." She managed to keep her face from frowning.

He closed his eyes for a moment and sighed. "Sometimes it's hard to feel young in these trying times."

"I saw the photographs of Kitty in the newspapers ... she's a pretty girl," said Hazel, blinking a couple of times.

"Yes – all this is taking a heavy toll on her. She's not really cut out for this type of life – politics."

"It's certainly not everyone's cup of tea. There has to be a supreme sacrifice if you want to make a difference in politics." She leaned towards him and whispered, "It has to come before everything else."

His eyes had a faraway look. "I just feel at times ..."

"What, Michael?"

"I feel the enemies that have been chasing me for so long will crowd in on me and catch me and tear me apart ... until there is nothing left ..."

She reached forward and held him tightly. "They'll have to get through me first, Michael, and I will never let you down."

The next night, 5 Cromwell Place was filled with society figures as Hazel hosted a party for Michael.

"I am so glad to have finally met the legend!" said Clementine Churchill to Hazel. "He's wonderful, isn't he?"

"Quite so!"

"Too bad he is spoken for! I can see a number of the ladies are taken with him," said Clementine as she observed a group of women around Michael, listening to his every word.

"Yes – I had better go rescue him. He's meant to be making friendships with the ministers – not their wives!" said Hazel as she went over, broke through the coterie and led Michael away.

CHAPTER 65

The next couple of months passed by in a flurry of activity.

Michael travelled to London a lot, meeting with the British cabinet. Hazel was always there waiting for him, organising his meetings, his schedules, driving him around to make sure he got to where he needed to on time. Sometimes he even stayed at 5 Cromwell Place as opposed to the coldness of a hotel. They grew closer and closer.

When in Ireland, Michael was constantly touring the country, giving speeches, garnering support for the Treaty.

Kitty had thrust aside the fears and suspicions she'd had after reading that revealing letter from Michael to Lady Lavery. Her instincts told her to be cautious and not do or say anything she might later regret.

She also tried to hide her resentment at how little time he was giving her. She even attended one speech he gave to an enormous crowd in Dublin. She marvelled at the thousands of people that were gathered there, all focused on the one figure who stood on a podium, commanding their attention and their emotions as he delivered his words. As she stood there amongst the crowd, she was full of pride and admiration for him. But also fear. She could hardly recognise this impassioned speaker as the tender, teasing man she loved.

As the words bellowed from his mouth and he shook his fist in the air, Kitty shivered. She saw the people around her become intoxicated by his vigour and enthusiasm. His energy and his words were literally seducing the crowd into cheering and applause. For some reason she felt scared by the crowd's reaction. It was too ebullient and she was scared of how easily Michael stirred this reaction. Such power would inspire much love but also some hate, Kitty feared.

Nevertheless, the severe opposition to the treaty did not go away until it was decided to put the decision to the Irish public in a general election. The situation became inflammatory in April when dissidents opposed to the Treaty stormed the Four Courts complex in Dublin and held it under siege. This was Ireland's principal courts building, located on Inns Quay. The situation was hugely embarrassing, not only for Michael and the fledging Dublin government, but for the British government. The other source of disharmony was the new Irish constitution, many parts of which the British were objecting to.

With all these issues, Hazel acted as a trusted intermediary. She was somebody both sides knew they could trust to inform them privately what the other party was thinking and how far they could be pushed.

"The British cabinet thinks the Constitution you have drawn up is too – communist – in nature and tone," said Hazel one evening at the end of May as she and Michael were enjoying a gin and tonic in the drawing room at 5 Cromwell Place.

"Communist!"

"I believe they used the term 'Bolshevik'."

"Ireland is the most conservative country in Europe! We could hardly have a Bolshevik constitution!" declared Michael.

"Be that as it may be, it will need to be toned down if the British are to accept it. The last thing Britain wants is a Bolshevik neighbour on her doorstep! Especially with the growing power of the Labour Party in Britain. Although I must say I like the look of their leader, Ramsay MacDonald."

Michael stood up angrily. "So I change the constitution and prove all my opponents and enemies in Ireland right – that I am merely a puppet of Lloyd George and the British!"

"Whatever you may be accused of, Michael, the fact is you need Lloyd George and the British now. You need the arms they are supplying you. If they suddenly stopped backing you at this stage and the Treaty collapsed, where would that leave Ireland? The full evacuation of the British troops out of Ireland is not complete – they could halt the evacuation at any minute and claim that, as you can't bring law and order to Ireland, then they will!"

"So they expect me to turn my troops, Irish troops, against other Irishmen in order to take back the Four Courts? It would result in civil war!"

"But you can't just continue to let those men occupy the Four Courts. They are laughing in your face and the face of the British government!"

"I can't turn my men against fellow Irishmen – I can't!" insisted Michael.

The next morning, as Hazel drove Michael to Downing Street they discussed the forthcoming election.

"If you win this election, as you will," said Hazel as she turned the automobile into Downing Street, "then it will show the people are in support of the Treaty and De Valera and the rest of them will have nowhere to go in their opposition."

"They might have nowhere to go – but they still aren't going to go away!"

"Anyway, let's just concentrate on the business at hand and the meeting with Lloyd George today – and getting the new Irish Constitution passed without any further interference from them!"

"Easier said than done!"

"Best foot forward!" insisted Hazel as she pulled up to the pavement.

The policemen outside 10 Downing Street quickly approached and opened the doors of the automobile.

The usual journalists were gathered on the street.

"*Michael, how are your meetings with the Prime Minister progressing?*" called one.

"Fine, thank you," said Michael as he and Hazel got out and headed for the door of Number 10.

"*Michael – are you and Lady Lavery having an affair?*" called another, causing Michael to stop in his tracks and stare at him.

Hazel saw Michael's face turn to anger as he began to make a move towards the journalist. "Michael!" she hissed. "The Prime Minister is waiting!"

Michael glanced at her, then glared at the offending journalist before turning and, taking Hazel's arm, quickly heading inside the building.

The following day Hazel was having lunch at home with John.

"You are quiet today, Hazel."

"Am I?" She snapped back to reality. "Just a bit distracted – thinking over the meetings of the past couple of days."

Suddenly the dining-room door swung open and Alice came storming in, waving a newspaper.

"Alice! Whatever is the matter?" asked Hazel.

"*This! This is what is the matter!*" cried Alice as she flung the newspaper down on the table.

Hazel picked up the newspaper and saw an article about Michael's visit to Downing Street the previous day.

The article's headline read: MICHAEL COLLINS ARRIVES IN DOWNING STREET WITH HIS SWEETHEART

The article made reference to Hazel so there was no doubt as to who the 'sweetheart' was.

Hazel's mouth dropped open.

"What is it?" asked John, reaching over and taking the newspaper.

"*We are disgraced!*" cried Alice.

"Alice, dear, calm down – they will hear you all the way to Buckingham Palace," said Hazel.

"It's libel! I'll sue!" said John.

"You'll do no such thing, John Lavery!" snapped Hazel. "You'll ignore it as I will."

"You'd want to be sure of your facts before you sue, John, as Oscar Wilde found to his cost!" said Alice.

"And what is that supposed to mean?" demanded Hazel.

"Well, is there any truth in it? That you are his sweetheart – his lover!"

"Alice! Young ladies shouldn't say such things!" admonished Hazel.

"And married women should not be cavorting around London with young Irishmen! You are a disgrace, Mother!"

"Alice, I have never been able to control what people say about me – your stepfather understands that."

"You could control the opportunities you hand to people to gossip about you! I've had to put up with years of innuendo and gossip about you! You've encouraged outlandish behaviour from everyone from Charlie Vane-Tempest-Stewart to Shane Leslie, for the sake of your own vanity. But this latest liaison with Michael Collins has now hit the national press – have you no shame?"

Hazel went to say something, but suddenly found her eyes fill with tears.

"Excuse me!" she said, rising from the table and, unable to hold back the tears, rushing from the room.

Alice turned to John, exasperated. "Have you nothing to say on the subject?"

"No – no, I don't, Alice," said John, placing the newspaper on the table. "And neither should you. It's really none of your business, or anybody else's for that matter."

Alice shook her head. "I don't understand you! Why do you continually allow her to make a fool out of you?"

"Hazel has never made a fool out of me. She has never been unfaithful to me, I know that for a fact. She loves me as I love her, and we have had to go through hell to have our life together. Neither of us would do anything to jeopardise that."

"But how can you stand these rumours?" she said, snatching up the newspaper and waving it in the air.

"Because that's all they are – untruths, rumours, gossip. Your mother and I do not care for such things. If we did, we would be over years ago."

Alice sat down at the table, trying to understand.

"Poor Alice!" He smiled at her and patted her hand. "I've sometimes wondered is there anything crueller than for a girl to have a beautiful mother. There is so much that is hard for your mother to understand and accept – insecurity, vanity – and the knowledge that one day that beauty will go and the fear that its departure will leave her with nothing ... and that is the day the problems will only begin. Charlie, Shane and Michael – all of them and more besides – they are no more to Hazel than water is to a plant. It feeds her self-perception – it validates her as a person." He smiled kindly at her. "Now I would be very weak indeed if I let that upset me, wouldn't I?"

"Oh, John!" Alice suddenly burst into tears. "I've always known, but I only realise now just how very kind you are."

"Now, now!" he said, taking a handkerchief and dabbing her eyes with it.

"And how cruel I am!"

"Not cruel, but perhaps a little harsh. But perhaps you can find it in your heart to give your mother a little kindness with this subject as well? She's terrified, Alice. She's getting older and she's terrified of what that will bring. Don't you remember a few years ago when she fell into a depression, after the car crash?"

Alice nodded. "It was a dreadful time."

"I always fear it may happen again. So, if she gets a little lift from a silly love poem from Shane Leslie or is made to feel important being Michael Collins' friend, then what of it? If it keeps out those black moods she is prone to and keeps her the vivacious, wonderful, witty and unique person that we both love so much, then is it not a small price to pay?"

Alice rose from the table and rushed to John who embraced her and soothed her as she sobbed.

Alice gently opened the door of Hazel's bedroom a little and peeped inside. The curtains were drawn, and Hazel was lying under the covers.

"Mama?" said Alice gently as she crept across to the bed and sat down. "I'm sorry, Mama, I truly am."

Hazel turned her tearstained face to Alice then sat up and hugged her tightly as they both cried.

"*Shit!*" muttered Michael under his breath in his suite at Claridge's as he saw the 'sweetheart' comment in the morning's newspaper. He sighed loudly as he flung the newspaper across the room. This was all he needed – loose allegations like that appearing in the press with the general election in Ireland coming up. It would be seized by his opponents as evidence he was in bed – literally this time – with the British. After the Princess Mary allegation, he did not need any more insinuations that he was a playboy in London, hobnobbing with high society. Nor did he need the scandal of being associated with a married woman, with an electorate as deeply Catholic as Ireland's. He needed to be more careful, but the reality was that Hazel had become his closest ally and he just couldn't do without her. He could not imagine life without her. He could tell her everything and anything. When he was with her, he was looking into a mirror almost, they were so close, and he knew she felt the same way. But he needed to try to curb how he felt. This was a losing game that had no future. His future was Kitty.

"Kitty!" he muttered. He needed to make light of the 'sweetheart' comment in the press and write to her immediately to dismiss it as farcical. He raced to his writing desk.

Kitty reread the letter she had received from Michael that morning.

My Dearest Kitty,

Please see enclosed a cutting from today's newspaper. With great amusement I see they have labelled Lady Lavery as my 'sweetheart.' Between bouts of laughter I am contemplating having a word with my solicitor to bring lots of lovely libel action!

I'm meeting Lloyd George at noon, so will sign off for now. Things not great here, terrible pressure, I long to see you,

M.

CHAPTER 66

The following night Hazel was in Michael's suite at Claridge's as they discussed the day's events.

Hazel stood up and, taking their two empty glasses, went to the drinks cabinet.

"Lloyd George is furious," said Michael. "He said the Irish have proven what everyone was saying – that we can't run our own affairs. He said if the situation in Dublin is not resolved, the British will have to intervene."

"And what did you say?" asked Hazel.

"I told him I'd fucking wrap up the country as a present and hand it back to him myself!"

He closed his eyes with exhaustion. She stood up and went to the drinks cabinet.

"More champagne?" she asked.

"Why not?" he said, before giving a cynical laugh.

"What's so funny?" she asked, handing him his refilled glass and sitting beside him.

"This!" he said, gesturing around. "This is exactly what my enemies accuse me of! If they could see me now – sipping champagne in a luxury suite in Claridge's with a very beautiful titled lady!"

"With your sweetheart – even?" She looked at him cynically.

"You saw the newspaper?"

"Of course. It was shown to me by my daughter, who was rather upset by it. We managed to calm her down."

"We?"

"John and I."

"He wasn't upset by the article?"

"Well, initially he threatened to sue, but no – these things wash over John quickly."

"I don't know if he's a saint or a fool," said Michael.

"Why should he be either?"

"I think no matter how much time I spend in your company, I will never understand the upper classes," he sighed, shaking his head.

She shrugged. "Why bother trying to understand – what's there to gain from the exercise?"

He turned and looked at her, trying to understand her apparently nonchalant attitude to life.

"The trouble is – if the truth be known, Hazel, and leaving aside my need to see you – it's no longer a chore for me to come to London. I never thought I'd say this, but I look forward to being here. I enjoy it here – I enjoy the people I know, the new friends I've made. I admire them and that is not being in any way a traitor to my own country – just a recognition that there are admirable people on this side of the Irish Sea too."

"I'm glad," said Hazel. "That is what I've been working to achieve. It's the only way forward."

"But, most of all, Hazel, I look forward to meeting you. I miss you when I'm not with you. When I am in Dublin, I turn to discuss something with you or get your opinion and feel sad – sometimes angry – that you are not there beside me."

"Michael," she whispered. "I feel the same. Life is empty without you."

"I've never met anybody as beautiful or sad as you, Hazel. And I just want to make you happy." He reached forward and stroked her face gently.

"What about John? What about Kitty?" she said.

He pulled her close and began to kiss her.

Hazel looked at her reflection in the mirror and, biting her lip, looked back at Michael who was asleep on the bed. Her mind was whirling, confused, upset, but at the same time elated. She looked at her watch and saw it was three in the morning. She thought of John at home and was overwhelmed with guilt. She needed to get home quickly. She tiptoed across to the bed, taking a last look at Michael before slipping from the room.

CHAPTER 67

Kitty did not need to be told by Michael about the article in the newspaper referencing Hazel as his sweetheart, as she had been already told by enough people about it and had ordered a copy.

Reading his letter again, she didn't think Michael was in any way serious about suing for libel – he wouldn't have time for such things in the first place. He was dismissing the remark as a joke not to be taken seriously, but Kitty had been hurt by the remark. Michael was her fiancé – everyone knew it by now. They had even been photographed by the press together at the races last month. For him to be associated with another woman, a married woman, was disrespectful to all parties concerned. But she, Kitty, hadn't done anything to attract this attention. Michael and Hazel Lavery had, by being in each other's company continually. Kitty knew Michael had come to rely on Hazel completely in London as his go-between with the British government. But why had he, or the Irish government, come to rely on a society artist's wife? Surely there must be better diplomatic channels?

Kitty didn't think she was an overly jealous person but she knew there was something going on between Michael and Hazel – she had seen that letter he had written. But how serious their relationship was, she didn't know. Her instincts still told her to be cautious. She knew how strong an emotion jealousy was and could be. Hadn't she used it during her own romantic machinations to capture Michael's heart? She needed to control it.

"You have a guest!" announced Molly, standing in the doorway of the parlour.

"Who is it?" asked Kitty, looking up.

"Good afternoon, Kitty," said a voice, and Harry stepped into the room.

"Harry!"

They stood staring at each other, Harry with a speculative look on his face while Kitty couldn't conceal her shock.

"Sit down, sit down, Harry," she said, taking a seat herself. "Great to see you. Tell me how you've been keeping."

A loud knock sounded and Molly appeared at the door, hands on hips.

"I suppose ye'll be wanting tea now?"

"Yes, Molly," said Kitty.

"And cake with it?"

"Yes, Molly, of course."

Molly grunted and left.

"She's as hopeless as ever," Kitty said to Harry.

"So I see," he said with a smile.

Having managed to regain her composure, Kitty began to chat about things as mundane as the weather while waiting for Molly to bring in the tea – which she soon did, slapping down the tray unceremoniously and departing.

Kitty poured and they settled back to sip tea and nibble fruit cake.

"You look very well, Kitty," Harry said.

"Thank you, Harry."

"Mick's still in London?"

"Yes, I think he's back in a few days," she said, blushing despite herself.

"In time for the general election," said Harry.

"I suppose so." She shrugged.

"Whether he wins the election or not, Kitty, I and the others will never accept the Treaty. Does he not understand that?"

"I'm not sure, Harry. You'd have to talk to him yourself about it."

"He's become impossible to talk to. He has such tunnel vision – his way or no way," said Harry, his voice becoming bitter.

"He's just trying to achieve peace," said Kitty.

Harry sat forward. "But does he not understand that he is leading us into anything but peace? There's going to be a civil war, Kitty. The country is going to be ripped in two."

"Is this what this visit is about, Harry? You've come to canvas me to change Michael's mind. You've had a wasted trip if that's the case, as he would never seek my counsel on such matters."

"No, I guess I'd be better off speaking to Hazel Lavery."

Her eyes widened in shock at his comment.

"I'm sorry – that was – unnecessary," he said. "Old friends shouldn't say things like that to each other."

"Are we still old friends, Harry? All of us – you, Mick and I? Are we friends at all after everything that has happened?"

"I'll always have your best interests at heart, Kitty. I'll never stop caring about you, despite everything."

"But not Mick? The friendship is gone?"

"We are just on two different sides of the fence – there's time yet for him to pull this back from the brink. If he doesn't – I don't know where this is all going to end."

She suddenly shivered.

"Are you alright?" he asked.

She nodded. "Somebody must have just walked over my grave. I sincerely hope the decisions you are taking have nothing to do with my rejection of you, Harry ... no, I don't expect you to answer that ... but it was the hardest decision I ever had to make, because I cared – care – about you greatly. But I fell in love with Mick and nothing could shake that, nothing can shake that ... I had to go with my heart." Tears welled up in her eyes. "But I hope you can forgive me if I treated you in any way unkindly or carelessly. I am truly sorry for any pain I've caused you, Harry –" She broke off as she tried to stifle the tears that now streamed down her face.

"Oh, Kitty, come here to me!" he said, getting up quickly and going to sit beside her on the couch where he put his arms around her.

"It's all such a mess," she said as she sobbed into his shirt.

"It will all work out, my darling, it will all work out for the best," he said as he stroked her hair.

"Are you sure you won't stay for dinner?" Kitty asked as she walked Harry to the door.

"No, I'll be on my way. I have an election meeting this evening in my constituency." Harry was defending his seat in Roscommon, the neighbouring constituency in the forthcoming general election.

"Will we see you again soon, Harry?"

"Of course, sure you are on my way down to my constituency so I can drop by any time."

"I hope you do ... you're welcome any time," she said.

He nodded and walked across the pavement to his automobile.

"Look after yourself, Harry!"

He nodded and smiled before starting the automobile.

She watched him drive down the busy street until he disappeared.

CHAPTER 68

As the insurgents were still occupying the Four Courts buildings in Dublin, the British government's frustration with Michael grew. Hazel feared that Lloyd George would order British troops still stationed in Ireland to attack the buildings and take back control of them. She knew if such action was taken the Treaty would be dead in the water, along with Ireland's fledging independence.

In those first few days of June she tirelessly tried to arrange meetings for Michael with British politicians to try to smooth over the situation. But they would not even meet him. Hazel's charms could not even work this time on Winston whose frustration had built to extreme anger.

In a way the heightened political turmoil was something Hazel was grateful for, after her night with Michael. Neither of them discussed it as they threw themselves back into politics. It was as if they were so close they didn't have to mention it or discuss what had happened. But as Hazel looked at Michael, she knew it had brought them even closer together as soul mates. She didn't regret what had happened, but she did feel very guilty over John.

Hazel called in as many favours as she could, particularly with Shane Leslie, and finally managed to get Winston to agree to a meeting with Michael.

Winston was staying at Philip Sassoon's country house in Kent and Hazel drove Michael down.

He looked out at the beautiful countryside as she drove him along the country roads.

"Do you know what I wish?" he said as he looked out at the beautiful countryside. "What?"

"I wish the two of us could just keep driving. Just keep driving further and further away from all this shit."

"Run away together?" she said, smiling at him.

"If you would have me," he said and smiled back.

"Don't, Michael. It's too hard to even think about. Sometimes I wish I had never met you ... and sometimes I wonder how I ever lived without you."

Michael and Hazel waited anxiously in the reception room of Philip Sassoon's huge manor house.

"For goodness' sake!" snapped Hazel as she paced up and down. "Where is he?"

They had been waiting over an hour. Hazel marched over to the bell and rang it.

A footman arrived in a couple of minutes later.

"Where is Mr. Churchill?" she demanded.

"He's painting, my lady."

"Painting!" she exclaimed in exasperation. "We are here trying to avert a bloody war and he's painting!"

The butler appeared at the door. "Mr. Churchill will see you now."

"About bloody time!" said Hazel as she marched out.

As they followed the butler, Michael urged, "Calm down, Hazel. Losing your temper won't achieve anything."

"Things must be bad when *you* are advising me to calm down!"

They were shown out onto the patio where Philip was sitting and Winston was at his easel, painting the grounds.

"Good afternoon, Hazel," said Philip.

"Afternoon! Are you sure it isn't evening we've been kept waiting for so long?"

"Young men must learn to have patience!" Winston said as he glared at Michael.

"And middle-aged men must learn to have manners!" retorted

Hazel as she walked up to his painting and inspected it. "It could do with a lightening of the shade you've painted the grass – it's too dark!"

"Really?" he said, peering at his own painting.

"I haven't come all this way to talk about grass paintings!" snarled Michael.

Winston looked at Philip and raised his eyes to heaven.

"You are lucky I agreed to meet you at all," said Winston. "Only out of respect for Hazel did I agree. You are putting us all in a very precarious position."

"I am!" retorted Michael.

"Letting those vagabonds keep control of the law courts in Dublin! We are on the verge of sending in the troops and bugger your independence! Not to mention your half-baked crackpot of a constitution!"

"Winston!" said Hazel. "You must not do anything at this stage to upset the applecart. We are days away from the election. If Michael and his party win then he has the people's backing –"

"And if Mr. De Valera wins, we all have nothing!" retorted Winston.

"*Can you not just wait a few days until the election is over!*" Michael exploded. "*Who has no patience now?*"

Winston looked at Philip who nodded.

"I will call off the wolves in Westminster," Winston said. "But I warn you, Michael," he pointed at him, "if you don't bring law and order to your country soon – I will!"

CHAPTER 69

Hazel hardly slept the night of the sixteenth of June, the night of the general election in Ireland. The next day she waited for news as the tallies of Ireland's first election for its new parliament came in.

To her delight, the people overwhelmingly voted for Pro-Treaty deputies.

She raced to her desk in her sitting room to write Michael a letter.

> *My darling Michael,*
>
> *Bravo! I am thrilled with the result of the election in Ireland and this clear declaration by the people of their support for you and the Treaty. I only wish I was there with you to celebrate this joyous day. I hope for everyone's sake now the opposition will realise they are fighting a losing battle and give up their position. More pressing, Michael, is the continual occupation of the Four Courts by the insurgents. I know you are loath to take arms against your fellow countrymen but, Michael, the threat from Winston is quite real. It would be disastrous for Ireland at this stage to suddenly have British intervention on the streets of Dublin again! Oh, how I miss you, Michael ... I think of that last night before you went home and the longing I had to go with you or keep you here! Either, as long as we would be together ...*

Michael read and reread the letter from Hazel. He held the notepaper close to his nose to see if he could smell her scent. He missed her terribly. He looked at the other letter he had received that day – from Kitty. She was discussing their wedding. She said she had been discussing with Maud the possibility of having a double wedding with her and Gearóid. She criticised him for not writing longer letters to her. She was always criticising him for that. He defended himself, saying he hardly had time to sleep, let alone write long letters. But the truth was he was writing long letters to somebody else – Hazel. He didn't know why but every time he sat down to write to Hazel, he had so much to say to her. So much to discuss and ask her opinion on. So much information to give her to feed back to Churchill and the others. He just didn't have anything like that to write to Kitty about, to fill up pages of notepaper. But he knew it was more than that. When he wrote to Hazel, he pictured her beautiful face reading what he wrote. He pictured her smiling or frowning or laughing. He wanted to stir those emotions in her. He even wrote her love poetry. All the time, he felt amazed that a woman like Hazel would be interested in a man like him.

He had a heavy heart as he thought of Kitty and Hazel. He felt torn in two. The same as he felt politically. He had so much pressure being heaped onto him to attack the insurgents and oust them from the law courts. But how could he do that? How could he order an attack on his former friends and colleagues? Including Harry. Kitty had written to him that he had visited her. A few months ago, knowledge of a visit like that would have inflamed jealousy in him. Now he just felt hope that all was not lost with Harry. That perhaps he could rely on this old friendship – that, when push came to shove, Harry could not abandon him.

Michael sat at his desk and thought hard as he began to pen a letter to Harry, appealing to him not to take the side against him.

The week after the Irish general election, Sir Henry Wilson was returning to his home in Eaton Square in London. Sir Henry was a man who regarded himself as Irish and had a home in County

Longford, a celebrated hero from the Great War and the military advisor for the Belfast government. He got out of his taxi and was making his way to his front door when two men appeared beside him and opened fire. He was shot six times in the chest, two of the shots being fatal. Two police officers and a chauffeur were also shot and wounded as the men tried to escape. They were surrounded by a crowd and arrested by other policemen. The men were Irish Republicans.

The assassination sent shockwaves throughout Britain. The establishment and public were outraged at the coldblooded murder of such a respected war hero and politician. Rumours began to circulate the assassination was on the orders of Michael Collins. If not him, then the insurgents in the Four Courts in Dublin were blamed and Michael's lack of will to crack down on them was blamed.

Either way, John felt the wind of change in public opinion changing – and changing for the worse. A stack of hate mail arrived for him in the days that followed the assassination. And the hatred was not just reserved for the Laverys but directed at Lloyd George and Churchill as well for indulging the Irish nationalists.

"I am being accused of being the friends of a coldblooded murderer!" declared Winston to John and Hazel in their drawing room.

"Well – so am I, if that makes you feel any better!" said Hazel.

"Madam – it does not make me feel in any way better! How could it? The fact that I and my good wife have socialised here with Collins and his ilk, in this very room, has us all tarred with the same brush!"

"We are sorry, Winston, if we have led you into any embarrassment," said John.

"But not sorry for trying to smooth the path to peace!" said Hazel.

"What path to peace has been paved when a man like Sir Henry is coldbloodedly murdered on his doorstep by Irish Republicans?"

"What's happened is tragic, Winston. But we can't let it derail the progress we've made," urged Hazel.

"*Madam!*" shouted Winston, slamming his hand on the arm of his chair. "I and the British public have had enough. I am announcing an ultimatum in parliament tomorrow. Either Collins goes in and takes back the Four Courts and brings order to Dublin, or we will send in the British forces. Last chance!"

"To fight with his countrymen – or fight you!" said Hazel.

"*Yes!* Now – I must get back to Westminster and prepare my speech for tomorrow." Winston stood up

John rang for Gordon.

"Show Mr. Churchill out, Gordon," said Hazel, sighing. "Good day, Winston!"

"Good day!" said Winston as he marched out of the room.

"Poor Michael! He's being put in a terrible dilemma!" said Hazel as she paced up and down.

"Hazel – I wonder should we go on a holiday for a while. Tangier perhaps? Until all this quietens down?" suggested John.

"Tangier! Certainly not, John!"

"I am just worried about where all this will lead! It seems to be getting worse and I am very concerned about our safety."

"Let's not panic, John!"

"When an MP is being shot outside his home in London and we are in the thick of it, I think there is every reason to panic."

There was a knock on the door and Gordon came in.

"Yes, Gordon?" said Hazel irritably.

"Forgive me, my lady, I didn't want to announce it while Mr. Churchill was still here, but there are two other guests waiting to see you – friends of Mr. Collins."

"Friends of Michael's! Well, show them in at once, Gordon!" said Hazel.

"And who the blazes are these men!" snapped John in despair.

A few minutes later Gordon showed two men in. Hazel recognised them as being part of Michael's entourage when he was staying at Cadogan Place.

"Good afternoon, Sir John and Lady Lavery," said the darker-haired man, handing Hazel an envelope. "Mick asked me to give you this."

Hazel opened it, pulled out a letter and quickly read it.

"Due to the heightened atmosphere since the assassination, Mick has appointed us as protection for you," said the man.

"Protection?" asked John.

"Bodyguards," said Hazel. "Very good. I'm sure you are famished. Make your way down to the kitchen and Cook will make you lunch. Tell Gordon that you can sleep in the rooms over the garage. Ask him to make up beds. It's quite cosy there."

"Thank you, ma'am," said the men and they left the room.

"Hazel – have those men got guns on them?" asked John.

"I expect so – otherwise they wouldn't be very good protection, would they? I knew Michael wouldn't abandon us and would make sure we were safe."

"But do you not see how dangerous the situation has become for us, if even Michael feels we need bodyguards?"

"Purely a precautionary measure, I am sure," said Hazel. "Now, I had better write to Michael without delay and tell him that Winston is on the warpath – literally!"

CHAPTER 70

Michael felt it was the hardest thing he ever had to do. He had been doing everything to avoid giving the order to attack the insurgents in the Four Courts for weeks. He was loath to take up arms against his fellow countrymen. But now, fate had taken the decision out of his hands. It was either take back the Four Courts forcibly or have another British invasion, the Treaty torn up and a return to foreign occupation.

On the twenty-eight of June, the order was given by Michael and the Irish government to reclaim the Four Courts. Vicious fighting broke out and the buildings were in flames two days later. An explosion and fire destroyed the Public Records Office which was part of the complex, together with census returns and thousands of baptism, marriage and burial records. Fighting broke out on the streets of Dublin and the city's main streets were reduced to rubble as the country descended into civil war.

Charged with leading the government forces, Michael resigned his position of minister in the government and was appointed Commander in Chief of the army. Just as it was left to him to fight the war against the British, he now had to lead the fight against his fellow countrymen.

Kitty and Michael wrote to each other continuously. But Kitty saw his letters were becoming shorter and shorter as the pressure mounted on him and the civil war spread throughout the country.

He wrote to her, telling her he was now General Michael

Collins, Commander in Chief of the army. All she could think of to reply was to write: *More trouble I suppose.*

Everything in Michael's life seemed to be trouble. They kept trying to arrange to meet, but it was next to impossible with Michael's schedule and the war ongoing.

Maud walked into Kitty's bedroom.

"Kitty – you've been in your room all day – are you ill?"

"No, I'm not ill," she said, turning around. "Just writing to Michael."

Maud came and sat beside her. She saw she was clutching a letter.

"Another letter from him?" she asked

Kitty nodded. "Only a short letter – he was rushing – as usual. This time to fight this new war against his former friends ... including Harry."

"Gearóid said Mick is under terrible pressure. He's never seen him so bad. He fears he's at breaking point."

"I can tell that from what he writes – but why doesn't he turn to me to support him?"

"Perhaps he feels he doesn't want to burden you. Perhaps he feels you can't cope with it?"

"Perhaps he's right," said Kitty, throwing the letter on the dressing table. "Another bloody war – and Mick in the middle of it. What kind of a life can we ever have together?"

"You knew all this when you got together with him, Kitty."

"But I fear he's changed. I fear he doesn't look at me the way he used to. I feel I'm not good enough for him anymore, now he's used to all that high life in London."

"That's nonsense, Kitty! Mick adores you, it's plain for everyone to see."

"When was that?" asked Kitty.

"Sorry?"

"When was the last time anyone saw us together? I fear I can't give him what he needs. They say the women in London were chasing him. They said he couldn't leave the house without him being propositioned as if he were some movie star!"

"Sure Mick wouldn't be interested in any of that, Kitty!"

"Something has happened to him ... I'm not stupid. I can sense it ... there is somebody else in his life. Somebody I have to fight to get his love back from her."

Hazel had received another lengthy letter from Michael that morning. She devoured the letter, absorbing every detail about the new war that had enveloped Ireland. He poured his heart out to her, telling how it was unbearable for him to now have taken up arms against his former friends and colleagues. She savoured the passages where he wrote that he needed her and missed her.

He had asked her and John to come to Ireland and she was making plans for them to visit. She longed to see Michael again, to support him and to help carry the load. She had decided that John should be there in his capacity as a renowned war artist, to paint the scenes from the civil war that was unfolding there.

That afternoon, John's daughter Eileen paid them a visit.

"I passed two unsavoury-looking men sitting in a motorcar outside the house on my way in," said Eileen.

"Ah yes, they would be our bodyguards," said Hazel with a giggle.

"Bodyguards?"

"Michael arranged them for us. Purely a precautionary measure. It makes me feel rather like the Queen!"

"Of Ireland, perchance?" said Eileen, raising her eyes to heaven.

"Speaking of which – we are to go to Ireland."

"Good lord – when?"

"At the earliest opportunity."

"But is there not a war – another one – unfolding there?" asked an astonished Eileen.

"Of course – that's what takes us there! It's what your father does best – documents war!"

Eileen looked at her father. "But, Papa, you are now sixty-six years old – is it not time to take life a little easier rather than put yourself in the middle of a war?"

"I feel I should be there to paint what is unfolding – the birth of a nation," answered John.

"A baptism of fire, more like. Well, I think it is quite insane!"

"Well, you would, Eileen," said Hazel. "But your father and I are more community-minded. The new Irish government needs our support."

"I take it you mean Michael Collins needs your support?" Eileen said cynically.

"Amongst others. They have even offered us the Viceregal Lodge to stay in during our stay – we declined naturally."

"That was wise – it might be bombed! So where will you be staying?"

"Well, all our Irish friends have invited us to stay – the Earl of Kincard, Daisy Burke-Plunkett. But we'll stay in a hotel – we'll have more freedom that way." More freedom to come and go to see Michael, she thought.

"And what of Alice while you are on this excursion? I take it she'll not be accompanying you?"

"No, of course not. I have a full itinerary organised for her during our absence – she will not be bored!"

There was a knock on the door and Gordon entered, announcing, "Mr. Eddie Marsh, my lady."

Winston's private secretary entered the room.

"Eddie!" said Hazel excitedly, jumping up and going to embrace him and greet him with a kiss. "So glad you called! I received a letter from Michael this morning."

"Good, Winston wants to know what exactly is going on over there."

"Let us retire to my sitting room and we shall discuss it," said Hazel, linking Eddie's arm to lead him out. "Neither Winston nor anyone else could accuse Michael of being soft on the insurgents now! He has shown the world he is on the side of law and order – at great personal cost, may I add. Soon I will be in Dublin and will be able to send first-hand accounts of the war back to Winston directly! I shall be in the thick of it!"

Eileen watched Hazel and Eddie walk out, leaving her alone

with her father.

"I often wonder is she quite mad!" she said, shaking her head.

"Because she does not want to spend the day in Harrods but has a keen interest in the political world?" said John cynically.

"But who in their right mind would want to go into the middle of a war? Do you want to know what I think?"

"Not really."

"I think she is a sad and lonely woman who is seeing her youth and beauty slip away and she sees Ireland as a way to make her relevant again. It makes her feel important. She has built Ireland into some romantic notion in her head with, of course, Michael Collins as the romantic hero and herself as the heroine!"

John became angry. "Don't *you* start on those ridiculous affair rumours!"

"Are you sure it's not true, Papa? For I have never seen anyone so anxious to rush into a war. My generation lived through the Great War, Papa. It was my generation that suffered the most – so many were killed or wounded. And I can tell you this – men, or women, do not rush off to a war unless they are desperately searching for something that is missing in their lives."

"I want Hazel to be happy!" John slammed his fist on the arm of his chair.

"I know! But can't you see – you are so desperate to make amends for not being an attentive and good husband to Mama before she died, that you are going way over the top to be the ideal patient and loving husband to your second wife! And all the time you are actually repeating the same mistake with Hazel as you made with Mama!"

"How?" demanded John.

"By throwing yourself so much into your work – into your bloody paint pots – that you cannot see what is going on under your nose! Hazel is clearly in love with Michael Collins!"

He looked at her but didn't respond.

She grabbed her gloves and stood up. "I'd better go. William will be wondering where I've got to."

"William – who you had an affair with when your first

husband was fighting the Germans on the front – and he subsequently divorced you for your adultery? Perhaps you should judge people by your own standards, Eileen."

"Or perhaps I am more qualified than most as an expert on human behaviour after my own follies and divorce," she said as she walked to him and bent down to kiss his cheek.

He watched as she left the room and closed the door behind her.

CHAPTER 71

Michael sat at his large desk in his rooms at the Portobello barracks where he had moved since the civil war erupted. He had a large map of Ireland stretched out on the desk before him.

Dublin, although the city centre was in ruins, was now under the control of government forces again. He had just finished writing a letter to Kitty. Now the city was safe again, he was attempting to organise for her to come to Dublin. The push to bring the whole country under control was still ongoing. What would be most difficult to regain control of were the vast southern areas of Cork and Kerry.

There was a knock at the door and Gearóid came in.

"We need to keep up the push into the South," said Michael, gesturing at the map.

"Mick …" said Gearóid, his voice trembling.

"What is it?" said Michael, looking up and seeing Gearóid was close to tears.

"It's Harry … he's been shot," said Gearóid as Michael went white as a ghost.

Now that Dublin was back under government control, Kitty had been planning to go there as quickly as possible for a reunion with Michael. But then news came of Harry being shot. She had run down to the church and spent hours praying and lighting candles. She anxiously awaited news from Dublin where he was in hospital.

Three days later, when she came back from the church, she found Maud crying in the parlour.

"Maud?" asked Kitty, her voice trembling.

Maud looked up and shook her head. Kitty rushed to her and they held each other as they sobbed.

"Gearóid said Mick wept like a baby when he heard the news – he's inconsolable," said Maud.

"Oh, that it has come to this!" sobbed Kitty.

As she looked around the parlour through her tears, she had a flashback to three years before. They were all there – Harry and Michael, Gearóid and all the family, laughing and dancing to music. She had a vision of Michael and Harry sitting on the couch together, roaring with laughter over some long-forgotten joke.

CHAPTER 72

Hazel and John disembarked at Kingstown Harbour in Dublin. It was a beautiful sunny August Monday. As they made their way through the crowd of passengers Hazel felt a burgeoning sense of excitement to be in Ireland again. She could not wait to see Michael.

She desperately wanted to be with him and to support him. The civil war had put him under more pressure than ever before. The deaths of former friends and colleagues were having a severe impact on him, particularly the death of his close friend Harry Boland. As if the civil-war casualties were not bad enough, news had come that Arthur Griffith, the man who replaced De Valera as President, had died the previous day. Hazel herself felt very saddened to hear of Arthur's death as she had entertained him at 5 Cromwell Place many a time during the treaty negotiations the previous year. And she knew it would be another bitter blow to Michael to lose the steady hand of friendship Arthur provided. It meant Michael was even more isolated and the success of the fledging assembly rested firmly on his shoulders.

There was a group of dignitaries waiting for them at the port.

"Welcome to Dublin, Sir John and Lady Lavery. Your car awaits, if you would care to follow me?" said one of the men as his colleagues rushed to take the luggage from the boat's porters.

"We are delighted to be here – to be home," said Hazel as she followed the men to the government car awaiting them.

The government car brought John and Hazel to the Royal

Marine Hotel in Kingstown where they were shown to their suite which had views out across the lawns to the sea. Hazel waited anxiously for Michael – they had agreed to meet for dinner at the hotel that night. As the evening drew in, she changed into as sequinned black gown and brushed her hair out while John changed into his suit.

"How do I look?" Hazel asked, spinning around.

"You look beautiful, Hazel, as always," he assured her.

She turned and checked her appearance in the mirror again.

As John watched her, he believed it was not for him that she was checking her appearance.

Finally, there was a knock on the door. Clutching her evening bag, Hazel rushed to answer it.

"General Collins is waiting for you downstairs, ma'am," said a porter.

"Excellent, thank you," said Hazel as she swept past the porter and down the corridor to the staircase.

John reached into his pocket and tipped the porter as he left the suite.

Hazel reached the foyer and anxiously looked around but couldn't see Michael.

"Where is he? General Collins?" she demanded of a passing porter.

"I believe he is in the reception room," said the porter, pointing to a closed door where two policemen were positioned.

"I am Lady Lavery," she said, walking past them, pushing at the door and swinging it open.

A lone figure was standing in the bay window, looking out across the lawns to the sea, his back to her.

"Michael," she whispered, closing the door behind her.

He turned around and they stared at each other before she turned the key in the lock behind her. Then he strode to her and they embraced and kissed.

"I have missed you so much," he whispered to her.

"And I you. The only thing that kept me going was receiving your letters." She pulled away from him and looked at him. "You poor thing! Between losing Harry and now Arthur dying – I know how much both of them meant to you."

He leaned forward and kissed her again.

Then they heard voices outside and she pulled away from him.

"*John is on his way down,*" she hissed. "*Unlock the door! Hurry!*"

She quickly went to the mirror and checked her make-up as Michael unlocked the door.

Hazel swung around from the mirror and adopted a light-hearted tone. "I am famished and I know John is as well so let's hope the food is good here!"

"I believe it's the best," said Michael and the two of them walked out into the foyer where John had just arrived downstairs.

"John, it's so good to see you again!" said Michael, approaching him and shaking his hand.

"And you, Michael. I am so sorry to hear about Arthur Griffith," said John with a sympathetic smile.

"Thank you, John. I know he thought very highly of you during our visits to 5 Cromwell Street last year."

"It all seems so long ago," said Hazel as she looked happily at Michael.

In the dining room they sat at a table inside the window. It was now dark outside.

Dinner was served and they began to eat.

"Winston and Lloyd George are very happy, Michael, that you've restored law and order to Dublin and are sure to have the entire country under your control soon," said Hazel.

"They forced my hand – what choice did I have? And I've lost friends – good friends," said Michael sadly as he looked down at his plate.

Hazel reached over and placed her hand on his. "Everyone knows the sacrifices you've made."

"Do they?" asked Michael, looking up into her eyes.

John looked uncomfortably down at his wife's hand on that of their dinner guest.

"Any word of Mr. De Valera?" he asked quickly.

Hazel removed her hand from Michael's and, taking up her glass of wine, took a sip.

"I believe he might be in Cork, with the insurgents," Michael said. "I am still trying to negotiate a peace with them – to give them a way out with pride – rather than for this battle to drag on with more death and casualties."

"Well, yes," Hazel put her hand on Michael's again, "but they must understand there is no going back now. They must accept things as they are, as negotiated by you and Arthur, bless him, and the rest last year in London."

Outside, in the grounds of the hotel, the night air was warm and humid as an insurgent lay hidden in the trees. His gun was aimed squarely at the dining-room window inside which Michael, Hazel and John were having dinner.

He waited impatiently to get a clear shot at Michael, but Hazel was seated next to him nearest the window. Every time the sniper had Michael in clear view, Hazel leaned forward, blocking it. The sniper took aim again.

"What of your fiancée?" asked John, the question prompting Hazel to remove her hand from Michael's again.

"Kitty – I haven't seen her for so long. It was too dangerous for her to travel to Dublin while the city was under siege and I couldn't get down to visit her. We write all the time. She's been badly affected by Harry's death – they were very close."

"Of course," said Hazel sympathetically, hiding her guilty pleasure at the news Michael and Kitty had not been seeing each other regularly. But she was also uneasy that she should feel pleasure on hearing this.

"But I am seeing her tomorrow," said Michael.

"Oh?" Hazel was surprised.

"She's coming to Dublin – well, just outside Dublin – to Greystones, down the coast from here. It's finally safe for her to travel."

John smiled. "Excellent! I'm sure you cannot wait to meet her after the prolonged absence."

"Absence does make the heart grow fonder, as they say," said Hazel. "She was the – sweetheart, to use that dread word – of Harry before you, was she not?"

"That she was. So, tomorrow, our meeting will be tinged with sadness for both of us. We were great friends, the three of us." His eyes welled up.

"This tragedy will probably bring you and Kitty closer," said John. "Tragedy can do that."

"Or tear people apart – one or the other," sighed Hazel.

Michael nodded sadly and was about to speak when two policemen came up to their table.

One bent down to speak to Michael.

"We have found an enemy sniper in the grounds of the hotel, General," he said quietly.

"What?" Hazel looked out the window into the darkness.

"He is under arrest. You were the target, General, but Lady Lavery was obstructing his view."

"Oh my!" said Hazel excitedly.

"Can we close these curtains, please!" John urgently called to one of the waiters.

The waiter quickly obliged.

"We could have all been shot dead!" exclaimed John, horrified.

"Not all of us, John!" said Hazel. "They were just after Michael. If they wanted to shoot us all then they would have shot us all! I was obstructing the view, did you not hear?"

"General, you need to return to barracks without delay, in case there is another attempt on your life tonight," said the policeman.

Michael turned to Hazel. "I had better go. I'll telephone you tomorrow to make our next arrangement ... I think you might have saved my life tonight."

Hazel's eyes widened in amazement. "Yes, you need to go. We'll talk tomorrow."

Michael nodded at her and then at John before marching out of the restaurant with the police officers.

"How remarkable!" said Hazel, her head in a spin from it all.

"Hazel, let us go to our suite – I really cannot endure any more drama for tonight!"

"Yes, of course," said Hazel.

As they emerged into the foyer, they heard gunfire from not too far away.

"Michael!" gasped Hazel.

It was two in the morning and Hazel was sitting at the window in their suite, looking out at the moon's reflection in the sea. John was asleep, but she was unable to. News had come earlier that the gunfire they had heard was an ambush on Michael's car. Hazel had desperately tried to find out more but was unable to.

There was a knock on the door, and she went quickly to answer it.

"General Collins in on the telephone in reception for you, Lady Lavery," said the porter.

Hazel was overwhelmed with relief as she made her way down to the reception and took the phone.

"Michael?" she said urgently down the phone.

"Hazel, I'm fine – my car was ambushed down the road from the hotel, but I was travelling in the next car. Two lucky escapes in the one night."

"Oh, Michael! I was terrified something had happened to you. Terrified, I tell you!"

"I knew you would be worried, so I thought to telephone you. I'm sorry I had to rush off earlier from the meal – little did I know I was rushing into an ambush."

"You must remain strong, Michael – don't let them frighten you – that is what they are attempting to do!"

"I know. I can only marvel at you, Hazel. Being told there was a sniper outside, and you didn't show any fear at all."

"It is only you I have concern for, Michael." She paused and then whispered, "*I love you!*"

There was a silence on the other end of the line before he said, "I'll speak to you tomorrow. Goodnight, Hazel."

The telephone went dead.

CHAPTER 73

Michael made his way down the corridor to Kitty's room in the Grand Hotel in Greystones. He remembered the argument he had with Kitty in London when she predicted his would be a life of hotel rooms, never having a proper home of his own – of their own. As he went from the Laverys' hotel last night to Kitty's hotel the next day, he thought she might be right.

He steadied himself at her door. It had been so long since they had met that he was overcome with nerves at seeing her again. He took a deep breath and knocked.

A few moments later, Kitty opened the door.

"Kitty," he whispered as she fell into his arms.

As they moved inside the room and closed the door, she started to cry.

"Will you stop – or you'll set me off as well!" he demanded, his eyes welling up.

"I'm just so glad to see you, Mick, and so lonesome after Harry," she said through her tears.

"I know, I'm the same," he said, sighing heavily,

They walked down the beach across from the hotel in Greystones, arms around each other.

"I wanted to go to Harry's funeral," said Kitty. "I desperately did, but I felt I wouldn't be welcome. Why would I – after what I did?"

"I wanted to go too – or at least send a letter of condolence, but it would have only hurt his family – no doubt they blame me for ruining his life and taking his life. To tell the truth, I blame myself as well. The guilt is mighty."

"I go to Mass each morning and pray for him and pray for you – that nothing will happen to you."

"Ah, sure they couldn't catch me! They tried last night and got themselves arrested for their attempt."

"Last night!" said Kitty alarmed. "What happened?"

"They ambushed a car they thought I was in, but I wasn't in it."

"Where was this?"

"Kingstown. Coming back from dinner with the Laverys."

"The Laverys!" she said, suddenly halting. "What are they doing in Dublin?"

"Over to support me and the Irish," he said.

"Support you! Isn't that what *I'm* here for – to support you? You don't need Hazel Lavery for that!" she said angrily.

"I need all the support I can get, Kitty!"

"And how long is she here for?"

"I don't know. We haven't discussed it."

She shook her head as she walked on. "I don't know, Mick, I really don't know what's going on with you!"

"What are you talking about?"

"If somebody told me a year ago that Mick Collins would be out with a London society lady, I would say they were crazy! And here you are!"

"She has been a very good friend to me and to Ireland."

"Oh, don't we know! She's a real *sweetheart*!" She spat the word out.

"Oh, so this is all about what they wrote in the newspaper – I thought I dealt with all that in my letters!"

"Because of everything that has been going on and the pressure you have been under, I have forced myself to remain quiet about the whole situation with Hazel Lavery. But enough is enough! Here she is now, over in Dublin! It's not just about the article in the paper calling her your sweetheart, although that is bad enough! You're the talk of London! I've heard it back from people. You've let your celebrity go to your head. I've heard there is a society lady in London who would give anything for the notoriety of having one night with Mick Collins! How does that make you feel about yourself? Proud or embarrassed? I hope for your sake it's embarrassed!"

"It is neither as it's a lot of nonsense! Hazel said there is always gossip in London as it's just the kind of place it is!"

"Well, if Hazel says it then it must be correct! I take it that *Hazel* is the society lady they are all gossiping about!"

"Kitty! Will you stop with your smart mouth!" he pleaded.

She waved her hands in the air. "I can see the change in you, Mick! The letters – they get shorter and shorter – the frequency less and less!"

"I am so sorry that I do not have time to sit down and write you a letter several pages long when I am trying to win a war and under threat from snipers!" It was his turn to be sarcastic.

"But you have time to go for dinner with Lady Lavery!"

"Her husband was there sitting across the table from us!"

"And what of your letters to her? I bet they aren't a few lines written as an afterthought, are they?"

His face went red with embarrassment.

Her eyes widened as she marched off down the beach "The look of guilt on your face!"

"Kitty!" He raced after her, catching up with her and putting his hands on her shoulders. "My letters to Hazel are different as I'm talking about politics with her and passing on information to hand to the British government."

"Whereas I am just your fiancée." Her voice was low and sad.

"Kitty – I love you!" he said.

"Do you, Mick? Do you really love me anymore? Or are you just in too deep and you feel you can't get out? If you could – if you had the option – who would you choose? Hazel or me? And I don't want to even hear your answer to that question."

She shook him off and began to march along the beach back to the hotel.

"*Kitty!*" he shouted after her.

Kitty was in her room in the Grand Hotel with the door locked while Michael knocked loudly on it from the other side.

"*Kitty! Will you open this fucking door!*"

She walked quickly to the door and unlocked it.

"What is it?" she demanded.

"Will you let me come in, please?"

"No, Mick! We've said enough for one day. I'm tired and not feeling well. We're both shell-shocked after Harry's death and you're now in grief over Arthur's death as well. I need some time and you need rest before you give your speech at Arthur's funeral tomorrow."

"But we need to talk, Kitty!"

"I'm here for the week – we'll have plenty of time to talk," she said as she closed the door and locked it.

She leaned against the door, her face creased in worry. She was filled with terror. The truth was she was too frightened to talk further with Michael that night, too frightened of what might come out in anger and what might never be able to be repaired. As it was, she had barely restrained herself from attacking him about the letter to Hazel that she had actually read.

CHAPTER 74

Th next morning Michael dressed in his full military uniform to attend the funeral of his friend and colleague Arthur Griffith. As he followed the coffin through the packed streets if Dublin, he was laden down with sadness over the loss of Arthur and Harry and the other casualties of the war. As he looked at the sea of faces he was passing he knew the people were now chiefly relying on him to steer the country back to normalcy.

And, as he gave a speech at the graveside, giving the impression of being a tower of strength, little did the people know he was being torn in two as he thought of Kitty and Hazel.

That evening Michael went to the Royal Marine Hotel again for dinner with the Laverys. After the incident there from two nights previously, Hazel asked for dinner to be served in a private function room where a gramophone was brought in by the hotel staff and music played.

"It's best not to take any chances," Hazel said as they sat at the beautifully laid table.

"I imagine after being stared at all day at the funeral, you appreciate the privacy, Michael," said John. "You can at least eat your dinner in peace without your fellow diners looking at you."

"This is perfect," said Michael gratefully.

John studied Michael and Hazel intently over dinner. The lingering looks, the casual touching of each other's hands. It came so naturally to them, neither were aware they were doing it.

"I wonder would you mind terribly if I retired to bed early?" he asked after they had finished the main course of roast duckling.

"But pudding hasn't been served yet," said Hazel.

"I think I've had my fill," he said, standing up. "Goodnight, Michael."

"Goodnight, Sir John."

Hazel waited until he was gone from the room before asking, "How did it go with Kitty yesterday?"

"She's not good," he shook his head. "She knows about us, or strongly suspects to the point that she can't ignore it."

"About us?" Hazel asked.

"That we are in love," Michael said.

As horrified as Hazel was to hear Kitty knew this, she was equally as excited to hear Michael say it.

"She thinks I no longer love her – that I've lost interest in her," he said.

"I see," she said. "And have you – lost interest in her?"

"I don't know. I still care about her deeply, I know that. But so much has changed in my life and I don't know if we have what we used to have in common anymore. Do you understand that?"

"Of course! You are now a world leader, Kitty still a simple country girl," said Hazel.

"She was never quite that, Hazel! She used to cut quite a dash on the Irish social scene, she orders clothes from Paris and has travelled in Europe. She's quite sophisticated, in her own way."

"In her own way, but not in your way anymore, Michael."

"She has sacrificed everything for me – *everything*! Her engagement to Lionel, her relationship with Harry – a future she could have had with Harry. She's heading towards thirty – I can't leave her now."

"But you can't marry somebody just because they are heading towards thirty! Out of duty! I've done that once myself with my first marriage– and it's a cold and awful place it brings you to, I can tell you!"

"What should I do, Hazel?"

"I can't advise you what to do, Michael. Not on this one. This is for you and your heart."

"But what about us? Where does this leave us? Could you ever – ever – leave John and build a life with me?"

"Leave John?" She whispered the words as if the thought had never crossed her mind before.

"Well – isn't that what you want?" he demanded.

Hazel stared in Michael's face, the face that she had fallen in love with. But his words panicked her – *leave John.*

"I – I love you, Michael, but everything's moving so fast!" she said.

"If two people are meant to be together, then there's no point in fighting it," said Michael.

The music on the gramophone played on into the night. Hazel and Michael danced slowly as the music played. As she held him tightly, Hazel never wanted to let him go – but the seriousness of the situation was beginning to hit her. John was asleep upstairs, Kitty waiting a few short miles away, and yet when she looked up into Michael's eyes, nothing else seemed to matter except being with him.

It was three in the morning when Hazel gently opened the door of the hotel suite and slipped in. She was surprised to see the chandelier was fully lit and John was still up, sitting at the window, with a bottle of whiskey beside him.

"John – I thought you would be long asleep by now," she said, walking over to him.

"I decided to stay awake for you," he said.

"You'll be a grouch in the morning! You know how you need your sleep –" She stopped short as she saw a stack of letters on the table beside him, her letters from Michael.

"What are *they* doing there?" she asked.

"I hope you don't mind – I was curious, so took them from your bag to read."

"I *do* mind! How dare you read through my private letters, John Lavery!" she said as she scooped them up in her hands.

"Well, I didn't think they were that private as you have shown them to Shane Leslie and Eddie Marsh and Winston –" said John.

"Only parts of the letters! Parts to do with politics – the rest is –"

"Personal," John finished the sentence for her. "Very personal indeed, Hazel."

"Michael and I have a personal relationship – what of it? He relies heavily on me!"

John sighed loudly. "Let's face facts, Hazel – he is clearly in love with you. I can clearly see that from how he is with you and, if I had any doubts, those doubts are cast aside having read those letters."

She looked at John, unsure how to react. She quickly tucked the letters away in her bag.

"How Michael feels about you is not of too much concern to me – although I'm somewhat surprised that a man with as hard an image as he has resorts to such sentimental hogwash in his letterwriting to woo a woman! After all, Michael is just the latest in a long line of men who have been in love with my wife."

"Well, then! What of it?" she said light-heartedly. "He may join the queue, such as it is!"

"The difference being that this time, as opposed to the flirtations with the Shanes and the Charlies, *you* are also in love with *him*!"

Her mouth opened as she frantically searched for something to say.

He watched her stand there like a statue.

"Hazel?"

She didn't know what to say or how to react. But hearing him say the words, looking at him, she knew there was no point in denying the truth.

"It's true," she said. "I can't deny it … I am in love with Michael … completely, utterly, absolutely in love with him."

"Oh, Hazel," he sighed as he shook his head and stroked his forehead.

She kept her voice matter-of-fact as she continued, her eyes free of any emotion. "I can't explain it and I don't think I even want to try and understand it – but when I am not with him, he is all I think of … when I am with him, nothing else matters … when I look at him it is like looking at myself, we are that close." She looked down at the floor.

"It's an infatuation, Hazel. A spell which must be broken."

"I don't want it broken," she whispered.

"Hazel, you need to start thinking straight. You've let this get out of hand – if you let it continue it will destroy you."

"I don't care … I don't care about anything but to be with him."

"Hazel, apart from the obvious lunacy of the situation – what kind of a future could you ever have together? Where could you go – where could you live? It would be the biggest scandal since – ever! You'd be rejected by society – he'd be ejected from his position of power in Ireland. You would both be pariahs!"

"Society!" she mocked. "Would I miss it? Endless lunches and dinners and parties, discussing tennis and fashion and other people's children! Can't you see how pointless it makes me feel? Can't you see the only thing that gives me meaning – gives my life meaning – is when I am with Michael, immersed in real life – his life!" Her voice cracked in desperation.

"But if this came out about you and him, his life in Irish affairs would be over. It would be ten times worse than what happened to Charles Stewart Parnell. And what of his fiancée – this girl Kitty?"

"She knows. Michael told me this evening that she knows."

"Hazel – you are standing on a cliff edge. It is not too late to turn back, because that fall off the cliff is a very long way down. Stop letting the mirror deceive you. You need to face reality. You are a twice-married woman in your forties – a mother with a daughter about to reach adulthood. He is a decade younger than you – how long do you think this relationship would last in the real world? Where will you be in ten years' time when your looks are gone, and he is most probably without children and blaming you for robbing him of his chance at a family? You will have no position in society. And you may mock that position, but you have never been without it. It is very cold out there – just think of your sister Dorothy and what awaited her."

"Oh, John," she started to cry, "I never thought you could say anything so cruel."

"And I never thought, despite everything, that you would ever think of leaving me."

He stood up and left the suite.

Trying to stifle her sobs, she went to the bed and collapsed on it.

CHAPTER 75

Kitty looked at the photograph of Michael on the front of the newspaper, taken the previous day at Arthur Griffith's funeral. As she studied the photograph her heart felt a pang of sympathy for him, but she was filled with terrible sorrow. Just a short time ago she had been so happy – happy at finally being with the man she had been searching for all her life. She thought back through the years and all the suitors that had pursued her. She had played them all like a fiddle as she partied throughout the midlands and Dublin, even getting engaged to poor Lionel on the way. But none of them, not even her dear lovely Harry, had captured her heart like Michael had. Sometimes through those years she feared she would end up on her own because she was being too choosy. She didn't know what being in love was like, but she knew she would know when she felt it. And she did with Mick. How ironic that the love of her life, after such a long search, now seemed to be in love with another.

She went for long walks on the beach. She prayed in the church, she prayed in her hotel room. She waited to hear from Michael.

Then he sent a telegram saying that he would be calling to her on Friday. She couldn't wait to see him but was terrified of what the visit would bring.

Michael sat in his quarters at the barracks in Portobello, staring at the map of Ireland on his desk. There were lots of markers on the

409

map, identifying enemy positions. But he couldn't concentrate. All he could think about was Hazel and Kitty.

Emmet, now his Chief of Staff, walked into the room.

"We've had another victory in Galway. An enemy unit wiped out and we've taken back control of the area," said Emmet.

"Are there many dead?"

"None on our side, four on the other."

Michael put his head in his hands. "Four! Four sons, four brothers, four husbands, four fathers, four friends ... perhaps our friends, men who were our friends and comrades!"

"Michael – are you alright?"

"We need to keep the pressure on the other side to negotiate – before this whole country falls apart at the seams," he said, staring at the map. "I'm going to travel to Cork on Sunday. I want to do a tour of duty there."

"Cork! But, sure, that is still very much enemy territory, Mick!"

"It's my home county and they are my people. And I want to see my people ... I need to see my family there," said Michael, his voice quiet and slow.

"I strongly suggest delaying that visit until we have secured the territory. It's not safe, Mick!"

"Make the plans, Emmet. We'll be travelling down on Sunday."

Hazel had never seen John in a mood like this before. He usually was so blasé, rarely getting disturbed or anxious about anything. She had given him enough reason to be disturbed and anxious over the years. His words had stung her to the core the other night. And yet she knew he was just trying to jolt her into reality and save their marriage. The problem was she was besotted with Michael.

She was on the telephone in the hotel reception to her good friend Elizabeth Burke-Plunkett, the Countess of Fingall, commonly known as Daisy. They were both invited to attend a dinner party that night at Sir Horace Plunkett's estate in Foxrock. Horace was a cousin of Elizabeth's husband and he and Elizabeth had a close friendship.

"George Bernard Shaw is coming too," said Elizabeth.

"Oh, good," said Hazel.

"He would very much like to meet Michael Collins. As would Horace, of course – they would have many issues to discuss." Horace was an agricultural reformer and pioneer of agricultural cooperatives – he saw this as the way forward to relieve Ireland of poverty and dissension. "Any chance you can bring him along?"

"Well, yes, I was hoping to meet him today, so I'll ask him to come along tonight," Hazel said, looking across the hotel lobby into the dining room where she could see John eating his breakfast.

"Excellent! We can't wait to meet him. Well, he'll probably be the next president now that Arthur Griffith has passed away."

"Yes, probably," said Hazel.

When the call was over, she picked up the telephone again and asked to be put through to Michael at his headquarters in Portobello.

"Good morning," she whispered. "Did you sleep well?"

"Not really, I had a lot of dreams – bad ones. I'm travelling to Cork tomorrow."

"*Cork!* But you can't, Michael. There are too many rebels there – you will be too much at risk!"

"Sure, there were two assassination attempts on my life here in Dublin during the week, Hazel. I'm as safe there as anywhere."

"I sincerely doubt that!" she insisted.

"Besides, I want to go home and see my people and try to reach out to the rebels there to stop the fighting … I need to see you today before I go."

"Well, that's why I was telephoning you. We've been invited to Sir Horace Plunkett's tonight. George Bernard Shaw will be there. Excellent opportunity for you to meet them all. They could be very helpful to you in the future."

"I was hoping to meet you on your own," he said.

"Well, I couldn't let my friends down, Michael. It won't be a long night – we can talk after."

"I'll call for you at six."

"Perfect! I'll see you then."

She joined John in the dining room.

"I was just speaking to Daisy. We're invited to Sir Horace Plunkett's estate tonight – Michael has been invited too."

"Michael!"

"They are all desperate to meet him," she said with a shrug.

"I won't be going, Hazel. You can take him on your own."

"But that's just childish!"

"What? That I won't accompany my wife and her lover to dinner and pretend nothing is the matter? Hazel, you have been involved with the British aristocracy for far too long and adopted their ways! But may I remind you that I am not, regardless of my knighthood, a real member of aristocracy. I am a self-made man from Belfast. And you are from the Mid-west of America, again a place that would have very different social mores from those of the British aristocracy!"

"Well, please yourself then and don't come!" she retorted.

"Your trouble, Hazel, is that you want to have your cake and eat it! You want Michael, you want to remain married to me and you want keep your position in society! I'm sorry, but that's not on! I will not be one of those husbands who looks away while his wife carries on with another man. I've looked away for years as you flirted shamelessly through the upper echelons of London society. I will not now look away while you sleep with a farm boy from West Cork! You're going to have to choose and choose soon! Follow your heart or follow your head, but I won't share you and I won't be made a fool of!" He threw his handkerchief on the table and marched out.

CHAPTER 76

There was a knock on the bedroom door. Kitty checked her appearance in the mirror before going to open it.

Michael was standing there. He looked very tired and not his usual exuberant self.

"Can I come in?"

"Of course," she said, holding the door open for him.

He walked in and she closed the door. He stood staring at her before she went to him and held him close.

"I'm sorry for everything, Kitty. I never meant to hurt you."

"Oh, sure I never meant to hurt anybody either – it's what happens though in love and war."

She gently pushed him away and went to sit on the couch in front of the window.

"Have you decided what you are going to do?" she asked then.

"Yes, I'm going to Cork on Sunday."

"Cork! What are you going there for?"

"First, I need to be seen there to show we are in control of the whole country."

"But you're not, are you? According to the newspapers anyway."

"There's still fighting going on. That's the second reason I'm going, to try and stop it. And I want to go home, Kitty. I want to see my family and friends at home. I need to see them."

"Well, I can understand that, if it's safe for you to go ... but what I meant by my question about what you're going to do was: have you decided what you are going to do about *us* – you and me

– and Hazel Lavery?"

His eyes filled with tears. "But, sure, we're engaged, Kitty! The deal is done!"

"What kind of an answer is that?" She was aghast. "I was engaged to Lionel and I skipped out of the arrangement quicker than Lanigan's ball! I don't want you to marry me because you feel *obliged* to!"

"I'm telling you that I'll marry you and I love you and that's an end to it!" he said, his voice rising.

"But I don't want you to tell me that!" she said angrily, jumping to her feet. "I don't want you tell me anything! I want you to *feel* it!"

"Ah, you want too much!" he snarled.

"I want to know the man I am marrying loves me – and no one else! Is that too much to ask? I don't want to be married to somebody in love with somebody else – maybe that's fine for other people, but not for me! I could be married a dozen times over by now if I wanted that kind of arrangement!"

He sank down on his knees, putting his face in his hands.

She went to him, got down on her knees and cradled him.

"But, Mick, I can't be happy unless you are happy too ... I know what it's like to care about two people deeply at the same time. I felt that way about you and Harry. But in the end my heart told me I was in love with you and I chose you. And that's what you need to do now – choose! And if you choose Hazel, then so be it. I'll understand. I'll be heartbroken but it will be the right thing for you to do, to go with her if you truly love her."

He looked up into her face. "You're wonderful, Kitty."

She sighed as she hugged him. "So are you, Mick."

As Michael sat in the back of his chauffeur-driven car leaving the Grand Hotel, his mind was still in turmoil. As he looked around the quiet village, he remembered the times he had come here every week during the War of Independence, to bring food and money to De Valera's family while he had been campaigning in America. Now De Valera was in hiding somewhere on the other side of the civil war. He thought of how he had become engaged to Kitty there, in October the previous year. It was one of the happiest days of his life. So much had changed since that day. He hadn't even met Hazel then. As he thought of Kitty back in the hotel, he leaned forward to the driver and told him to go to the house of a close friend of his who lived in the village – Doctor Brendan Leigh Doyle.

The car pulled up outside the house. He got out, walked up the path and knocked on the door.

"Ah, Mick! Is it yourself! Come in!" said Brendan, beckoning him into the hallway before calling to his wife. "Victoria – it's Mick Collins!"

Victoria came out of the kitchen and kissed Michael. "Mick – what a pleasant surprise! You're just in time for tea!"

"No. I'm not stopping. I was just passing so thought I'd drop in."

"Sure you don't come and see us enough, Mick – but we all know how busy you are," Brendan said.

"You look tired," said Victoria.

"I'm fine. I'm off to Cork in the morning. And I just wanted to ask you a favour. Kitty is staying in the Grand Hotel close by – will you mind her for me? Just look in on her while I'm away and make sure she's alright?"

"We will surely, Mick," said Brendan, suddenly becoming concerned. "Is everything alright?"

"It is, when I have good friends like you," he said with a smile before turning and leaving.

Victoria and Brendan stood at the door and waved him off as the car pulled away, before exchanging a concerned look.

CHAPTER 77

That evening Hazel walked down the steps of the Royal Marine Hotel where she had been informed by the manager that General Collins was waiting for her in his automobile. She was surprised to see he didn't have his usual escort with him, only one driver. The driver opened the back door and she got in and gave Michael a hug.

"Where are your bodyguards?" she asked as the driver sat in and they drove off.

"I decided not to bring them tonight. After the attempts during the week I thought I was being too conspicuous driving around with an escort – drawing attention to myself. More discreet this way."

"I don't know if that is wise," said Hazel doubtfully.

"Where's John?" he asked, ignoring her unease.

"He's not coming, Michael."

"Why not?"

"He knows what's been happening between us, Michael."

"Oh no!" Michael sighed in horror.

"I'm afraid he's given me an ultimatum. To stay married to him or leave him for you."

He looked out the window silently.

"Michael?"

"I just feel great shame," he said as he rubbed his forehead. "I respect John so much. He's been a great friend to me and for him to know that I have been … with his wife. I hardly recognise myself these days."

416

"Events have changed you – they have changed me too."

"Changed for the better or for the worse?"

She didn't answer.

"Well, Kitty has effectively given me the same ultimatum."

The car drove in through the gates of Sir Horace Plunkett's estate and up to the manor house, Kilteragh. As Michael observed the stunning sprawling manor he became unnerved. It was one thing mixing with London high society, quite another to be mixing with the Irish Anglo-Irish aristocracy in his own country. They had been the sworn enemy for generations.

As the automobile pulled up outside the house there were several other expensive automobiles parked outside. The butler and two footmen hurried down the steps to open their automobile door and escort them up the steps into the house.

Michael gaped at the gigantic hallway as they were led across it and into the drawing room.

A tall regal-looking woman approached, arms outstretched in welcome.

"Daisy!" said Hazel, using the name her friends called her, as she embraced her.

"Hazel! Looking ravishing as usual!" Elizabeth had a jolly no-nonsense approach to life.

"Bless you for noticing, darling – we do our best!"

Sir Horace, a thin bright-eyed man in his late sixties, approached.

"And, Horace, thank you for the invitation, so nice to be back at Kilteragh," said Hazel, embracing him.

"And lovely to have you back, my dear Hazel," he said, smiling. "Where's John?"

"A headache, or a migraine, or one of those irritating pains artists get – oh!" Hazel broke off. "George Bernard Shaw! You wonderful man!" She threw her arms around the famous writer.

Michael stood at the edge of the small group, shifting awkwardly from one foot to the other as he watched Hazel play to the crowd like the great performer she was. As if she had just remembered Michael was there, she turned to him with a flourish and announced, taking him by the hand, "Everybody – this is the famous – the infamous – General Michael Collins!"

"We are delighted to meet you! Naturally we've heard so much about you!" said Elizabeth as she shook his hand.

"A great pleasure," said George Bernard Shaw, shaking his hand.

"Likewise," said Michael.

"I thought half the Irish army would be in attendance!" said Horace.

"No, I'm afraid it's just one car this evening, Michael thought it better to travel low key," said Hazel as she took a glass of champagne from the butler. "Well, he has endured two assassination attempts this week alone. On Tuesday we were dining in our hotel when a sniper was found on the grounds. Seemingly *I* was blocking his aim at Michael!"

"Hazel, I think I should be shaking in my shoes if I were in your position," said Elizabeth.

"It will take more than that to unnerve me!" said Hazel.

"It's no wonder poor John is down with a headache!" said Horace.

Michael was very quiet throughout the dinner as the others chatted and laughed. He felt tired and emotionally exhausted. He felt out of place and, as he looked at Hazel, he thought how comfortable she was amongst these people. She was in her element there.

Afterwards they retired to the drawing room.

As Michael spoke to George Bernard Shaw, Elizabeth sidled up to Hazel.

"Well – what do you make of him?" asked Hazel, as her eyes remained focused on Michael.

"If I have to be honest, I would say I am a little disappointed," said Elizabeth.

"Disappointed!" said Hazel, turning quickly to face her.

"Yes. I had expected him to be witty and funny and charming company – instead he hardly said two words over dinner!"

"Well, he's had quite a week, Daisy, between Arthur Griffith's death and the assassination attempts and he is devastated after the loss of his friend Harry Boland."

"Oh, yes, I know. '*Uneasy lies the head that wears a crown*' and all that – but after hearing how he took London by storm, I think I was expecting a little more than a farm boy. But perhaps what is exotic to the London ladies is commonplace to us Irish ladies?" Elizabeth smiled and moved on to talk to Horace.

Elizabeth's words had hit home and Hazel felt wounded and deeply disturbed. She tried to shake the feeling off as she watched Michael chat to George Bernard Shaw but negative thoughts and fears welled up in her. She tried to imagine her life if she did leave John and form a relationship with Michael. Where would they go? Where would they live? His career would be destroyed, that was certain. And she would lose her place in London society amidst a scandal the likes of which had rarely been witnessed before. Although she always enjoyed being a celebrity, would she enjoy notoriety? And what about John ... her wonderful, loyal, patient John. Could she really ever hurt him? Could she ever do without him? She felt dizzy from the whirl of emotion going through her as she realised that it was as John had said – she was standing on a cliff edge and it was a long way down.

"Are you sure we can't persuade you to stay any longer?" asked Horace as Michael and Hazel were leaving.

"Very kind of you, but I am travelling to Cork in the morning. Thank you for your hospitality," said Michael.

"Thank you, dear Horace. I shall be in touch," Hazel kissed both his cheeks before she and Michael walked out and down the steps to the car.

As they drove down the long avenue, Hazel said, "Are you alright, Michael? Everyone commented how quiet you were."

"I don't feel that well. I shouldn't have gone there tonight."

"Oh, I'm sorry. I thought you would enjoy it."

"I felt ill at ease. Those people were decent and interesting – rebels and reformers in their own way! – but they aren't my kind of people, Hazel. I'm not one of them and never will be."

"I did suspect you felt uncomfortable amongst them ... but, they are all good friends of mine."

"I know. But it just made me realise how different we are. I'm from a different class and culture. I didn't notice it as much in London, but I do here in my own country."

Hazel's heart sank as she heard him echo Elizabeth's words.

Michael reached forward and pulled back the dividing window.

"Yes, Mick?"

"We're not ready to go back to the hotel yet – take us for a spin somewhere, up in the hills."

The driver turned around and headed further into the country.

"What are we going to do, Hazel?" he asked.

"I don't know, Michael." She looked at him despairingly and shook her head.

"All I know is there is a broken-hearted girl in a hotel room in Greystones and a broken-hearted man in a hotel room in Dublin," said Michael.

"Look, I didn't ask to fall in love with you and I'm sure it was the last thing on your mind to fall in love with me – but it happened! Guilty as charged!"

"But ... what kind of a life could we have together?"

"You would lose everything."

"So would you."

"You would have to give up your position," she said.

"Of course ... if they couldn't accept a relationship with a married woman for a Protestant like Parnell, they certainly won't accept it for a Catholic like me."

"So, we couldn't stay in Ireland?"

"It would be impossible. We'd be ostracised. Same goes for England, I imagine. We would have to go to somewhere where nobody knew us or, if they did, couldn't care less about Ireland and our past."

She sighed as she looked out the window. "I'm too – old to begin in a new place where nobody knows me."

"America is the only place we could go to."

"America? But Americans *do* care about Ireland! So many have Irish ancestry and they have given the cause such financial support! We could never hide away there. Besides, I know so many people in America – I promised myself I would never go back after Dorothy died. It wouldn't be starting afresh for me there – it would be anything but! And there is Alice to consider. Her whole life is in London. I couldn't just transport her to America."

They fell silent for a while, both brooding on an uncertain future.

Hazel was thinking about her daughter.

"And what would our affair do to Alice's marriage prospects?" she said at last. "What family would allow their son to marry her with a divorced mother mired in scandal?"

"That's true," Michael whispered, as if to himself.

They fell silent again for a while, then Michael spoke.

"Hazel, would you really still want me if I no longer had my position?" he asked.

"I'm not in love with you because of your position, Michael," she said.

"Are you sure? Is it not my fame, my reputation that attracts you? Strip that away and I'd be just an ordinary man."

"I love *you*, Michael."

He sighed. "But, Hazel ... have you thought ... what work would I do? Who would hire me?"

"I have money, Michael."

"And I would be what?" he said gently. "A kept man?"

Tears started to roll down her face.

"I'm sorry, Hazel. I'm just trying to face the hard facts."

He leaned forwards and tapped on the window again.

"Pull over," he said, indicating to the driver who pulled in to the side of the road.

"Let's go for a walk, Hazel."

She nodded as he opened the door and helped her out. They were high up in the hills, the city spread out below them and the sea beyond that, the full moon lighting up the water like silver.

They walked along the country road.

"I have never loved anybody like I love you, Michael. But I've let these feelings carry me away. I got caught up in the excitement and the drama – I needed it because sometimes I just look at my life and, when I take away the parties and the fame and everything else, it just feels empty. I want my life to have meaning and I run around desperately trying to fill the void and you fill it completely. For the first time in my life, the void is filled. But how long would that last? If we left Ireland, we would both lose everything that gives meaning to our lives." She looked up at the shooting stars that were crossing the clear August night sky. "I'm afraid our love is as beautiful but as transient as one of those shooting stars ... I could never leave John. He's been too good to me. He's my security and, most of all, he knows me. He understands me. He knows all my faults and weaknesses, and not only does he forgive me for them, he loves me for them."

They stopped walking and he pulled her close to him and kissed her.

"So this is the end?" he asked.

She nodded tearfully.

"What about you? Will you go back to Kitty?" she asked.

"If she'll have me," he said.

"Of course she will – she's in love with you. And she's a very lucky girl."

"We had better get back," he said.

Back at the car, Michael opened the door. Hazel got in and he followed.

Suddenly there was a gunshot and the window on the side of the car shattered.

"*Get down!*" shouted Michael as he grabbed Hazel's by the back of the neck, pushed her down on the seat and fell on top of her.

There were more shots as the snipers opened a volley of shots on the car. The driver sped away as quickly as he could down the country road as shots continued to be fired.

Hazel was shaking as she arrived back at the Royal Marine Hotel and made her way up to the suite. It was after two in the morning. The sound of the gunshots was still ringing in her ears. She had come so close to death.

In the suite she walked to the bedroom and, opening the door, turned on the lights.

John awoke with a start and sat up to stare at Hazel who was standing inside the door in her coat and hat.

"We were fired upon!"

"W-w-w-hat?"

"We were being driven back from the dinner party at Horace Plunkett's when out of nowhere a barrage of shots came at us!"

"Was anyone hurt?"

"No, but only by luck! Glass was shattered, bullet holes through the metal – I am lucky to be alive."

"Do you need to see a doctor?"

"No. I need to see a barman."

She went to the drinks cabinet, poured herself a strong gin and downed it in one.

"Michael is alright?" asked John.

"Yes, he has had a lucky escape yet again."

She came and sat on the side of the bed and took his hand.

"And I have had a very lucky escape. I am a very lucky woman, John Lavery."

"Yes, you could have been killed!"

"Not just that. I am a very lucky woman to be married to a man as wonderful as you. How do you put up with me?"

"I am quite happy to put up with you – as long as you are happy to put up with me."

"Well, I am not going anywhere any time soon, so we shall just have to put up with each other."

She leaned forward and kissed his lips.

"All – that – is over now?" he asked.

"All *that* is over," she confirmed.

Michael was being driven back to his quarters at the barracks. As he looked at the shattered glass, he realised he had been lucky yet again – despite his massive carelessness. What madness had made him venture out without his bodyguards? And walk unprotected along a country road at night? If they had opened fire while they walked, he and Hazel would now be dead. But, of course, they would have had to follow at a distance, park their automobile and approach stealthily on foot. He must have been watched all evening by his enemies. Clearly, they knew about his relationship with Hazel and that had made her a target as well. Due to her connections with the British government, the relationship would be viewed as dangerous in some quarters.

What he and Hazel had was wonderful, but he had to now move away from her and let her follow her own destiny and her own life. He would not be responsible for her death.

And his life was with Kitty. He hoped it wasn't too late.

CHAPTER 78

The next day Kitty received a letter hand-delivered to her from one of Michael's aides. She sat in the hotel conservatory and carefully opened it.

> *My dearest Kitty,*
> *This is, as ever, a short note as I am about to leave for Cork. My heart and mind have been tormented since we last met when I think of your beautiful and sad face. As soon as I arrive back from Cork, we need to set a date for the wedding. Tell Gearóid and Maud, no more delays – if they want to have a double wedding with us then they need to get a move on! Counting the days until I see you again,*
> *I am sorry for everything I put you through and I love you dearly,*
> *With all my love,*
> *Michael*

Kitty folded the letter and held it tightly.

"Thank you," she whispered, smiling to herself.

Hazel was having a nightmare as she twisted and turned in the bed at the hotel. She was seeing Michael and was desperately trying to reach him, but he was always out of reach.

"*Michael ... Michael!*" she called in her sleep and then suddenly she sat up and screamed.

"Hazel?" gasped John beside her as he struggled to sit up and turned on the light.

"What's wrong?"

Her face was as white as a ghost's.

"He's dead," she whispered. "Michael's dead ... I saw it as plainly as I see you."

"Nonsense, you were having a nightmare, that's all. Probably brought on by the shock of the gunshots a couple of nights ago."

"He's dead. I know he's been killed," she whispered again as she reached out, grabbed John and began to sob loudly.

Kitty was putting on her hat in her hotel room. She had planned to go into the city that day and do some shopping. She planned to visit some bridal shops and start looking at wedding dresses.

There was a knock on the door.

"*Coming!*" she called and went to answer it.

There was a man standing there, with two police officers behind him.

"Kitty, I am a friend of Mick's – Brendan. I live here in Greystones," said the man.

"Ah, yes, I've heard him mention you many a time – so nice to meet you!" Her smile faded as she saw all three men had tears in their eyes.

"Is something the matter?" she asked, a chill running through her.

"Mick was killed in an ambush in Cork last night, Kitty – he's gone," said Brendan as the tears fell down his face.

Kitty turned and went silently to a chair and sat down.

"Was it quick?" she whispered.

"We don't have the details, Kitty ... not yet ... Can we do anything for you?"

She shook her head, feeling numb.

CHAPTER 79

The tall elegant woman made her way up the steps of the Royal Marine Hotel and across the lobby to the reception.

"I am here to see Lady Lavery. Can you tell her Elizabeth, Countess of Fingall, is here."

"Elizabeth?"

She turned to see John standing there.

"John!" She went and threw her arms around him. "Isn't this the most awful news about Michael Collins? Why, we had dinner with him at Kilteragh on Saturday!"

"We are all quite shocked. Though in a way I don't know why we should be – Michael was going around with death at his shoulder for a long time – he had that many lucky escapes."

"In a way that makes it worse – he gave the impression he was indestructible. To find out he was merely human like the rest of us ..." She shook her head. "Do you know any of the details ... how he was killed?"

"He was travelling in a convoy through the countryside in Cork, a remote area, when the convoy came under attack – an ambush. The others wanted to flee but Michael insisted they stay and fight. They got him with a single bullet, to the back of the head."

"How horrific – the poor man!" Her hand sprang to her to mouth in shock. "How is poor Hazel?"

"Distraught! Inconsolable! Come, and I'll take you to her. You are very good to come so quickly."

Taking her by the arm, he led her upstairs.

Elizabeth was sitting beside a weeping Hazel on her bed, attempting to console her. John had left the two women alone.

"Such a terrible shock for you," said Elizabeth. "It's impossible to think he is gone."

"I'm heartbroken, Daisy. I don't know how I'll survive. I love him."

"Everybody knew how close you both were. You were the best of friends."

"It was more than that. I *loved* him and he loved me. He wanted us to run away to America together!" Hazel blurted out.

"I see!" Elizabeth was shocked. "I knew there were the rumours about the two of you but I never for a moment believed them."

"He was my soul mate. John knew. But in the end I couldn't leave John. We've been through too much together."

"And what about the girl Michael was engaged to? The one whose photograph was in the newspapers?"

"All I know is that Michael loved me with all his heart and now he's gone." Hazel started sobbing again.

"Oh, dear, dear!" said Elizabeth, taking Hazel into her arms and soothing her. "I understand they are bringing his body back to Dublin by boat along the coast?"

"They said it would be easier that way, rather than by road with all the bridges and roads destroyed around the country due to this bloody war!"

"Will you go see him – when he arrives?"

"Of course," said Hazel.

"Well, I shall go with you. You need your friends at a terrible time like this."

On the Thursday Michael's body lay in the chapel at St Vincent's Hospital in Dublin. He would remain there for twenty-four hours for family and friends to visit before being brought to lie in state the next day. Hazel steadied herself as she walked up the steps into the hospital, holding Elizabeth's hand.

John had not accompanied them as he had been given permission to paint Michael later that day.

"It's a great honour for you, John. Capturing this for posterity. I imagine it will be the most important painting you will ever do," Elizabeth said.

John indeed felt honoured. His own emotions were going through a maelstrom. There was something peculiar about painting the portrait of the dead man his wife was in love with. For John, work came first. Art came first. There was no life if it could not be captured in art, there was no art if it could not be captured in life. He had spent his own life capturing moments, everything from weddings to baptisms to war on canvas. Michael's death was the next instalment in that mission, and he must put aside his own personal involvement. Besides, John was grateful this gave him an opportunity to see Michael alone and for Hazel to pay her respects without him being there. John felt this was one thing they needed to do separately.

"He looks so peaceful," whispered Hazel as she stared down at Michael's body laid out. There was a bandage across the top of his head.

"Apart from the bandage you would think he was just sleeping," said Elizabeth.

"Was it all worth it – was any of it worth this?" said Hazel.

Elizabeth looked at her friend with real concern. Hazel had gone into deep grief. Michael's death had shaken her to her core. She wondered how she would ever recover.

The door opened and a nurse came in. "I'm sorry, but there are more guests expected to arrive shortly."

"Ah, I see, we'll go now," said Elizabeth, taking the hint that they had outstayed their allotted time.

"I'm not going yet. I'm staying with him," said Hazel.

Elizabeth looked at the nurse and shrugged.

"It's Mr. Collin's fiancée who is expected to arrive shortly. The family have asked all other guests to be gone before she gets here. Naturally, she wants time alone," explained the nurse, trying to sound as sympathetic as possible.

"Of course!" said Elizabeth.

She turned to Hazel and put both her hands on her shoulders.

"Hazel, we really have to go now."

Hazel silently allowed herself to be led from the room, her eyes never leaving Michael.

As Elizabeth was helping Hazel into the automobile outside the hospital, another automobile pulled up and two women got out dressed in black. One woman was crying but it was the other woman who drew Hazel's attention. She recognised her as Kitty Kiernan from her photographs in the newspaper.

As Kitty walked up the steps of the building, Hazel gazed after her. It struck Hazel that both of them knew Michael so well and yet they didn't know each other at all. Almost as if Michael had two separate lives. In a way, Hazel reasoned, he had.

CHAPTER 80

The morning of the funeral Elizabeth waited for Hazel and John in the hotel lobby of the Royal Marine. She sat on a couch reading the headlines of the newspaper which were all about the funeral.

"They say there will be hundreds of thousands of people there," said the waitress as she cleared away glasses from a table.

"I daresay there will be," said Elizabeth, putting the newspaper aside as she saw Hazel and John come down the stairs. Then her mouth dropped open when she saw what Hazel was wearing.

She got up and hurried across to them.

"Hazel! You're wearing widow's weeds!" she gasped.

"Yes, what of it?" asked Hazel from behind her black veil.

"But you simply can't!"

"Why not?"

"Because you are not his widow! Honestly, Hazel, you must go back upstairs and change at once!"

"I will do no such thing! Michael would have expected me to wear widow's weeds."

Elizabeth looked at John who appeared shell-shocked and broken.

"Pardon us a moment, John," said Elizabeth as she grabbed Hazel's arms and pulled her to a quiet corner of the lobby.

"Hazel! You simply cannot attend the funeral wearing widow's weeds! You will be the talk of the town! Not just this town but London too – and Paris and New York and every other town there is!"

"Let them talk, I don't care! I want everyone to know what Michael meant to me and what I meant to him."

"You are trying to advertise your relationship with him! You are blatantly trying to claim him as yours and you don't care if you disgrace yourself in the meantime and humiliate John and Kitty Kiernan as well!"

"I just miss him so much and I don't want to be forgotten. I want people to know we loved each other."

"But it's not your place to do so at his funeral. It's Kitty's. Whatever went on between the two of you in his life, Hazel, leave him to her in his death. Do the decent thing."

Hazel began to weep but finally nodded. "I'll go up and change."

"Jolly good – we'll wait for you in the car outside."

Elizabeth shook her head and walked over to John.

"I can't get through to her – she isn't making any sense on anything," said John.

"She's in shock and grief-stricken, John. She doesn't even know what she's doing herself," said Elizabeth, trying to make John feel better about seeing his wife in widow's weeds for another man.

Kitty stood by Michael's grave in Glasnevin cemetery. Maud stood on one side of her and Gearóid on the other. Strange, she thought, how the four of them were supposed to be at an altar together getting married and instead they were at a grave. There weren't many people left at the graveyard by the early evening. The funeral as expected had been massive, with Michael being given a full state funeral. But now most people had gone home.

Kitty looked up from the grave and around at the small groups of people still gathered around, huddled together in small circles. She didn't recognise any of them, but she was sure she would recognise all their names if she heard them, from all the stories Michael had told her.

She suddenly spotted a very glamorous woman dressed in furs. She was with another well-dressed woman and an older man. She immediately recognised her from all the magazine photos.

"That's Hazel Lavery," said Kitty to Maud.

"What's *she* still doing here?" snapped Maud.

Kitty suddenly began to walk towards Hazel.

"*Kitty!*" Maud hissed after her but was ignored.

Hazel was speaking to Elizabeth. "I'm not sure how long we'll stay in Ireland now –"

"Lady Lavery?" Kitty called her from behind.

Hazel turned around and was shocked to see Kitty there. They stared at each other, almost disbelieving, finally meeting someone each had heard and thought so much about.

"I am –"

"I know who you are, Kitty," said Hazel.

They continued to stare at each other.

Hazel cleared her throat and said, "I'm very sorry –" but her voice broke as she began to cry.

Kitty watched her cry for a few moments and then reached out and took her in her arms. The two women hugged tightly.

EPILOGUE

NINE YEARS LATER

1931

Cecil B Beaton stood back from his camera and studied his model. Lady Hazel Lavery was reclining on a chaise longue in her husband's studio in their home at Cromwell Place. Cecil had been commissioned to take some photographs of the famous woman for *Tatler* magazine. He had become quite friendly with Hazel since he himself had become a fixture on the London social scene as a famous photographer. Like everyone, he found Hazel to be witty, charming and insightful. As he studied her that afternoon, he tried to guess her age. She had been around for so long that he reckoned she must be past the half-century mark and yet she still looked remarkably young. Many rumours circulated as to the source of Hazel's continued youthful appearance. Cecil would like to believe the theory that amongst all those hundreds of portraits her husband Sir John had painted of her, there was one hidden in the attic at 5 Cromwell Place and that Hazel was a female Dorian Grey.

"There is a rumour circulating that John is to be appointed Lord Lieutenant of Ireland and you and he are to take up residence of the Viceregal Lodge in Dublin," said Cecil as he fiddled with the camera.

"There was talk of it, but I cannot see that happening at this stage," said Hazel. "Times have moved on and I don't think they would particularly want me in Dublin anymore. I'm too much associated with the past."

Cecil stopped fixing his camera and looked up at her.

"With Michael Collins?" he said.

"Not just Michael ... the Irish want to move on and forget the past – the Civil War. They don't want to know me anymore."

"I wouldn't say that! They made you the face of their new currency – using your image as a personification of Ireland. Surely that shows the esteem they hold you in?"

"Yes, we were thrilled when the Irish government asked John to design their new currency and I was so moved when he used my face as the image."

"A great honour," said Cecil. "It is usually only kings and queens that appear on currency notes."

"My reward perhaps for services done for the country ... but I always saw it as a parting gift from Dublin as they didn't want me involved in their politics anymore."

"Why, when you were such a good friend to them?"

"Most of the people I had known and been friends with were either dead, killed or too old. Some resented the influence I'd had during the treaty negotiations – and afterwards the sway I held over Michael."

As Cecil studied her, he was eager to ask her about the rumours that circulated about an affair between her and Collins. But he suspected he would not get a straight answer from her.

"Do you go to Ireland much these days?" he asked instead.

"Not so much," she sighed.

"But in a way you'll never leave there now – with your face on every pound note in the country!"

Hazel's eyes became misted over as she said, "Do we ever really leave the places we have been? Does a part of us haunt the places we have been – or do the places we have been haunt us?"

"Your involvement with the Irish rebels and the foundation of the Irish state is fascinating, Hazel."

She smiled. "All I wanted to do was to help as best I could. Oh, people accused me of all sorts – people have always accused me of all sorts. They said I sought fame or infamy, excitement and danger through my relationship with Michael Collins and the others during that time. But when it comes to my time for leaving this world, I can look back at my life and say that it mattered. That I mattered and that my life had meaning. That I was more than just a face."

The door opened and John walked in.

"Sorry for disturbing you, but I've just ordered tea in the drawing room and wondered if you cared to join me?" he asked.

"Oh, yes – tea please!" said Hazel cheerily, standing up.

"Yes, I think we deserve a tea break," said Cecil with a smile.

"How is your photography going?" asked John, walking over to inspect the camera equipment.

"Excellent. But then how could it not – with Hazel as the subject? She is the ultimate professional."

"Well, I should be by this stage of my career – how many times have I sat for my portrait!" Hazel said.

"She's the best," said John, smiling proudly at her.

"Only because I learned from the best," said Hazel as she walked to John, smiling at him. "This is just relaxation, John – I have such a busy week ahead of me. Dinner tomorrow night with Ramsay MacDonald at Downing Street, lunch the next day with dear Winston –"

As Hazel continued to rhyme off her week's schedule and John listened, Cecil watched the couple link arms as they walked from the studio.

There seemed nothing particular to set the woman apart from the other women who walked down the street in Dublin that day. She was just a normal housewife going about her business on a normal day, running her suburban house in Rathmines on a tight budget as times were hard, being a good wife to her husband and mother to her two young sons. She was just another well-groomed housewife and there was no hint that she had once occupied a pivotal role at the heart of Irish politics. As she walked along, she wondered how many people on the street would even remember her name by now.

It had been very different a decade ago. In the months after Michael's death, Kitty had received thousands of letters of condolence.

Letters from people she had never known or even heard of. People who had known Michael, people who had just met him briefly or people who had never known or met him but felt the need to put pen to paper to commiserate and to reach out to a grieving young woman. Kitty had become a symbol of tragedy for so many as they mourned Michael's untimely death. The letters had kept her going as she fell into despair. The need to read each letter and write a reply gave her a purpose. It was as if in his death Kitty could finally be the woman he always wanted, protecting his legacy.

But then the times had moved on. The civil war had ended, and in its wake left a broken divided country. People wanted to forget about the bad years, the wars, the hatred. As the country began the task of rebuilding, people were almost afraid to talk about the past. Afraid to open old wounds and find out the person you were speaking to might not be on the same side as you. It was too painful to remember so people chose to forget. And with that Kitty soon was forgotten too.

Then, as she entered her mid-thirties, still deeply mourning Michael, she met a handsome ex-army officer called Felix Cronin. Felix hero-worshipped Michael Collins and fully understood how the special place he held in Kitty's heart took precedence over everything else for her. Felix never tried to replace Michael and, in a way, felt it a privilege and honour to marry his hero's fiancée. As for Kitty, there was much about Felix that reminded her of Michael. She had to make a decision: would she remain for ever a woman in mourning or at least try to rebuild a new life? So, they married.

Kitty walked into a draper's shop and started looking at the materials on display. The first thing she looked at was the price, the design second. She smiled to herself when she remembered a time when it had always been the opposite, in the good old days when she was at the heart of the Kiernan business empire. Things were different now. Money was always short. Felix drank too much, she had large doctor bills due to her failing health, and life in this new Ireland was a struggle. The cost to rebuild the country had been massive and investment was lacking due to the instability created by the wars.

Kitty finally chose a fabric and ordered a section.

"It's a beautiful shade, isn't it? It will go lovely with your colouring," said the shop girl who looked at the elegant customer as she cut the fabric and decided she might have been a looker in her day.

"It's certainly a cheery colour," said Kitty.

The shop girl folded the fabric up and put it in a brown-paper bag.

"That will be three shillings and two pence, please," said the shop girl.

Kitty reached into her bag for her purse. She opened it and took out a one-pound note. Ireland had broken away from using British sterling as its currency three years previously and now had its own currency like all independent nations. Kitty stared at the note as she had done hundreds of times before. It was a beautiful design with the haunting image of a woman's face on the front of it, a women who personified Ireland. Sir John Lavery, the artist, had used his wife Hazel as the model. Kitty smiled wryly to herself, thinking not for the first time that she would never, ever be free of Hazel Lavery. Every time she went into a shop or a bank or a post office – every time she bought or sold something, she would have Hazel Lavery, with her enigmatic expression, gazing at her from the money she was handling. As Kitty slipped further into oblivion, Hazel Lavery had been immortalised as the face on millions and millions of pounds.

Kitty walked down the street they lived on and opened her front door. She put her shopping down on a side table in the hall. She listened but could hear no noise and realised the child-minder Moira had not brought the children back from the park yet. The eldest, Felix, was now five and had been named after his father. The youngest was two and they had named him Michael Collins Cronin. It had raised some eyebrows that she had named her son after her dead lover, but her husband Felix understood and fully approved. And that was what she loved most about Felix: he never questioned or felt intimidated about her love for Michael. He accepted it as a fact of life. Felix might not be the best husband in the world and often they did not get on, but Kitty would always love him for that understanding.

She walked down the hallway and into the kitchen to make herself some tea. Then she came back down the hallway and into the front parlour where she sat down on the couch and gazed at the painting that was on a stand in the corner of the room. The painting had been there since the day she and Felix had married and moved into that house. It was a portrait of Michael Collins by Sir John Lavery that had been painted during the treaty negotiations in London in 1921. After Michael died, the Laverys had gifted her the painting. Having the painting allowed Kitty to believe she had a part of Michael still with her. And for that, if nothing else, Kitty would always be grateful to Hazel Lavery.

The End

AUTHOR'S NOTE

Hazel Lavery died in 1935 at the age of fifty-five after falling ill. Her untimely death sent a shock wave through London society, with Winston Churchill becoming often depressed, missing his close friend. It is interesting to contemplate what role Hazel would have assumed for herself as Churchill's advisor and confidante when he became Britain's wartime leader a few years later, if she had lived. A role she would no doubt have relished.

Hazel's face continued to appear on Irish banknotes for the rest of the century, only finally being replaced in 2002 with the introduction of the Euro as Ireland's currency. John Lavery outlived his wife by some years. During the blitz he left Cromwell Place and went to live with his stepdaughter Alice who had married an Irishman and was living in Kilkenny. He died there in 1941, aged eighty-four. His reputation as a world-renowned artist has flourished in the decades since.

Kitty Kiernan died aged fifty-three in 1945 of Bright's disease. She was buried in Glasnevin cemetery as close to Michael Collins' grave as was possible.

The Lavery mansion in Kensington later played a role in another famous liaison. In the last part of the twentieth century the building became a gallery owned by antiques expert Oliver Hoare who had a relationship with Diana, Princess of Wales. John's famous studio became known as the Lavery Room. At time of writing the building is being renovated and will be an art exhibition centre.

As Ireland fought for its independence, Michael Collins became internationally known as a figure of mystery, daring and tactical genius. It is amazing to think that he had time for a personal life during those critical and hectic years, living life on the run and being the most wanted man in the empire. However, the exact opposite was true. Perhaps it was the danger of living under the constant threat of capture or death, but Michael and the people in his life lived life to the full – perhaps with the knowledge that they might not be there tomorrow. His relationship and subsequent engagement to Kitty Kiernan is laced with intrigue and tragedy. The infamous 'love triangle' with Harry Boland has all the hallmarks of a Greek tragedy and I hoped in this novel to be able to show the emotions Michael, Kitty and Harry must have enjoyed and suffered during this time.

Kitty was a fascinating person. A woman with little or no interest in politics, she is now almost viewed as an afterthought in history. And yet her relationships with Harry Boland and Michael Collins put her at the very heart of the epic story of Ireland's struggle for independence. Often viewed just as a tragic figure in the aftermath of Michael Collin's death, I wanted to show her as the vivacious, fun but complex woman that captured the hearts of not just one but two of Ireland's heroes. I also wanted to draw attention to intriguing and little-known elements of her life, for example the assassination of the police constable in her family hotel and the fact her sister Maud was engaged to and married Michael Collins' close friend and second cousin Gearóid O'Sullivan – the man who raised the tricolour over the General Post Office during the Easter Rising. These elements undoubtedly brought Kitty much closer to the furnace of what was happening during those dangerous and turbulent times and contradicts the image of her as being only a remote romantic figure on the fringes of events.

Then there is Lady Hazel Lavery. Considering the pivotal role she played in Ireland's independence, it is perhaps unfair that she isn't more widely known and appreciated. Her image gazed enigmatically from Irish banknotes for decades and yet she remained largely unknown. Hazel's work for Irish independence and commitment to bringing peace to Ireland has not been properly acknowledged. Perhaps it was the fact she was a titled

London society hostess that alienated her from another legacy she might have enjoyed in an independent Ireland. Or perhaps it was the controversial friendship she had with Michael Collins that made her an uncomfortable player in Irish history.

It is impossible to say exactly what the real relationship between Michael and Hazel was. The sequence of events in this novel follows an actual timeframe. When Kitty wrote to Michael saying she had heard there was a society woman in London in pursuit of him, she must have had insecurities regarding her fiancé and the new and very unexpected position he found himself holding in London high society once the truce was called. Clearly Michael and Hazel had become very close. And this closeness became well known at the time with the newspaper referring to Hazel as his sweetheart.

I wanted to draw attention to the last fateful week of Michael's life when the Laverys travelled to Dublin, and the pivotal role Hazel was playing in Michael's life by then. Hazel and Michael had grown so close that they did spend much time in each other's company during that final week – the last of his life. Piecing together the chain of events, they did go to Kilteragh for the dinner party and met George Bernard Shaw, unaccompanied by Hazel's husband John. After the dinner party they did go for that drive in the mountains where they were the target of an assassination attempt.

By Hazel belligerently attempting to wear widow's weeds to Michael's funeral the next week, there is a clear indication that she wished to be seen by the world as the woman in Michael's life – regardless of the severe hurt and humiliation this would have caused both her husband John and Kitty Kiernan. But an actual affair could have still been just a fantasy in Hazel's mind. Their relationship is a mystery and here I have tried to join the dots of that mystery. But the only two people who knew what really happened between them were Michael and Hazel.

A Great Beauty is an author's interpretation of the events.

Now that you're hooked why not try
By Royal Appointment
also published by Poolbeg

Here's a sneak preview of
the Prologue

By ROYAL APPOINTMENT

PROLOGUE

1871

Queen Victoria sat on her couch in the audience room at Windsor Castle as the Prime Minister William Gladstone was shown in. As she watched him respectfully approach her, she was not looking forward to the meeting. She had never liked Gladstone. He was austere, a perfectionist who never tired of pointing out perceived imperfections in others. Even Victoria was not exempt from his disapproval.

"Your Majesty," said Gladstone as he bowed to her.

"Prime Minister." She nodded to him.

"I understand the Prince of Wales has been ill? How is his condition?" enquired Gladstone.

"He is poorly, Prime Minister. He has taken to his bed in Sandringham but is getting the best of care and I have no doubt will recover soon."

"Typhoid is a terrible illness. But I do not need to tell you that, ma'am, when it caused the premature death of your dear husband."

"That, amongst other things," muttered Victoria under her breath.

"With the Prince falling ill and the approach of the tenth anniversary of your husband's death, I thought it might be an apt time to discuss concerns surrounding the royal family, ma'am," said Gladstone.

"I should think these events make it anything but an apt time, Prime Minister," said Victoria.

"Perhaps so, but the issues need to be discussed in any case."

"What exactly needs to be discussed?" Victoria said curtly.

"Ma'am, I do not think I can remember a time when the royal family have been so out of favour with the country as they are now."

"Out of favour?" Victoria sounded more irate than concerned.

"Ma'am, the press is openly critical of you and the public is equally dissatisfied."

"The press is always critical and the public never satisfied. To try and make them otherwise is a fruitless exercise."

"You have not been seen in public for many years, ma'am. The country is beyond puzzled at this stage at your continued absence from public life and, quite frankly, angered by the perceived neglect of royal duty."

"Prime Minister, may I remind you that I am in deep mourning for my beloved husband." Victoria's tone was at its most icy.

Husband *and* first cousin, thought Gladstone, wondering whether the close blood relationship had made the attachment excessively intense. "I understand that, ma'am, but the country does not. They think that two years, maybe three or four, may be sufficient to be in deep mourning. But ten years, ma'am? The country is perplexed and your popularity is at its very lowest."

"My aim never was to be popular, Prime Minister. I have done everything out of a sense of duty."

"Indeed." Gladstone bowed slightly. "But the situation has now become so unsatisfactory that the press is openly questioning the need for a monarchy at all and calls for a republic are getting stronger every day. May I remind you that Napoleon the Third has just been ousted in France and that country has become a republic again?"

"There is no need to remind me, Prime Minister. I assure you that I am fully informed of international affairs, despite what you may think. Your fears of Britain becoming a republic are unfounded – that will never happen here. One thing you can always be sure of in Britain is monarchy and rain!"

"Ma'am, I have urged you before that if you feel you are not up to performing your duties in public then you should allow the Prince of Wales a role in government and let him represent you. At least then the country would have a royal presence, rather than this gaping void we have had for ten years."

"That is quite out of the question. My son is simply not ready to assume an official royal role and I will not jeopardise this monarchy by giving him a role that he is not prepared for."

"But, ma'am, the Prince desperately wants the active role that you are denying him."

"What he *desperately* wants and what he is capable of are two entirely different things."

"I think him more than capable," objected Gladstone.

"And I think I know my own son better than you do."

"The reality is – because the Prince has been denied an official role by you – he too has become deeply unpopular. As he has no official function, he and the Princess of Wales are seen as frivolous and uncommitted. He has acquired the image of a playboy more interested in parties and alcohol, amongst other things, with his decadent set – the Marlborough set, I believe the press calls them – than showing any interest in his royal duty."

"If the Prince has that reputation, then perhaps he deserves it and it is through no fault of mine that he acquired it," said Victoria.

Gladstone looked at the small dour-looking woman dressed as always in mourning black and realised he was wasting his time. He and previous prime ministers had tried to make her see that her all-consuming grief, along with her distaste and distrust for her son, was destroying the institution that her husband had worked so hard to build up during his lifetime. The situation was now so critical that her family's future was in real jeopardy, but she refused to see it.

There was knock on the door and a footman came in.

"Excuse the interruption, ma'am, but an urgent telegram has arrived for you from Sandringham," he said.

Victoria nodded to the footman and beckoned him to come to her. She took the telegram and as she read it she paled.

"What has happened, ma'am?" asked Gladstone.

Victoria stood up. "The Prince of Wales' condition has deteriorated rapidly. They have asked me to go to Sandringham without delay."

"But – I thought he was recovering?"

"That was what we were previously informed. I must go, Prime Minister."

"Of course, ma'am, and I hope the news is better when you arrive at Sandringham."

Victoria nodded and quickly left the room.

As Victoria's carriage drove through the grounds of Sandringham to the main house, she was overwhelmed with a terrible sense of foreboding. It was December and it would soon be the tenth anniversary of her dear Albert's death. It was true what Gladstone had said, that typhoid was the official cause of his death. But everyone in the family knew Victoria had other ideas about that. And, now here she was, nearing the tenth anniversary of her husband's passing and being told that her eldest son and heir was suffering from the same illness and that he was in grave danger. Victoria knew that she would not have been sent for if the doctors did not think the situation was extremely serious. She could not help thinking that history was repeating itself. That she would lose her son in the same terrible fashion as her husband at the same time of year. As she thought of her son – Bertie as he had always been known to the family and close friends – she could not even imagine him being sick or physically impaired. He was a young man of thirty, a father to five children. He was always so strong-looking and cheerful. Victoria could not imagine a person so full of vitality being struck down so young. But life could be cruel – had the same thing not happened to her husband at a young age? And she had never recovered from the shock of that. And now she was being blamed by her prime minister for not appearing in public when she felt every day was a case of mere survival without her darling husband.

She thought of her relationship with Bertie. How they had become so distant from each other in recent years. As the years passed by, they had grown ever more estranged from each other. She had lived in her court of mourning, Bertie had lived in his court of decadence. There had been nothing in common between the two courts. But, through it all, she had never imagined that anything could happen to him, that he would ever fall ill or that his life could be in danger. She knew how sometimes doctors could get things wrong and how her own family were prone to exaggeration – she could only hope and pray that this was the case.

The carriage came to a halt and she was assisted out. Inside, she was escorted through the vast rooms and corridors of Sandringham.

Her daughter Alice and her husband had been visiting from Germany when Bertie had taken ill. Alice, who prided herself on her nursing skills, had remained to nurse her brother. As she was escorted down the corridor to the room Bertie was in, she saw Alice deep in conversation with Bertie's wife Alexandra outside the door. Victoria knew she had to be strong for them all. Not only was she the head of the family and Bertie's mother, but she was also the queen. She knew in this time of crisis she had to show strength.

As she reached the two women she could see they had been crying.

"Mama!" Alice came and kissed her cheek.

"Your Majesty," Alexandra managed to say as she tried to pull herself together in front of Victoria, but her tall elegant figure was trembling.

"How is he?" asked Victoria. "How is our dear Bertie?"

"We must prepare ourselves for the worst," said Alice.

"I fear there is no hope," said Alexandra as she raised her handkerchief to her beautiful face to stop herself from sobbing out loud.

Victoria suddenly felt weak and held on to a nearby chair for support.

"But – this cannot be – it just cannot be," she whispered. "Not Bertie . . . I had been informed he was improving."

"He had been, Mama, but then he had a relapse," said Alice.

"I must go to him at once," said Victoria.

Suddenly she could hear the sound of groaning coming from the other side of the door.

"You must prepare yourself, Mama, he is quite delirious. Sometimes he is not making much sense. He will not recognise you."

Victoria nodded. "Take me to my son."

Alice nodded and, offering her mother her arm, led her to the door and opened it. As Victoria entered the room she could see a group of people gathered around the four-poster bed – doctors, nurses and some of the household staff at Sandringham. With Alice's support she walked across the room.

The medical staff stepped away from the bed and bowed to her.

Then Bertie came into full view. She saw his deathly white face, his brow covered in sweat, his eyes closed as he tossed and turned alarmingly on the bed.

She let go of Alice's arm and went to the side of the bed.

"Bertie, my darling Bertie, it's your mama," she said.

But he seemed not to hear her as he continued to toss and turn.

"Bertie!" Victoria reached out, took his hand and held it firmly.

He gripped his mother's hand and looked towards her. "I need to go – I need to go now and see her," he gasped.

"He's not making much sense, Your Majesty," said the doctor beside her. "He hasn't for some time – it's the fever."

On the other side of the bed, Alice took a cloth and wiped Bertie's forehead as Alexandra tried to suppress her tears.

"Bertie – can you hear me?" Victoria said, squeezing his hand tightly to try and get a response.

"You don't understand!" he said, his voice rising. "I have to go and meet her now – she's waiting for me – she's been waiting for me all this time."

"Who – my dear? Who is waiting for you?" asked Victoria.

"Nellie – Nellie is waiting for me. Can't you see? I can't keep her waiting any longer. I must go to Nellie – I must go to my Nellie now!"

Victoria's eyes widened in shock. She looked across at Alexandra and Alice who looked utterly horrified.

"I must go to Nellie now," repeated Bertie. "I must see her – I must see her now."

Also by Poolbeg

The LEGACY *of*
ARMSTRONG HOUSE

A. O'CONNOR

2017 – At Armstrong House, Kate and Nico Collins are looking
forward to a bright future with their young son Cian.
When archaeologist Daniel Byrne arrives in the area to investigate life
there during the Great Famine, he soon crosses paths
with Kate. Through Daniel's work, Kate is horrified to
discover that a vicious sexual assault occurred in their home in the
1860s when the occupants were Nico's ancestors Lord Edward and
his wife Lady Anna. Kate sets out to use all her investigative skills to
discover the circumstances of the crime, the identity
of the victim and the guilty party.

1860s – After Lawrence, the long-awaited heir to the Armstrong
Estate, is born Lord Edward and Lady Anna take great joy in
watching him grow up. But somebody else is watching
– Edward's cousin Sinclair who has always felt cheated of the
Armstrong legacy by the unexpected birth of Lawrence. As Anna's
past comes back to haunt her, life at the house is a tangled web of
deceit, blackmail and betrayal that shatters in the summer of 1865.

2017 – As Kate's detective work edges closer to discovering the truth
behind the assault, she and Daniel uncover a mystery that goes much
deeper. Kate realises that if the truth is ever revealed it will not only
destroy the legacy of the Armstrong family
but also her marriage to Nico.

ISBN 978-178199-821-2

Also by Poolbeg

On SACKVILLE STREET

A. O'CONNOR

1869 – When Milandra arrives to live on Sackville Street as a young
widow, she becomes the talk of Dublin. Firstly, she
scandalises society by refusing to wear the mandatory widow's weeds.
She then sets her sights on marrying young solicitor Nicholas
Fontenoy, despite the fact he is already engaged to Bishop
Staffordshire's daughter, Constance.

But is there something darker behind Milandra's professed love for
Nicholas? As she attempts to lure Nicholas away from Constance, a
chain of events is set off that leads to bribery,
blackmail and murder.

1916 – Now in her seventies, Milandra is one of the wealthiest and
most respected women in Dublin. Back in her mansion on Sackville
Street, after spending Easter with family, she is astonished to be
confronted by a gunman. She fears he has come to rob her, but
quickly realises she has been caught up in
something much bigger.

Then, as Dublin explodes with the Easter Rising, Milandra's
granddaughter Amelia desperately tries to reach her grandmother
who is trapped in her house at the very centre of the conflict.
Meanwhile, events unfolding on Sackville Street
will unravel decades-old mysteries, secrets that were
to be carried to the grave.

ISBN 978-178199-868-7